TEMPTATION OF
THE FORCE

STAR WARS
THE HIGH REPUBLIC

TEMPTATION OF THE FORCE

Tessa Gratton

RANDOM HOUSE
WORLDS

NEW YORK

Published in the United States by Random House Worlds,
an imprint of Random House, a division of
Penguin Random House LLC, New York.

RANDOM HOUSE is a registered trademark, and
RANDOM HOUSE WORLDS and colophon are trademarks of
Penguin Random House LLC.

Originally published in hardcover in the United States
by Random House Worlds, an imprint of Random House,
a division of Penguin Random House LLC, in 2024.

ISBN 978-0-593-72311-1
Ebook ISBN 978-0-593-72310-4

Printed in the United States of America on acid-free paper

randomhousebooks.com

2 4 6 8 9 7 5 3 1

For Matt and Joanne Gratton, my dad and mom,
the first *Star Wars* fans I ever knew

THE **STAR WARS** NOVELS TIMELINE

THE HIGH REPUBLIC

Convergence
The Battle of Jedha
Cataclysm

Light of the Jedi
The Rising Storm
Tempest Runner
The Fallen Star
The Eye of Darkness
Temptation of the Force
Tempest Breaker
Trials of the Jedi

Wayseeker: An Acolyte Novel

Dooku: Jedi Lost
Master and Apprentice
The Living Force

I THE PHANTOM MENACE

Mace Windu: The Glass Abyss

II ATTACK OF THE CLONES

Inquisitor: Rise of the Red Blade
Brotherhood
The Thrawn Ascendancy Trilogy
Dark Disciple: A Clone Wars Novel

III REVENGE OF THE SITH

Reign of the Empire: The Mask of Fear
Catalyst: A Rogue One Novel
Lords of the Sith
Tarkin
Jedi: Battle Scars

SOLO

Thrawn
A New Dawn: A Rebels Novel
Thrawn: Alliances
Thrawn: Treason

ROGUE ONE

IV A NEW HOPE

Battlefront II: Inferno Squad
Heir to the Jedi
Doctor Aphra
Battlefront: Twilight Company

V THE EMPIRE STRIKES BACK

VI RETURN OF THE JEDI

The Princess and the Scoundrel
The Alphabet Squadron Trilogy
The Aftermath Trilogy
Last Shot

Shadow of the Sith
Bloodline
Phasma
Canto Bight

VII THE FORCE AWAKENS

VIII THE LAST JEDI

Resistance Reborn
Galaxy's Edge: Black Spire

IX THE RISE OF SKYWALKER

A long time ago in a galaxy far, far away. . . .

TEMPTATION OF THE FORCE

Worlds suffer inside the formidable OCCLUSION ZONE, where Marchion Ro and his band of Nihil marauders, untouchable by the Republic, rule with an iron fist.

Jedi Master Avar Kriss has escaped from this occupied space and, along with fellow Jedi Elzar Mann, leads the Jedi and Republic in a desperate fight against the Nihil and their Nameless creatures.

But a new danger now threatens the galaxy. A mysterious BLIGHT has begun to spread randomly across worlds, slowly infecting areas and turning all life in its path to dust. . . .

Prologue

Porter Engle drifted.

It was not the first time he'd died—or nearly died—nor was it likely to be the last. Someday the final death would arrive, and he would be one with the Force.

The last clear memory he had was of standing over the void of space, on the torn edge of a ship, his lightsaber lost, his shoulder bleeding, and that old Mirialan grinning desperately at him from above: "Goodbye, Porter Engle."

Goodbye, Porter Engle.

You are not alone.

No, that wasn't—

Porter groaned softly and fell back into drifting.

He remembered screeching metal, the hiss of a lightsaber blade against *beskar.* He remembered sending someone off—*you are not alone*—again, always sending others away, watching them leave, driving them off—

No.

It had been Avar Kriss this time, determined to make it, filled with a fire of hope.

He remembered white braids whipping like ropes and a laugh, chasing after that laugh, chasing after promises, tears, and lightsabers clattering to the ground all around him like an avalanche.

General Viess. Older. Stronger. *Goodbye, Porter Engle.*

Then, on the tattered metal edge of what once had been a hangar bay, Porter remembered sitting down to welcome the Force. He had closed his eye and let the pain diffuse into light, the blood sticking to his skin a warm reminder of the life he was leaving.

It drained out of him, and he listened to the Force. He felt other beings scrambling in the ruined ship, heard the wail of steel, the burst of engines, and the whisper of blades cutting through air: the Force all around him.

Porter Engle had never sought death, though through his long years, it had often come calling, but now he could welcome it through the Force.

Except.

Porter was here. On a bed with a thin mattress. It gave oddly, like a material pulled over metal bars. A cot. His head throbbed, and his shoulder tingled. There was a noise he should be able to recognize. It was familiar. Rhythmic.

By the Force, his body ached.

He was alive.

Not quite ready to open his eye, Porter let his breath deepen again and internally studied his situation. He wore what felt like a thin clean robe. He smelled medicine and a soothing astringent smoke, like incense maybe. No shoes on his feet. No eye patch. A bandage was wrapped on his left shoulder where Viess had stabbed him. He could move his fingers and toes.

All told, not a bad summation.

This was a small room, based on the echo of that familiar rhythmic noise.

Oh, it was only music.

Someone in the room was playing some kind of harp, though not especially well.

As Porter focused, he heard the sound of breathing and the ruffle of clothing. A distant, muffled thrum of life outside well-insulated windows. So a city, perhaps.

Porter reached with the Force and identified one other being in the room. They felt mostly at ease, if frustrated by something. Not an immediate threat.

Below them more beings moved, alive with the Force. He was on the second story of a building. Alone with the musician.

Slowly, Porter turned his head toward the musician and opened his eye to daylight.

The player was human, by the looks of him, wearing a black tunic and robe with bright-red ribbons tying his sleeves tight to his forearms as he stood over a horizontal harp and gently picked out a song by tapping the strings with little hammers. Concentration pulled his young, handsome tan face into a frown, and strands of black hair fell from a messy topknot.

The human looked harmless, and Porter's wounds had been tended, but better not take chances.

Carefully, Porter settled himself and welcomed the Force toward him. He waited until he felt it gleaming around him, sharp as a hundred blades, humming in his mind like kyber.

He moved.

Porter leapt up and swept across the room between two strikes of the hammers, ending with his side against the human's back and one arm around his neck—too loose to kill, too tight to allow for a struggle.

The human froze.

"You're, ah, awake," he said.

Porter grunted. "Who're you?" he said, voice dry and cracking. Unused for the Force knew how long. Maybe it had been a day, maybe weeks.

"Cair," the young man said quietly. His hands slowly lowered the hammers, placing them gently against the strings of the harp. *A dulcimer,* Porter thought. He'd seen them before.

"Where are we?"

"Seswenna City."

Porter nodded, his right hand clenching, inadvertently tightening that arm around Cair's neck. "How did I get here?"

"I rescued you," the human said, and for the first time Porter detected a tone in his voice: lighthearted, purposefully gentle, the way one might speak to a wild predator.

Porter had been a lot of things in his long life, including a predator. A hunter. It wasn't his natural state or his preference, but this was still the Occlusion Zone, and the Nihil were still in charge. He'd closed his eye on a fracturing Nihil ship and opened it here. The most logical explanation was that this Cair was Nihil, too. Despite his music, despite Porter's lack of restraints.

Snorting, Porter shook the young man slightly. "Rescued me, ah? How? That ship was littered with Nihil and only Nihil."

"Well," Cair admitted, "I do sometimes run supplies for them."

Porter sucked air through his teeth.

"But!" Cair was fast to explain, his hands lifting urgently in surrender. The left hand was a prosthetic made of black alloy. "I do it to keep my clearances, you know, against scav droids, and to be able to move around. I smuggle under their noses. Information, goods, sometimes people, but that's more difficult."

"Difficult is what this story is to believe," Porter said, more cranky than usual because of all the things he didn't know, as well as his aching shoulder and the expanse of anger growing in his guts. "I'm to understand that a non-Nihil Nihil just happened to come across me, get me out of the wreckage, and nurse me to health?"

Cair shrugged abortively under the weight of Porter's grip. "Not . . . not so hard to believe if you trust the Force."

Porter barked a laugh and again tightened his arm around Cair's neck. "The Force?"

"Let me show you something, old man," Cair said, turning his head to show Porter the gleam of a dark-brown eye and the edge of his grin.

For a moment, Porter did his best to stare into that eye, feeling his way with the Force to discern if Cair was setting him up. He sensed an earnest nature, a thrill of fear and excitement. Nothing more.

Well, Porter hadn't made it this long without throwing himself off a few metaphoric—and literal—cliffs. "All right."

Releasing Cair in one swift motion, Porter stepped back and tightened his fists at his sides. He was the blade. And the Force was with him.

Cair darted past the harp and quickly moved around the cot where Porter had been unconscious. On the other side was a small metal table with several drawers. Cair pulled the top one open, and Porter tensed, calling on the Force in case the human took out a blaster.

But it was no such thing.

In the young man's hand was a lightsaber—Porter's lightsaber, which had gone rolling away from him on the ruined deck of General Viess's ship. Porter stared at it as Cair flipped it and offered the hilt to him.

"I haven't known many Jedi," Cair said. "But I'm from the Core and didn't always live out here. I wasn't always trapped under Nihil cruelty. I know a lightsaber when I see one, and I know Jedi even without their robes."

Something about the words settled heavily on Porter's shoulders. He drew a long breath and reached out for his lightsaber with the Force.

Cair let go and the weapon flew the short distance to gracefully land in Porter's palm. It felt like years since he'd held it. "How long since you found me?"

"A little more than a month," Cair said. "You had to be in stasis for a while, because of your injuries. And also, honestly, I don't have access to the finest medicine under Nihil occupation, so it took me a while to safely track down the right help."

"That hand looks pretty fancy," Porter said, though he was starting to believe the kid.

"It's a long story," Cair said glumly, flexing the black prosthetic. But his attention spiked again, and he stepped eagerly toward Porter. "Listen, I know how the Force works. It had to have led me to you for a reason. I'm trying to help people out here. I can't do what Jedi do, but regular people are doing our best."

"I've seen it," Porter murmured. In the past year, he'd seen so much, good and terrible.

"You can help. I know a lot about setting up undercover operations, spying and smuggling, but I don't know about tactics and—"

Porter shook his head. "Stop."

"But—"

"Look for a human named Rhil Dairo and for an Ugnaught pilot named Belin, who's been doing runs for the Nihil like you. They'll help you."

"Oh." Cair blinked as if his mind was working overtime.

Porter said, "I'm not your prisoner, am I?"

"No!" Cair said, eyes wide with surprise.

"I'm leaving. Where are my things?"

Cair pointed to a bin beside the cot. "Boots, belt, jacket are in there."

Porter nodded and put it all on, then strode for the only door.

"Wait!"

Porter ignored him, gripping his lightsaber in his hand. It felt so right. He knew where he needed to go.

Before he touched the door release, Porter paused. Turning only his head, he said, "If you meet other Jedi, if you hear of them, don't mention you saw me. Don't mention I'm alive."

"Why not?" Cair looked incredulous.

Porter pressed his mouth into a firm line and held the young man's gaze. His missing eye really wanted to open, the phantom awareness of it clear even after all this time. He was going to need a new patch.

He said, "I don't need any Jedi trying to find me. Where I'm going, they can't follow."

With that, Porter Engle hit the door release. It swished open.

Cair said, "Tell me your name, at least. I won't give it away."

"Sure." Porter nodded almost to himself, but he said, "Porter Engle."

"Thanks. Goodbye, Porter Engle, Jedi," Cair said. "If the Force is with us, I'll see you again."

It should have been nice, to hear faith in the Force from someone out here in the Occlusion Zone. But Porter could only think of where he was going. Of what lay ahead.

Goodbye, Porter Engle.

Chapter One

CORUSCANT

Avar Kriss walked quietly down the corridor of the Jedi Temple, a ceramic bottle of sourstone mead in one hand, a box of keldov nut pastries in the other. When she reached Elzar Mann's quarters, she paused, tucking the liquor under her arm, and flattened her palm to the cool metal door.

In most of the Temple, the song of the Force flowed peacefully, easily. This place was no exception. She pushed her awareness outward, reaching for her friend. He was in there. A small smile played on her lips, but before she could knock, the door slid open. Elzar was scratching at his beard, but his hand fell away at the sight of her. "Avar."

"Elzar." Her smile faded into something soft and expectant. "I'm leaving in the morning."

"I know." That was all he said, staring at her.

Avar waited, studying the thin lines of stress at his eyes, the way those eyes focused on her, unblinking. His beard had grown full, though he kept it trimmed shorter than Stellan's had been. He wore only the innermost layer of his temple robes—white tunic and white pants—and his feet were bare. When he noticed her glance down, he moved his toes against the thin carpet.

"Can I come in?" she asked. She wanted to add, *The last time I left you, I did it badly. I don't want to leave without you again. Without us.*

"Of course." Elzar backed up and Avar followed, pushing the pastry box against his stomach.

"Are these from Tal-Iree's?" he said in a hushed tone.

Avar grinned. "It's exactly where it used to be, down that alley in the Jadeite neighborhood."

"I'll get plates." Elzar hummed a little in pleasure as he went to the corner cabinet.

"And cups." Avar set the mead on the floor, then removed her boots and hung up not only her cloak but the outermost gold layer of her robes as well. After a second thought, she took off her belt and light-saber, too.

In the six weeks she'd been back from Nihil-occupied territory, she hadn't grown used to the layers of appropriate Jedi attire again. She embraced the Temple uniform for what it symbolized, though: being a part of a whole, a melody in a great symphony. It was unfortunate that this new mission would require her to remove it. Meanwhile Elzar had always hated the formal robes, and he wore them every day now. They'd both had to adjust.

Avar bent, stretching her hamstrings and calves, and grabbed the liquor.

"There are three buns," Elzar said suddenly.

She looked up, startled. He stood at the counter, where two small plates and cups were stacked on a dark tray, and looked down into the open pastry box.

Avar swallowed. "When I walked into the shop, I was so overwhelmed. It smells exactly the same, the menu is the same, the eat-in stools are just as chipped, that old painting over the pickup counter is the same. I ordered what I always ordered without thinking, and when I realized, I couldn't bring myself to make any corrections."

Elzar nodded and put all three buns onto the tray. When he turned to her, he was smiling sadly. "Already making yourself at home, I see," he teased.

"The mess in here is too familiar not to," she teased back.

Elzar's quarters were as basic as any in the Temple, except the small table, low bed, meditation platform, and every built-in shelf were covered in odds and ends. Mostly machinery, tools, pieces of computers, and datapads. Some rags and robes were tossed over the back of the sole chair. Avar nudged a pile of what looked like scraps of droid plating away from the foot of the bed and plopped onto the rug. She leaned against the bed and unstoppered the jug of mead while Elzar joined her.

She busied herself by pouring for them.

"Did you water it down?" Elzar asked.

"Pinkapple juice," she said lightly. Locating some had been the reason she was in the Jadeite neighborhood in the first place. Cutting the sourstone mead had always been for Stellan's sake, when they were fifteen and goofing off. Not because he opposed the alcohol, but to sweeten the flavor.

With full cups, they saluted each other and drank. It wasn't as good as when they were kids—probably because they weren't getting away with anything anymore. They hadn't had any idea what was to come back then. Of course, nobody ever did, but when she was a teen, Avar had thought she'd be an exception. She, Elzar, and Stellan: all exceptional.

She'd been right, in a way.

Avar picked up one of the nut buns and tore through the dark-brown crust to the rich crumb. With her chin she gestured toward the table. "That looks like parts of the Sunvale device."

"I've been experimenting with different alloy shielding and the most flexible style for the construction to make the devices more adaptable to different kinds of ships. The innards—the wiring and coding and slicing—I don't touch. I barely understand what Avon and Keven have designed for processing."

"I'm glad you're helping." Avar bit into her bun and leaned her shoulder against his.

"I couldn't let you go back across that Stormwall without a piece of me along with you."

She nearly inhaled nut bun at the dedication in his simple words.

Avar knew how dangerous this mission was. The newly invented technology for crossing the Stormwall was untested. She would be co-ordinating Jedi and Republic Defense Coalition—RDC—efforts to determine the feasibility of the tech and leading forays back and forth. There was every chance it was a one-way trip. The Stormwall remained practically impenetrable. She should know: She'd been the first person to escape after a year of trying.

She said, "Once we get the process down, it won't be very exciting. Just making jumps back and forth, evacuating people and delivering goods to Maz Kanata's contacts inside the Occlusion Zone. Maybe some of the Jedi still alive over there, who . . ." She trailed off, thinking of Porter Engle, who had sacrificed himself to distract the Nihil's General Viess from Avar's escape. It was difficult to imagine the great Blade of Bardotta dead. But not even an exemplary Jedi could survive an exploding ship or the vacuum of space.

Shaking herself out of it with a sip of sweetened mead, Avar said, "It will be mission after mission, each time with different priorities, different goals. Rescues and relief work."

"Sounds good. Sounds like making a difference out there." Elzar's tone was rife with the subtext: *Better than the politics here. Better than anything I'm doing.*

"Danger, experimental use of the Force, questionable allies. Sounds like," Avar said, glancing at him from the corners of her eyes, "a mission perfect for Elzar Mann."

He grimaced. "It's better for me to stay on Coruscant."

"Why?"

"I've been here, liaising between the Council and the chancellor, for nearly a year and a half. It would be disruptive for me to leave. The chancellor trusts me."

"El," she said gently, with only a slight censure. His answer was a line for the Senate or the public. Maybe fellow Jedi. But not her.

For a long time, he was quiet. Avar could hear him in the Force. It had been awful last year, not knowing if she'd hear him again—the comforting, necessary harmony of his familiar song. Not having it when she reached for it had taught her a lot about what she needed. Who she was.

Avar grabbed Elzar's bun and tore it apart. She held a chunk up to his mouth, and he smiled a little, eating it. As he chewed, his attention drew inward.

At different times in their lives, they'd been as close as two beings could be. She knew him better than anybody, and she could tell Elzar was aware of the real answer to her question. He was searching for the version he wanted to share. What he was willing to tell her.

A long time ago, he'd have told her anything. He'd reach for her first even when it was inappropriate according to Jedi teachings. Oh, how she wished for that now. Avar had spent too long holding him at arm's length, putting distance and sharp words between them, because of her own misunderstandings about selfishness and attachment, duty and worth. Now she understood that the whole she was part of meant nothing without Elzar in it.

Only it was his turn not to be ready.

Avar pulled her knees up to her chest and leaned her arms across them. She'd made so many mistakes, especially in the final months of Starlight Beacon's existence. She chased after anger under the guise of doing her job, spun too near revenge, and nearly gave in to the dark side. After the Drengir, the discordance of the dark side had been so loud. So Avar simply wasn't there for the fall of Starlight, for all the people who died: civilian, crew, Jedi—everyone. And in the aftermath, when she should have reached back for Elzar Mann when he held out his hand in grief and love, she pushed him away and left. Left Elzar, left Republic space, left herself.

Trapped in the Occlusion Zone, Avar had found herself again. She'd begun to make connections—with Porter Engle, that cranky Ugnaught pilot Belin, Rhil Dairo—and once she started working with others again, she'd rediscovered the melody in her own Force song.

She'd come home.

But there remained work to do, and she was leaving again on an uncertain mission, against awful odds. This time she wouldn't abandon Elzar without a fight. They needed each other. So she pushed a little. "Is it because you can't face the Stormwall again?"

Elzar closed his eyes, looking calm to a stranger maybe—but to Avar his struggle to maintain his expression radiated clearly from the tightness of his lips and the shift of muscles in his temples. "When was the last time I did something right?"

Avar sucked in a surprised breath. He hadn't failed *her*. Elzar knew— she'd told him—how much she'd needed to hear his message. How he'd been her anchor even from impossibly far away. He'd made mistakes, but just like Avar, he came home again in the Force. So many people here, including the chancellor herself and the Jedi Council, listened to his thoughts. Trusted him.

"I know," he murmured as if he sensed the direction of her thoughts. "I know I can solve problems sometimes. I'm stubborn, relentless even. When I want something for myself, I can find a way to get it. But when something goes wrong . . . it's so easy to give in to rage. I can't stop feeling it."

Touching his knee, she said, "You can't stop feeling things."

Elzar hummed a note of neutrality.

"We've all given in, the past two years," she said. "We've all failed."

"And we get back up and try harder."

"Yes."

"But what if it's not enough? Some things can't be fixed."

"Is this about what you did on Starlight?" Avar took a deep breath. "You tried to tell me on Eiram, when I was blaming myself for what happened and couldn't hear it. You would . . . honor me by trying again, now that I can listen."

"I'm doing better with it," he began. "Accepting that it happened. If I hadn't tried to tell you, I might have just repressed it and let it fester. The words sat with me, though, while you were gone. I thought about it over and over, until I just accepted that it happened. The part I can't accept is that it could happen again. The rage I felt watching Grand Master Veter be executed like that . . . and after the . . . when the flotilla . . . what if I only hold on to myself when there's nothing I can attack? Nothing I can take my rage out upon?"

Avar squeezed his knee.

"Chancey Yarrow was there. Right there. She'd been our prisoner because she was working with the Nihil. But that day she was working to fix Starlight, and I killed her. I didn't think about it or feel any hesitation—I just struck. Every excuse is too thin. It was darkness. It wasn't who I think of myself as or who I want to be. And it cost us everything."

"Not everything." Avar glanced up at him and gasped silently at the tear trailing down his cheek. "Come here," she whispered as she pulled him against her. Elzar hugged her waist, and Avar felt tears in her own eyes.

This was how it should have been immediately after Starlight. Them, together, holding each other. But Avar had rejected him, again, and a big part of her could hardly believe he trusted her enough to keep trying. She wasn't sure she deserved his trust.

Avar had left him. But Elzar never let go of her. Even across the Stormwall, countless light-years, misunderstandings, anger, failure, loss, a year of grief and struggle—no, more than a year—he had never let go.

Avar knew, as completely as she knew the Force, that Elzar Mann would never let go of her. Even in rage.

Once it would have upset her. She'd have believed it meant their relationship was too narrow, too selfish. A tangle of emotions and hormones and boundary-pushing attachment.

She didn't believe that anymore. In Elzar's voice, when he'd reached for her across those light-years, across the Stormwall, Avar had felt a fathomless, rolling faith. In herself. In the Force. In hope.

Surrendering to all of it made her stronger. Realizing and accepting that she was in love with him made her stronger.

She was afraid if she told him that right now, he'd be the one to run away.

"Stellan," Elzar started, but he swallowed the rest. Avar gave him time. She breathed, gently tapping her heartbeat against his shoulder. Finally he said, "Stellan would have told me to get right with myself, with the Force. And then he'd have wanted me to tell the Council. Seek support."

"That's right," she agreed, ignoring the things she herself had not told the Council.

"I miss him. All of them. But him."

"Me, too," Avar whispered through a tight throat.

Elzar shifted, lowering to lie fully on the floor with his cheek on her thigh. Avar combed her fingers through his hair and stroked his tear-damp beard. He talked about what it had felt like, the cold horror of what he'd done and the distorted fear of those Nameless let loose on the station. He told her about how awful those hours on Starlight had been, and of his final moments with Stellan. And he told her about leading the RDC flotilla to batter the Stormwall only to watch helplessly as so many lost their lives. Again. He told her he knew it was selfish how badly he wanted her back, needed to hear her answer his calls.

Avar listened. She listened to his voice and to the melody of his Force. And she whispered his name to him, whenever he needed to hear it.

In the morning, they woke in a heap on the floor, groggy and tearstained. They laughed softly at each other and shared a cup of caf. Avar could see the weariness still in him. His fear and anger mirrored her own heart. But this was better. They could get through it together. They would.

As Avar started for the door, Elzar grabbed her hand.

"Every time you return through the Stormwall, send me a message."

Avar cupped his cheek, then tweaked at his beard. "I promise."

They stared at each other for a moment, breathing in tandem. Avar reached for him, heard his note in the song. Felt him reach back. It wasn't quite the strength of the connection they'd had once. But it was good. It was a new start.

Then, at the exact same moment, Avar and Elzar parted, and each Jedi Master got back to their work.

Chapter Two

Marchion Ro had been bored for a very long time.

Bored, weary, furious. Occasionally rising to some vicious circumstance that should have filled him with glee at least, or sometimes twisting a knife he'd planted long ago only to feel the bare echo of satisfaction.

The things that once drove him had become duties.

But this, *this* was interesting.

He stood at the prow of a barge, one hand on the rail. The barge hovered low over a forest of crystals as tall as a human adult. This entire side of the moon had been engineered into a growing field for the raw hestalt and false kyber crystals. For over a year the moon had glinted with smoky gray and pink quartz fractals—the crystals harvested every month and transported to the Lightning Crash space station to be inserted into Dr. Mkampa's power array. From there they powered his Stormwall.

It was cold here under the pale-blue Norisyn sun, but Ro didn't mind. He'd weathered much worse. What was a nip in the air to a man who'd battled lyleks bare-handed and navigated the Veil, a man who had brought the Republic to its knees and kept it there?

He stood with the stillness of a predator, black eyes fixed on the spikes of crystal just below his barge.

"It's beautiful," said an Evereni woman standing beside him.

Ro ignored her.

"I've never seen anything like it, and it was built for you," she continued, her voice soft with wonder.

Ro had been hearing her voice for a long time, softer against the anger and irritation of his father's. But she had only recently begun to appear. She was usually older than him, with the telltale red streaks of Evereni age in her long black hair. She wore pristine white. Her skin was dark gray, her teeth sharp, and her big black eyes as soulless as his own. Sometimes her mouth dripped blood.

She was only a manifestation of an old Evereni talent—or curse: seeing their ancestors. But Marchion Ro did not speak to the dead if he could help it.

He leaned out over the edge, then lazily touched the starter to rev the barge's engine. It hummed quietly as he pulled it back, drawing the lengthening shadow away from the particular line of crystals he studied.

Several days ago he'd been informed by his secretary, Thaya Ferr, that some sort of plague had begun to affect the crystal farm here on Norisyn's fifth moon. There were no theories as to the source, for the workers tending the crystals had simply stopped sending their reports, and the last harvest transport had set down on the moon and never left. Dr. Mkampa complained at her lack of replacement crystals—and she needed them immediately, for the pressure of the basalt bath and delicacy of her arrays cracked crystals beyond repair quite regularly. The complaint ran up the proper channels until it reached Thaya, and Ro was willing to admit to himself that some things happened more smoothly with the advent of Ghirra Starros's structural organization of his Nihil. He'd rather dig out his own eyes than admit it to anyone else. Thaya had presented Ro with a handful of options for who should be dispatched to look into it, but Ro had been, as was often the case these days, bored.

"I'll go myself," he'd said, and that was that.

The *Gaze Electric* orbited the moon now, a long dark shadow against the thin sky. Ro had taken a shuttle down to the empty barracks and calmly confiscated this heavy barge equipped with winches and laser cutters to harvest and haul the hestalt and false kyber. There was no sign of living beings, the harvest transport abandoned. Blaster marks scored a few of the buildings, but no bodies remained. *Perhaps there has been a jailbreak of sorts,* Ro thought. Perhaps nothing had gone wrong, but the workers had fled. It made little sense, though. If insurgents or anti-Nihil or Jedi had come to the Norisyn moon, they'd only have done so to hurt the manufacture of his crystals, which they'd have had to find out about in the first place. Stumbling upon the moon accidentally was extremely unlikely even for the Force-supported Jedi. In that event, they'd have done more than free a few measly workers—they'd have destroyed his entire harvest.

The harvest was not going to survive, but the longer Ro studied this plague, the less he was bothered by the massive loss. All he saw was incredible potential.

"It spreads from there." The Evereni ghost pointed to the epicenter of the plague.

Half the field of crystals glinted under the blue sun; the other half was dull, chalky, diseased.

A gray-white dust seemed to spread from a single point, consuming everything in its path, in every direction. Turning the hestalt blades and false kyber columns into something new. Something dead. A void of energy and life.

The plague did not confine itself to the crystals, either. It covered the granular matrices of various minerals of the moon's surface from which they grew the crystal. And toward the horizon, where the growing field became a tundra, the grasses and shallow dirt were all consumed by the gray plague, too.

Ro steered the barge along the edge of the field, staring at the desolation.

"It's rather peaceful," said the old Evereni woman. He knew her name but would not deign to think it. "Do you think there is freedom in peace?"

Ro ground his teeth to keep from answering her. The barge swung around toward the small settlement, and he could see the fingers of plague reaching into the living quarters. The flora was nothing but calcified skeletons and dust, and the semi-organic walls of the barracks fared little better. It was the steel and plastics that retained their integrity, but even those showed the beginnings of being affected. Infected?

"You're supposed to answer that there is peace only in death, little Evereni," the old woman said with a smile. "But you never do what you're supposed to, isn't that so?"

Ignoring her amused glance, Ro angled the barge back to the plague line at the heart of the crystal forest. He lowered the barge until he could nearly see his reflection in a bright facet of false kyber. He put both hands on the rail and stared. Studied. Waited.

The false kyber was beautiful, it was true. If he spoke to the dead, he would admit as much to his ancestor. Blue and green and pink glimmered deep in the smoky walls of the crystal as it pierced up. But the plague had reached it. Little filaments of dust-gray, like crawling soot, nested at the crystal's base. Ro stared, breathing carefully, and waited.

In his infinite stillness, he could see it eat.

The blue sun hid behind the planet Norisyn, and Ro watched.

Stars appeared and a vast darkness spread over the crystal farm, and Ro did not move. He blinked and he breathed but did nothing else.

Next to him, the dead Evereni didn't even blink. She didn't need to.

All through the brief night, Marchion Ro stood beside his great-

great-grandmother, and together they watched the plague of nothing-ness creep up the length of the false kyber.

When the first white light of the moon's dawn haloed the planet, she said, "It eats the kyber faster than the hestalt. It ate the grass and fibrous windows of the barracks faster than the alloy frame. I wonder . . ."

Ro barely narrowed his black eyes against the morning light as he continued to watch the progression up the long vertical facet of crystal.

"I wonder . . ." the Evereni woman murmured again, herself leaning over the rail of the barge.

Marchion Ro activated his comlink. "Thaya, send someone down here with meat, the first three things you can put in a bag, along with several different designs of handheld weapons and that three-legged tooka cat that Bas Ear'lasr has been feeding in my hangar bay."

"Yes, Eye, immediately," Thaya replied at once.

It did not take long for a shuttle dispatched from the *Gaze* to land on the edge of the farm. Ro steered the barge over it and tossed the barge's ladder down toward the top of the shuttle. He commanded the Nihil with his deliveries to emerge from one of the upper maintenance hatches and climb up.

Shortly, a Nihil whom Ro had never paid attention to before—and hardly intended to start now—clamored over with a bag that thunked onto the metal floor of the barge, and a second bag still held over his shoulder. The latter squeaked and hissed, and tiny claws pierced the material.

Ro grabbed the moving bag and dumped the flailing tooka cat out over the rail.

It yowled but landed well on its three legs, talons slipping against the angled face of a crystal to finally rest on the mineral matrix below. Or what remained of it, here where the ashen plague had eaten every-thing.

Ro watched the tooka cat pick its way along the calcified crystal farm. Its tall ears pricked toward the only sound in all the landscape: the humming engine of the barge.

"What is this?" the Nihil snarled, fear shamefully detectable in his voice. He was a heavily tattooed human with the bright-blue eye painted across his entire face.

Overcompensation, Ro thought dismissively. Instead of ordering the Nihil to dump the contents of the second bag over the edge, he grinned at the human with all his sharp teeth. "An experiment," Ro said and shoved the human against the rail. He punched up into his solar plexus, driving the breath from the man, then tipped him backward over the edge.

The man hit the ground with a hard thump and groan. Ro smiled down at him.

Beside him, the old Evereni woman sighed. She leaned against Ro's shoulder. He felt nothing as he commed the shuttle, instructing it to return to the *Gaze.*

Ro held vigil again, ignoring the yells and complaints of the fallen Nihil, letting the shrieks of the tooka cat wash over him. The little purple-striped tooka cat with its tall ears died first. It was not consumed quickly, but neither was it as slow a crawling death as the false kyber suffered.

The human Nihil climbed over spears and blades of crystal, running for the settlement. But there was nowhere to go. He'd been infected, and the shuttle was long gone. The Nihil cursed up at Ro and spat on the ground as the plague-ridden crystal farm crumbled under his boots. That one did not die until the next brief nighttime, when the plague reached his chest and turned his lungs to dust.

It was so slow. So excruciating. The effect was so—

"So familiar," his ancestor whispered. "Like the Leveler's power."

Marchion Ro didn't speak to the dead, but sometimes he listened.

Chapter Three

Jedi Master Avar Kriss closed her eyes and listened to the singing Force.

It surrounded her, the melodies tumbling over one another, a harmony of stars and beings and breath.

She centered herself in its cradle, ready.

When Avar opened her eyes, she raised them from the controls of the navicomputer before her to the spread of stars. There was no hint of visual distortion, no buoy or blinking fence post. As far as she could see, there were only distant suns against the blackness of space. But she was staring at the Stormwall.

"I'm ready at your mark," she said softly to Friielan, the RDC pilot next to her.

Friielan nodded. They were half Theelin with dark-copper skin, vivid-violet hair, and a warm but sharply focused demeanor earned through the loss of their immediate family on Valo. They said, "The device is fully loaded and ready to deploy."

Avar smiled softly to herself, glad for the obfuscating language.

What they were doing was dangerous and experimental, not so mundane as Friielan's words made it sound.

Since Avar had left Coruscant—and Elzar—she'd been back and forth across the Stormwall six times. Today would be her seventh.

When Avar had first escaped the Occlusion Zone on the ruined *Cacophony*, it had taken desperation and luck and the sacrifice of good friends. Now it took courage, a pilot, a little machine invented by a young genius named Avon Sunvale to trick the Stormwall, a series of time-phased Path-oriented codes stolen from the Nihil and run through the navicomputer via the Sunvale device, and someone confident to input the hyperspace route coordinates in real time without mistakes.

She and six other Jedi had managed the feat, including Stellan's former Padawan Vernestra Rwoh, who'd been instrumental in gathering the technology for the Sunvale devices to work. But even with their expertise and the Force, two of the missions had failed. Jedi Knight Ilsan Kowal had died along with his RDC pilot, and the second failure lost them not only Jedi Master Forsyth Wry, guiding one of Maz Kanata's pilots, but also five refugees making the jump back with them.

Avar emptied her mind of the potential consequences and past failures and focused on the way ahead.

It was only Avar and Friielan heading into the Occlusion Zone with supplies, information, codes, and messages all useful to various people in Nihil space. These border crossings were too risky for doubling up on Jedi, despite the Guardian Protocols in place prohibiting individual Jedi missions. They didn't use Longbeams or ships that required a larger crew for similar safety reasons, especially for a mission like this that was only a quick smuggling trip, that poked holes in the Stormwall. Avar would fly them to the prearranged coordinates and trade her cargo for the O.Z. cargo, then return. In theory, the return required the same effort and the same risks, but in reality, Avar had learned the trip home was significantly more difficult for her.

Because the return cargo was always people. People desperate for help, who were fleeing the Nihil in this dangerous way, whose lives depended on Avar's ability to direct their ship along a specific, safe hyperspace route.

Last year, Avar's song had been distant and discordant as she struggled alone in the Occlusion Zone with grief and anger. Then she'd begun working with others, and as Avar had grown to feel like part of a team again, she'd found the hope and strength to escape and return home to the Jedi and Elzar. Being on a team didn't end with distance. The parts of the galaxy divided by the Stormwall were still their galaxy. Avar could finally hear the full, gorgeous song of the Force again without distortion, for the first time since Starlight fell, when Stellan and Maru and so many others died.

And Avar understood that going forward her work needed to be out here, on the edge of Republic space—doing, acting, helping. That was her role on the side of the light. Not planning and leading as she'd so often done before. Now Avar went where the Force needed a single note to ring bright.

A clarion.

The people she helped save included refugees, politically important Republic citizens, and children. They clamored for rescue, buying or earning their place in these missions. Avar didn't know how they were selected, and part of the deal brokered by Maz Kanata between the various groups of freedom fighters organizing in the Occlusion Zone and the Jedi included that the choice of who exactly was rescued would be left to the fighters in Nihil space. Jedi could request specific targets, but the final determination was up to their allies.

Avar trusted their contacts by now because not only were her passengers often people who would not have been able to pay for special treatment, but there were always children in the groups. Two of her trips had saved *only* children. Their survival had been wholly in her hands, and so far she'd managed to keep all her temporary charges safe.

"Initiating Sunvale device and hyperdrive. You have forty-two seconds," Friielan said, their bronze fingers flashing over the dials.

Avar breathed softly and let her vision blur. She sank into her ready state of meditation, and the bright song of the Force lifted around her again, just like turning up the volume on a playback device.

She knew the long strings of numbers that made up this hyperspace route. She understood their rhythm. But now Avar let the Force make the coordinates into a refrain for her to sing back.

Friielan counted down the final moment for her, and when the Theelin said, "We are *go*," Avar leaned in and let the route flow out of her mind and into her hands. She inputted quickly, precisely, and felt the shudder and hum of the *Blue Range* leaping into hyperspace.

Avar breathed through the moment when any explosive flash would abort their mission, unafraid of the quiet silence of immediate annihilation against the Stormwall's gravitational fluctuations. Those fears were for nightmares. This moment was for focus and the joy of Force communion.

She put in the next coordinates just as precisely.

The Force melody pulled her along, and Avar was simply a voice in its infinite choir.

Avar focused on the melody of hyperspace flight and listened for the cues from the pilot. She added the next coordinates and the next, and after the final numbers slipped flawlessly from her fingers, she released a long, soft sigh.

The *Blue Range* dropped back into realspace with a light shiver.

"Arrived at rendezvous coordinates," Friielan confirmed with relief in their voice.

Avar allowed herself a smile and a moment in the warm glow of success.

A spike of anxiety touched Avar through the Force, coming from Friielan. Avar looked up at the viewport.

Stars glittered, and so did the metallic shells of dozens of scav droids.

She felt her body go cold. The rendezvous coordinates had come from the same sources—why would it be a trap now? Why bring them right to a Nihil dead zone?

Friielan cursed under their breath and brought the ship around. Avar dashed across the cockpit to the communications station and started the scanner. "Any sign of our contact?"

Through the viewport, Avar saw scav droids whirr to life, drifting speedily toward the *Blue Range*.

"Incoming in ten . . . nine . . . I'm powering shields," Friielan rushed to say. "Do you have other coordinates for jumping away, or should I start the navicomp—"

Avar studied the readout on the comm, ignoring the army of dots indicating the scavs. "There's a personal shuttle ahead, but it's a Nihil designation. *Blood Vulture*," she said grimly. She glanced up as a scav droid shifted, its spindly legs aimed right for the port.

Just then the cockpit filled with a stranger's voice. "This is the *Brightbird,* code *Theljian snow dogs are known for loyalty.*"

"Oh," Avar said, and pressed the mic, ready with the response. "*Plinka is the best girl.* Please tell me you have accurate scav codes."

"On their way to you," the cheerful voice promised. "Sorry for the scav surprise—we're testing out a few ideas and hoping the Nihil would never think to look for us in the middle of these nasty babies."

"More than a surprise," Avar said tightly. "I hope your codes are accurate."

"Incoming," Friielan said, their voice high with nerves. "And re-transmitting . . . now."

Avar kept her attention locked on the many-legged droids, doing her best not to remember the sound of their saws and claws tearing into the hull of a ship like it was made of Sentuvian cheese.

Suddenly the scav droids froze in place.

They hung, floating as if their strings had been cut all at once. The codes had worked.

"Thanks, *Brightbird,*" Avar said. "*Blue Range* ready to couple. Can you come around?"

"Copy, transmitting coupling codes," came the stranger's voice.

"I'll go down to manually lock the tether," Avar said. It was unnecessary, but Avar liked to be there to help any children maneuver through the gravity-free docking tube.

Friielan nodded. "I've got the control."

Avar made her way through the ship to the belly level where the air lock was. The *Blue Range* was a midsized transport with three crew levels, minimal weapons, strong shields, and a backup hyperdrive just in case. There was a turbolift, but Avar used the quick-access ladder behind the captain's quarters to slide down to the lowest level. She made her way to the hold where the docking ring was. There she activated the clamps and tether, then waited for word from Friielan.

The pilot commed down, linking Avar in with the two ships. The cheerful voice from the *Brightbird* said, "Initiating dock," and Avar listened to him and Friielan quickly and competently maneuver together while the *Blue Range* hissed and whirred comfortingly around her. It was easy to push away the knowledge of enemy territory, of the creepy scav droids waiting just past the hull, silently sleeping.

The docking ring lights blinked blue, then red as the locks engaged, and air hissed as the tube equalized. Once the red lights flashed off, Avar turned the clamp that would unlock the door itself. A warning beeped to remind her of the potential of vacuum, but Avar hushed it and swung the ring door open.

She stepped up into the lightweight tube and held on to one of the handles to hold her balance. It was only a few paces across to the *Brightbird,* and already people were pulling themselves through. Avar put a pleasant smile on her face, knowing she looked like any regular flight crew, not a Jedi. Except for her lightsaber, she continued to leave the trappings of the Order behind while she worked across the Stormwall. It hardly mattered, because her face was so well known these days, but Avar didn't find it useful to tempt anything.

The first man to reach for her hand was an older human Avar recognized. Surprise lifted her eyebrows before she realized she should have expected him.

The man was Marlowe San Tekka, and behind him was his husband, Vellis.

Avar had last seen them on her trip to Naboo right after the Great Hyperspace Disaster, when she and Elzar approached the San Tekkas for their expertise on hyperspace. And one of the most recent expansions of part of the Stormwall had consumed Naboo. The San Tekkas were exactly the kind of high-profile people in need of a quick escape.

"Marlowe San Tekka," she said, grasping his hand and pulling him gently to the ring. "Welcome to the *Blue Range.*"

"Master Kriss," he said, sounding rough and weary. "I wasn't expecting you."

"Perhaps you ought to have," his husband, Vellis, groused softly behind him.

Avar smiled. "Watch your step," she said, helping them through.

Several others followed, including human adults and three older children all dressed in variations of Naboo styles. But behind the line of Naboo citizens was a stout Ugnaught whom Avar recognized instantly.

"Belin?" she gasped, a grin spreading.

The Ugnaught popped his head up, grinning back around his tusks. "Jedi," he said. "Sorry you have to be back over on this piss-poor side of the galaxy so soon."

A small round cam droid zipped up over his shoulder, blinking and beeping softly. Belin rolled his eyes, but they twinkled at Avar as he said, "Rhil's here, too."

Avar stepped back to let the Ugnaught in, and he swept her up in a big hug. He hugged so hard it startled a rare laugh out of her.

"I had no idea you were working with our allies over here," Avar said when he released her, and she patted her jacket back in place. "I should have known."

"I'm not usually on these kinds of runs," Belin admitted. "But Rhil and I need a favor from the Hero of Hetzal."

Chapter Four

INSIDE THE OCCLUSION ZONE

Avar commed up to Friielan, asking the pilot to come help the refugees settle while she slipped over to the *Brightbird* to retrieve their data load of messages and intel. She sent each new member of the *Blue Range*'s party up the lift with a shoulder clasp or gentle smile, promising she'd return shortly and they'd be across the Stormwall in no more than an hour.

They understood the reality of the risks or they wouldn't be here. Avar didn't need to remind them. Better to project surety and hope. Too many of them burst into tears when they heard her name.

When the last refugee headed to the next level, Avar turned back to Belin. It was good to see him after nearly three months, and in a way she hadn't expected. They'd met during the last trying weeks of her imprisonment in Nihil space. It had seemed a chance encounter, because Avar hadn't expected to find such a staunch ally when she hijacked a Nihil supply ship to steal their grain for starving people. But Belin had latched onto her—and her mission—immediately. He didn't let go until he met Rhil Dairo, and chose to stay with the former Republic reporter and keep the mission going when Avar left the O.Z.

Belin had been caustic and gritty but reliable. Avar had trusted him. She was glad for the chance to repay him with whatever favor he asked.

Still, she felt a slight unease at the way he'd phrased his request for help. Belin had been with her on Nihil-occupied Hetzal.

"It's good to see you," Avar said, walking to the docking ring.

"You, too, Avar," Rhil Dairo called from the open mouth of the *Brightbird*'s matching ring.

The little cam droid zipped across the tube, nearly slamming into Rhil's chest.

"After you," Belin said with a cheeky bow of his head. Avar reveled in the warm camaraderie as she used handgrips to pull herself along the tube toward Rhil. She had friends across the galaxy, especially in the Order and on Coruscant, but it was so good to remember she had them in Nihil space, too.

Rhil Dairo grinned as she reached for Avar to pull her into the *Brightbird*. The brown-skinned human woman had her cybernetic augmentation back. The last time Avar saw her, Rhil had retained only the machinery built into her temple and around her eye; the visor and connection to the cam droid had been missing.

Rhil grasped her hands. Despite her big smile, her voice was quick and professional when she said, "Thank you for coming over. It won't take long."

"What exactly is the favor?"

"Let's let the mastermind explain," Belin grumbled behind Avar. The Ugnaught hit a few switches to put the docking tube in standby.

"Sure, Belin," Rhil said. She gestured at the droid hovering over her shoulder. "This is Tee-Nine. Not currently recording, but I still see what he sees."

"I'm glad you've reunited."

"Tee-Nine was on Bentora, where I lost him in the first place." Rhil reached up almost as if she were tickling her droid's underbelly. "He was our first rescue mission."

T-9 whirred and clicked as they led Avar into the *Brightbird*.

It was a small, old-fashioned prospecting ship, like many of those found in the Outer Rim. Fitted and refitted for different lives. This one had clearly begun as state-of-the-art, though the lines now were out of style, with plenty of scoring and scars and a few signs of typical messy Nihil updates. Avar wondered if it had ever had a functioning Path engine.

"What have you been doing since I saw you last?" Avar asked as they led her up a spiral stair and into a galley lounge.

"It took us a while to make contact with useful allies," Rhil said. "Even once I started broadcasting my own stories on those old Eeex frequencies. We moved around a lot, so we were less likely to be caught, and looked for better substations to push out the broadcasts with more power. It was Cair who found us, actually." Rhil smiled. "Belin was not impressed by Cair's approach. He used a Nihil battle song to deliver a coded message."

"Made my ears bleed," the Ugnaught said, coming up the spiral stairs into the galley with them.

"That's just an old man's taste," came a new voice—the same cheerful one that had greeted Avar and Friielan when they arrived at the coordinates.

Avar turned toward the corridor that probably led forward to a cockpit. Her hand automatically shifted toward her lightsaber, but she lowered it.

"Avar Kriss," Rhil said, "this is Cair San Tekka, the center of this side's insurgent web."

"One of them, at least," Cair San Tekka said with a grin. "I used to prefer the term *anarchist* in my youth, but these Nihil bastards really ruined that for us." The young human man was in his twenties and stood tall and lanky, hip cocked to one side. He wore a tight black flight suit under a tattered black jacket tied at the wrists with red ribbons. His skin was tan and his black hair in a messy topknot. When he grinned at Avar, his upturned brown eyes wrinkled with smile lines. He put his hands over his chest and bowed with a definite air of flirtation.

Avar let her amusement show, but not her surprise at finding someone so young in charge of so much. "Cair San Tekka?" she said lightly. "Related to Marlowe and Vellis?"

"Yep, yep," he answered. "They're my second cousins removed a time or two, but we all mostly just call them uncles. You probably know how San Tekkas are."

"I'm making some of that dirt tea," Belin said, stomping to the line of panels on the galley wall. "Let's get this moving before something goes wrong with your scav camouflage."

"Good thinking," Cair said. He glanced at Rhil, who nodded and led Avar to sit on the bench around a very old real-wood table scoured with stains and stripped lacquer.

Turning to Rhil, Avar lowered her voice, though it could still be heard by everyone. "Have you heard anything about Porter?"

Rhil immediately shook her head, looking sorrowful. "The *Foregone Catastrophe* was destroyed right in the air above Seswenna, and Nihil and scavengers were on it immediately. General Viess survived, and maybe Porter did, too, but . . . we don't know anything."

"We would know if he was captured by the Nihil," Cair San Tekka said. He swept back his long jacket to sit dramatically on a stool, then settled his folded hands on the table, making it obvious his left hand was a cybernetic prosthetic. It was sleek black alloy with dark-red joints, matching his whole aesthetic. It made sense he was related to the San Tekkas of Naboo, if he could afford something like that.

Avar let herself hope. If anybody could have survived that wreck, it was Porter Engle. "Belin said you had a favor to ask me."

"I do. We do." Cair shifted his energy from frenetic into serious and meaningful, almost as seamlessly as a Jedi might. Whatever else he turned out to be, Cair San Tekka was obviously a performer. His brown eyes met Avar's earnestly. "You know Belin and Rhil, so I'm sure you can imagine what Rhil especially is capable of. She's become a voice for the underground here in Nihil space. Sending messages of hope mostly, and coded hints about how to reach out for help if people can find them. She's great." Cair slid Rhil a quirked grin.

The reporter nodded, clearly used to his flirtatious air.

From the station preparing tea, Belin snorted.

Cair didn't let his smile waver. "We make morale drops whenever we can—basically implanting streams into different comm buoys or system frequencies to disrupt Nihil comms and get our message out. So people will know, remember, and believe that there are people here, under the Nihil, working for good." The young human leaned in. "You must know that the best way to keep people going is to give them a goal to aim for. Even if it's just something as unknown as—"

"Hope," Avar finished for him.

"That's right." Cair San Tekka nodded. He flattened his hands on the old wood table. "We want you to record one—or ten, honestly, as many as you have time for."

"Messages for your 'morale drops.'" Avar tried not to frown. She understood. She did. But there were consequences.

"Exactly." It was Rhil's turn. "If you, Avar Kriss, Hero of Hetzal, can speak to them for us, it will be more powerful than anything we can say. You made it out. You keep coming back to help."

Avar shook her head. "But I don't want to provoke anything. Boasting that I can get in and out of the Stormwall is a mistake."

"Not a boast," Rhil said. "A promise."

Belin set a tray of four steaming mugs on the table. "They already know you come in and out, Jedi," he said, giving her a mug.

"Do they?"

"Yes," Cair said. "You've been doing it for weeks, making a nuisance of yourselves according to my best Nihil source."

Rhil said, "But they don't know how you're crossing. That isn't something they can discover with a morale drop."

Avar narrowed her eyes on Cair San Tekka. "Who's your source?

How did you make this connection? Are they the one providing the rolling Path codes to cross the Stormwall? If you have a spy in the Nihil, you should tell me."

Cair's grin sharpened. "I won't. But I'll tell you I trust him with my heart."

Belin groaned.

Rhil said, "They're married. Don't get him started."

That was not what Avar had expected. She paused, staring at Cair San Tekka. She listened intently to the Force, to her instincts honed by decades of training. Everything in her and outside of her said, *He's telling the truth. They're all telling the truth.*

But Avar wanted to press. The main reason that the Jedi and RDC could do nothing more than these small missions right now was a lack of intelligence. If a source in the Nihil had access to the Path codes, surely they could help the Jedi locate the central source of the Stormwall's power. Then they could bring in an attack group to actually end this. "Tell your source we need to know how to bring down the Stormwall."

"I'm working on him," Cair said.

"We can protect him if we have to. Get him to Republic space, keep him safe. That's a promise the 'Hero of Hetzal' is willing to make."

"I'll tell him," the young man said with a bit of a bite.

"All right." There wasn't much else Avar could do at the moment. She took the hot mug but didn't drink. "If I record a message for you, won't the Nihil retaliate?"

Cair San Tekka tapped a cybernetic finger against the table. "They will. But"—he leaned forward to cut off Avar's protest—"they already kill whomever they want. They will kill a hundred people tomorrow and a thousand the next day. If they're going to do it regardless, shouldn't we do everything we can to—to mitigate the emotional and spiritual damage? We can't control who dies out here; we can only try to make the living remember there's something worth fighting for—hope, right?"

Avar studied the younger man. Passion burned in his gaze, but there was a rare purity to the notes the Force offered her, as if risk for him remained theoretical, sympathetic. Not desperate. Not like he'd ever been broken by the Nihil. She sensed anxiety in him, yes, but no devastation. It hurt Avar to think it was only a matter of time before that changed. But she couldn't deny the truth and faith in him; it reverberated through the Force like a shock wave. Avar was glad there remained people like this young human, who were willing to act solely on principle.

Belin sighed roughly. "Jedi, even Rhil has come around to this kid's propaganda."

Cair made a bright, offended noise, but Rhil smacked the Ugnaught on the shoulder with a laugh. "It's the truth, Belin," Rhil said, showing her teeth in her smile. "I know my best weapons."

Watching the three of them—a cranky pilot, a kidnapped reporter, and a raggedy freedom fighter—engage in a friendly argument about the most dangerous, volatile storytelling filled Avar herself with hope.

"All right." Avar smiled back at the trio. "Let's do this."

Chapter Five

Jedi Knight Burryaga was frustrated.

The forest world of Oanne was one of the few places he'd ever visited where he was the one capable of vocalizing the primary indigenous language, but he still couldn't manage to communicate.

His friend Jedi Knight Bell Zettifar was doing his best.

"It won't last forever, I promise," Bell was saying, going to one knee beside the leader of this colony of Elia-An. The medicine artist—the title of the leader according to the translator droid—stood at the height of Burry's thigh, exactly tall enough that Burry struggled not to settle his large hairy hand on her downy head. The Elia-An had stiff bristles instead of fur or hair, but they were lined with exceedingly soft-looking down in iridescent colors of emerald and blue and pearl that matched the heartlines of their nativity trees.

The medicine artist patted Bell's arm and trilled a short line that reminded Burry of a higher-pitched dialect of Shyriiwook. "Can't matter if—burnt out," the translator droid said. Part of the Elia-An language included the shifting of bristles around their necks, and the droid didn't catch it well. That only compounded the communication issues.

They'd been on Oanne for three days, alongside a preliminary evacuation team with the Republic Defense Coalition. Oanne was the only inhabited world in its system, mostly left alone to exist and provide certain Republic interests with a particular fungus that grew on the roots of the planet's geriatric nativity trees and could be used as a very efficient electroconductor that didn't leave a traceable signature. A few generations ago, the Republic had made a trade deal with the Elia-An colonies, welcoming them into the Republic. In return the Elia-An had asked for scientists to help them understand the symbiotic gestation they shared with their nativity trees and attempt to form alternative arrangements for offworld travel. There were files and files of information Burry had scanned on his way to Oanne, gathered especially by a Ho'Din specialist. But nobody had successfully created an artificial or even temporary natal chamber for the Elia-An that mimicked their nativity trees well enough for the people to reproduce.

Therein lay the problem facing the RDC and Jedi: Oanne was extremely near to the Stormwall's current border, and there was every likelihood of Marchion Ro expanding the border again soon—in the haphazard, unpredictable way he'd taken to doing since Master Avar Kriss's escape. Oanne would be consumed. The Elia-An faced a choice: remain and be occupied or massacred by the Nihil, or leave their homeworld.

Bell was determined to convince them they must leave, and he was sure that it would only be temporary. Burry was less certain.

"The Nihil might set fire to your forests, that's true," Bell said with a frown. "But if you're here, you'll die, too. If you evacuate with us, you have a chance."

"Doesn't the Republic want us for our—" The translator droid stumbled over the name of the fungus.

Burry didn't need to hear it. "No," he said sharply in An-An, startling everyone.

Bell slid him a surprised look, but the medicine artist tilted her head to look up and up at Burry.

Burry met her vivid-green gaze. The bristles along her neck rippled, shimmering green-blue to blue-green.

Gently, Bell said, "Maybe it's true the Republic wants your mushrooms, but not me and Burryaga. We want to keep you safe."

"Our forest can't leave," the medicine artist said to Burry, her trill and growls both soft and pretty.

Softening his Shyriiwook to better reflect the An-An vocalizations, Burry told her that the forest couldn't be saved at all if the world fell to the Nihil.

The medicine artist looked sad. It wasn't only the color of her bristles that said so: Burry could feel it radiating off her through the Force.

He glanced at Bell to see the slight pout of Bell's lower lip that the human got whenever he almost understood a more complicated sentence of Burry's. Bell didn't like how much he still relied on interpreters sometimes. Bell's reliance didn't bother Burry, but his determination to learn filled Burry with warmth. The first time he'd realized Bell was studying Shyriiwook, Burry had burst into Bell's little quarters and picked him up off the stool. There hadn't been room in the bunk to twirl him around, but that didn't stop Burry from trying. His master, Nib Assek, had made the effort for Burry so she could communicate with her Wookiee Padawan, but Bell didn't have the same kind of impetus. Bell was just a good friend and strong Jedi who knew it showed respect and that there would always be nuances an interpreter would miss. Bell wanted to understand his friend.

When Burry had been trapped in that cave at the bottom of the Eiram ocean, starving and tearing out his own fur to send messages that might not survive, he'd known that the chances of anyone even finding, much less understanding, his little totems were slim. But the hope had remained, lodged in his diaphragm like a cough, that somehow Bell would see them. That Bell's nature, his drive to understand, would save Burry. It had.

The medicine artist reached out with her seven-fingered forehand— the Elia-An had an extra set of arms that were shorter with smaller claw-tipped fingers they used to hook into their nativity trees—and patted Burry's stomach as high as she could reach. It was right above his belt, where the brown of his robes crossed. Then the medicine artist touched her own stomach over the interwoven strips of sashes that served as her clothing. She said something the interpreter droid couldn't translate. It sounded like the Shyriiwook word for "chiming bells": *Arryssslesh*.

Her name. Burry touched his stomach where she had. He answered her with his name in his native language.

"Come," she said, waving over her shoulder as she trotted deeper into the forest.

Burry glanced down at Bell, then grabbed his friend's elbow and hauled him up. They followed the medicine artist. The interpreter droid tromped after.

The forest thickened. This was a grove of nativity trees, which had smooth green-black bark that developed a single furrow up the center as they aged. Most here were older, parents to generations of Elia-An. Their branches spiked upward like wine flutes made of bright-blue filament, and their leaves, with the same downy feathering that covered the Elia-An, shifted in the planet's breeze. Between the nativity trees, smaller flowering saplings grew, spreading toward one another into a lacework of milky-white branches just low enough that Burry had to duck and walk in a crouch. He tried to avoid crushing the grasses along the narrow Elia-An path, but his feet were too large. When the blades bent and broke, they smelled like spice and their nectar glimmered like star algae. It lit the forest from below, and Burry thought it was beautiful.

Beside him, Bell said, "It's beautiful."

Burry roared a soft agreement.

It was easy to understand why the Elia-An didn't want to abandon their forest, even for a little while. If the Nihil came here, they'd turn it into ashes and smeared nectar.

Burry tried to let go of the anger he felt when thinking of the destructive determination of the Nihil. Better to rest in this lush forest teeming with the Force. It felt strong and connected, in the way of a healthy ecosystem. Burry, empathic as he was, sensed the emotions of the nativity trees. They were more like their sentient Elia-An counterparts than most trees Burry had encountered. He wondered if any Force users had tried to transplant the nativity trees into a starship's arboretum. If the Force could communicate to the trees the necessity of letting go their roots here, to survive, that might be a solution.

The medicine artist brought them into a meadow filled with bright-yellow insects floating around—no, they were seeds. Or insects. Burry found himself purring slightly in amusement. It didn't matter. Everything here was connected on more than just the level of the Force.

"Ah, um," Bell said.

Burry glanced back. Several of the insect seeds had settled in Bell's hair like a string of jewels. Burry laughed softly and told Bell he looked very pretty. Bell grinned. It was good to have moments like this, reminded of these pockets of peace and beauty out here next to the Stormwall. They'd spent so much time chasing and fighting, nearly dying again and again. The people here on the edges of Republic space were desperate, and Burry had let himself feel that, too. He was hyper-aware of sudden changes, of the potential for everything to explode or fall apart at a moment's notice. When he went to sleep, he always expected to be woken up with emergency alarms blaring.

At the far end of the meadow was a nativity tree so large around that six Wookiees with joined hands couldn't quite encircle it. It had multiple seams, and around it several Elia-An sat in tiny nests of downy filaments with their eyes closed, their extra limbs raised to hook into tendrils from the tree.

"This is a Grandfather tree," the medicine artist said via the droid. "This one no longer nurtures our fruit but helps those who wish to be parents pair with a younger tree. The memory in this Grandfather helps us locate our seed-heart."

Burry nodded, though he didn't understand the terms perfectly.

According to the Ho'Din scientist, the most accurate description of the relationship between the nativity trees and the Elia-An was that the people were the seeds to be cross-pollinated. The Elia-An moved from grove to grove, drifting with their communities to new trees.

"Come," the medicine artist said again. Burry went to her, and to his surprise, she took his hand and placed it on the warm, smooth trunk of the Grandfather tree.

"We cannot leave them," she said. The droid's translation was emotionless, but Burry could feel the grief and certainty in Arryssslesh's trill. He closed his eyes and leaned into the tree. The Grandfather tree was sad, too. It knew. It longed, it . . . Burry felt the pang of pride and sorrow along with something less easily definable, but Burry thought it was like a promise of letting go. As if the Grandfather wanted these Elia-An to go, to save themselves.

He knew if he said that, Arryssslesh would be even less inclined to evacuate.

She put her small seven-fingered hand over the back of Burry's, sandwiching him between her and the tree. Burry breathed deeply, and the Force thrummed throughout him—throughout the whole forest. It felt like home to him. The Force was a galactic forest, leaves and branches and pillars and roots, the complex array of animals and vines and lichen, fungi and viruses and worms that made up the variety of the living Force. This forest, in particular, had grown in a balance. Take one part away and the others would be bereft.

The Nihil had cut off part of the galaxy from the rest with their Stormwall. If they cut through the Oanne system, Burry was not sure the Elia-An could ever recover.

They shouldn't have to leave.

Bell stepped nearer and, asking permission with his eyes, put his own brown palm to the bark of the Grandfather tree.

Burry could feel his friend join the connection more directly.

"Is it better," Bell asked gently, "to die together, or to live apart with the hope of regrowing?"

Tiny spots on the Grandfather tree began to glow. They lit up in sequence, one after the other, a trail of light rushing up the lines of bark like shooting stars aiming high. Burry gasped. Bell laughed.

Arryssslesh's bristles tipped with the same light.

Burry understood. They were one. There was no such thing as apart. Not right now.

He really wanted to hug the whole tree, and so he did. He fell into the Force, into the rootwork and interlocking lace of the branches. He let himself have a moment, this moment, invited to connect with an intricate web of Force.

Something—something not too far from here—drew his attention through the layers of Force and emotion. A pull. A . . . hunger. It could be a dying nativity tree or a body of water, something slightly diseased maybe. He'd ask Arryssslesh—she would know.

But first Burryaga pushed his awareness toward it.

A harsh electronic bleep cut through his thoughts.

Burry jerked back, and Bell flailed for his comlink. "Sorry," Bell gasped. "Sorry." He thumbed the alert off and stepped back from the tree. "This is Bell Zettifar. What's going—"

"Jedi!" came the tinny voice through the comlink. "You're needed back on the *Tractate*. There's a distress call from the neighboring system and we—" The comlink distorted. They were deep in the trees, after all.

In his softened Shyriiwook, Burry promised Arryssslesh that they would return, then he followed Bell's trot away from the Grandfather tree.

"I'm sorry, can you say that again?" Bell insisted.

"It's Drengir!"

Burry stopped in his tracks. Drengir—sentient, vicious, meat-eating plant monsters. Here. On the Stormwall border.

"Burry, come on," Bell said, shock echoing in his voice.

They ran.

Chapter Six

CORUSCANT

Jedi Master Elzar Mann was definitely not hiding.

He was absolutely not avoiding anything. In the dark of a narrow storage closet on the twenty-seventh floor of the Senate building.

He was meditating. A very important part of a Jedi's day.

Just because he'd ducked in here before anybody could drag him away for an impromptu meeting didn't mean it was a very deliberate act of a not-at-all-desperate man. He had been rushing down a plush corridor between a meeting with a resource committee whose exact designation he couldn't quite remember and his daily one-on-one with the chancellor when one of the chancellor's secretaries had waved him down to cancel the meeting. This was right in front of Senator Toon's second aide, whose four round purple eyes brightened immediately at the news that Elzar suddenly found himself with ten minutes of free time to go over the allocation of Jedi Knights with the RDC on the border. Elzar had managed a stiff smile and grabbed JJ-5145's arm so quickly the droid stuttered to a halt. "I'm sorry," he said to the aide. "Forfive was just dragging me to an emergency comm, so I'll definitely get back to you. Forfive, can you find a minute or two for the RDC allocation this afternoon or, even better, tomorrow..." and Elzar dragged the droid down the hallway fast before the aide could do more than gape. Once they rounded a corner, he said, "Belay that, Forfive, and instead find me an empty room right now."

Luckily, Elzar found his own empty room before JJ-5145 could plug into one of the panels to access a map. Unluckily, it was a closet.

"With your unexpected free period, Master Elzar, might I suggest you attend to one of the prioritized items on the action-item list I've compiled, beginning with—"

"Thanks, Forfive, but just do me a favor and guard the door for, ah, at least twenty-five minutes. No comms, no emergencies, no interruptions, all right?"

The copper face of the droid tilted inquisitively, and it scooted back, then forward again on its rollers. "Master—"

"Thanks!" Elzar said and closed the door, leaving himself in the dark.

Before he could enjoy the shadows, automatic lighting glowed up. Elzar scowled and swiped the control panel to darken it again. He'd seen enough: shelves and panels with drink services for multiple types of teas and liquors and gaseous straws, refrigeration and heaters, and a long line of carafes in every material lined up like tiny security guards. Presumably there were a lot of meeting rooms on this level of the wing, and if anyone needed refreshment, Elzar had found the place to go.

He dropped to the floor with his back against the far wall and closed his eyes. It was cool and noiseless in here, thanks to whatever sound-proofing the Senate building specialized in for the privacy of its members.

With all the meetings and arguments he'd been caught up in, it had been a struggle to find times to connect with the Force. When he slowed down for just a moment, he began spiraling into thoughts of everything the Jedi and Republic hadn't done, couldn't do, and, worse, the things he firmly believed they needed to do but were stymied by politics. Elzar might scream if he had to argue once again with Senator

Toon about why they should be helping any civilizations on the Storm-wall border who wanted aid, not just those with resources valuable to the Republic. All lives would be devastated if they were swallowed up by the Stormwall, not just those of importance to shipyards or harvest processing. He'd absolutely spit transparisteel screws if someone tried again to convince Elzar they were wasting the potential of the missions Avar was leading. Elzar couldn't remind people yet again that the reason they didn't send a star cruiser across instead of a transport was because there was no useful target. They didn't know where Marchion Ro was from moment to moment, and they had no idea where to find the central hub of power running the Stormwall because it was a small space station that apparently moved. And what was the point of liberating a world such as Ryloth when the world would simply remain in Nihil space as long as the Stormwall was in effect? Yes, they could run missions back and forth, but the priority still had to be finding a way to bring down the damn barrier. And no, of course they didn't trust former senator Starros, but they still had to act like her representing the Nihil to the Senate mattered.

Elzar did wish he could be present the next time somebody said anything snide to Lina Soh's face about the chancellor sharing a meal with the Nihil representative.

But at this exact moment, it was only himself and the Force.

Elzar breathed and reached out.

The Force roared around him, crashing waves, and Elzar felt buffeted by the strength of it. His connection to the Force was immediate and vigorous even in this little dark bubble of a closet. If all that was required of Elzar was communion with the Force, he'd be unstoppable. But if the Force was a roaring ocean, he was a ship bobbing and tossed chaotically, barely managing not to drown even after all this time. The Force brought waves of contrary voices with it, a tide pulling him in every direction. He heard too many voices: everyone in his meetings tugging for this or that, the members of the Jedi Council, Chancellor Soh saying his name like he knew what he was doing, like he could do anything at all, JJ-5145 with its action items, Master Yoda discussing fear, Azlin Rell's *I see myself in you,* senators and techs on the Stormwall team, the pleading cries of the dead—the dead he owed, the dead he made. And Stellan's voice, calm and urgent, Stellan laughing. And Vernestra Rwoh, once Stellan's Padawan and now a determined Jedi Knight who had spoken Chancey Yarrow's name to Elzar and promised Elzar he would never be as good as her former master. Avar's voice. Avar, Avar, Avar telling him, *I trust you, Elzar.*

Avar who was out there again, crossing into Nihil territory again.

Elzar tried to focus on only the wordless Force, the rhythm of it matching his breath. It was dark, quiet, and still in this closet. Like a deprivation garden or meditation cubby. He should be better than this. After all his failures, he was trying. Trying to keep going. Do the work. Any of the work anyone required of him. All of it.

He went through the paces, the steps he'd used to connect to the Force since he was a youngling. It worked. The Force was right there with him, only it was so loud. It was too much, crashing from every direction.

If Elzar narrowed his attention, he might miss something.

If Elzar didn't listen to every voice, what if the solution drifted right by?

He let the cacophony crowd around him. At least it was strong. He had to be strong now, after his failures and missteps. They all did: The Jedi were flailing against the Nihil and the Nameless, and they didn't know the path forward.

Spending so much time with Chancellor Soh and politics in the past year had taught him that even if the Jedi didn't know what they were doing, they needed to pretend to. He had to sweep into his meetings with confidence, even if it was mostly faked. He had to leave his guilt and uncertainty for the solitude of the night.

Elzar breathed.

The Force swelled around him—loud, messy, without a singular voice.

Master Yoda had told him to trust the Force. To listen to what it would say. Avar said the same.

Elzar was trying.

After the disastrous attempt to breach the Stormwall he'd led, which caused so many lives to be lost for nothing, Avar had come bursting out of Nihil space in her captured ship, offering hope for everyone in the form of old hyperspace prospecting technology. The lost routes hadn't been enough to break through again—not when the Nihil had adjusted the codes in her wake. But Avar herself had escaped with a hint for the solution. Then weeks later, Vernestra Rwoh also escaped, along with the young Avon Sunvale. Elzar was one of a small number of people who knew that Avon's true surname was Starros, and that she'd defected from her mother's side and thrown completely in with the Republic, tirelessly attempting to help the task force breach or break the Stormwall. Avon had created something that used what Vernestra and Avar had both figured out with the help of the Force: a machine to mimic the Path engines and trick the Stormwall, but it only worked with a skilled, brave, determined Jedi. And even then, it didn't always work.

Of course, Avar Kriss led those kinds of missions. She was the most skilled, brave, determined person Elzar had ever met. And the Force sang with and through her.

Elzar wanted to be worthy of her again. Of her friendship, of working at her side. Both things he'd had when they were young. But most of all, he wanted to be worthy of the trust she insisted she already—always—had for him.

Focus, breathe, Elzar told himself.

He couldn't.

The Force was strong, but it did not want to talk to him. It wanted to shove its way down his throat and drown him.

Elzar sighed, leaned back against the closet wall, and reluctantly admitted to himself he was wasting his time. There was too much to do, to know, to hear. He couldn't sit here struggling with meditation.

Standing up, Elzar made his way to the door and keyed it open.

"Master Elzar!" JJ-5145 jerked in a little half circle. "Your allotted time has not completed its course, and so I—"

"It's fine, Forfive," Elzar said wearily. "I couldn't concentrate. Let's get back to work."

"Excellent, Master Elzar."

They headed for the level with Elzar's tiny office. It was as near to the chancellor's as propriety and the rules of political courtesy allowed—in other words, at least ten levels down. But Elzar used it for the occasional meeting that needed neutral ground, to read massive reports, and to take comms from longer-range contacts and the Jedi on the border. As they went, JJ-5145 described the prioritized items on his list, starting with an official memo—a memo!—Elzar needed to draft about the current reasoning behind how the Jedi were spreading themselves along the shifting Stormwall border to aid the RDC in voluntary evacuations of the worlds most in danger of being swallowed by Nihil space the next time Marchion Ro decided to arbitrarily expand random sections of the wall.

The Jedi weren't supposed to have to explain themselves in such a way. The Jedi guided themselves at the side of the Republic, not as weapons or guards for hire or wise old monks with good advice. Elzar shouldn't have to do any of this. But at the same time, the Republic was stretched thin, dealing with all the usual local conflicts and system-wide natural disasters and labor strikes on top of the constant, extreme, imminent threat of Nihil invasion.

This bureaucracy wasn't exactly what he'd been excited about growing up to do when he was a youngling.

But Elzar wanted to serve. He did. And right now he needed other people, Jedi Masters with a better understanding of the goals of the Order and the Force itself, to tell him how. This was where they'd put him: serving between the Chancellor's Office and the Jedi Council. In Stellan's shadow.

Every time he'd tried in the past year to push past his role here, to drive himself beyond the nexus of politics and meetings, it had gone horribly wrong. Elzar's instincts failed him. His work as a tool of the Force had failed him.

He couldn't fail anymore. Not the Order, not the Force, not himself. Not Stellan.

Elzar swept into his small office, activating the false window that made it seem like the room looked out over the dazzling glow of Republic City, instead of being a windowless cubicle stacked deep in the sinew of the Senate building. JJ-5145 continued speaking its list, something about a joint query from the RDC and the Temporary Emergency Rehoming Committee, who wanted to pull Jedi from the Oanne system, which Elzar honestly didn't even recognize, but surely he had read some report about Jedi being assigned there to help.

He turned to wave JJ-5145 off and make some instant caf of whatever sort was stocked in his drawers when the comm on the corner of his beat-up steel desk pinged.

Avar.

Elzar knew immediately it was her.

He hurried around to acknowledge and saw the comm was from the Font-Alor system, near the Stormwall. Elzar let himself smile. Maybe the Force had talked to him after all, pushing him to get off his ass in that storage closet so he could be here just in time to answer.

The connection trilled, and Elzar smiled. "Avar."

"Elzar." Her voice flooded the small room, and even JJ-5145 seemed to settle at the cheer and confidence she exuded across sectors and stars. "I made my seventh run."

"I knew you would," he said, a half-truth. The statistics of these Stormwall missions weren't something he liked to think about.

"It was good. The people I'm working with are doing so much good. I can't wait to tell you everything."

Elzar sat in the chair and leaned his elbows on the cold desk. She always contacted him immediately upon returning to Republic space. She said it grounded her and gave her a soft goal that never changed from mission to mission; he knew it was to calm him down.

"I want to hear everything," he said, unable to keep the low longing from his voice.

"I'll tell you this now," she said. "I saw Rhil Dairo and the pilot Belin I told you about. They've been working to disseminate hope and promises throughout Nihil space. I'm proud of them. Rhil seems to be eating better."

"Good." Elzar relaxed just a little into a casual tone. "You should give them a message of hope from the Hero of Hetzal," he teased.

Avar's laugh was bright. "I did! I wasn't sure, given my history with Ro. I was concerned about provoking him, but I thought of something you said."

She paused, and Elzar met the copper gaze of JJ-5145. He didn't know what she was going to say, either.

Avar continued, "You were worried about jumping to conclusions, about acting too fast and soon. But I think I've been doing the opposite. Too conservative. Not acting when I can."

"Avar, you haven't stopped acting," Elzar protested. "You survived across the Stormwall and escaped, and you brought us data that lets you go back and forth now. I know how dangerous it is—that's why the Council established so many rules for who could make those jumps and who couldn't."

"I know."

Elzar wished he could see her face. See the shape of her lips to read where her stress cut most deeply.

She said, "But I'm doing what I'm told."

"You say that like it's a bad thing."

Avar laughed again, softly this time. "I recorded a statement for them. I think it's probably less exciting and stirring than they were hoping for."

It was Elzar's turn to laugh. He missed her so much. "I imagine it was exactly what they wanted, if they asked you."

He heard a sigh and could almost see Avar's quiet smile.

"Are you heading back?" he asked.

"Not yet. I'm rendezvousing at the *Axiom* with Vernestra. We have a window to wait for comms and see if we need to jump back once more this cycle. Then I'll head back."

"All right. I'll be here, drowning in datawork. Can I tell the chancellor about Rhil Dairo?"

"Yes. I'll have a full briefing ready for her and the Council. I think this is going well, but it's not enough."

"Neither is evacuating the borders. It's too complicated, it's too expensive, and I'm not sure it saves anything in the long run. In these circumstances, is it better to be a refugee or an occupied community?"

"The answer is probably different for everyone."

"And it's hard to convince people here on Coruscant and within the Core that they should be giving up their resources for what-ifs or inevitabilities."

"Try not to let yourself grow bitter, Elzar," Avar said gently. "If you start to, join me out here."

Elzar shut his mouth. He couldn't do what Avar was doing. He couldn't do much of anything. This arguing and backbiting charm suited him better. It did. "I can handle it here," he said, a little too hard.

After a brief pause, Avar said, "May the Force be with you, Elzar Mann."

"I know the Force is with you, Avar Kriss," he answered, aiming to tease.

But he didn't think it landed lightly enough for that.

Chapter Seven

RILIAS II, INSIDE THE OCCLUSION ZONE

Cair San Tekka had been a lot of things in his relatively short life: a spy, a musician, a secret husband, a security aide, a secretary, a punk kid, a troublemaker, a pilot, and now a smuggler and freedom fighter. He wasn't the only one running various rebellions throughout Nihil space, and several such rebel groups had found ways to access the constantly changing anti-scav codes to allow for safer travel out here on the frontier, as well as a comm subroutine channel that made it through the Nihil comm embargo. Cair managed those things, too. But what he had that nobody else had was someone who provided him with frequently updated time-phased Path codes that could be used by the Jedi to penetrate the Stormwall.

And allies with ships of their own.

Those ships were what allowed Cair to be down in the central water garden of Rilias II, huddled in the bowl of their foris alloy funnel. The funnel had been built a few generations ago as a decorative fountain the size of a small building, out of a metal mined on one of their moons that allowed for an exact resonance with the minerals found in their perma-scatter clouds. The funnel gathered thin trickles of water all day and night from the water garden, and at sunrise and sunset most days of the year, when the light filtered through the clouds, it hit the alloy funnel. The funnel's reverberation caused particles in the air to vibrate into little rainbow stars.

It also amplified certain audio frequencies.

Cair shifted the strap of his harness to better reach the small panel that was part of the controls in the base of the funnel. He balanced against the sloped, slippery wall with his feet and worked quickly to remove a datachip and replace it with his sliced frequency emitter.

This would be the fifth morale drop he'd personally led, but the first that included a visual component.

Ever since he'd met up with Rhil Dairo last month, she'd been angling to find a way to include visuals in their drops. Symbols and smiles, she'd insisted again and again. Cair hadn't disagreed with the sentiment, only the practicality.

But today they had means and opportunity.

It was a three-pronged setup: Cair down here slicing the funnel to match the necessary frequencies, Rhil up in orbit with the *Brightbird*— or as it was known in these parts, the Nihil transport *Blood Vulture*— and Belin ready in his ship on the other side of the sparkling felsic cliffs edging the city. Rhil had dropped the refitted comm buoy with her newest broadcast, active to the frequencies Cair matched with the funnel, and Belin would fly over the city, releasing a hydro-spray to activate the clouds prematurely. Then their show would begin.

Cair finished his slice and hit the countdown monitor he'd brought. It synced up with the similar countdown embedded in his artificial hand. He grinned. So far, so good.

Climbing out of the funnel took a bit of time, but Cair hooked his legs over the edge and found a seat on a broad ruffled lily pad. He leaned back on the soft moss and tilted his head up. The teal sky was striped by thin blushing scatter clouds, and every once in a while, a personal shuttle zipped past.

Rilias II had been hard hit by the Nihil, but its central government had capitulated faster than many, giving in to demands for total surrender and allowing regular Nihil rioting missions under the cover of "tax collecting." Neighborhoods had been razed and anybody who fought back taken into custody or killed. It was a horribly typical story of the past year in the Occlusion Zone, but thanks to quick thinking or cowardly leaders, enough of the populace and riches had been sacrificed to semi-mollify the Nihil.

That just made Cair's job more important. He had to remind people they needed to fight. And they could survive. There was hope. It was worth reaching out, worth trying. Everybody needed to be trying.

The water garden shuddered under him as the city's inner mechanisms opened the underground rivers. It was nearly time.

Cair tried not to feel too deeply about the moment of peace. Waiting was the only peace he got these days. The peace between planning and action.

As always, he pretended he could feel the Force thrumming through everything, connecting him to the lily pad and water, to the air and atmosphere, to his allies in their positions, to the stars beyond, to his family—all of whom were in Republic space now, thank the Force. Cair wasn't strong in the Force in the least, but he'd been raised to trust it anyway. Sometimes he pretended so well he could actually feel it in his bones.

The countdown alert notified him he had a minute, and Cair got up onto his feet. He stood at the edge of the funnel as if he didn't have a care in the world. Security teams— the local constabulary indebted to the Nihil now and oppressed by them—could see him if they looked. If Cair was seen, he might be shot on sight. Or he might be cheered.

But Cair felt deeply that he needed to be seen. Somebody would tell the story: A human had been here and caused this disruption. Not from space, not from the distance beyond the Stormwall. Someone here. In the flesh. Risking death and torture to bring them this message.

Cair stood, ignoring the fear. This was worth being afraid. Worth death. It had to be. He'd spent too much of his life serving only his family's benefit, making underhanded business deals instead of music, toying with industrial espionage instead of new wavelengths for his dulcimer. He was good at creating trouble and spycraft, and he'd never regretted prioritizing what his uncles and parents pushed him toward. Until he met somebody even better at such games, and married him.

Of course, with the Nihil occupation, nothing was a game anymore. Cair had done his best to lay low, help those he could, and keep himself from putting a target on his husband's back. He hadn't known what else *to* do.

Now he knew.

He'd seen people sacrifice everything to keep their families alive. He'd witnessed far-flung San Tekkas disregard profit and exploration and everything Cair thought made San Tekkas San Tekkas just to save a handful of people in danger. They'd been more than brave, risked everything, left it all behind, not for glory or profit but for *hope*. He'd lost his hand learning to make the same choice.

It still wasn't easy to do. But every time Cair chose hope, it got a little less scary.

Warm wind brushed strands of messy black hair across his face. He made himself smile. That would be the last thing he did, if it was the last thing he did. His dramatic husband would say, *Running should be the last thing you do, you fool.*

Cair heard the high scream of Belin's engine before he saw the glint of the ship out at the line of felsic cliffs.

It was time.

Cair twisted a tiny red dial on his black-metal hand, and it snapped with a frequency. The funnel hummed in answer.

The rest was up to Rhil and Belin.

Suddenly Rhil's voice blasted throughout the sky: "Greetings, free citizens of the frontier! This is your friend and ally Rhil Dairo, and today we have a message from a hero you all know!"

Cair laughed. Rhil's broadcast would travel from buoy to buoy until the Nihil managed to stop it.

The funnel thrummed harder, and there came Belin, streaking across the sky in his sharp-nosed shuttle. Behind him trailed a shimmer as the hydro-spray clung to the lower atmosphere, ready.

Cair raised a hand to Belin, who vanished over the distant horizon. The spray caught the sunlight and the funnel flared.

"Hello, this is Jedi Master Avar Kriss," the Jedi's voice rang out.

Everywhere in this system, and hopefully the neighboring as well, and in every Nihil ship and city with comms that could be reached, Avar Kriss spoke to those listening.

But here on Rilias II, held in shape by the rainbow frequencies of the alloy funnel, Avar Kriss's face looked down like a god.

If Cair knew Jedi at all, he knew she'd hate the comparison. But Cair relished it. He grinned and laughed again. And before he hightailed it to his mark to be picked up in a hurry, he stood there, watching and listening.

"I bring a message of hope, though it is difficult to hear. But listen, please. Even I am familiar with despair. I know it. That feeling when everything is too much, when the pressure of looking for anything inside of tomorrow is overwhelming. It hurts. I know it, too. In times like that just remember who you are—who you want to be. Who you can be. Focus on that. Fight with me, if that is who you can be. But if you cannot, you do not have to fight. I won't ask that of you. There are people already fighting for you. For all of us. All I am asking of you today is that you live. Live today, and try to find hope tomorrow. This is Jedi Master Avar Kriss. Help is on the way."

Chapter Eight

INSIDE THE OCCLUSION ZONE

Porter Engle ran hard. Panic tore down his spine in a way he hadn't experienced in a long time, possibly ever. He had to get *away.*

The fear kept him from breathing, but he could still run.

He clenched at his lightsaber, powered down, and shoved past two Nihil, knocking them aside roughly.

He had to get away. Get far enough away.

Careening around a corner, he burst through a set of thin wooden doors. Pain streaked his temple and shoulder, making him stumble. Porter kept running.

Noise followed him, yelling and blasterfire, but he turned and turned again, finally falling down a short flight of stone steps into a courtyard.

Too-bright light cut at his vision, the sun glaring off the diamond-stone bricks all around. Too bright, too painfully bright.

Porter dropped to his knees, gulping for air.

He was—

He was—

Porter's ears stopped ringing. His head ached. But the fear was gone. Vanished completely.

Carefully standing, Porter looked around and darted behind a column.

Breathed.

The Force flooded toward him when he opened to it: cold and comforting as the glow of his lightsaber blade.

With the Force he listened, reaching out.

The compound was crawling with people. Nihil.

A pocket of—

Porter shied away from it.

He'd been so close. For weeks he'd been waiting on this world, one of the few places Viess regularly visited. It wasn't an operations base for her so-called Ministry of Protection but a personal retreat, it seemed. Across the Occlusion Zone, people feared Viess's army and her lieutenants, because they dropped in wherever they liked to raid and plunder, as if every world in Nihil space was their personal playground. But this one Viess herself preferred, according to rumors. Maybe it was the glinting pink triple moons the locals called Hearts in Alignment. Maybe it was the riftfeather brandy made from a spring at the foot of the mountains that bubbled and tingled like laughter. Maybe it was the luster of the diamondstone flats, quarried into blocks to build the towers of the city.

Viess had always appreciated all the luxury money could buy— almost as much as she enjoyed murder and violence.

Porter didn't care what drew Viess back here again and again; he only cared to catch her at it.

He'd infiltrated the manor she'd claimed, ready to surprise her and cut her down. His clothes were layered leather and scuffed armor, and he even had a spiky mask dangling around his neck. It wasn't a gas mask, but from a distance it could've been. He'd darkened his hair and gotten ahold of a belt nearly the shade of Nihil-blue paint. Porter was not above looking like his enemy.

He'd been so close.

Porter had watched Viess's cruiser descend through the night sky, blocking out two of those three pink moons. He'd watched, and he'd slipped in through the Nihil guards as easily as just looking bigger and tougher and more furious than any of them.

As he'd moved deeper and deeper in, dread had built in his chest. First a tiny prick like a heart palpitation. Then a pain, a tight band around him, hooked under his ribs. He kept going, pushing the dread away. He could manage.

Then he'd heard her laughter, sharp and high as it had always been, and he was right back there, on the planet of blades. Viess had said, "*I am a killer of Jedi.*"

Porter slammed into the next room with a roar.

Terror roared back.

It filled his mind, scouring him clean of the Force, of plans and memories, until he was only panic. There was no Force, no Porter.

He ran.

Alone in the courtyard, Porter came back to himself. He kept his eyes closed against the sunlight bouncing awfully against the diamondstone. This city was a nocturnal one, because under the light of the moons, the stone glimmered pleasantly. This daily onslaught of sun was an attack on the vision of most people and creatures who hadn't evolved alongside the city.

But Porter could use the Force and the smoked lenses of his fake Nihil mask.

Dragging it over his face, he kept his awareness of the Force blasted open and quickly made his way out of the compound. He avoided Nihil.

Even when he was totally free of it, he kept moving through the alleys and streets of the city. He kept going, keeping to the shade where he could, because to walk down an avenue at the height of the day would give him away.

Eventually Porter found a tree with fan leaves wide enough to shelter him, and he sat down hard. He tore off the mask that covered his face.

The sun set and locals emerged. They crept into the streets to quietly open shopfronts, silently acknowledging their neighbors where once, a year ago, there might have been loud teasing and twilight greetings. Smells of rich caf and fried breads reached him, but not conversation or pleasant hawking from the carts and shops in this district. Porter clawed his fingers around his skull bulges. Their lives continued, though through the Force, he felt the edges of their strain. They tried to live, to do more than survive, but worry coated everything. They moved around him as if he were a plague carrier. He might as well have been, marked as Nihil the way he was.

Porter wanted to help them. Free them. But he couldn't return to where those creatures were. He couldn't get past them. He'd been so close, but he was unable even to locate Viess when they were near.

He should go back, drive through them even if it killed him. It was fine if this was a suicide mission now. Porter wouldn't be surprised to die in this endeavor.

As long as Viess died with him.

Porter pressed his hands into his eyes, willing the thoughts away. It wasn't his way. These thoughts were tinged with darkness, with despair. He knew better. He did. It was only the creatures leaving their prints inside him. Fear and this emptiness.

Hopelessness settled in the streets. Even as the moons rose and the diamondstone buildings began to shimmer and glow, and Porter felt it all.

Then he felt a ripple. A murmur of voices, and he opened his eyes.

Several locals clustered around one of the carts, one that sold replacement parts for droids and tech. Everything here was patchy these days.

They were listening to something playing on a handheld holoprojector.

Porter stood.

He walked toward them, using the Force to soothe his way so he didn't startle them.

He knew that voice, the one from the holo.

". . . times like that just remember who you are—who you want to be. Who you can be."

It was Avar's voice.

"Focus on that," she said. "Fight with me."

Porter welcomed the bright relief washing through him. She was alive, Avar Kriss was alive, and that meant she'd made it out. And then somehow made it back.

". . . find hope tomorrow," she implored.

He knew what to do. He knew in a flash how his strategy had been wrong. And he knew how to make it better.

For the first time in a while, Porter Engle smiled.

Chapter Nine

THE *GAZE ELECTRIC*,
INSIDE THE OCCLUSION ZONE

The moment Marchion Ro returned to his *Gaze Electric*, he commanded the vessel to jump to Hetzal Prime.

He strode for his private quarters, pushing through the She'ar in his way. His secretary, Thaya Ferr, kept up, quickly biting out a report on the information she'd received while he'd been on the surface. She was a soft-spoken but reliable human, and Ro assumed she spied on him or would soon begin to. Still, she organized information and pursued his commands with dedication most in the Nihil did not have. Most of his followers feared him or craved his regard and power. Ro sensed little of that in Thaya, but the mystery of her ambition was not interesting enough to hold his attention.

"Where is Di'ir?" Thaya asked as her report ended.

Ro wondered if Di'ir was the Nihil he'd shoved over the rail of the barge, or the tooka cat. He didn't answer, and Thaya drew her own conclusions.

The *Gaze* shivered as it jumped into hyperspace.

Thaya said, "My lord, is there anything you'd like prepared for the ministry meeting?"

Ro scoffed. He reached up and jerked his helmet off, turning his head just slightly to give her a narrow look. "Ghirra knows I only attend to her bureaucratic inventions because I find it amusing. She and Viess will bicker about the Jedi without providing me with any solutions to their continued incompetence."

"The Minister of Advancement will be attending," Thaya said delicately, referring to the Ithorian scientist Boolan, who kept himself isolated most of the time, working with the Levelers that Ro had gifted him. Few usable results had come from that avenue thus far, either. Ro would almost prefer Boolan focusing on his experiments instead of attending Ghirra's meetings. But he liked watching them maneuver against each other, and he wondered what she had invented to bully or blackmail the fervent Ithorian into showing up.

"When we arrive at Hetzal," Ro said, "I want a list of any reports or rumors you've received concerning planet-wide blights or droughts, any kind of sickness or plague that destroys everything in its radius. Include any news of my Levelers being reported in places we know they have not been. Especially strange disappearances near Wild Space."

"My lord," she acknowledged.

"And tell my *ministers*"—he put all the disdain in his voice—"the meeting will be on the *Gaze*. They can come to me."

With that, Ro stormed onward alone. He quickly put his hand to a panel that revealed an inner corridor angled sharply down into the bowels of the *Gaze*. His ancestors had slipped many a secret tunnel into the ship, along with pockets of hidden rooms never marked on any schematics.

This took him directly to the small chamber below the throne hall where he kept the personal histories and items too precious to be destroyed. Unless someone who was not Evereni attempted to penetrate the sanctum. Then it would self-destruct.

Ro touched his thumb to the spike above a tiny analysis pad. The spike was carved from the fang of an Evereni, melded to the black metal with a strip of gold. He cut his thumb, and dark blood slipped down to drip once, then twice, onto the pad.

The indicator light slowly transformed from blue to red, and the door before Ro irised open.

The ghost of the woman upon whose tooth he believed he had just cut himself waited inside.

Ro ignored her. He especially disliked when she appeared in this youthful form, wearing pale robes and blue waving lines across her face instead of blood splatter. He walked past her to the ceiling-high wall of storage compartments and began opening them.

He spent the journey to Hetzal riffling through the family history contained therein. He found little that was unfamiliar, having read through and listened to everything when he was a boy. It was not something his father had appreciated—the man cared only for cruelty and conquest—but his grandmother introduced him to the potential usefulness in anything related to the name *Ro,* despite how mad and strange his great-great-grandmother's records became before she died.

The ghost sang softly to herself as he worked. A lullaby with words he did not recognize that perhaps were not words at all. Ro gritted his teeth and ignored her.

There was nothing to be found in this place that mentioned anything like the husking of an entire crystal forest.

Ro hesitated before beginning the recorded journals of his great-great-grandmother. He didn't want to give voice to it again. She had rambled about freedom and home, about her hunt for their people and her gradual descent into violence. Ro had found it useless as a child; it would be even more so now.

"Maybe it's something I did," the ghost whispered into his ear, startling him enough that he looked right into her Evereni-black eyes.

Marchion Ro sneered.

Putting himself at the center of everything was a trait he shared with her. He knew it was a flaw of ego. Maybe it was a reaction to the genetic memory of being rejected by their own homeworld. But unlike her, Ro had built an empire around himself.

The ghost smiled at his sneer and danced back, her bare gray feet silent against the floor. She had lompop flowers in her hands, and she reached out, letting a small pink one fall from her fingers. It touched the metal tile and the tile turned to ash.

From the place the flower landed, the gray ash spread slowly, eating away at this sanctum.

The ghost dropped another flower, and the same thing happened. She began to hum her song again.

"Get out," Ro said with quiet, deadly threat. He'd rather his father any day than this madwoman.

The ghost twirled away, vanishing before she reached the door. The illusion of the ashy blight pockmarking his storage room vanished with her.

Putting it from his mind, Ro returned focus to his task.

By the time the *Gaze* dropped out of hyperspace and Ro began his ascent from its guts, he'd found nothing to indicate his predecessors had encountered anything like what he'd seen on Norisyn.

Thaya was waiting for him as soon as he emerged from his private corridors and handed him a datapad. "There isn't much, my lord."

"Unsurprising." He'd peruse the information while Ghirra led her little meeting. It was likely to be a long one, given Ghirra had been in Republic space for most of the past few weeks.

But as Ro headed for the throne hall, he noticed small footprints carving a path in front of him. Perfectly shaped into bare feet, they marked the floor of his ship with chalky residue. As he followed them, Ro realized that a feeling he hadn't experienced in quite some time was building under his skin.

In the throne room, the ghost waited on the dais beside the throne, her legs tucked under her and her expression dreamy. From where she sat, the blight spread, creeping up his throne and down the steps in streaks of ash. As if she carried it with her and set the blight where she stepped or dropped her flowers.

"Ro," Ghirra Starros said, standing at the head of a dark table set before the throne. General Viess lounged across from Ghirra, with her hip hitched up on the table.

Neither of them saw the ash consuming the surface of the table, making its way with little tributaries of blight toward them. Ro stopped. At the far end of the table, his father sat, tapping a claw on the edge of the table—another source of blight.

Ro drew his attention away from Asgar with the ease of long practice. He stared at Ghirra and Viess coldly, without speaking, then cast his gaze toward the far door where Boolan entered, dragging braided charms and long, tattered robes. He wondered if the Ithorian scientist had been successful in his experiments yet. Perhaps Ro would not allow Boolan off the *Gaze* without one of his altered pets in custody.

Ghirra spoke, but Ro only had eyes for the way her hand and arm were slowly turning to ash. Viess replied, and he saw dots of the blight on her face, like freckles spreading. He hoped Viess went first, and he could watch her chest and ribs dissolve before it took her withered old heart. He hoped she'd be afraid.

Ro climbed to his throne, where the little ghost played idly with the end of her braid and patted the seat.

Setting the datapad on his thigh, Ro watched as Ghirra brought the meeting to order. He smirked at his so-called ministers, at the trappings of organized power Ghirra relied upon. Titles and hierarchies, when all that was necessary was the blowing strength of his storm.

The illusory blight consumed the table, reaching Boolan finally. It turned the superstitious charms dangling from his staff into chalk, and they crumbled. His metal appendages froze and darkened. The Ithorian spoke, and Viess laughed. Her neck was nearly all pale-gray stone.

"—Eye? Are you even listening?" Ghirra's voice penetrated his thoughts.

Ro glanced at her and grinned with all his teeth. Her arm and collar were ash under the vibrant green of her gown. "Why should I?"

Boolan stood up and left.

Ghirra angrily leaned forward and jabbed a finger against the holo-projector set before her on the blighted table.

The earnest face of Avar Kriss was projected in light blue over the table. ". . . people already fighting for you," she was saying. "For all of us. All I am asking of you today is that you live. Live today, and try to find hope tomorrow. This is Jedi Master Avar Kriss. Help is on the way."

Ghirra stood and glared at him, and Viess raised her black eyebrows. They both expected him to be furious about the Jedi. To lash out.

He did not. Their bodies were turning to ash.

Though it was true that he did not like this news. Jedi growing bolder in their whispering attempts to cross his Stormwall meant nothing good for him. If they could not destroy the wall itself but only pick at its cracks, they'd realize soon enough a more focused target would suit them better.

Ghirra said, "They are spreading this message everywhere, undermining so much of what we—you—have done, my lord."

"Let them!" Viess said, smacking her green hand on the table. The Mirialan in her shining armor leaned toward Ghirra. The armor did not so much as gray with the blight, even as Viess's tattoos flaked off her cheeks. "The Jedi are secretively crawling through the Stormwall like rats, Ghirra. That is good. We are winning if they fight for scraps."

"The Jedi will pry open larger and larger holes," Ghirra said smoothly. "That is their nature. Stubborn, determined, and convinced of their own righteousness. The whole might of the Republic will be right behind them."

Ro drummed his fingers on his throne, watching the creep of the blight. He agreed with her, but the last thing to do would be to accede to their fearmongering. "If you are worried, send out more raiders. Catch the Jedi rats as you have been profoundly unable to do. Use the Levelers. Tighten the wall. I will expand it again and again."

"There is only so much the Lightning Crash can power," the senator answered. She folded her delicate brown human hands together in an effort to calm herself. Ro liked being able to read her so easily. Learning her tells had been one of the only things he enjoyed about having her in his bed. "Especially given the so-called leadership there. It's hardly being run to your standards, my lord."

Ro let his smile grow. He recognized this was a move against Viess, who ostensibly assigned such things as Lightning Crash security under the auspices of Ghirra's ministerial organization.

Viess made a false moue of sympathy. "I'll take care of the Lightning Crash if you think it's so vulnerable," she said. "It would be my pleasure to finally squeeze the life out of that insolent Graf. He wasn't exactly a volunteer, and he has always been without loyalty. Wiping clean the whole crew starting with him should be the best solution. I hope it won't cause you any trouble—weren't you familiar with his family before you turned coat, Ghirra?"

Ghirra laughed once. "Familiar enough not to mourn the loss of a single one of them."

"Charmed, as always, to be your ally," Viess said through clenched teeth.

"Hmm. Did I miss your report on the status of the queen of Naboo and *her* allies? Or did you not manage to capture any of them in your conquest?"

"I don't need the queen. The rest have bowed to me just fine."

Ro stopped listening again as they began discussing the general's takeover of Naboo and establishment of a military base there. She'd created bases all over his territory. Ro skimmed through the reports on the tablet Thaya had given him, slowly choosing where to look next for this blight. He had more questions about it. There—one world in particular looked promising, as there'd been rumors of Drengir nearby as well. If the Drengir were returning, Ro could certainly fold those creatures back into his plans. Best to look into it.

"—always spies!" Ghirra was saying. It caught his attention, but when he looked at her, Ghirra's eyes were chalky gray-white, like little moons in her face. It was disconcerting. He liked it.

"We have ways to remove them from *my* ministry," Viess said.

Ro appreciated how Viess and Ghirra always seemed at each other's throats. It suited him for his Tempests to work against one another. They'd kill each other, and he could enjoy the show. Whoever replaced them would be stronger. Hungrier.

"You can't catch them all, especially in an organization such as the Nihil, where the ethos is officially everyone for themselves," Ghirra said silkily. "You must simply assume there are spies and act decisively, quickly, before they have time to pass along their information."

At Marchion's knee, his great-great-grandmother sighed.

The throne hall was consumed by ash in sharp streaks and lightning flashes, turning it into a ruined, husked version of itself.

Marchion himself remained unaffected.

Maybe it's something I did, the ghost had said earlier as she dropped ashing flowers and blighted footsteps in her wake. Maybe it was. Or maybe spreading it was something *he* could do.

Ro smiled.

This was exciting.

Chapter Ten

THE *GAZE ELECTRIC,* INSIDE THE OCCLUSION ZONE

Ghirra Starros found it truly stunning sometimes how little foresight went into basically everything in the galaxy. Not just with regard to the Nihil but across the Republic, too. So many people acted without considering the potential ramifications or desired consequences of their actions.

Some days that made her work easier. If she was the only person predicting a variety of political outcomes, she was the only one prepared for anything.

The thing that allowed her to predict the actions of Marchion Ro was his explosive nature. When Ro was in the picture, it was best to prepare for widespread disaster and chaotic fallout. The worst-case scenario. That was why the Republic couldn't stop him: They assumed an order existed to the way things were done. When one's organization strove for benevolence and justice, it was difficult to imagine specific atrocities.

That was Ro's specialty. Or it was supposed to be. Lately his inattention to, frankly, everything was not something even Ghirra had planned for. She'd assumed his heavy fist would be the pressure keeping the Nihil together, and that her job would be to use that pressure to place the inevitable cracks where she wanted them.

Once Viess promised to cleanse the Lightning Crash, it had been apparent to both of them that Ro wasn't listening, and what was the point of prolonging everyone's suffering? After she and Viess shared an antagonistic but knowing glance, Viess clapped her hands and departed without much fanfare. Ghirra marched up to Ro and smiled. The Eye had blinked and then peered at her with those awful black eyes. His gaze flicked around her face until he smiled back at her, crooked and dangerous.

Almost deranged.

She tilted her chin, aware that Marchion Ro was looking through her, not at her. "If you look at everyone the way you looked at us during this meeting," she said as coldly as she was able, "more of your people will think they can risk putting a dagger in your throat."

"Would you like that, Ghirra?" Ro purred.

"You know I would not," she snapped. "As little as I'd mourn your loss of blood, you're supposed to be building something here."

"That's what you think I'm doing," he said, waving dismissively.

There was something wrong with him.

It was an insane thought to have, of course. He was a reckless, vicious megalomaniac and always had been. She knew it and had always known it. She'd walked that knife's edge for months, using it, fearing it, relying on it. She'd ignored it, even when sharing his bed, because he was a reckless, vicious megalomaniac who *won*.

This was something different. His thoughts weren't on the *Gaze* with them. Weren't on further suppressing the Republic. She had no way to know in which new direction he was looking. That spelled disaster for her: the end of her preparedness.

Ghirra gave her best mocking curtsy and swept out of the ridiculous dramatic throne room on his terrible flagship. Just outside, two of her Nihil aides waited, and they fell in to flank her as Ghirra attempted to project only certainty and calm while seething inside.

If Marchion Ro turned his attention away from the Republic, from the Jedi, and even from the Nihil, things were going to get so much worse. Ghirra was going to have to get his attention back or find someone to replace him. The alternatives—giving up everything she'd worked for to go on the run, being hunted by the Republic, ending up imprisoned or dead—were unacceptable.

As Ghirra headed for her shuttle, she told herself she was overreacting. Ro was wily and determined and focused. If not focused on his previous goals, then on *something*.

She needed to find out what.

Ghirra reached the small private docking bay where more Nihil guards loyal to her waited. Or rather, as loyal as Nihil could be. These days Ghirra thought the money and stability she provided counted for a lot. Not all Nihil imagined themselves raiding and destroying into infinity. Once settled on her ship, there were several informants and assistants she needed to message, a few of Viess's spies to feed various bits of semi-false information, and a schedule of events to plan for her next foray home to Hosnian Prime.

Stepping up to the docking ring, Ghirra opened her mouth to tell Jayd, her best Nihil aide, that she wanted to go directly to her own cruiser instead of detouring down to the Hetzal palace, but was interrupted by a side door swooshing open.

"Minister Starros," said the harsh young voice of one of Ro's human aides: the little blue-haired spy Nan.

Ghirra raised an eyebrow and paused, waiting.

Nan stomped up to her, fists on her waist. "The Eye has a message for you."

"Oh? I only just saw him." If this was some attempt at spywork, it was clunky. Nan was usually less obvious than this, if clumsy.

"He wants to know where your daughter has been."

All trace of patience wiped itself from Ghirra's expression. It was a good gambit of Nan's to get Ghirra's ire up. Ghirra easily let herself lean into fury. "At school," Ghirra snapped. "As he well knows."

"Do you see her when you go to Republic space?" Nan blinked her big eyes innocently.

"Naturally," Ghirra lied. Ghirra had not seen Avon in months, not since she'd allowed Avon to return to Coruscant for university and the child had run off instead. Avon had vanished from Ghirra's networks without a trace, no doubt with the help of Deva Lompop, the Nihil bodyguard Ghirra herself had given her. Avon had stolen plenty of Ghirra's credits, presumably to finance this change in her identity.

"Oh, I'm glad to hear, and surely the Eye will be as well, that you know where she is."

"Is that all he wants now? I'm in a hurry."

Nan paused, then shrugged. "We know where to reach you."

Ghirra turned without farewell and strode through the docking ring.

Message delivered loud and clear, she thought bitterly as she snapped at her crew to get them on a route back to Republic space. Someone—if not Ro himself, then someone high enough in the ranks for Nan to pay attention—was looking for Ghirra's daughter. Possibly for Avon's own merits: She was cunning and a genius, and she knew too much about the Stormwall. But probably they wanted Avon to use her against Ghirra, because it would absolutely work.

Ghirra needed to find her first.

Before jumping to hyperspace, Ghirra Starros recorded a message. She'd considered the benefits of such an action the moment it became clear that Viess would be purging the Lightning Crash of at least outsiders and those with untested loyalties.

Ghirra had considered it and dismissed it as unnecessary. But now she had a better reason than paying back a debt that had been questionably owed in the first place.

The message simply stated, "It is time for your tenure on the Lightning Crash to end, Xylan Graf."

She sent it quickly and directly to his private codes, then did her best to put it from her mind.

Avon was hiding from Ghirra in Republic space, focused on countering the methods her mother would use to seek her, the avenues and resources she was aware her mother possessed, which were restricted naturally, because of her alliance with Ro. But for some reason Xylan had gone out of his way to save Avon's life before, and presumably he was involved indirectly at least in the tangle of information that the Jedi had received about the Stormwall. Avon had never pretended to want the Nihil to win, and she'd repeatedly let Ghirra know how much she hated the choices her mother had made.

Avon wouldn't be hiding from Xylan Graf, especially if he returned to the Republic with the valuable information of a reformed traitor. And Xylan couldn't hide wearing his snow dog's fur in an ice storm. When he found Avon, Ghirra would, too.

Chapter Eleven

THE *TRACTATE,*
REPUBLIC SPACE

Burryaga finished reading the after-action report on the last known Jedi encounter with Drengir and immediately closed the screen. He sat at the sturdiest chair in the comm station on the bridge of the RDC ship *Tractate* and tried not to let out an involuntary whine.

The smell of singed fur jerked him out of his concentration, and he absently patted out the little smoldering section of hair near his knee. At least it wasn't the hem of his mission robes this time.

Ember, the charhound who followed Bell everywhere, rubbed her bony cheek in the same spot, eliciting a spark. Burry purred at her but gently shoved her off. She could tell he was upset. That wasn't good. Burry centered himself in the Force. He let his concern and frustration fall away just enough that they didn't spike his emotions or shift anything noticeable in his physiology.

"Don't worry," Bell said from the second chair in the shared station. "You're definitely coming with us this time, Ember. Fire is one of the only consistently useful weapons against these creatures."

Burry patted her stiff fur in agreement.

"If all else fails, you can pee on it," Bell promised.

Burry startled, and Ember's ears perked. But Bell was grinning at Burry, and the humor shook off another layer of his frustration.

"Did you find anything to suggest where this Drengir came from? And why it appeared now?" Bell asked, smile fading but not going away.

Burry shook his head. He'd mostly been reading about all the ways not to bother trying to kill them.

The Drengir had appeared after centuries of dormancy around the beginning of the conflict with the Nihil, seeded all over the galaxy to distract the Jedi and cause pain and chaos. Drengir were a carnivorous botanical species who were very tough to kill—and killing them was the only way to stop them, unfortunately, unless you could put them in permanent stasis. They had razor-toothed mouths eager to eat flesh, surrounded by tentacle-like vines barbed with poisonous thorns. They were connected to the dark side of the Force strongly enough to affect anyone from Jedi to people barely in touch with the Force with their miasma of darkness and dread. They didn't give up, even when sliced in half by a lightsaber, and shared a kind of hive mind—which was both a strength and a weakness, as it led to their defeat right before the Battle of Valo. Master Kriss had led a team to their homeworld and stopped their Great Progenitor. The Great Progenitor and other captured Drengir had been locked in stasis within Starlight Beacon when it fell. The reports suggested the Drengir would be unable to recover from the loss quickly, if at all.

This seemed pretty quick to Burry.

"Dropping out of hyperspace," called the *Tractate*'s pilot.

"Put us in orbit over the outpost," Captain Amaryl Pel said, then she turned to Bell and Burry. "You sure you want to take your Vectors only? I can send a team with you."

Burry stood to his full height, settling his hand on the long hilt of his lightsaber.

Bell answered, "As long as the outpost commander hasn't encountered more than one, I think we'll manage."

"Very well, Jedi." Captain Pel smiled crookedly. "But do call if you need support. I've read those reports on the Drengir, too."

Bell slid his gaze to Burry. "We'll keep that in mind."

They dropped down to the moon and landed in tandem at the port attached to the science outpost, which barely had room for two Vectors. Felne 6 was a small rain forest moon with no immediate exports or ores or gases or slimes easily harvested, but its atmosphere made it excellent for certain kinds of long-term science experiments.

Or so the project leader, a turquoise-skinned Duros woman who blinked her big red eyes very fast, told them hurriedly as she led them to the southern edge of the walled outpost. The walls were electrified because of the rather large flying beetles that made their home in the upper canopy of the rain forest.

Burry clapped a hand on Bell's shoulder when his partner winced at that. This moon teemed with life, and the Force flowed eagerly and strong. Burry had to make an effort not to reach for it, in fact. Bell seemed on edge with a similar fuel. And Ember trotted along with a wag of her tail—despite the suspicious glances the Duros scientist kept shooting her. Burry understood it was aggressive of them to bring a charhound to a giant tinderbox.

The scientist told them one of her techs had gone missing two days ago, and when they sent out a search party, the party encountered a section of the rain forest blackening with rot. That was one of the telltale signs of Drengir—along with missing people and local beasts of burden. Fortunately, the outpost didn't have any children, and nobody else had gone missing. But Bell assured her that possible Drengir was a good reason to reach out to the RDC and Jedi.

"Oh, it's not just a possibility," she said, her lipless mouth drawing an even thinner line. "We saw it. It roared at us and reached with its vines as it dragged along a copse of sarcran light trees. We ran, and it did not give chase."

"Which way?" Bell asked.

She pointed. "Only two kilometers. We have some speeders, but to be honest, the ground here is covered in so many layers of roots and vines, the repulsors don't always work. The copse of sarcran is beside a bend in the river, though, where a karst promontory flattens the ground some."

"Thanks," Bell said. "Let's go, Ember."

Ember bounded ahead as Bell and Burry began their trek.

The air was thick and dusted with floating pink seedlings. The project leader promised nothing was toxic this time of year, as long as they didn't eat anything or touch the green sap of the strik weeds, which they could identify by their vivid-black grapes. Burry led the way after Ember, striding confidently along fat roots and using heavy vines for leverage. Bell only struggled a little, cursing and laughing at himself every once in a while.

Burry was gladdened at Bell's light mood. He kept his feelings open to sense any hints of danger that might come from other sources. He called out once to Ember when the charhound sniffed something too closely and sneezed a little puff of flames. They saw only one of the giant insects: a huge moth with white-scaled wings that batted lazily on the branch of a tall tree. Beautiful.

When they drew near the Drengir, it was obvious.

The pale-white light of the system's sun didn't change, nor the chattering songs of local birds and the buzz of insects. Not at first. But Burry slowly noticed a strange creeping feeling, like something just outside his peripheral vision. Except it wasn't a physical sensation so much as one through the Force.

Then the chatter of the forest slowed and stopped, and they stepped into a quiet zone.

The breeze ruffled the wide blue-green leaves of the upper canopy, and red vines swung. Flower petals dropped. Color and sunlight shifted, layers of shade sliding against each other, and the roots glistened with vibrant silver moss. But there were no singing birds or treefrogs or ylvrin chirping to one another. Only his and Bell's footsteps and the huff of Ember's eager breath.

It was eerie.

And then Burry felt the darkening of the Force.

It was as if the air itself grew weighted and cold. Burry could see flowers and the hints of violet sky, but he felt like his life was muffled.

Burry looked at Bell, who'd gone tight around his mouth. Their gazes met, and Bell unclipped his lightsaber. Burry brushed his fingers against his own weapon but left it in the heavy holster.

The sound of the rushing river cued them to being near the place the Drengir had been seen. The water tumbled over rocks and fallen mossy trees, sparkling green with sunlight and algae. The ground under Burry's feet leveled out as he entered the karst promontory. And he smelled the sweet scent of rot underlying everything else.

Grasses bent over, sickly yellow and black-spotted in streaks that pointed toward a huge pile of what looked like forest compost. Tangled vines and shadows, a few ruffled fringes that might have been leaves.

Ember growled.

The huge pile of vegetation shivered.

It moaned.

"Oh, no," Bell said.

The Drengir stirred, moving as if it tried to lift itself up. It vocalized something in a rumbling, hissing voice, but not recognizable words.

Burry felt a wave of dread hit him, and he clenched his hand around his lightsaber. The Drengir felt like a pit of despair, pulling at him, and Burry's head ached. He knew this despair—it was the bottom of an ocean, slowly running out of oxygen, nobody looking, nobody reaching out, nothing, no connection, alone, alone, *alone.*

Ember darted forward, spitting fire.

Bell followed her.

"*Stop!*" Burry shouted. He thrust out a hand, nudging Bell away with the Force.

Bell stumbled in surprise, turning to Burry with a wrinkled brow. Bell, who never gave up. Bell, who never would. Burry breathed deeply. Couldn't his friend feel it, too?

"Come back, Ember," Bell said, patting his hip. He thumbed on his lightsaber, and the green blade hummed to life.

Burry walked nearer to the Drengir. It stank of old plants and fallen leaves. And blood and rancid meat. Burry's nose twitched. He reached out again, feeling the edges of the Drengir's miasma. It was dark, dreadful, angry, but that wasn't all.

"Burry, what are you doing? Be careful," Bell said urgently.

Vines snaked toward him, but halfheartedly. This was nothing like the ferocious, deadly monsters described in all the reports.

Burry's heart pounded as he approached, touching the energy of the Force. He pushed on it with his own feelings and his sense of self. It was almost like a caress.

The Drengir shoved hard, rejecting him with a sharp, painful spike of the Force, echoed in the Drengir's bellow of . . . sorrow.

It was dying, Burry realized, sadness draining him. He said as much to Bell.

"What—dying?" Bell crouched several meters away, holding Ember around the neck.

The Drengir shuddered again, and vines rolled away from the low center to reveal that red maw, beaked and fanged, and Burry fought back a shiver of his own. The whole creature roiled with feelings. Burry needed to stop letting it in. He wanted to pet it but knew better. He wanted to soothe the creature even though it was a monster, even though it would eat him and Bell and every sentient being on this moon. It would snatch away children and kill them slowly. He only felt this way because it was trying to make a connection to use him. Burry shoved it away, which was easier than it should have been, according to everything Burry had read.

"Let's finish this?" Bell said, but he sounded uncertain.

Burry shook his head. It was already dying. All they had to do was wait.

Burry sat cross-legged with his long lightsaber hilt across his lap and held vigil for the dying Drengir.

Bell and Ember remained a bit farther off, ready in case Burry was wrong.

He knew he wasn't. As he sank deeper into meditation, Burry could feel the subtleties of the Drengir's sorrow. It was lonely. Cut off from the other Drengir, from the hive mind. Something had happened to cut that tie.

Burry wanted to ask, and he touched the boundaries of the Drengir with his feelings. But it wouldn't let him in. Given the stories the Wookiee had read, perhaps it was for the best.

Though Bell pulled out crinkling packets of rations, he only fed them silently to Ember and didn't suggest leaving. He walked a perimeter once or twice as the sun set and the sky turned a jeweled royal purple and the rain forest glowed green and pink from its algae.

The Drengir moaned and it rolled, but it continued to slowly die.

Burry opened himself up to its final thoughts and feelings.

The Drengir didn't understand what was happening to it, either.

When the sun rose on the sixth moon of Felne, the Drengir was dead.

Burry knew immediately, and his shoulders drooped, but he didn't move from his meditation. He had felt something he needed to process, and so it took a while before Bell noticed the Drengir had died, had sunken in on itself slightly, as if malevolent energy had kept its vines thick and its stench hungry. He walked to his partner and nudged Burry's shoulder.

"Burry?" Bell said. On Burry's other side, Ember snuffled her muzzle into the thick hair along the Wookiee's neck.

Burry sighed, gathered himself, and stood. He said they needed to

report the death and request permission to investigate any other Drengir appearances nearby.

Bell looked at him for a moment, and Burry wondered if he'd have
to rephrase for his friend's growing, but limited, Shyriiwook, but then
Bell nodded decisively and said, "All right. I agree. Tell me why."

Burry stood up, his gaze drifting to the pile of vines and fibrous
monster. He tried to think of the simplest way to explain the roiling
emotions he'd sensed. The Drengir was lonely. And scared. Cut off
from family.

"Afraid? Is that what you said?" Bell asked in a hushed tone.

Burry nodded. He gripped his lightsaber tightly and glanced at
Ember. It was time.

"Ember," Bell commanded gently, and gestured to the remains.

The charhound puffed herself up with sparks and, with a choking,
coughing hack, set the remains aflame.

Chapter Twelve

CORUSCANT

Elzar held a shallow bowl of water cradled in the lap of his crossed legs and touched the surface with a finger to create quiet ripples.

He let his vision blur along with them, recalling the sway of ocean against his body, the physical sensation mirroring the visual ripples. The Force rippled out from the bowl and from himself, reaching out and pulling back in. It was a tiny ocean. Enough to represent everything the Force could be, but not enough to drown him.

In and out.

Connected to the vast, deep sea of the Force, Elzar felt calm. He closed his eyes and gave himself a moment to remember the dark side. The times he'd touched it. Only a handful, but they made an impression. On Valo, he'd let it happen. Chosen it, even if briefly, knowing the consequences. But on Starlight Beacon, it had chosen him instead.

That was the thing he feared.

Elzar sank into the memory of what it had felt like when he murdered Chancey Yarrow.

The flood of rage and desperation echoed in him now: accurate, implacable, but cold. It hit like a sudden wave crashing against a beach, not the tsunami it used to be.

He let it wear at him, becoming part of him.

Slowly, a little bit more every day, he accepted what he'd done. Only when he accepted it could he be sure it wouldn't happen again. Elzar could almost hear Orla's voice. Telling him to get back in the water. Stay there. Hold there.

"Master Elzar," came JJ-5145's crisp voice, much less soothing than the memory of the Wayseeker. "The Jedi Council is summoning you!"

Luckily, Elzar wasn't startled and didn't spill a drop of water. He was more than used to the droid's interruptions. Truth be told, if JJ-5145 ever acted calmly and without urgency, Elzar would have him analyzed for bugs.

Elzar stood smoothly with the water. "Thanks, Forfive." He handed the droid the bowl. "Take care of this for me?"

A summons like this right now had to be the will of the Force. He'd been working on accepting his mistakes and moving past them—with them—and telling the Council about Chancey the way Avar suggested and Vernestra demanded.

Elzar wanted to do right by both of them and by Stellan.

Vernestra Rwoh had been Stellan's Padawan, and a few months ago, she'd been the second Jedi to escape the Occlusion Zone after Avar. Upon her return, the young Mirialan had confronted Elzar about Chancey Yarrow. Vernestra was friends with Yarrow's daughter, and they'd discovered the cause of her death while spying on the Nihil.

Stellan had been proud of Vernestra, and because of it, Elzar had a childish desire for her to like him. And it was fairly obvious she did not. Elzar couldn't compare to her master, after all.

But Vernestra had been right about Chancey: Even if Elzar was dealing with his actions himself, the Council needed to know. The weaknesses of all Jedi were Council business, especially when they kept putting Elzar in charge of things.

It was time to tell them. His progress in coming to terms with what he'd done and the consequences was . . . fine. This was a hurdle he could overcome.

Whatever the Council wanted today, he'd listen, do what they asked, then make his confession.

"But, Master Elzar," JJ-5145 said, wheeling after him in the tight quarters. "I can go over possible reasons for this emergency session with you on the way."

"It's fine, and I doubt it's a real emergency, or we'd already know what went wrong." Elzar paused. "I'll find out when I arrive."

The droid wheeled back in surprise. Elzar tried not to be offended, smiling wryly. "Just wish me luck."

"Er, may the Force be with you, Master Elzar."

"Thanks."

Elzar left his quarters and strode for the lift in one of the outer spires that would take him up to the Jedi Council Chamber. He wouldn't back down this time. He couldn't.

Elzar swept into the Council Chamber, cloak flapping behind him. It had been ages since he'd worn plain Jedi mission attire instead of these more formal temple robes. The stark white and gold made a difference when he was in the Senate building regularly: Various senators and their aides found reassurance in the pristine nature of formal Jedi dress. He thought fleetingly of Avar, who barely even wore a mission uniform these days.

He had to push the thoughts of her away. There was no use fretting. Avar would be fine. She would send another message after her next mission. Elzar had more urgent needs to worry about right now.

As Elzar took his place before the circle of Jedi, Grand Master Lahru said, "Elzar." Several others nodded. Grand Master Yoda nodded a little from his low perch on a cushion.

Every one of the Council members was physically in attendance. None wavered in place as a blue holo. Elzar hadn't seen them all together since they'd welcomed Avar home. Whatever this was, it was important. He readied himself. It was as good a time as any to make his confession.

First Elzar glanced at the two empty seats: Stellan's and Grand Master Veter's. The sight of them filled him with sorrow and a flicker of his old fury at the last moments of Veter's life. Those seats were both empty because of the Nihil. Because of Marchion Ro. The anger hummed, but Elzar let it flow away and turned his gaze around at everyone else. "Masters," he said.

Yoda stood with a little hop, tapping his walking stick once for attention. "Elzar Mann, a question, we have for you."

The rest of the Jedi Council stood, too. Elzar took a deep breath to stop from backing up in surprise.

"Long it is that this seat has been missing a Council member," Master Yoda said, indicating Stellan's chair.

"Too long," murmured Master Adampo. The gold Jedi Order emblems piercing his ears flashed in the light as he gently shook his head.

Elzar bowed slightly in acknowledgment.

Grand Master Lahru inclined his head, his long cranial fin making him the tallest in the room. "We want you to accept the position."

Now Elzar was startled.

No—he was shocked. He had no idea what his face was doing.

Master Ada-Li Carro smiled. "Yes, you."

Grand Master Ry Ki-Sakka was smiling, too.

"Avar—" Elzar began, unable to help himself.

"Walks a different path than once she did," said the older human Teri Rosason. "As do you."

The Jedi Council fell quiet as Elzar absorbed their solemn gazes.

He wanted to turn in place, to spin around and stare back at each of them. They couldn't possibly mean it. He wanted to demand detailed reasons. Out of everyone they could offer this to . . . it couldn't be him.

"I killed someone," he blurted out.

Silence continued to reign for a drawn-out moment, and Elzar couldn't believe how fast he'd lost any semblance of control of this situation. That had not been how he'd intended to make this confession. But he couldn't possibly be the right Jedi for this job.

"Killed, have we all," Yoda said almost tentatively. Or as if he were talking to a child.

Master Murag raised both graying eyebrows, inviting Elzar to go on. He swallowed. He breathed. And he told them.

"When Starlight Beacon was falling, one of the Nihil prisoners escaped and was trying to stop the crash. She . . . her name was Chancey Yarrow. She was working for Marchion Ro, developing weapons, but ultimately she wanted to save us, save the Beacon, even if only to save herself." Elzar let his gaze drift to the floor, remembering the darkness of that room, the sound of Nan screaming at him. The smell. There was always a smell when a lightsaber cut through something. A cold, clean, electric smell, even when it was flesh.

Elzar didn't push the memory away. His heart beat faster. "I killed her the moment I saw her digging into a panel. I acted in anger and fear. And Starlight fell."

It sounded so simple when he said it. Awful but simple. A chain of events, no more.

But it was so much more.

"We know now she was behind the technology that led to the Stormwall." Elzar made himself continue. "If she were alive, we might understand it. We might . . ." Elzar shook his head. So much of the galaxy suffered in ripples from that murder. Just like his finger disrupting the surface of the water.

"Relish it, you did?" Yoda asked.

Startled, Elzar frowned. "No, no, of course not."

"And when did you know you'd let go of the light?" asked Master Teri Rosason with her creaky old voice.

"Immediately." Elzar shook his head. "I was horrified right away. But that's not the point."

"What is the point?" Yarael Poof's head tilted at the end of his long, long neck.

Elzar opened his mouth but nothing came out. He understood they needed him to be able to articulate this, and he could, but the context should have been a confession, not them *offering him Stellan Gios's Council seat.*

The Jedi Council waited patiently.

He wasn't worthy of Stellan's legacy.

"The point . . ." Elzar began, "is not that she died by my hand. It's that I didn't weigh anything. I didn't consider. The world was exploding around me, and I gave in to the chaos, to the desperation. I didn't maintain myself as a Jedi. The circumstances are no excuse. What I was going through—what all of us on Starlight went through—should have made me better, not worse."

"You think Master Gios would condemn you for it?"

"Yes."

"And do you condemn yourself?"

"Yes." Elzar hesitated before making himself continue. "I'm trying not to. I'm working on it, on accepting my mistakes, because they're part of all that makes me who I am."

Yoda tapped his walking stick on the floor again. "What better action should you be taking in response, hmm?"

"I shouldn't have to do it in the first place," Elzar said, knowing he sounded incredulous.

"No Jedi is perfect, Elzar Mann," said Grand Master Lahru. "It is how we choose to serve Light and Life every day through the Force that makes us Jedi."

Elzar lowered his eyes. "I know. We learn that as children. But knowing it and living it are different."

"Even members of this Council, mistakes can make." Yoda shook his head.

Elzar couldn't help thinking of Azlin Rell, the former Jedi Master whom Yoda had sought for so long, returning with him to Coruscant last year. Yoda had sought Rell in the hope he could provide resources the Jedi could use to face the Nameless, and so far he hadn't done so, to Elzar's knowledge. There remained a chance, but how did one weigh that kind of hope against the dark side itself?

Yet it did allow Elzar a moment of insight into what Master Yoda meant. Choosing the light—any kind of choice—always left room for mistakes. For making the wrong choice. Elzar nodded. "I believe I understand you."

"Yet you also believe your actions disqualify you from holding a position among us?" The Thisspiasian master Oppo Rancisis tugged at his layered beard.

"Yes," Elzar said. How could he stand where Stellan had stood, given the choices he'd made?

The Jedi Council members shared a moment, glancing around at one another, and for all Elzar knew, they were talking in ways he couldn't hear.

Before long, Master Yoda said, "Believe that you are disqualified because of this new information, we do not. Your choice it is, to revere your mistake so highly."

Elzar wanted to protest the phrase "revere your mistake" because that wasn't what he was doing. His hesitation was born of a healthy respect for lifelong tendencies he continued to learn how to temper. He'd certainly argued plenty with the Council before. This time he stopped. This wasn't about policy or rescue missions or about where to send their resources. This was just about him and his future at a time when some nights he couldn't sleep because he feared none of them had a future at all.

Slowly, Elzar asked, "Will you tell me . . . why do you want me? You don't believe I'm unworthy of this seat, but what makes you think I'm worthy of it?"

"Elzar." Ry Ki-Sakka walked to him and clasped his shoulder. "New Council members are not meant to replace the old on the Jedi Council. That's not what this is."

Elzar's gaze fell to the shiny floor. Once again, he felt young. Too young, too fragile for the weight of all this. How did they manage it?

The expectations of an entire galaxy? Stellan's shoulders had always remained straight.

Ry said, "We don't replace. We add. We expand. It would not be Stellan Gios's seat you would take. It would be *yours*."

For a moment Elzar was frozen in place. Then he swallowed and bowed. "May I have time to consider your words before I make my choice?"

"Certainly, Master Elzar," Soleil Agra said, speaking for the first time. "We have needed new voices among us for months. A few more weeks will make little difference."

"We hope," Master Yoda said with a teasing lilt to his reedy voice.

Elzar flicked his glance at the shortest Council member. He certainly did hope with every part of him that he wasn't about to make another mistake.

Chapter Thirteen

REPUBLIC SPACE,
BORDER OF THE OCCLUSION ZONE

The *Blue Range* rendezvoused with the RDC star cruiser *Axiom* at the edge of the Font-Alor system, and Avar concentrated on helping the refugees transfer themselves to the guest quarters for their journey to the nearest station. It wasn't until she'd stopped in her own temporary bunk to clean up and change and head for the crew mess that she ran into Jedi Knight Vernestra Rwoh.

Avar smiled. She wasn't close to the young knight but felt a kinship because of their mutual connection to Stellan. She vividly recalled teasing Stellan, about a year after he had taken Vernestra on, that *of course a prodigy can only be trained up by a prodigy.* Stellan had made the expression he saved for when he was being too mature to stick out his tongue, and told her he didn't see how Avar could tell the difference anyway.

Vernestra waved wearily, looking like she'd just walked off a mission of her own. Avar tracked back in her head as she wandered over to the pantry to pick something basic to eat, remembering that Vernestra had been on an on-the-ground rescue mission in Nihil space for the past six days. It was the kind of mission Avar didn't allow herself to be assigned, thanks to the weight of being so recognizable. She couldn't do that kind of fieldwork without cause. Especially now that she'd made the holo for Rhil. Besides, the Mirialan had different contacts on the Nihil side, including her own former Padawan Imri Cantaros, who was still working undercover in the O.Z. the way Avar had when she was trapped all last year.

Unlike Avar, who'd immediately changed back into standard Jedi mission attire, Vernestra wore brown robes without any insignia; the only obvious marks of her status were the lightsaber and a few of the less overt design elements of her belt. The only permanent change to Avar's attire was that she no longer wore her diadem, having sold it last year for food to help people on Merisee in the Elrood sector, and she tended to pull her shorter blond hair back into practical tails. Vernestra meanwhile had chopped her purple hair above the shoulder and seemed to have aged a decade, despite the longevity of her species.

It reminded Avar of how much the Jedi had changed, not only individually but also as a whole, in the wake of devastating defeats. And the looming threat of the Nameless. Jedi weren't used to losing—they weren't even used to constant fighting. Of course, there had always been strife across the Republic and those in need whom the Jedi strove to aid through the Force. Bad things always happened. But Jedi like Avar and her peers, and Vernestra and hers, had come up in the Temple during a time of widespread prosperity and—if Avar made herself admit it—glory. The Jedi Order was grand and wealthy with knowledge and strength and resources, well suited to the task of managing peace and justice alongside the Republic.

Then the Nihil came, their target the Republic itself and everything it stood for. Alongside it, the Republic's Jedi allies—their guard dogs, as Avar had heard the Order called. And the Nihil brought with them Marchion Ro's strange, horrifying creatures who devoured the living Force, stripping it away and leaving behind only fear and ashes. The chaos of the Nihil was a foil against the Republic, but the Nameless were a brutally efficient enemy of the Force itself.

Jedi had something to truly fear.

In some ways, Avar thought, the worst thing Marchion Ro had done to the Jedi was take away their certainty. It had been a piece of their very identity.

"You look upset," Vernestra said as Avar joined her at a long table in the corner of the mess with a glass of fiz water and a nut-berry-honeychip protein bar. The two Jedi were isolated from the few crew stragglers in here at this hour.

Avar smiled a bit sadly. "Just thinking about . . . courage, I suppose."

Vernestra's eyebrows lifted. "You?"

"Me," Avar said with a little laugh. She knew how she was viewed, but she also trusted anyone who'd worked closely with Stellan. And anyone doing the work Vernestra had set herself to. They were absolute peers now. Some of the stories Avar had heard of Vernestra's exploits—half of them rumors—convinced her that Stellan would be proud of how ferocious his Padawan had become. How ferocious she'd had to become in the face of the Nameless. Avar softened her voice. "I don't remember ever having to choose to be brave when I was a youngling or a Padawan. I studied and meditated and went out with my master and my friends, eager to face challenges. I experienced nerves and anxiety, of course, but nothing overwhelming. I don't remember thinking about fear except as something to accept and dismiss. As almost irrelevant."

The Mirialan Jedi glanced down at her bowl of some kind of hot cereal. "But the Nameless compel us to."

Avar nodded. "I still am not . . . afraid very often. Sometimes, but always on behalf of others, for others, for potential danger, but it isn't like the inevitability of the kind of fear the Nameless demand. The relentlessness."

"The panic," Vernestra admitted plainly.

"You've faced one."

"Yes. No." Vernestra's gaze went distant, and she shivered. "I've been close enough to feel the effect, to lose myself. But I wouldn't say I faced it, exactly. If I'd been alone . . ."

"We need better methods to defend ourselves against them. Or work around them."

"Or we need to stop fighting them ourselves. Maybe it's a weakness we can't avoid. Retreat. Let those who don't sense the Force lead the charge against them. Or security droids."

The idea turned Avar's stomach. Retreat was necessary sometimes, but to assume it would be necessary, to let others do the fighting on behalf of the Jedi, galled her. There should not be any place a Jedi could not or would not go in service of the Force. Avar held her silence, not wanting to burden Vernestra with her reservations when her fellow Jedi already bore so much.

Picking apart her nut bar, Avar gave both of them a moment to compose themselves before asking after Vernestra's latest mission across the Stormwall.

"It was a rescue. We heard through Takodana of a cell of resistance fighters who had been on the run after their city was destroyed by Nihil—lucky Nihil who stumbled upon them. They included one of the informers who've been providing the group with anti-scav codes . . ." Vernestra sighed and dropped her spoon into the last of her uneaten cereal. "It was successful, but now a new informer will need to be sourced."

"Or the pressure on those remaining might grow too tight and they might snap."

"Exactly. I'm not sure if the end result is fortunate or unfortunate. I tell myself it's not part of my duty to know. That doesn't sit well, either."

Avar huffed. "It's different, doing this sort of work, isn't it? I was the marshal of Starlight Beacon. I've led strike teams and large-scale battles, not to mention what happened at Hetzal. But these days it's just me and my pilot throwing ourselves across hyperspace to try to save a few people at a time."

"I'm good at it," Vernestra said slowly.

"You are. I think I am, too. Better, maybe, at this kind of mission than those at the grander scale, despite my particular gifts. Grand leadership is for Stellan—" Avar stopped. She still thought of him like this sometimes: vital and living and only a comm away. "Now Elzar."

Vernestra's gaze flicked away at the mention of Elzar. She knew about Chancey Yarrow, about how the woman had died. Avar considered opening the subject, but as she studied Vernestra and listened to the Force, brushing her awareness against Vernestra's song, Avar could hear that Vernestra was fine now. Concerned, not entirely certain of herself, and young, but fine. Strong enough for what she needed. Elzar was the rattled one, the Jedi who continued seeking his place in this war, in this new Order. Vernestra Rwoh didn't need the counsel of Avar Kriss, who'd made as many mistakes as Elzar, as many as Vernestra had or would in days to come.

The only person any of them wanted to talk to was Stellan. Avar could wrap herself up in the steady baritone of his Force song. It had always been so vivid, but it worked best as part of a whole. A harmonizing line. A charming countermelody.

Ah, he would be so annoyed with them.

Avar hummed a soft note under her breath, letting the loss and grief drift away, melt into her again. She was getting better at this: accepting her feelings without allowing them to hurt or control her. Amazing how long it had taken her to achieve it. How long and how much suffering.

Just before she popped a chunk of nut bar into her mouth, the mess intercom chirped. "Master Kriss, this is Captain Ba'luun. A Nihil ship just dropped out of hyperspace in Republic territory at the same mark your *Blue Range* did. We're jumping back to the mark in three—two—"

By the time the captain said "One" and the ship hummed with the quiet lurch into hyperspace, Avar was on her feet and across the room.

It sounded like Nihil had followed her out of the Occlusion Zone. That shouldn't be possible, unless one of her refugees had a tracking beacon or was a spy. She flicked the intercom and said, "Captain, how many Vectors are berthed on the *Axiom*?"

"Three, Master Kriss."

Avar spun around to catch Vernestra's eye. The Mirialan nodded, grabbing up their discarded food. Avar said, "Vernestra and I will get two powered up and ready to deploy."

Together they dashed through the cruiser to the fighter bay, bypassing RDC crew heading to their own battle stations.

"How long is the jump back to your exit coordinates?" Vernestra asked as they took turns hopping down the ladder, landing hard on the metal floor of the bay.

"A few minutes."

"It can't be a coincidence," Vernestra said. "It's not a public beacon on this side."

Avar only shook her head and let the Force draw her to one of the sharp Jedi Vectors lined up like sleek, deadly stars beside a row of RDC fighters. The likelihood of a Nihil ship exiting at the exact same place as her route through the Stormwall was so small as to be impossible. The only reason it could happen besides one of the refugees betraying them was that the Nihil knew Cair San Tekka's data—they had caught him, or Belin and Rhil, or possibly had infiltrated his group long ago and chose now to reveal their hand. Because of Avar's message.

Vernestra touched the Vector beside Avar's, and they both unlocked the cockpit bubbles.

Avar called, "May the Force be with you, Vernestra!" and climbed into hers.

She settled quickly once the transparisteel bubble closed around her, first opening communications from the Vector to the bridge of the *Axiom*. She confirmed Vernestra's engagement with her fighter. Then Avar opened her feelings to the Force and the second skin the Vector could become.

"Ready over there?" she commed to Vernestra.

"As ready as I ever am," Vernestra said wisely. It made Avar smile.

"Ready to launch on exit from hyperspace," she told the captain.

The Force flowed through and around Avar, ringing the Vector. She closed her eyes as she waited for the *Axiom* to drop out of hyperspace. Avar didn't pilot Vectors often—as she'd told Vernestra, she'd more frequently led from a cruiser or Longbeam deck in the past decade—but Avar had never grown out of the thrill they gave her. They were like an exoskeleton of strength that melded perfectly with her own strengths. She liked the maneuverability and power, the necessity for total communion with the fighter's internal processes. The reliance on her own focus, her own skills.

Captain Ba'luun's voice filled the cockpit: "Arriving now."

The *Axiom* dropped and instantly the alarms rang; the fighter bay energy field sparked blue and dropped. She smiled grimly to herself and launched into the stars.

The Vector dipped instantly and spun around, and Avar loosed her senses into the fighter.

"Nihil ship holding location at the Republic beacon," Ba'luun's voice rang in the cockpit. "No fighters of theirs scrambled."

"Coming around," said Vernestra.

Avar set her lightsaber onto the keypad and it locked in magnetically, keying open the weapons for use. Avar pushed up the speed of her Vector and zipped ahead of Vernestra, who fell into flank.

The rush of coming battle raised Avar's body heat, and she pushed it down, focused on the mass of the Vector and the appearance of the Nihil ship. It was bulky and snub-nosed, with blasts of paint and scoring like many Nihil ships. Cannons aimed in every direction as if a child had glued sticks haphazardly around a toy. It was smaller than the *Axiom,* and Avar was confident that, unless the Nihil had a secret weapon or trick up their fuel lines, they and the RDC could take it.

"Nihil ship," Ba'luun's voice rang out over comm channels. "This is the Republic Defense Coalition ship *Axiom,* and I am Captain Ba'luun. You have entered Republic space. Stand down immediately and return to your space or you will be destroyed."

Avar thrust her Vector to the port side of the Nihil ship as Vernestra swung opposite. They darted back and forth like little fireflies with the greater *Axiom* rising behind.

Suddenly, a forward bulkhead on the Nihil ship exploded. Pale gas billowed out and flames flickered, then evaporated into the vacuum of space. Avar double-checked, but nobody had fired.

A second explosion in the belly of the ship flared vivid blue, bright enough that Avar blinked at the afterimage. "That was the Path engine," she said on the private channel to Vernestra's Vector.

"Nihil ship!" Ba'luun commanded. "Stand down! If you require assistance, stand down and it will be provided."

Just then, a top panel of the Nihil ship, along the neck beside the cockpit, blew. Avar saw living beings evacuated into space. Their limbs flailed as the ship vented.

Lights flickered along the spine of the ship, and in tandem three cannons detached, tearing away strips of the hull.

"What's happening?" Vernestra asked.

"I have no idea," Avar replied, nudging her Vector nearer. "Perhaps sabotage?"

Captain Ba'luun's voice emerged again. "This is your final chance, Nihil ship."

"—need! No need!" drawled a response, crackling and almost too loud. "We're here to surrender."

Avar felt the stutter of her surprise shift through the body of the Vector. She reached out and flicked her comm switch. "Nihil vessel, this is Jedi Master Avar Kriss. Who are you and why should we let down our defenses to believe you?"

"Ah, Master Kriss! Just who I was looking for. What a pleasure to meet you. I assure you, I have no designs on your lovely little Vectors or our Republic."

"Avar!" Vernestra hissed through their Vector-to-Vector comm. "I know that voice!"

"I'm Xylan Graf, of the Core Grafs, and I can now state more accurately that I don't come to surrender so much as rescue myself from the clutches of those dastardly Nihil—but I also come bearing a gift! I can tell you how to destroy the Stormwall."

Chapter Fourteen

SARUMO, INSIDE THE OCCLUSION ZONE

It was the middle of the night in the northern parts of the supercontinent of Sarumo, the burnt-out fields lacking the usual activities of the daytime, as desperate farmers continued to coax life back into them. The streets of the once-lovely, if blocky, capital city were silent. Here, unlike some planets in Nihil territory that had made the transition of power more seamlessly, the citizens had been pressed into harshly policed districts: Farmers toiled constantly to regain the lost agriculture, former merchants and traders now worked in quarries and mines, displaced children were left to run their own gangs in the absence of education or families, and there was a small district of wealthy people, who had sided with General Viess when she handed the whole planet to Marchion Ro last year.

Some refugees had fled to the south, whose ice deserts and tundras were useless to the resource-hungry Nihil. If they survived, they did so barely.

Porter Engle slipped under elegant marble beams of the peristyle court of the sprawling manor that once had served as General Viess's barony and alflacow ranch and now was an operating base for her

Ministry of Protection. The first established, in fact, and rarely inhabited by the minister herself.

For once, Viess's absence served Porter just fine.

Using the Force, he muffled his presence. *You-don't-see-me, it-was-only-a-shadow, just-a-night-bird-taking-wing.*

The sleepy nighttime patrols were easy to fool.

Porter moved silently, divested of his Nihil costume for this mission, wearing plain dark notice-nothing clothes instead, with a cowl pulled low over his brow. His lightsaber was wrapped with a strip of gray cloth to keep the hilt from gleaming. Porter could still ignite it if everything went sideways and he needed to fight his way out.

At the rear door, he waited patiently, at one with the Force, until a patrol approached. Porter breathed nothingness into the air, whispering commands to the dull ears of the two Nihil. They didn't even glance his way, but when the door opened, he followed them inside. They didn't notice that, either.

Porter kept pace with them, murmuring commands through the Force, unconcerned with being seen by others: He looked as if he belonged at first glance, despite the plain clothes. He walked with them, near enough that it should be impossible for him to be an enemy. Any fellow Nihil would assume he was guest or prisoner.

The Nihil turned off toward the smell of grilling meat. Porter didn't follow. That wouldn't be the right way. He ducked into an alcove and reached out: The Force flowed out and back in, and Porter sensed the whereabouts of the Nihil guards. He sensed where they slept in barracks, where they ate a quiet meal in a mess nearby, where several stood in constant vigilance near the center of the manor. That was his goal— what else would they guard but their general's office? Or if it was something else, he should investigate that, too.

Peeking out, he glanced quickly for signs of security droids or cameras that might see him and record him. He wasn't too concerned about his presence being noticed after the fact. But he needed to get where he was going first.

Rounding the corner at a jog, he followed the path toward the mystery office, ducking around a cracked statue of some sort of tree. There were two Nihil guarding the wide double doors. He'd have to approach directly unless he could . . . Porter reached out, closing his eyes. Yes, if he backtracked, he could take a different route and come up alongside them instead.

He did it, encountering only one Nihil, whom he dispatched with a sudden punch. It knocked the Nihil back into the wall with a thump, sending them unconscious. Porter dragged them into an empty room.

Returning to the general's office from the side hall, he slipped quietly against the wall, focused on the two Nihil. He removed a small coin from his pocket and, with a nudge from the Force, sent it zipping as far down the opposite hall as he could. It pinged, and both of the Nihil masked heads jerked toward the sound.

One said, "I'll check it out."

The other only grunted and watched his fellow dash away.

While his back was turned, Porter slunk up behind him and whispered with a subtle Force command, "You heard something inside the general's office."

"I heard . . ." The Nihil spun and immediately slapped the controls, opening the door and bursting in, blaster raised.

Porter leapt after, grabbing him around the neck in a choke hold. He spun them and used the Force to rip the Nihil's blaster from his hand and fling it away. He clapped his hand over the Nihil's mouth to keep him quiet, cutting off his airflow until he hit the ground and slumped to the side. Porter picked up the Nihil's mask and held it like a shield.

Then Porter waited. It didn't take long for the guard's partner to return and make a confused noise at the open office door. She stepped in, beginning to raise her blaster. Porter grabbed her wrist and yanked her inside. He punched her in the face with the Nihil mask. Her visor cracked, and she slammed into a shelf. Porter gestured with his hand, and the Force shut the office door.

The second Nihil groaned and lifted her hand to her comlink. Before she could initiate it, Porter had her in his grip again, a hard lock around her neck. He pressed. She passed out, too.

Porter was barely breathing hard. The Force rushed in his ears like the high-pitched singing of lightsabers, bright with energy and cutting through the air as if a hundred Jedi were going through forms. A comforting sound to Porter, who'd always felt best in the Force when he could focus it through a blade.

The office was not as large as he'd expected, but it dripped with the trappings of wealth. Gleaming precious metal and rainbow starwood inlaid with gemstones. Local vir-silver lace covered the desk, and the pelt of a spotted ice phoenix spread over the polished tile floor. When Porter touched the lighting panel, two floating chandeliers detached from the arched ceiling and began to emit a pale glow. Just enough for him to stride forward and begin riffling through the very real, very rare books, a few scrolls made of a stiff local plant fiber, and drawers of datacards.

The whole place smelled like a sweet flower he couldn't identify and a musk some whispering voice of the Force said must be the remnants of the Nameless here with her.

Porter didn't have a lot of time, but he had enough. He grabbed a few star maps and memorized the names of the books. He looked for anything out of place: items that didn't quite belong, which Viess must not have acquired here or which already had had their spots in this office before she commandeered it. He needed to find the things she'd brought herself. Things of importance to her specifically.

Porter had spent weeks hunting the Nihil Minister of Protection—what a gross bastardization of the terms—the way a Jedi might hunt any political enemy or generic Nihil. By the rules. Tracking ships, observing Nihil movements. Asking locals, acquiring tracking beacons, slicing comm frequencies.

So far he'd chased behind her, unable to grasp her. She stayed ahead of him by moving and by surrounding herself with soldiers and monsters.

Porter had to change the game. Avar's message had said she was coming—the Jedi were coming. He was running out of time to get Viess himself.

He'd been treating her like a mercenary, like a wealthy feudal lord. Like a messy, power-hungry Nihil intent on destruction and violence. He'd acted like a Jedi.

Viess was surely all of those things. But she was both more and less than their combined meaning. She was an individual with specific wants and needs, just like Porter was a specific sort of Jedi. She had changed in the hundred years since she'd taken his sister from him. So had Porter changed.

It was time for him to stop hunting her like a Jedi after a Nihil, and get to the bones of it. He would study her, get to know her. Understand what drove her intimately and immediately, not just broadly. Then he'd use that knowledge to predict her and find her.

Porter would become the perfect hunter for only Viess.

Just the two of them.

Everything else could fall away.

Chapter Fifteen

NABOO, INSIDE THE OCCLUSION ZONE

It was difficult to look out the viewport at the devastation Naboo had suffered. Cair San Tekka had been born here, though he hadn't grown up on the planet. He'd spent most of his life closer to the Core, in school and then training in various aspects of the family businesses before going undercover as a security agent with Graf Enterprises for a little bit of corporate espionage.

The edges of Theed still glimmered with refined marble, gilded decorations, and the mist from the glorious waterfalls. But marks of the Nihil invasion remained: dark scouring scars from cannons, wreckage of the planetary Royal Space Fighter Corps, the lone tower remaining from an ancient suspension bridge that collapsed when the plasma shook the city and the power went out. And here and there, Cair could see the bright-blue eyes smeared large across the domes and rose marble walls. It was a jarring note in a city that favored the warm colors of sunrise.

Cair dropped the slick yacht beneath one of the arcing waterfalls spilling away from the south side of the Naboo capital. This was his third ship since leaving the *Brightbird* on the dark side of a dead moon.

He'd taken a beat-up fighter with only enough power to get him to the Chommell sector and transmit the right anti-scav codes. On the new colony on Jafan, he grabbed the hauler he'd bribed some mechanics into hiding for him in a spaceport partially abandoned, thanks to the Nihil presence in the sector, then made the quick jump to Naboo. Cair was able to slip down to the swampy base of one of the cliffs on the south side of Theed to switch from the hauler to the pristine San Tekka family yacht he'd hidden among the flora.

Two months ago, Cair had been struggling to run his new insurgency from the run-down backwaters of Seswenna, with few resources easily accessible and most of his energy spent bribing and threatening people too afraid of the Nihil to fight hard. Then the Stormwall had expanded again, this time swallowing most of the Chommell sector, including Naboo.

With communications suddenly down and no possibility of help from the Republic, the Nihil had invaded with almost embarrassing ease.

It wasn't just any Nihil, either, but Viess herself. Marchion Ro's general was a brutal old Mirialan who arrived to personally subjugate Naboo. Probably because the planet was known for finery and riches. After she pummeled the capital with a barrage of ion attacks, the plasma mine shafts on the outskirts and beneath the very buildings of Theed had trembled and grown unstable, knocking out all power planet-wide. Energy fields collapsed, and planetary defenses could barely respond. The Royal Naboo Security Forces could get only a third of their ships moving at all. There'd been essentially no resistance to Viess's takeover. The Gungans stayed withdrawn inside their underwater cities, and the queen was spirited off by her guard so quickly and thoroughly she'd not yet been found. Cair hadn't been able to discover a whisper of truth about whether she was even still on the world.

Cair himself had raced to Naboo so fast he'd broken several of his own rules about covers and secrecy. His uncles Marlowe and Vellis had surrendered along with the regional and planetary governments of

Naboo. They'd had no choice, given the widespread forced disarmament and the attention of Viess herself. The San Tekkas handed over quite a bit of money as tribute to the Nihil general as a way of maintaining the pretense of freedom on the now-occupied planet. Everyone with resources or a title who was trapped on Naboo had done similarly. Thanks to the easy surrender, the less-rich populace had managed better than those on other Nihil worlds—at least those who survived the initial raid. Cair had snuck in and pretended to have been on Naboo all along, a useless spoiled scion of the San Tekkas. It wasn't a bad cover, especially once Viess took her flagship and left the planet in the violent care of lesser Nihil pirates.

It didn't take long for Cair to convince the uncles to quietly allocate some of their hard funding for the use of his freedom fighters, especially once he promised he could get them to Republic space. Using San Tekka money was easier than the intricate siphoning of his husband's credits, which were sprawling, hidden well, and often soft in comparison. The bribes had allowed him to get the uncles offworld and eventually to Avar Kriss, presumably safe and sound with family on the Republic side of this mess.

As Cair flew low against the river that led away from the city center and toward the San Tekka family island compound, he made lists of everything he needed to organize over the next few days while performing his indolent-heir act. The louder he was, the less likely anyone would notice that Marlowe and Vellis had escaped quite so soon.

But first, he really looked forward to sinking into a long nap with Plinka, his husband's six-legged giant Theljian snow dog, curled around him like a shaggy blanket.

When the nose of his long yacht darted around a cluster of white stone spires dripping with tiny waterfalls blasting out over the expanse of a lake, Cair pulled back and cursed with every word he'd learned in every seedy spaceport.

The San Tekka compound matched the marble-elegant aesthetic of Theed, despite being kilometers away on the outskirts, rising from the center of a vast lake like bubbles of twilight turned to towers and domes. Most of the architecture had survived Viess's bombardment, at least overtly, and from a distance one might not even realize the site was under siege.

But where San Tekka pennants usually billowed from thin poles around the circumference of the grand entrance dome, this afternoon the green and pink remnants were overlaid by a holodisplay of General Viess's personal crest.

She was back, and instead of taking up residence in the royal palace, or the planetary defense corps fort with its long-range comm Cair would love to get his hands on, she was *here*.

General Viess was setting up shop in his family seat.

Cair spun the yacht around immediately, muttering curses under his breath.

He dipped the yacht under the nearest mainland waterfalls and settled it quickly on a rocky outcrop. The moment the engines cut off, Cair was out of the pilot's chair and dashing to his small quarters in the rear of the ship. He dug into his closet and pulled out a brighter-red coat. He stripped off layers of black, leaving only his undershirt and trousers. Quickly he layered a silk vest with a long pink skirt and a vivid-red sash, loosely knotted. The red coat went over it all. Cair tore his hair out of the topknot, finger-combed it until it was properly disheveled. He took one of his wrist ribbons and looped it around his throat like a lazy necklace. From the panel beside the bed, he pulled out lipstick and smeared some under his ear, rubbing it in like a love bite. He dragged a bottle of wine from under the bed, and in the bathroom, he washed his mouth with it, spitting the big gulp out in the sink. He spilled a few drops on his lapel and then rubbed his eyes, reddening them and smudging the leftover liner.

This would have to do.

After a second thought, Cair took another swig of the wine, but this time he swallowed.

Back in the pilot's chair, he lifted away from the waterfall and flew less steadily toward the compound's ground-level landing pads. They were around back, on a long slab of polished, gleaming stone. Usually he'd prefer the shelf landing pads that clung to the towers like crescent mushrooms, but the ground was where the general's people would be.

He flew lazily, with an idle hand, and ignored the comm burst asking for his name and identification. Cair pushed back the ship's codes only, as if offended to be asked at all.

When he landed, a scatter of Nihil in their haphazard steel-and-leather uniforms moved back. They were splattered in that pretty blue paint that had come to represent nightmares to everyone in the Occlusion Zone, their spiky gas masks hanging from their belts or pushed up on their heads like angry hats.

Still ignoring them, Cair slowly put the yacht through its landing sequence. He took a few deep breaths, then stood up and bent over, hanging his head upside down. Blood rushed into his cheeks and temples, throbbing gently.

As he made his way to the exit, it was easy to put a sway in his walk. A sexy, slightly hungover sway.

The moment the landing doors slid open, discordant music filled his ears. Maybe that was what had been throbbing, not his head. It wasn't exactly Nihil-raiding wreckpunk, but only barely more pleasant. Cair plastered on a grimace and put his black-metal fingers to his temple as he stomped down the ramp.

"What is going on?" he demanded of the Nihil at the base.

The many-times-pierced Kerkoiden raised a blaster in answer. "Tell me your name or you won't have a face."

Cair grimaced delicately and waved his hand in front of the blaster. "Please, you're in my house, surely you should be introducing yourself to me."

"You know who we are," the Nihil sneered.

"I suppose, though by that same logic you should know who I am, too."

"The cousin," said a Twi'lek with scarification in waves around the base of his lekku. "Where have you been?"

Cair peered at him, pulse racing, and gently nudged the Kerkoiden's blaster barrel out of his face. "Wherever I like. And now I need a drink and a long bath."

"The patriarchs of your clan have vanished, and you expect us to believe you had nothing to do with it?"

Cair pinched his expression into a pout. "Did they take the jadeite coins? Those are my favorite."

The Nihil peered at each other. The Twi'lek finally said, "The general will want to speak with you."

"She should join me for dinner," Cair said, pushing past them to head inside. The music truly was giving him a headache. He'd wash up, put on a better version of his costume, and have Ino'olo get some of the crystal linflower liquor from the wine cave. Suffer through a tense dinner, then get that nap with Plinka.

"No, now." The Twi'lek grabbed Cair's arm hard enough to bruise, and he yelped. The Nihil ignored him, dragging him along despite Cair's protestations and glares.

He was taken into the family's private tower and all the way to the observation deck via the luxury glass turbolift that some enterprising Nihil had sliced to play a song that sounded like a crash landing. Cair had never missed his dulcimer more—though he hadn't had much time or energy to relearn how to play it since losing his hand. Hopefully he'd be able to get some practice in with the one he kept here on Naboo. There were a few jigs Plinka enjoyed.

They passed several of the household staff, most of whom ducked nervously away from the Nihil and Cair, none of whom knew Cair as anything more than the indolent, spoiled scion he pretended to be. Only Ino'olo knew more of the truth. Cair didn't see the young woman, though she usually paid attention to his comings and goings and waited to greet him. A sharp rock formed in Cair's gut as they approached the grand doors of the observation deck.

There she was—Ino'olo, her head lowered, her hands clasped tightly before her. She peeked up at him from under the elaborately puffed hairdo but looked away again immediately. Scared.

Cair was in trouble.

He lifted his chin arrogantly as the Twi'lek punched the door panel and shoved him onto the observation deck.

An energy shield created domed protection from the elements here but also gave the wide marble and polished-cambylictus-wood-paneled room the illusion of being open to the air. The view was spectacular: The distant skyscape of Theed rose in pale colors that gleamed in the sunset, the vivid-violet sky streaked with thin-edged fire-orange clouds and the rolling foothills stabbed with crystal spears and jutting pink granite. Two of the moons hung in hazy crescents.

The general stood with her back to Cair, stiff-shoulderened and caped with fine blue. Her armor gleamed in the light pearls set into chandeliers that hovered near the top of the energy dome.

And between them, chained with heavy electro-alloy, was Plinka.

Cair made a shocked sound and Plinka whined. She was taller than him, even sitting, with shaggy white hair and six legs. All of her eyes were pink-rimmed with pain or fear. "What is the meaning of this?" he demanded, stepping toward the big snow dog.

"Don't move," the general said softly.

Cair froze. The general turned slowly.

Unable to take his eyes off Plinka, he scanned her for any sign of injury. There was nothing he could see. His guts twisted. What had she done to Plinka?

"I'm surprised you returned," Viess said coldly. She walked to him, her boots clipping on the ballroom floor.

"This is where my dog is," Cair spat.

"Funny you should call her that." Viess stopped beside Plinka. Her dark hair was bound up under a helmet that trailed a veil of thin material over her neck. Her armor gleamed immaculately with intricate metal inlay. She studied him with an eyebrow raised, as if he were nothing. Black diamond tattoos marked the green of her cheeks.

Cair asked, "What do you want? Why are you here instead of the palace?"

"It's being refitted for visits from the Eye himself. I would never deign to set myself up there. Especially not when this manor has everything the palace has, being so defensible and with such a useful port, a perfect view of Theed. And its own power generators. Not to mention a shockingly decadent wine cellar. We can live here quite comfortably and keep Theed itself defenseless."

"Who would attack you here?" he demanded. "We've turned over the resources and treasures you've asked for."

"I have plenty of enemies. All the strong do." Viess thumbed the hilt of the sword at her belt. "Tell me where Marlowe and Vellis San Tekka are."

"I don't know."

"Where were you, then, these past days?"

"In the city!"

She eyed him, blue eyes hot in her green face. "With a paramour?"

"With a lot of people."

"You want me to believe you simply wandered off for a bit of love-making?"

"And gambling," he said, jutting out his chin. "There's a lot of good trouble to be had in a Nihil-run city like Theed."

Viess laughed. "I see."

Beside her, Plinka trembled hard enough Cair could see it. He wondered if the chains held her in stasis. "Let Plinka go. You're scaring her."

Plinka's lips curled back from her sharp teeth.

The general drummed her fingers on the hilt of her sword. "Let me tell you a story, Cair San Tekka."

"Just what I always wanted."

She smiled magnanimously. "I was recently speaking with Ghirra Starros about rats. Rats crawling through cracks in walls, and how you just can't get rid of them carefully. What matters is speed and decisiveness, yes?"

Cair opened his mouth to joke, but panic stopped it in his throat as the general moved in one fluid step, drew her sword, and sliced along the side of Plinka's throat.

Cair leapt forward with a cry, running to Plinka's side. The dog made an awful gasping sound, and the chains shorted out. Blood seeped from the wound, flooding into the white fur. Cair caught Plinka as she tumbled, throwing his arms around her. He helped lower her, but she was so heavy. She landed half in his lap as he fell to his knees. "Plinka," he said, struggling to hold her and strip off his coat. He balled it up and pressed it to her neck. Blood gushed but didn't spurt. Maybe—maybe...

His breath stuttered as Cair tried to focus. He pressed hard, then yelled, "Help! Get a doctor!"

Viess pointed her sword at the doors and said, "Stay."

Gritting his teeth, Cair focused on stopping the bleeding. Plinka blinked at him, whining.

"It's all right, girl," he murmured. "Just stay still."

A cold blade sticky with blood touched his jaw. Cair froze. The blade lifted his chin until he was forced to look at Viess.

"Worry less, human. The Theljian snow dog's primary cranial artery is tucked beneath the spine."

Cair's mouth dropped open. The Mirialan could know that only because she was an experienced mass murderer. She lowered her gaze to his neck, where his own pulse throbbed, probably visible to her, seeing as it was so vulnerably close to the surface.

Viess continued, "You haven't heard the point of my story."

Cair swallowed, the smell of cool snow dog blood filling his nostrils.

"We—Ghirra and I—were discussing the need to establish a new hierarchy of Nihil working on the Stormwall, since that's where any flaws in our armor are likely to be. Dr. Mkampa cared about exactly what one might expect from a Nihil-backed scientist: power and continued support for her research. And Xylan Graf cared about so little, you know, I wondered if it must have been an act. Best to get rid of them both and start over. But if I killed everyone working on the Lightning Crash, I'd need new people to run it, wouldn't I?"

Her voice faded behind the ringing in Cair's ears. Had she already done it? Already massacred everyone on the Lightning Crash? Had they had any warning? Cair clenched his jaw, tightened his hold on Plinka, and tried not to throw up.

"—and Ghirra reminded me that in the absence of our former experts, we have some of the foremost *Republic* experts on hyperspace right here on Naboo, and how convenient that I've already conquered it!" Viess smiled, as if not only pleased but overjoyed.

Former expert. Former.

Cair was definitely going to vomit.

"Too bad they're gone." Viess crouched, smoothly shifting so that her blade didn't move at all, even as she reached Cair's eye level. "Their drunken, silly cousin was gone, too. But do you know what I did find here, waiting eagerly for me?"

Cair didn't answer. He couldn't open his mouth. His hands were going numb with Plinka's cold blood.

"Since you've come home, Cair San Tekka," the general asked sweetly, "tell me, what are you doing with Xylan Graf's dog?"

Chapter Sixteen

Xylan Graf was pure chaos, and Avar almost regretted letting him on the *Axiom.*

First of all, he brought suitcases. Two of them. He piloted and docked a small transport shuttle normally attached to the Nihil ship he'd flown—stolen?—from Nihil space. Avar had secured her Vector, Vernestra right behind her, when Graf landed. They were joined in the welcoming party by several RDC soldiers with blasters ready and Captain Ba'luun herself—a stout Thisspiasian with her thick hair and beards braided uniform-style. She slithered quickly but regally across the docking bay to Avar's side.

"You know this Xylan Graf?" Ba'luun asked.

"No, but I've heard of the Grafs, and he knew several of the right names," Avar admitted wryly.

"I know him," Vernestra said breathlessly, as she dashed to Avar's other side. "I don't trust him, but he did help us on my first mission across the Stormwall. I could be mistaken, but I suspect he's the person who's been supplying us with the time-phased Path data."

"Good place to start," Captain Ba'luun said as the transport shuttle hissed and its lower hatch popped open.

A fancy metallic suitcase fell through, landing with a crack on the floor. A second followed it.

One of the soldiers laughed.

A ladder descended and first one polished boot, then another, followed by vivid-teal silkensteen trousers, several layers of ruffled tunic skirt, and a tight jacket. Then the whole overly pretty dark-skinned human Xylan Graf hopped the final rungs. He spun and spread his arms with a flourish and a charming grin. He certainly looked like a rich fop more than a Nihil escapee.

Before he opened his mouth, Captain Ba'luun gestured for her soldiers to surround him and said, "I see you took the time to pack."

Xylan fluttered his dark eyelashes. His eyes were electric blue, too vivid to be natural in a human. "Why . . . Captain, is it? I've had these bags packed and ready to go for absolutely months. Always safer to be ready to run at the first opportunity when one is hostage to Marchion Ro."

Vernestra shifted beside Avar, and Avar reached to touch the Mirialan's wrist. They'd see how this played out at first.

"And you chose now to what? Defect? We'll have to do some investigating." Ba'luun nodded to a soldier, who stepped forward with her blaster ready.

Xylan Graf held up his hands. "No need, no need. I'm no danger, I promise—I really just need a ride to Coruscant, maybe a meal and bath, nothing like a cell, you see." As the soldiers nudged at him with their weapons, one going so far as to pat him down, Xylan looked around, eyes wide. "Wasn't there a . . . ah! Yes!" He waved. "Master Avar Kriss! Yoo-hoo! Don't let them hurt me, would you?"

Vernestra snorted a laugh.

Though Avar hadn't been feeling too amused, Vernestra's reaction loosened a knot that had been forming at the base of her neck. Avar said, "It's all right, Captain, I can take Mr. Graf to settle in and explain."

But Graf noticed Vernestra. Shock showed on his face in a flash, then he reconfigured the expression to haughty surprise. "Vernestra Rwoh! As I live and breathe, as they say on the frontier. Is that you? Now, here." He turned to Captain Ba'luun. "This is a Jedi who knows me personally. I'm sure she'd vouch that I have no ill intentions toward your ship."

"I wouldn't go that far," Vernestra said.

"Vernie," Graf said imploringly.

The shift in Vernestra's energy from relatively open to sudden dangerous irritation had Avar glancing at her sharply. Vernestra smiled at Graf in a decidedly unpleasant way.

Xylan Graf's expression froze. "Vernestra," he corrected himself apologetically.

Slowly, Vernestra looked to Avar, and Avar nodded for Vernestra to proceed. The younger Jedi had the history here, and she absolutely had the skills. She could handle it. One thing Avar had learned well during her year in the Occlusion Zone was to sometimes hold back her natural tendency to take charge. Her instincts had always been to throw herself into leadership because nobody could do it the way she did. And Avar was good at leading, at accepting and beating challenges. But in Nihil territory giving herself away as an authority figure, or someone with any power at all, often got people killed. Not to mention it was prideful. She'd realized how to work to her strengths even when standing at someone's back, when taking a side seat because that was the will of the Force.

Vernestra said to Captain Ba'luun, "If your people can take Xylan's bags to the brig, we'll take him to get something to eat and he can have a chance to convince us he doesn't need to join them in the cell."

Xylan smiled sourly at her. But he bowed politely.

"You should join us, Captain," Avar said.

"I'd love to. We can use my command quarters." The Thisspiasian tapped the thick tip of her tail to the docking bay floor, and two of her soldiers jogged over to grab up Graf's suitcases. "Be sure to check them for explosives."

Xylan offered his elbow to Vernestra, and the younger Jedi rolled her eyes. He shrugged and said to Avar, "Lead the way?"

Captain Ba'luun returned to the bridge to bring the *Axiom* around for the jump to Coruscant. She'd join them in her command quarters shortly, and welcomed them to dig into her drinks station.

But the moment the Jedi with their sort-of captive stepped into the corridor outside the docking bay, Avar nearly ran into Marlowe and Vellis San Tekka.

Marlowe said, "Ah, Master Kriss, can you tell us— "

Behind Marlowe, his husband, Vellis, halted in shock, pointing over Avar's shoulder. "You!"

Marlowe leaned forward and scowled. "Xylan Graf."

Avar put her hand on Marlowe's chest. "Gentlebeings, please. Everything is fine, and we'll be entering hyperspace momentarily, soon to be on Coruscant. Please return to the room you were assigned."

"But—"

"*San Tekkas* like to blame Grafs for everything wrong in the universe." Xylan spoke gently, as if discussing a baby. Avar glanced back. Vernestra had a hand on Xylan's arm, but the only thing dangerous about Graf was his smile, eyelids lowered with either laziness or malice.

Avar sensed neither but rather attentiveness and a brand-new edge of something in Xylan Graf's energy. Something like panic. That boded poorly. Avar kept her awareness of the Force open and flowing.

"Grafs are the ones who—Master Kriss," Vellis said, pushing past his husband. "This man and his family paid for the development of the Stormwall technology. Xylan Graf was arrested on Coruscant and his assets seized over a year ago because of it. The Gravity's Heart fiasco."

Behind her, Xylan sucked in a sharp breath. He didn't move out of Vernestra's grip, though. He said, "True, but perhaps you should join us for the story I'm about to tell, Masters San Tekka. Since we wouldn't have that very same Stormwall—or the Nihil themselves!—without the aid of *your* family."

Avar felt momentarily like a boulder pummeled on one side by hail, the other by the ocean itself. She put out both her hands. "Stop. We will discuss this peacefully." She glared at Xylan. "This is not the Nihil. Threats and obnoxiousness will not get you what you want." She turned her glare onto Marlowe and Vellis. "This *is* the Republic, and we work through justice and mercy. Keep both in mind if you would like to participate in this conversation."

"Yes, ma'am," Vellis said, despite being her elder. Marlowe nodded. Xylan sighed like a put-upon cat.

Vernestra met Avar's gaze and shrugged a little as if to ask, *What can one do with people like this?*

Once the party had situated themselves in the commander's quarters with cups of caf, a tea service, and snacks, the *Axiom* had made the jump into hyperspace and Captain Ba'luun arrived, brandishing a small bottle of a poisonous-looking pink liquor.

Everyone but the Jedi partook, and Xylan Graf nearly melted with relief when he sipped the alcohol. "It's such an annoyance finding fine wines in the Occlusion Zone."

"Then you shouldn't have allied with the Nihil," Vellis San Tekka sneered.

"Perhaps," Avar said, "you should begin your tale, Xylan."

He smiled at her and looked to Vernestra and Captain Ba'luun, ignoring the San Tekkas. He said, "Years ago, I began working with a charming, brilliant—but ultimately rather unhinged—scientist named Chancey Yarrow, funding her research into gravitational distortions."

Avar blinked at the name but otherwise did not react. She knew this background from Elzar, and already Xylan felt calmer, though there remained an urgency to him. He believed his life depended on his words.

It was probably wise.

"The details are neither here nor there," Xylan said. "But once the

Gravity's Heart space station was destroyed, Chancey removed herself to a lab provided by Graf money where she continued her research. I—as the good San Tekkas were so kind to point out—had been alleviated of my positions within my family and stripped of resources. But I did manage to hide away quite a bit of funding in secure locations." Here Xylan looked pointedly at the San Tekkas. Vellis's face turned red, and Marlowe closed his eyes.

Avar sensed Xylan Graf was grandstanding to hide his anxiety.

"One of the assets I managed to retain was a station I was building alongside the Gravity's Heart—a backup, as it were. It's never a good idea to put all one's credits in one bank." Now he turned his pitying gaze to Avar, and she knew he was referring to Starlight Beacon. She did not react. Nothing he said could hurt her more than the loss itself had. The fall of Starlight had been her responsibility. She knew she couldn't have done a better job than Stellan and Elzar of protecting it, but she still thought sometimes that if she'd listened to Stellan, if she hadn't run off chasing the Nihil Lourna Dee, maybe something would have been different.

What had happened, happened. She'd left Eiram because of it. But she'd come back. She was better than before, more attuned to herself and the Force. A man like Xylan Graf couldn't scratch that.

Xylan continued, "Of course *my* mistake from the beginning was thinking anything like profit or science could make a difference to Marchion Ro or his pirates. When I took my vacation from the Republic in the aftermath of the debacle with Chancey, they caught up with me and my Gravity's Light. They essentially kidnapped me, and soon enough I found that they'd done the same to Chancey, moving her laboratories to my station and forcing us to continue our development. Ro wanted the Heart's technology portable and flexible. Blah blah blah." Xylan waved his hand. "We created the stormseeds and the Stormwall itself. I was hardly a willing participant, especially once Chancey died. At that point I was barely keeping myself alive." Xylan took a drink and drained his cup.

"Anyway, the Nihil turned the Gravity's Light into the Lightning Crash and proceeded to run and power the Stormwall from there. Ro and Viess want an impenetrable wall, but that is impossible. They don't care about the objective reality of the situation. They only care that I'm *failing to provide*. Especially because you managed to find a way through, dear Jedi, and now you continue jumping back into the mess as easily as if it's a piece of agron cake!"

"Sorry we made your life harder, Xylan," Vernestra said without sympathy.

He turned a flirtatious smile toward her. "You shouldn't be, I suppose, since if you haven't already guessed, I was the one providing the Path codes in appropriate bundles to your smuggling partners in Nihil space. I may have been forced to work for the Nihil, but I've always been on your side, you see."

Marlowe San Tekka crossed his arms over his chest while his husband snorted. Avar sensed hostility from them, but not anything about to set them off.

Captain Ba'luun poured Xylan another drink. She said, "If your station is powering the Stormwall and you're on our side, why not self-destruct to bring it all down?"

"Because it's *mine*," he pouted. But then he shook his head. "And I did assist in an attempt to do so once—but there were fail-safes in place. Anyway, destroying the station wouldn't be good enough. The effectiveness of the wall is what needs to be destroyed, not simply its power source. Kill a grand master and the Jedi Order still works. Blow up the Lightning Crash and the wall would only be down temporarily while Ro returned control to its original location on the *Gaze* and found a new power source. Yes, it would be a blow to the Nihil, and of course *now* destroying it is part of the plan. But in the long run what we need to do is render the wall irrelevant. Which is why I have come to you now with information on how to do just that."

Avar studied him, listening to the Force. It nudged around Xylan Graf and told her he was not lying. He was very worried but not lying.

If Elzar were here, he'd be able to differentiate better. Elzar had always been good at parsing people. "What changed?" she asked.

"Yes, what?" Vellis demanded. "You wouldn't destroy your precious space station before. You stayed with them. Why surrender now? Did they finally see through your lies?"

"Something like that must have happened." Xylan shrugged. "I learned Viess was making a total purge of the Lightning Crash's personnel and decided to take my opportunity to leave. But I know there is a home key to the Stormwall, one equation that unlocks the rest. Destroying the Lightning Crash would temporarily ruin things, and breaking individual stormseeds might be an annoyance to the Nihil. But the home key? Find it and *that* would render the Stormwall's very makeup irrelevant forever."

A thrill sang brightly in Avar's heart. She felt it vibrating through the Force. She truly wished Elzar were beside her, listening to this.

"So you have it?" Vernestra asked skeptically.

Xylan flicked his gaze to her. "Obviously I do. Take me to Avon Sunvale on Coruscant. She's the only person capable of deciphering it and the only person I will tell."

The San Tekkas scoffed in unison, just like old married folks, and Captain Ba'luun frowned through all her beards.

Avar took a moment to calm the sudden spike of surprise and suspicion that had struck her at the name *Avon Sunvale*. She'd been mentioned in the brief on Vernestra's first mission across the Stormwall, and was the same Avon who had invented the device that let the Jedi slip across the Stormwall. The Force was telling Avar this young human mattered more than just as a tech genius. She would ask Vernestra what more the Jedi Knight knew, but first Avar asked lightly, "What do you want in return?"

Xylan Graf shrugged. "Only my complete pardon. Oh, and to encourage the Republic to free Naboo immediately upon penetrating the Stormwall."

"Naboo!" Vellis cried.

"My dog is there," Xylan said. His casual tone clearly hid a deep concern.

"You mean *your husband*," Marlowe said.

"Shall we shift the conversation to San Tekkas? Do you want to talk about Mari San Tekka?" Xylan asked silkily. "And exactly why she helped the Ro family for so long? I could write an entire dissertation on the theory that the Nihil could not exist without San Tekkas. It's been a few years since my last doctorate."

Both Marlowe and Vellis were silent.

"Someone married you?" Vernestra said incredulously.

Xylan's smile grew toothy. "I believe everyone here, with the possible exception of our good captain, has met my husband of more than two years: Cair San Tekka, rogue musician and freedom fighter."

"He was meant to spy on you, and you blackmailed him and used him against us!" Marlowe snapped.

"What can I say?" Xylan shrugged one shoulder. "I'm just that talented."

Avar leaned forward and flattened her hand on the table. "As interesting as your marital—"

"Bliss," Xylan interrupted.

"Situation," Avar said firmly, "might be to your families and gossip nets, let's get back on target. You're certain you and Avon can decipher the home key to the Stormwall quickly, and you only want a guaranteed pardon and for the Republic to consider kicking the Nihil off Naboo first?"

"Yes. To an unspecified definition of 'quickly.'"

"Quickly, as in fast," Avar said, holding Xylan's vivid-blue gaze.

He fluttered a hand in acknowledgment. "I'm sure the Force will be with us," he said airily.

"The Force is always with us, Xylan Graf," Avar said. "What matters is what we choose to do with it."

Chapter Seventeen

Burryaga stood at the crumbling edge of a massive sink-hole. The prairie grasses around them hissed in a sharp breeze, glinting silver-gold in the overcast sunlight. Jewel-toned grasshoppers buzzed around, leaping in a frenzy of life. But the scored ground at the Wookiee's feet was like a deep, dead wound.

He and Bell—and Ember—had arrived this morning on Ronaphaven, an agricultural planet in a midsized system only two jumps from Felne 6. After seeing the dead Drengir on Felne 6 burn to ashes, they'd returned to the *Tractate* to make their reports and dig into any other possible Drengir sightings in the nearby sectors.

Burry scoured all kinds of data and news holos, while Bell wrote up an official request to the Council for resources to look into the problem for at least a few days. With the Guardian Protocols in effect, putting the whole Order on alert, such permissions were necessary. But it wasn't like they'd been doing much good with the evacuation projects along the Stormwall border. Negotiation and diplomacy were a necessary part of a Jedi's work, but Burry knew Bell especially preferred more direct action.

Burry couldn't pretend it wasn't easier to stay on the move and face challenges head-on. Anything else left a lot of room to remember what he'd been through, and lost, in the past two years. That dark ocean cave.

They'd come to Ronaphaven following a canceled request for aid from one of the local governors after several kelivan root farmers had gone missing and a whole season's crop had been lost. The governor had mentioned Drengir, but the alert that would usually accompany such a keyword never went out because of the cancellation. There were no Drengir on Ronaphaven.

Burry and Bell decided to investigate because Drengir were so huge and specific, it was hard to imagine anybody mistaking them for anything else. But if they'd been on Ronaphaven only to die like the lonely Drengir on Felne 6, it was definitely something the Jedi Council and Republic needed to know about.

They hadn't exactly been welcomed by the local governor, who complained that Jedi would only draw Nihil attention to their world, and the only thing additional Republic oversight had done for Ronaphaven so far was to muck up their already delayed shipments with questions and bureaucracy. He swore the Republic wouldn't find any fault in their regulations and labor force, and that their high-quality roots could be processed not only into standard cord fibers but also into a version so strong that even the Corellians wanted them for securing cargo on their new cruisers . . .

Burry tuned out the governor's high-pitched words in favor of listening to the Force and its flow. It wasn't as if the governor could converse directly with Burry anyway. Let Bell charm him.

Bell had insisted on their investigation, promising not to get in anybody's way, which wouldn't be a problem if everything went as smoothly as the governor promised. So they were given a guide and a landspeeder just big enough to fit Burry, and then sent off.

Now Burry, Bell, Ember, and their guide stared at the sinkhole.

This was common in Drengir encounters: The monsters dug tunnels through the roots of a world, making their dens where they could wrap their fleshy victims up in thorns and vines and slowly drain them of life and the Force. Then they ate the carcasses.

Burry glanced at Bell, who shrugged.

The Wookiee pulled his lightsaber off the holster on his belt. Then he jumped into the pit.

From below, Burry vaguely heard Bell entreating Ember to wait on the surface until called, then Bell hit the rough floor of the sinkhole beside Burry.

This patch was lit by the sun filtering down through roots, but beyond the long, narrow sinkhole's boundaries, various tunnels pushed out into darkness.

Burry reached out with the Force.

It was quieter here than in most places, dampened by the remnants of the dark side. The life of the place had been sucked dry. What remained were shades, old whispers. Burry hardened himself to it.

"This is creepy," Bell murmured.

Burry trilled back agreement. He brought his lightsaber up, gripping it in both hands as he thumbed it on. The blue energy thrummed to life and lit the way as Burry strode forward down one of the tunnels.

The darkness was broken only by the glow of his and Bell's blades glinting off dangling roots. When his big shoulders brushed the walls of the tunnel, dirt crumbled, skittering at their feet.

They kept going, following the traces of the Drengir.

Burry breathed carefully, focused on his connection to the Force. It wasn't only for any warning of danger, but also for comfort. This planet had its own rhythm and temperature, like any ecosystem. A specific thickness. Burry could feel how the Force shifted in these tunnels. It wasn't active, more like an echo: an emptiness quickly filling back up with life, because there was no possibility of a true void in any atmosphere. This was a world touched by the Force and Light and Life, and where the Drengir had been, all would be reclaimed.

Bell kept quiet, too, as the pair of Jedi wandered the tunnels. Though neither had personally faced Drengir before, this seemed to both like a warren that would have suited several of the massive botanical beasts.

Occasionally they tripped over large bones. Burry wondered what kinds of Ronaphaven prairie grazers had been the Drengir's victims here.

Before long, they reached the end of the tunnel, and Bell and Burry climbed up through the crust of Ronaphaven into the sunlight again.

Bell whistled for Ember: The charhound's sparks could be seen in the distance against the pink horizon. They'd probably covered only a kilometer from the sinkhole, though the tangle of tunnels had made it seem longer.

"They're gone," Bell said.

Burry quietly said he hadn't read anything about Drengir leaving a place without eating everything. And there weren't any remains here, so it was unlikely the Drengir who'd made the tunnel had died like the one on Felne 6. In fairly simple terms, the two of them tossed back some ideas about how Drengir might leave—on a ship, perhaps, or by using their connection to the dark side to possess some person who might fly them off.

Several people here on Ronaphaven had gone missing. Maybe they hadn't been devoured by the Drengir but had been made to act as escorts and pilots.

"But why leave?" Bell said. "There's plenty to eat here."

Burry didn't know. Gradually, he became aware of how strange he felt. No, the Force felt strange.

Burry sank to his haunches and touched the ragged grass with a large hand. Closing his eyes, he reached as far and wide through the Force as he could. He felt Bell, the brightness of his partner, and the sprawling emptiness left behind by the Drengir. He felt sparks of life in bugs and the blanket of prairie grasses, the edge of the sparse forest, and Ember's fiery eagerness. Their guide followed more slowly. In the distance, Burry could sense the teeming life of the farming community, the spaceport, and then the rising layers of a large city with processing plants and neighborhoods.

In the other direction . . . Burry jerked his hand back.

"Burry?" Bell said, frowning.

Burry shook his head, listening with his ears and with the Force.

The sensation from the other direction was not unlike the loneliness of the dying Drengir. But it wasn't as acute.

Standing, Burry started toward it.

"Where are you going?" Bell hurried after him.

Burry didn't slow down, muttering to Bell about a strange feeling.

"Ah, maybe? It's all strange. You're better at emotions than me, though. I'm not surprised if it's subtle."

Burry nodded and picked up the pace. He made his way along the edge of the forest, ignoring the calls from their guide and Bell's pinging comlink.

What he found defied explanation.

It was a section of prairie where the grass met undergrowth and a few elegant tall trees clung to the bank of a small pond. Only everything was ashy and gray. The ground itself, as well as the grasses, had turned into a pale stone of some kind, and in places seemed to have broken off, blown to ashes by the wind. The gray crawled up the trunk of one of the elegant trees.

"What is this?" Bell asked, staring in horror. "It looks like . . . like . . ." He leaned down, expression tight with anxiety.

Burry grabbed his shoulder a little too hard.

"Burry?" Bell gripped his friend's wrist hard enough to bruise anybody who was not a Wookiee. "Do you know what this is? Did the Drengir do it?"

Burry shook his head. This looked like the Nameless, not the Drengir. Bell knew it, too—Burry felt the tremors of fear and anger twisting off his friend.

Bell squeezed his eyes shut and visibly calmed himself. When he looked back at Burry, the echoes of the loss of his master remained, but Bell had himself under control. He frowned. "Could the Drengir still be responsible, though? Maybe it's a natural reaction to Drengir on this world."

Burry shook his head and gazed out over the strange grayish landscape. He didn't think so. There was nothing natural about this. It was too . . . empty.

Chapter Eighteen

It was the middle of the night on Naboo, and Cair San Tekka dragged himself off the floor of his chambers in the inner family tower. He'd huddled there beside Plinka for hours, holding her as she slowly healed under the state-of-the-art bacta patches that had tangled with her thick fur. He wished he had a sonic razor, or anything else that could easily shave her. But after the Nihil had dumped her here with him, it had been all he could do to find the bacta and plain bandages.

His left side pinched sharply. He was sure at least one rib was broken. General Viess hadn't been able to resist a kick.

Once Plinka was stable, Cair gave himself half an hour to despair. It wasn't as cathartic as he might've hoped, given the aforementioned broken rib. It was hard to sob when every gasp caused a shooting pain. He couldn't even settle at the dulcimer, though playing through a few scales would have calmed both him and Plinka.

When he could, he stripped and washed himself down, then wrapped a bandage around his chest. Field medicine had taught him that binding a broken rib tightly didn't actually help anything, but feeling the weight of the bandage reminded him to be careful. Even without proper care, though, this kind of injury healed itself as long as he refrained from too much exertion.

And he would rest, as soon as he sent his *I've been compromised* signal out to his comrades. Of his contacts, Rismo on Seswenna or Rhil and Belin were the most likely to reach out soon, and if they did, they might be traced. Cair had to warn them all off, regardless of how badly he wanted to speak to them because they might know about Xylan. Viess had casually assured him that Xylan was dead, but Cair couldn't—wouldn't—believe it. Not without proof. And surely with someone like the general the lack of gruesome proof was reason enough to cling to hope.

Cair dressed in dark clothes still shiny with embroidery and wealth, thanks to his role here. He quietly broke a liquor flute into a jagged knife and wrapped the end with a torn bedsheet for a handle. He grabbed his backup comlink from the hidden compartment behind the decoy light panel and then started pounding on the door.

He kept it up until his fist would've hurt if it had been made of flesh and bone instead of black alloy. Every once in a while, he punched the lock alert.

Finally, the door slid open, and before the Nihil guard could get out more than a grunt, Cair jabbed the makeshift glass knife up under the man's mask into the soft tissue of his neck. Cair twisted to grab him around the collar so that he fell inside the room. Cair cut through his neck and then slipped out into the corridor, locking the door behind him.

Heart pounding, Cair jogged quietly down the darkened corridor toward the turbolift.

His organic hand trembled with adrenaline, and he swallowed back the immediate memory of the death gurgles the Nihil had made. It wasn't his first kill, but the few before now had been at the far end of a blaster. Cleaner. Easier to ignore. The dark blood of that Nihil was currently splattered across his chest.

Suddenly, he wondered if Xylan knew how to get different types of blood out of different types of fancy material. Probably. Or rather, he would know the right expert to do it for him.

Cair needed to stop and take a breath, but he didn't. He turned a corner and walked right into a person.

She squeaked, jerked away, but Cair hissed, "Ino'olo!"

The young woman's dark eyes widened, then she sagged into him. "Master San Tekka, we didn't know what happened. A few of the staff fled as soon as Viess showed up, but the rest of us are playing our parts as best we can. We were taking turns walking past your rooms, but—"

"I'm all right for now, but it's bad, Ino. You should all get out of here." Cair pulled her by the elbow against the wall, looking in both directions for any movement. The corridor was lit by dim glowlights implanted into the corners of the ceiling. They cast a gentle, swampy green-white light.

"I can get you food or an—"

"No." Cair looked straight into her eyes. "Get out. The patriarchs are free, and everything I've done is burnt. You need to stay away from me. I'm caught. Done."

"Cair." She shook her head. The finery of her staff jacket glittered. There were even slender quartzlight strings woven into her elaborate hair. Cair touched one. He'd never mastered the Naboo San Tekka style of extravagance during his time here. He'd been too deep in spycraft. Which was ironic, given he'd been spying on a man even more extravagant than any San Tekka he'd ever met.

"Ino'olo, go. Gather anyone you can and just go. The general isn't leaving. This place is a bad place to be. You can do more good in Theed." She frowned. Her cheeks seemed to pink as she grew upset. "Don't die."

Cair grinned. "I have to stay alive for Plinka."

But Ino'olo didn't smile back.

Before they could continue, a cry sounded from the direction of Cair's quarters.

"Let's go," he whispered, pulling her along. "Get out!" He shoved her ahead of him, and he darted to the side into a small lift arch.

"Always come home," Ino'olo said as the elevator doors snapped closed.

Always come home, Cair mouthed to himself. An old San Tekka prospecting saying. Cair liked it, except that he didn't know where home was. He'd never had a chance to truly make one.

As the lift shot up, he thought of his mean, flippant husband, hoping with his whole being that Xylan was still alive. Xylan, who'd blackmailed Cair into marriage as if it were only another chit in a balance book. Cair had been shadowing Xylan for weeks by that point, sure he knew the Graf well, less sure of his own feelings. Out of nowhere, Xylan had presented evidence of Cair's espionage and said it was time to cut ties and run, or to bind himself to Xylan more completely. Xylan wanted to hide assets in layers of marriage contracts so the Republic— and his grandmother—couldn't find them. He'd seduced Cair with epic promises and legalese that should have been dry but instead sounded thrilling. Spying, forbidden romance, ancient rivalries ended in wedded bliss—it had appealed to Cair's rebellious nature. Besides, he liked Xylan, and Xylan absolutely liked taking Cair to bed.

None of that should have been a solid foundation for a home.

Then again, nothing in Nihil-occupied space was conducive to building any kind of future. That was what the fight was all about.

And Cair was running out of time.

If he survived all this, there was a song he'd been working on before he had to deal with relearning to play with his prosthetic hand. A song for Xylan and for himself, too, for every messy thing they'd already done and the possibilities they could achieve together. It was the kind of composition that was never finished. If he survived this, he'd play it, even though it would completely expose him to his suspicious, terrible husband. Maybe that was close enough to a home: the opening notes of an ever-evolving song.

The lift hit the top floor, and Cair burst out, already on the run.

He skimmed around the hallway to the access point, disguised by a gratuitous floral faux-gold panel, punched it, and threw himself up. He grabbed the ladder and clenched his teeth against a cry of pain as his ribs protested sharply. Fine, it was fine, it was almost over. Cair climbed. He slid into one of the side tunnels that marred these domes for plasma venting and countless wires and threads for communication throughout the manor complex. There was one tight turn, then he burst out into the open rafters. A narrow beam led to the maintenance shaft for one of the antennas for long-range communications.

When at his leisure, the crawl wasn't quite so harrowing, but at a run, he felt like he could lose his balance at any second.

Cair made it. He popped the shaft and climbed up onto the smooth surface of the dome itself. Wind shoved at him, but he was cupped in a small alcove from which the antenna emerged. He quickly connected his backup comlink into the presliced wire port and activated the secure frequency with those silly codes. *What is Plinka's favorite treat? Roasted Elienise field carrots.*

"Belin, come in. Belin," he said. "This is Cair San Tekka." Cair paused. Breathed three deep breaths, then said again, "This is Cair San Tekka. Come in. Come *on.* I don't have time for all the codes."

The dark midnight sky of Naboo glowed from distant Theed, but stars still gleamed, and that one straggling moon glared at almost full. Cair could see the black line of the distant rain forest. Hear the hiss of wind through grass and leaves.

And the sudden roar of a ship's engine.

"Belin!" Cair yelled, as if volume could reach across space faster.

"—Cair? —at you?"

"Belin!" Cair leaned his forehead against the cold metal of the antenna. "Listen, I'm done. The general is here and she knows I'm involved in . . . a lot. Warn who you can, and see if you can reach my husband through the regular means."

"—Rhil is—"

"No time," Cair interrupted. The noise of the ship approaching almost drowned him out. A light appeared over the edge of the dome. "Burn my current missions—don't try to reach me! I planned for this—talk to Rismo on Seswenna, he has fail-safes."

"What are you going to do?" Belin's grumpy voice was clear suddenly through the crackle.

"Try to survive. And make sure Viess does not."

It was out of Cair's mouth before he even realized he'd made the choice.

Just then, a Nihil ship lifted into his sight, blocking the stars. Lights flared, and Cair flinched back. "May the Force be with you!" he yelled into the comlink.

"Better with you than—"

Belin cut out as Cair ripped the sliced wires away. Sparks landed on his cybernetic hand. Cair took the comlink in that prosthetic and crushed it into dust and shards of metal.

The Nihil ship hovered near him, and the engine pulsed as the boarding ramp lowered. Cair leaned away, exhausted and hurting, as General Viess herself stepped down the ramp. She held on to the hydraulics strut and said, "Cair San Tekka. I'm disappointed. Not surprised, but very, very disappointed."

"Glad to be of service," Cair said, too casually for her to hear.

"Get him," the general said. "This time, let's break him a little better."

Chapter Nineteen

CORUSCANT

Elzar was in a shop halfway across the Federal District of Republic City when his comlink pinged in the pattern designated for urgency that JJ-5145 had programmed into it and definitely overused.

So Elzar gave himself a moment to finish his conversation. "You've tested the resonance?"

Limal Pakt, the highly recommended and qualified metalsmith, fixed all four of her narrowed golden eyes on him. "As requested, it rings neutral so that the recipient will be able to select a focus if they so desire."

"Fantastic." Elzar smiled and touched the cool golden metal. The design was slightly thicker than the previous iteration, which suited the triplet of small star gems fitted into the central arcing arrowtip.

"Shall I wrap it for you?"

The comlink pinged again. "If you can quickly. I need to go." Elzar handed over the final payment and pulled his link from its clip on his belt. "Forfive, what is it?"

"Master Elzar, I was growing concerned you forgot the pattern established for emergencies—"

"What is the emergency, Forfive?" Elzar asked as the Dyplotid carefully wrapped the delicate crown in silk.

"You're required for a meeting with Chancellor Soh and some newly arrived Republic guests, which begins in three minutes."

Elzar grimaced and glanced out the tall windows at the gleaming cloudscrapers and flitting traffic. "I can't be there that quickly."

"I will inform the chancellor of your delay."

"Thanks." Elzar tucked the comlink away and thanked the metalsmith for her astonishing work.

"I hope it melds well with your Jedi Master's own metalwork," Limal Pakt murmured with a bow.

"It will. Master Flik-Lant will be able to finesse anything he needs, if it's necessary."

"Tell him I'd love to have a drink with him sometime to trade secrets." The Dyplotid raised two of her four brows, clearly teasing.

Elzar was sure he would not be telling Flik-Lant any such thing. The Jedi Master was particular about his specialty designing and molding the buckles of formal Jedi belts, elaborate pauldrons, bracers, and the fancier formal lightsaber holsters. Elzar ought to have gone to Flik-Lant for this design, because he'd done the original. But Stellan had been involved with the last one, and Elzar needed a clean break for this. Something else he would also not be telling Master Flik-Lant.

Tucking the package under his arm, Elzar made his way outside. The long ledge of the building's curved walkway was crowded with beings of all kinds who entirely ignored the Jedi pushing through them.

Elzar knew he should have flown one of the Jedi Temple speeders here instead of walking. But he'd thought he'd have a rare few hours free, and a walk always did him better than holing up in his office or one of the meditation chambers in the Temple. Now, though, he'd have to flag down an air taxi or hoof it. Elzar started speed-walking, keeping his eye out for pausing public transport.

It was an elaborate journey of spiraling stairs and mystifyingly thin bridges, past two mirroring pleasure gardens, a hundred-story mall, food stalls, and plasma stations, before Elzar finally reached the broad avenue leading up to the Senate building. He was sweating despite the planetary climate regulation.

The entire time the people of Coruscant behaved with utter normalcy. As if nothing were different now from two years ago.

If one didn't know any better, here on Coruscant one might think the Nihil didn't exist. That there was no massive gravitational distortion cutting off a shard of the galaxy. That Starlight Beacon hadn't fallen—it had never existed in the first place.

Elzar knew the Republic was vast. The galaxy was huge. But it rankled that so many people here in the capital itself could ignore what was happening out there. They were privileged enough and oblivious enough that the Nihil barely mattered. Refugees barely mattered. Elzar wondered what they thought of the broadcast death of Grandmaster Veter. He wondered if half the people he passed had even watched it.

The resentment tightened his chest, and Elzar caught himself. He fought the darkening of his thoughts.

Stellan would say the people who needed the Jedi the most were the ones who didn't realize it.

Avar would say what mattered was Elzar's relationship to the Force, and who Elzar wanted to be, not what these citizens understood.

Master Yoda might say, *These people's problem, it is not; yours, it is, Elzar Mann.*

Elzar didn't know what wisdom he'd give to a younger Jedi, someone who came to him with their own frustration. Maybe that it was best to choose how to look at the issue. Was it disregard that led these people to behave as if there were no threat? Or did they trust the Jedi enough to live their lives openly, easily, freely?

Maybe the point was that the Jedi—especially Elzar—needed to act to earn that trust every day.

JJ-5145 waited for Elzar at the end of the long entryway to the Senate building. The droid offered Elzar a rehydration packet with one arm and a change of robes with the other. JJ-5145 always remembered

Elzar struggled to make time to care for himself. Elzar downed the packet and stripped out of his plainer brown cape and outer robe in return for the pristine white-and-gold formal Jedi robes.

They hurried to the bank of lifts, and JJ-5145 keyed in the right floor. Elzar touched the silk pouch with the new diadem that hung from his belt, and then his lightsaber.

When he emerged onto the high level with all its bright sunlight and elegant arched passageways, he nearly ran over a young woman heading in the same direction.

"Pardon me," he said, catching her elbow. "Oh."

It was Avon Starros—known here as Avon Sunvale to obscure her association with her mother, Ghirra. She was a young human girl with dark-brown skin and black hair braided close to her skull with a puffed tail. She also had a really bad attitude. Elzar liked her. He liked who her mother was a lot less. But Avon had been working hard on behalf of the Republic for weeks down in the RDC labs with the other scientists and Jedi attempting to crack the Stormwall. Her advantage over the rest was that she'd had the opportunity to study live Path engines as they actively crossed the wall, having been ensconced with the Nihil thanks to her mother's questionable loyalty. Plus, Elzar understood she'd spoken directly with one of the people actually running the Stormwall.

With her was Keven Tarr, hyperspace technician and also a member of the Stormwall science team. Elzar nodded to Keven, trying to swallow back another apology. He'd harassed Keven for weeks leading up to their failed attempt to breach the wall.

"Are you going to this same meeting?" Avon asked, moving her legs faster to keep pace with Elzar.

"With Chancellor Soh?"

"Yeah. Do you know what it's about?" Avon scowled. "I'm busy."

"I don't. I assume, since you're here, it's about the Stormwall. But if it makes you feel better, I was dragged away from my business, too."

Avon shrugged. "Sure, I guess."

"They must have new information," Keven said eagerly.

Elzar tamped down a spike of dread. When was the last time he'd been given good news at a surprise meeting? He hurried on with the others, JJ-5145 trailing behind as its rollers worked as hard as they could.

A Republic Senate Guard stood outside the chancellor's office suite, but she knew Elzar and immediately pressed the access panel.

Elzar swept inside, cape snapping.

Beyond the greeting room, the chancellor's study doors were thrown open. Elzar could hear someone speaking urgently, something about a finite number of Paths, and he entered quietly, hoping to slip in and around the crowd unnoticed.

Then he saw Avar and grinned. Her gaze flicked to him, and she smiled back in a flash before returning her attention to the meeting. But Elzar sensed her excitement even through the tension in the room.

It *was* good news.

Elzar focused.

White light spilled through the skylights and windows, giving the impression of clear air, and Chancellor Soh sat at her pale wood desk with her twin targons lounging dangerously to either side.

Senator Toon was there leaning against one of the bookshelves, and Senator Izzet Noor who aided Toon in most of the defense coordination. There were a few aides Elzar didn't recognize, as well as the chancellor's primary aide, Norel Quo, and Vice Chancellor Larep Reza. Beside Avar was Jedi Knight Vernestra Rwoh, Stellan's former Padawan.

Avon Starros lit up at seeing Vernestra. Elzar didn't feel as glad, given their history. None of which was Vernestra's fault.

In the center of the room was a brown-skinned human in vivid-teal costume, speaking urgently. ". . . that's why we assumed it had to be a Path. They used to be dynamic, living routes while Mari was alive. She could create one almost instantly, but they needed to be retired almost as fast because of the complicated interacting dynamics of, well, absolutely everything in the galaxy. Those that remain, that we use for the

Stormwall codes, are not so much active, useful Paths for hopping around as extremely intensive strings of data."

"Because now a planet could move in its orbit and that Path would no longer be viable," Senator Toon said.

Before the newcomer in teal could answer, Keven Tarr said, "That's right, just as with all hyperspace routes the calculations need to be updated constantly. Which is why we have buoys."

"Mari's mind was essentially acting like all the hyperspace beacons across the galaxy at once," the human in teal said, turning to fix Keven with a narrow look, but his gaze touched Avon instead. He called out, "Avon, finally!"

And the young woman's smile transformed into a scowl. "Xylan Graf." Avon's tone dripped with dislike.

The Graf man responded, but Elzar didn't hear. In the past year he'd done his digging on Chancey Yarrow, the woman who'd invented the technology behind the Stormwall, and the name *Xylan Graf* was recorded in the same files. Graf had bankrolled Yarrow's work, been charged with sedition and stripped of his resources, then vanished.

It was all coming together.

Elzar felt the links forging themselves in his understanding. Links the Force had created or reinforced. He looked at Avar, and she already was looking back.

Chancellor Soh stood up. "Stop. Avon Sunvale, this Nihil collaborator has claimed that he has information you can use to end the oppression of the Nihil's Stormwall. Do you believe him?"

Under Soh's impressive countenance, the said Graf put his hands on his hips but kept silent. Avon said, "I don't trust him."

Xylan Graf spun to her, hurt painted too plainly over his face.

"But"—Avon glared at Xylan briefly before looking more earnestly at the chancellor—"he doesn't gamble if he doesn't think he can win, so we should hear him out."

Vernestra added, "He is the one providing us with the Path code bundles in order to spoof the codes and travel into the Occlusion Zone."

Xylan Graf smiled at her as if she'd hung the third arm of the galaxy. Vernestra ignored him.

"Very well." Chancellor Soh inclined her head. "Proceed."

Elzar watched as Graf eyed the chancellor, who was for all her power a small-statured human woman. She did have her giant cat bodyguards, though. Graf took in the whole room and obviously drew a shroud of performativity around himself. He said, "Avon here theorized that there needed to be a master key, so to speak, a primary data set from which Mari San Tekka unspooled all of her mathematics. Avon also believed it would be a specific Path, but there is no way to simply guess. So in addition to risking my life by essentially stealing the Path data for you, I've spent the past weeks looking into Mari San Tekka herself. I wanted to know who she was, why she did what she did. What she wanted. And there are so very many rumors about her among the Nihil."

"Did you find out anything useful?" Avon asked.

Xylan Graf grinned at her. "You already know it, Avon. That's the ridiculous, amazing piece."

Avon huffed impressively for a fifteen-year-old. "If I knew it, we'd have breached the wall. I've been running all sorts of scenarios, spinning through codes as fast as the computers can handle it. It's all guesswork."

"Just tell us," Senator Toon drawled. "Stop drawing it out for your own benefit."

Xylan didn't even glance Toon's way. Instead, he kept his attention on Avon. "Avon, you think with your brain, and that is how you'd create a key. I think with my wallet, and therefore would base a key on profit. Jedi think with, oh, justice, I assume. And San Tekkas, well, they've been the same for generations, ever since the first time they ruined some quick scheme of my family. Do you know what San Tekkas think with?"

Avon's whole body lit up, and she said, at the same time as Xylan Graf, "Their hearts!"

Avon immediately scowled, as if offended on her own behalf for agreeing with him.

"What does this have to do with the Stormwall?" Senator Toon demanded. Elzar was glad Toon was here to voice his own concerns. He glanced again at Avar, who nodded slightly at him. This was not a moment for the Jedi to take over. They could be allies here instead of leaders. That was fine. When it was time for action, they'd be ready.

"Her homeworld," Avon whispered.

Xylan Graf clapped.

"Can we bring it down or not?" Chancellor Soh demanded.

Avon Sunvale put her hands on her head, eyes flashing as if she was looking past all of them.

Graf answered for her, watching Avon with an amused expression. Elzar was glad, he supposed, that somebody could find humor here. "No, Chancellor, but if I'm right, you'll be able to get through. Straight through, as if there are no impulses or occlusions, no Stormwall at all. And I can direct you to the Lightning Crash, no matter where they've moved it, thanks to some proprietary Graf tech. Once you destroy that, you'll sabotage Ro's ability to maintain the wall."

That sounded almost too good to be true.

But the young girl turned to the chancellor. She leaned her fists against the desk. "I'll know in a few hours if he's right. You, Chancellor, and you, Jedi, get ready! We're going to do this!"

With that, Avon dashed out of the meeting.

Definitely too good to be true, Elzar thought grimly. He was going to need to work on his hope.

Chapter Twenty

CORUSCANT

Avar studied Elzar as the chancellor's meeting broke up in the wake of the young Sunvale's departure. Keven Tarr dashed after her, calling out something about reverse-engineering the Path mathematics with the right location. Xylan Graf thanked Senator Toon and the chancellor. Vernestra bowed and left, no doubt eager to remove herself from the formalities. The chancellor remanded Xylan into Republic custody until his solution could be proved and he'd properly earned his pardon. Xylan immediately complained.

Elzar started to join the argument between Soh and Xylan, but instead he caught Avar's eye and hurried to her side.

Avar held out her hand and he took it, squeezing. She said, "Hi."

"Avar," he answered. "You must be ready to rest, to . . . I need to stay, there's . . ." Elzar waved back at the heated discussion. He represented the Council and had to participate. "But will you have dinner with me later tonight?"

"Of course," she promised. "Go do your job."

He slid her a half-cocked smile and released her hand.

Avar caught the chancellor's eye to nod before she left. These days she was just a Jedi Master working for Light and Life. Listening to the Force and going where the Council sent her. A cog in the machine. She'd settled into such a role. She liked it.

Maybe that was part of the problem, she thought wryly. Avar walked with purpose but not urgency as she made her way out of the Republic executive building and headed for the Temple. Avar Kriss hadn't been built or nurtured to be a cog in a machine. She'd been made to lead. People—Jedi—had been telling her that for her whole life.

Look where that got her.

In the executive building, even in her mission attire, she found it easier to maneuver incognito. Even if aides or secretaries or reporters or senators themselves recognized her, they were used to fame, to the people who wielded power and effected change in the Republic. It wasn't like in Nihil space, where recognition sparked desperate hope or immediate capture.

But once she approached the Jedi Temple, the flow of the Force shifted. Attention fell upon her and stuck. Avar wished she had a deep cowl to pull over her face, then immediately admonished herself.

This was a pressure she could—and would—bear. The pressure of expectation, of hope, of having a name that rang across the galaxy. A name that united. It was what the Force had given her, and a tool she'd wielded for the light more than once.

You're our shining light, Estala Maru had said to her right before he died. Once she'd believed it. She'd been a beacon, no matter how undeserved, no matter how flawed.

Then Starlight Beacon crashed and burned. Avar had fled.

But she'd returned. She would keep reminding herself that she had fought her way back.

In the Temple, Avar focused on letting the weight of gazes and knowledge settle around her instead of a golden cloak, and refused to allow them to change her. Her choices would remain her own. They had to.

That was what the Force needed from her.

Focus.

If the Force was a song, Avar would be its tuning fork.

Nodding to a Temple Guard, Avar changed course and hurried to the archives to write up an addendum to the report she'd filed the moment the *Axiom* popped out of hyperspace into the Coruscant system. This one would include a note about the meeting and the promise of Avon Sunvale that in a few hours they'd be able to begin preparing a fleet to penetrate the Stormwall and attack its power source.

Avar went to the communal restroom to wash and change into one of the standard temple uniforms kept in the extensive wardrobes there. She sent a message to Elzar that she'd be meditating in one of the more secluded garden balconies reserved for Jedi Masters, and wasn't it good he was finally a master, too, and could join her.

He replied with a warm laugh.

It was nice that he was able to react without the tight defensiveness of last year and the years directly before it. Elzar didn't believe it, but Avar knew his work on Coruscant had been good for him. Now he needed to get out into the galaxy and let the Force guide him. The pieces of himself he'd allowed to narrow were ready to expand again. She wanted to be there when it happened. She wanted to wedge them open herself.

Avar picked her favorite meditation garden, a rather small crescent balcony off one of the higher levels of the Temple. It was a cool white-and-gray rock garden with three curling trees that bloomed with tiny violet flowers all year. A patch of dark-green carpet moss in the center was the perfect seat, and Avar settled down, falling quickly into meditation.

Coruscant was just as alive with the living Force as any populous planet. Though most of the native flora and fauna had been corralled and covered and changed, the life that replaced them thrummed. Countless beings with their own connection to the Force moved around her. Pockets of peace, lines of traffic, urgency and passion and the constant noise of engines and the hum of power generators. Avar could see the stars, and two of the moons following the sunset with thin crescent smiles.

Avar fell into the melody of the Force, into the ebb and flow. She listened, letting her questions flow out of her wordlessly, hoping they'd catch in the greater song and whisper something back to her. But just asking them was enough. It put her in active connection to the power of the light. She hardly noticed as her body lifted gently off the mossy cushion. She hovered, at one with the song of the Force.

Deep in her meditation, she felt the gentle touch of Elzar's presence as he sat beside her. He was a churning tide, a drum, a pulsing beat against her singing, and Avar sensed he couldn't quite fit the rhythm of his heart with hers. She slowed her thriving connection, reached with a hand that felt disembodied, and placed it on his knee. She did not even jolt a little as she touched down against the moss again.

She wanted him to know that a quiet, slow ebbing-and-flowing growth built just as strong a foundational root as her brighter, ecstatic growing. Slow like the sea turning the cliffs inexorably into a glimmering white beach, and sand falling into the reefs, catching in shellfish, and even more slowly turning to pearls.

Elzar squeezed her hand.

When Avar opened her eyes, he was looking up at the first wink of the third moon in the apex of the sky. Hours had passed since she began. Light from the cityscape glinted in Elzar's warm eyes. She could see the new lines of stress between his brows, drawing out from the corners of those eyes, but they were hidden around his mouth by the soft-looking beard. He was so handsome, Avar thought in an echo of her teenage self.

For a moment, she felt Stellan behind them, crouched with an arm around both their shoulders.

"Hi," she said again.

Elzar turned to look at her with a slow smile. "I'm so glad you came back."

Watching his smile, Avar wondered what she'd been so afraid of before. Giving in? She'd spent months adrift and alone. Without connections like this. Now she didn't want to tamp down her feelings; if anything, that was what had pushed her to run, to grow frustrated, to forget herself. She'd angled hard against fury and despair when fighting the Drengir and Nihil, giving no quarter to herself or others. That had been a mistake. Mercy was part of justice, was part of the light. Jedi needed to be merciful with themselves before they could understand mercy. Just with themselves before they could know justice. Give to and of themselves.

Avar felt light as she knocked her shoulder into Elzar's. "I did, and I came back hungry, so you should feed me."

"I'm sorry it took so long to get here. I was with the Council after I finished discussing things with Senator Toon and Admiral Kronara. The Council agree for once," Elzar said wryly. "If this is a real way to slip through the Stormwall and take out the Lightning Crash, we're all in."

"If?"

Elzar put his hand over hers on his knee. "It's hard to be hopeful," he admitted. "Hard to be eager again, ready again, when every other time for more than a year it's gone wrong. Longer than that, even, ever since Hetzal it seems like. Sometimes."

Things even went wrong between us, he seemed to think. Avar could almost hear it. Turning her hand over, she wound their fingers together. "We have to try, El."

Try again, she thought at him.

"I know. Practice."

"I think it will work this time," Avar said. "Neutralizing the Stormwall. It will work this time."

"Why?"

They stared down at their hands, not each other.

"Hope. Light. Life."

"Before . . ." Elzar took a deep breath and continued. "Before I was on Starlight with Stellan, I was working with this Wayseeker, Orla Jareni—"

"I met her," Avar said.

Elzar nodded. "She was helping me think about why I was pulled to the dark side, how to shift my relationship to the Force so that I could reconcile my emotions. But she died on Starlight."

Avar pressed her shoulder into his. "I was close to Estala. We worked together for months. I trusted him. I was with him when he—" She stopped, recalling the pain of being shoved into an escape pod, torn away from him. She should have stayed, should have been the one doing the shoving. Not have abandoned Starlight again.

"I'm glad you—" Elzar cut himself off. His eyes widened.

I'm glad you're the one who lived, he'd been about to say. Avar knew it. Felt it. She was breathless with it. She thought about Stellan Gios, their Stellan, and knew that he would be glad Elzar survived. Avar was glad, too. But it didn't diminish her grief for Stellan. They were just people. Jedi, bastions of hope and justice. But in the end, only people.

Elzar murmured, "I'm sorry. I shouldn't . . ."

"There's nothing you shouldn't say to me," Avar said just as softly.

Elzar squeezed their fingers together. "I have something for you." Still without looking at her, Elzar reached under the shadow of his cloak. He pulled out a silken bag and offered it.

Avar accepted with both hands. It wasn't heavy, but the object inside was an obvious shape. She swallowed back building emotions. Stellan and Elzar had given Avar her first diadem when she was Knighted. Elzar had handed it over shyly, but with a passion she hadn't recognized at the time. Stellan had laughed warmly at both of them, shaking his head like they were ridiculous. Perhaps they had been.

With hands that absolutely did not tremble, Avar untied the cord and removed the gold diadem.

"Elzar," she breathed, holding it carefully in her fingers. It was simpler and slightly thicker than the one she'd lost. A basic crown that arced down into a point that would settle against the center of her forehead, it was a soft rose gold, almost warm to the touch, and where her original had a single bright-blue gem, this one had three. The clear, shining blue quell stones were cut into four-pointed stars that caught the light and refracted into many purples and pinks and blues. "Three of them."

"It seemed right," he said so quietly she felt the words more than heard them.

Avar cradled the diadem in her lap. Tears prickled at her eyes, and she let one fall before blinking them back. "Do you remember why he was on Starlight?" she whispered.

"Jedi Council business."

She couldn't bring herself to look up at him. "I know I told you he was there to replace me."

Elzar sucked air through his teeth. "Avar . . ."

"It was the last thing he ever said to me. That I abandoned Starlight. And I did. I wasn't fit to be marshal. I thought I was doing it for the right reasons, and maybe they were. Maybe. But if I'd been better, Stellan would have been here." Avar looked up at Elzar, letting the ferocity of her feelings show. "He'd have been safe on Coruscant."

Elzar stared at her, and Avar couldn't tell if he was gutted or just trying his hardest to hear her.

She said, "It made it difficult to act at all. When you told me about what you'd done, it was easier not to react. To walk away. To run away. Leave you, hope you'd be safe. I didn't want others to be hurt or die because of my choices. And that's how I ended up trapped in the Occlusion Zone for a whole year." Avar laughed helplessly. "I thought I was alone, just because I didn't have anyone around me. But I found people. The Force didn't leave me alone. I struggled to listen every day. To hear the song of the Force and be that light, that clarion note, everyone expected me to be. I had to practice, like you said."

"And it worked."

"It *worked*." Avar laughed again, less helpless, more disbelieving. Sitting with Elzar here in this meditation garden at the Jedi Temple made her feel so young, despite it being reserved for masters, despite them being decades beyond their Padawan years. She gripped the bands of the diadem. "I'm practicing hope, Elzar. That's why I believe it will work. It's going to work. We're going to rescue those people in Nihil space like I promised. 'We're coming,' I said. And we are."

"All right," he said.

"And you're going with me."

Elzar grimaced. "I can't."

"You can, Elzar Mann."

"This is where I belong now."

"Is that what the Force is telling you?"

Elzar looked out over Coruscant again. "The Council offered me a seat among them."

Avar caught her breath, different reactions freezing her: elation and rejection primarily. Her lips parted but words didn't escape. Elzar glanced at her.

"I was surprised, too," he said.

All she could do for a moment was nod. Elzar in the formal Council robes; Elzar sitting in that circle . . . it felt wrong to her. But how could she say such a thing when he clearly struggled to trust himself, to find himself in the Force lately.

"I know you could do it," she said quietly instead. "You would be good. A strong voice. Keeping them from stagnating too much."

"But?"

"But do you . . . think the Jedi Council is your destiny?"

Elzar's eyebrows shot up. "It's been a long time since you talked about destiny, Avar."

She glanced down at the diadem in her hands. "It's been a long time since I thought maybe I haven't actually found mine yet."

Elzar didn't look away when she lifted her gaze back to his. She peered into his eyes, because when they were young, she'd assumed their destiny with the Force would be the same. Or at least run parallel. They'd be together in it, forever. She was starting to believe that again. The pull to him, the need for him—it couldn't be wrong. It didn't feel wrong.

Tell him, tell him, tell him, that voice whispered. She would. Soon. She could feel how close he was—how close they both were—to revelation. It was a heady feeling, knowing the edge approached. Knowing when the time came, they could tip right over. In trust.

"You'll make the right decision," she told him instead.

"I hope so. I'm just . . . unsure right now."

Afraid, Avar heard. Fear was such a rallying cry these days, with the Nameless wreaking their havoc.

Avar reached out and pressed her hand to his chest. "You called Stellan our polestar. But, Elzar, he'd agree with me you're the central gem here." She glanced at the three crystal stars set into her new diadem. "The heart."

Elzar scoffed. He actually scoffed at her!

Avar smiled. "Stellan was the brains, I'm obviously the brawn, so you have to accept the heart position."

His mouth tilted up in a tentative smile.

"Listen," she said. "Do you know what has always struck me about your experience of the Force as a great galactic ocean?"

". . . what?" His tone was suspicious, clearly expecting a trap.

"An ocean has a tide. A rhythm." Avar tapped her hand against his chest. "A heartbeat."

"Only if the planet has a moon or some kind of gravitational effect," he said mulishly.

"I'm trying to make a point here with a really good metaphor," she said with a glare.

"Apologies, oh Hero of Hetzal," he said, hands up in surrender.

Avar paused. "I barely remember the point now."

Elzar laughed. "You're delirious with hunger. I should feed you."

"You should do that. But wait." She tugged at his sleeve to keep him in place. "First. A rhythm—a tide—is part of a song. And there's a pattern to the movements of the stars. It's predictable, grand, like music. This rhythm—a heartbeat. You call the Force an ocean, I call it a song, Stellan called it a galaxy. But it's all the Force. We're describing the same thing. Just because mine is the best metaphor doesn't mean yours isn't effective."

"The best!" Elzar practically shoved her away.

"Not all worlds have oceans—have you been to Tatooine? You can't even sweat there! And stars burn out. They fall from the sky. But music . . . ?" Avar raised her brows, letting anticipation build. "Even the Nihil play a song."

Elzar choked on her name. "Did you just . . . ?"

Avar grinned. "I told you, it's the best one. It fits everything."

Shaking his head, he smiled at her. "I—"

Love you, he didn't finish.

Avar knew. She felt like she was being slingshotted toward something inevitable. "So listen to me. Go out into Stellan's galaxy with me. Fight with me. Unless you're completely certain the Force wants you here."

"Stellan—"

Avar put her fingers over his lips. He fell quiet.

Then Avar took up the diadem. She tilted her head contemplatively, slowly bringing it up until she placed it over Elzar's head to settle on his brow. He wrinkled that same brow, rolling his eyes up as if he could see it.

"There," she said. "A little bit of me. And this"—Avar tugged gently at his soft beard—"is a little bit of Stellan. So where is my Elzar?"

Elzar huffed. He didn't meet her gaze anymore.

Avar cupped his face so that her thumbs rubbed gently under his eyes. She soothed the skin there, stroking until Elzar finally looked up. "There he is," she whispered.

"Avar."

"We can do this," she said with all the conviction of daily practice.

Slowly, Elzar's mouth firmed into a line. He nodded. "We can do this."

Suddenly a harsh series of beeps sounded. They both startled apart.

"It's Forfive," Elzar groused, grabbing his comlink. Avar smiled because the diadem remained perched awkwardly on his head.

"Master Elzar! We've been summoned again, because young mistress Avon Sunvale was successful in her simulations! One hundred percent so! It's time to plan our assault!"

"Thanks," Elzar said. "We'll be there." He cut off the comm before the droid could continue.

"So much for food," Avar joked.

"So much for sleep," Elzar shot back.

They stood up, holding hands, and left the meditation garden in darkness and starlight.

Chapter Twenty-One

HOSNIAN PRIME

In a luxurious security suite in the lower dome of a personal cruiser currently in low orbit around Hosnian Prime, Ghirra Starros sat in the seat of her own making and tried not to fume.

"What do you mean you don't know where he is?" she demanded of the human Nihil Nan.

Nan grimaced, her youth and blue hair washed out from the patchy holo. "He took a shuttle from the *Gaze* with two of the Force Eaters and just jumped away. He said he'd be back."

"Without any of his She'ar?" Ghirra asked, doing her best to mask how appalled she was. Marchion Ro was many things, including reckless, but this was the first time since she'd joined him that he'd simply wandered off.

Nan shrugged. "He doesn't think they're worth as much as he lets on, especially since Arathab was murdered."

"In an assassination attempt," Ghirra ground out. Heavens, it would solve a lot of her problems if Marchion managed to get himself killed, but she'd rather see it coming. She was as prepared as she could be for such an eventuality—an inevitability, even—but without being able to more closely monitor and predict the situation, she'd be left grasping at dust. "Did he hear about the Lightning Crash?"

"Thaya relayed to him the whole report from the general," Nan said, her lips twisting. "That the techs and crew had been overturned—what a way to put it—and that Dr. Mkampa was still alive but in holding, currently arguing her case. He knows we lost that Graf. But I'm not sure he gave a tiniest rancor polyp about it."

Ghirra leaned back in her perfectly curved chair. "Do we know how Graf managed to evade Viess?"

"He must have been tipped off or had some very precisely timed good luck, which he somehow always manages. He took a ship through the Stormwall, and it's apparently in Republic hands, though some of the Nihil aboard scuttled the Path engine when they realized Graf was turning them in."

"As expected. I imagine the Republic will have whatever data he brought with him soon." Ghirra hummed, wondering how long it would take Xylan Graf to ingratiate himself with the Republic once again. And how soon he'd reach out to Avon.

"He'll go into hiding if he knows what's good for him," Nan said with a little snarl.

Ghirra reached for her datapad to make a note to check in with her contact in the Senate and perhaps her spy in the RDC as well. Perhaps there were rumblings already on Coruscant about Graf's presence. She suspected Graf would head for the chancellor directly with his knowledge of proprietary Stormwall technology, if he could. Negotiate for his own stake in the situation instead of relying upon his family. He had more leverage with the Republic than ever before. And hopefully he needed Avon to help him. Ghirra was counting on it.

"Who is running the Lightning Crash now?" she asked.

"A She'ar who was none too happy about it until she realized she could use the extremely fancy quarters Graf abandoned. Along with all his wine and cheese."

"Very well. Keep me informed and try to find where Ro's gone. Get me everything you can about where he's been in the past weeks."

Nan narrowed her eyes. "I want to bring it to you personally."

Ghirra spread her smile wide and dangerous. "Hoping to enjoy some Hosnian pampering?"

"You know what I want." Nan cut off the communication.

The petulance made Ghirra laugh lightly. She did know what Nan wanted: To survive. To be on the winning side. Ghirra didn't trust the little rat, but she did allow herself a small bit of pride at the knowledge that of everyone Nan had considered allying with in order to win, she'd chosen Ghirra. Of course, Ro and Boolan weren't real options. But Viess was almost as likely as Ghirra to slither out of this situation with her body and riches intact. Unless she allowed herself to continue running her military with her *feelings*.

Though there'd been Nihil-wide resistance to Ghirra's ministries and procedures in the beginning, in the months since she had begun making inroads with the Republic Senate, more and more Nihil had found ways to indicate to her they were interested. She had names and faces from all over the organization who would do a favor for her here or there in return for only a place in Ghirra's eventual success. Nan stood out only for being among the first—and for her nearness to Ro. Most of the time at least.

With a reluctant sigh Ghirra input her personal Stormwall comm codes again, activating a relay that would find the general.

Then she stood and stretched. She ran her hands along the beaded ends of her braids, pinched at her cheeks, and went to the sideboard for a glass of pale-pink moonberry juice. It was rejuvenating and filled with essential vitamins. And quite good with a nip of Hosnian pan-root gin. Perhaps Ghirra would indulge later.

Or send Xylan Graf a bottle, care of Chancellor Soh.

The luxury security suite was Ghirra's private sanctuary on her personal cruiser, which flew smoothly through the upper atmosphere of Hosnian Prime. She brushed her fingers against the control pad, and the dimming effect on the transparisteel bottom of the dome flashed away.

Ghirra was left with the impression of cool glass under her slippers, and all of Hosnian Prime spread beneath her feet as if she walked on air.

The thin blue clouds snaked over rich green forested hills. A river glinted like a ribbon of silver silkensteen. It rushed beneath her, colors spreading into the vivid blues and violets of the Vorashian Sea.

Ghirra wanted her daughter back, but she could admit to herself that perhaps their lack of connection now was further protection for Avon in the worst-case scenario of either the Republic gaining an upper hand and choosing to punish Ghirra for her Nihil collusion, or Marchion Ro giving in to a whim to kill her.

But that didn't stop Ghirra from needing to know where her child was and how she was doing. Avon's ability and willingness to hide from her mother—one of the most powerful humans in the galaxy—both aggravated Ghirra and filled her with pride.

The robotic voice of the dome's security system said, "Ghirra Starros, incoming signal from General Viess on Naboo."

Pulling herself together, Ghirra strode to her station and touched the ACCEPT button. She painted a smile on her face at the holo request.

General Viess's blue-washed face shimmered into existence in front of Ghirra. "Starros," she drawled, clearly in a good mood.

"I'd be slightly more concerned about the potential breach in the Stormwall we're facing than not at all," Ghirra chided.

"Ah, the Stormwall, what a nuisance," Viess said. "Keeps real battles from taking place, keeps people in hiding. Give me a full-frontal assault any day."

Ghirra paused, holding back on snapping commentary. Let her silence do her talking. Her silence and a slowly raised eyebrow.

The general's smile softened, somehow becoming more dangerous. "I see you're concerned."

"Merely interested in preparedness."

"And Ro?"

"Out and about."

This wiped Viess's smile away. "Again."

"Again," Ghirra repeated as lightly as a wisp of blown sugar.

Viess's jaw worked. She turned from the holo briefly, gesturing at something. Then she glanced back at Ghirra. "I have one of the organizers of the Jedi smuggling ring in custody. You were right, Ghirra—Xylan Graf was providing codes to them. Scav codes, coordinates for meets, and bundles of the Path data used to encrypt the Stormwall."

"You're on Naboo?" Ghirra tapped directions into her display to bring up a map of that sector near the Stormwall.

"Along with Graf's snow dog. Plinka. Did you ever meet her? It turns out he sent her away from the Lightning Crash some few weeks ago to live with his paramour here on Naboo."

"I'm deeply uninterested in such details," Ghirra lied. "But you should be preparing yourself for that assault you desire, if the Republic has Graf."

"You think he'll want his dog back?" Viess wondered with false concern. Then she laughed sharply. "I should kill it, save him the trouble of a rescue."

Ghirra tilted her head in a shrug. "Whatever you like, except don't lose Naboo. We need to maintain control over what we currently have under occupation. Look strong and undefeatable. And warn your so-called fleet to be prepared to defend the Lightning Crash."

"You think Xylan Graf can make that much of a difference? He's not that clever, and he strikes me as a runner more than a fighter."

"I think he'll have a vested interest in the fall of the Lightning Crash as well as winning a place on Coruscant."

"Either way, their response won't be immediate. We moved the station, and the Stormwall isn't suddenly more vulnerable than before. Why would they be able to bring in more firepower than recently? If Graf knew a greater weakness, he'd have handed it over to his lover already. He's just one of the top rats, Ghirra."

"You're the strategist," Ghirra said lightly. She couldn't blame Viess for underestimating Graf—she was a mercenary, and Graf, like Ghirra, was a politician. But Ghirra wouldn't make the mistake of doing the same to her own daughter. Or to the determination of Chancellor Soh and her Jedi dogs. Yes, the Republic and the Jedi lost repeatedly against the Nihil, but that was when Marchion Ro himself led. Ro was currently . . . unengaged.

It was worth contemplating whether maintaining Nihil occupation of Naboo or losing control over it suited her long-term plans better.

For a moment Viess stared unblinking through the holo. Then she leaned back in her chair. "Don't you worry about the Nihil looking strong, Ghirra. We *are* strong. And I've already begun a little counter-campaign of my own. Setting some bait and what have you."

"A trap."

Viess grinned. "But the Lightning Crash is not my immediate problem."

"It's all of our problem."

"Until the RDC blows it up."

"That won't exactly be a sign of strength," Ghirra said, barely resisting rolling her eyes.

"But maybe it will bring Ro back from his walkabout."

Ghirra held up a hand. "Whatever happens, he'll be prepared. He has enough backup plans to take a personal day or two."

"Personal, my ass," Viess said, then snorted. "Marchion Ro doesn't have a personal side. But every rumor and myth I've heard about those Evereni is that if they stop moving, they die. Stop hunting, they stop breathing. Ro was never going to sit idly on a throne and rule."

"Hmm," Ghirra hummed, eyes narrowing on the holo Viess. Ghirra disliked being reminded that oftentimes she and Viess thought alike. "Goodbye, Viess," she said and cut their call.

It was time to leave the protective bosom of her power base on Hosnian Prime and head back to Coruscant, Ghirra believed. If Ro was incommunicado, she could represent him and the Nihil interests however she liked. And let Ro and the Nihil see exactly why they should rely on her.

Chapter Twenty-Two

NORISYN, INSIDE THE OCCLUSION ZONE

Marchion Ro angled the barge over the broad swath of crystal farm. He flew it over the false kyber and hestalt formations spearing up like arrows of delicate pale ash toward the new edge of the blight. An air of death and delicacy lay over everything like a dreadful mist.

Ro thought if he so much as laughed too loudly, the entire field would shudder into dust.

The barge rumbled and sputtered as he paused it above the demarcation between ruined fractal spears and those still living. They glinted smoky and pale pink under the blue sun.

Checking his chrono, Ro estimated the time he'd been away. The distance from this blight line to the pale-green energy marker that glowed from the base of the research droid he'd dispatched before leaving was . . . extensive. Ro launched a second droid, with the command that it mark this new line and time. The droids would hover slowly along the former edge and the new, calculating the consumption rate and noting any inconsistencies.

His next experimental site was deeper into the blighted farm. The barge zipped along until Ro brought it around over the row of objects lined up. Now they were all completely consumed except for the last two. "Give me the summary, Seven-Nine," he said to the droid stationed here.

Thunking down onto the barge, the droid spat out a list of data, highlighting the conclusion that items brimming with life fell faster than items forged by minerals or complicated chemical processes or both, like transparisteel. In fact it was a shield built of a specific ancient alloy Ro had found in the family storage room on the *Gaze* that still retained a gleam of itself around the scalloped edge.

But the final item shone with untouched luminescence. Ro smiled grimly with burgeoning satisfaction.

It was one of his few remaining Leveler eggs, and it, alone of everything, was safe from this blight. The blight itself had crept close to the egg then moved around it without touching, as if the egg emitted a blight-specific energy field.

"The Leveler egg's energy readings indicate it is not well," the droid said tonelessly.

"Sick? Dying?"

"Unknown. Withdrawn, perhaps, or dying. Slowly. It is affected, but I can collect minimal data without being invasive. The information does not align with previous data I have access to on either the eggs or hatched creatures. Perhaps Baron Boolan—"

"No," Marchion said. "Don't share this data yet."

"Yes, sir."

In the corner of his eye, Ro saw the ghost of his great-great-grandmother leaning over the rail of the barge. Too bad shoving her over wouldn't hurt her. She said nothing.

On to the next phase of this experiment. He guided the barge quickly over the blighted crystal farm to the edge of stable land. Giving himself plenty of unblighted land, he set the barge low enough that he could vault over the edge and land easily. Before doing so, Ro turned to the quivering, silent creatures behind him.

The two Levelers huddled together, their limbs tangled and spines flicking up and down in what was likely distress. He could see the line of their ribs through emaciated white flesh, but their panting was silent.

Taking the rod from his belt, he held it before them. "Let's go," he commanded.

"Sweet things," the Evereni woman murmured, drifting to them. She caressed the long tendrils of the nearest and, as they stood on shaking legs, patted down its spine. The Levelers did not sense her but towered over her slight stature. She leaned against one, unafraid.

Ro kicked the gate at the rear of the barge open and jumped to the ground. "Come," he said, focused on the controlling rod.

First one followed, then the next. They hit the ground and stumbled. One bellowed.

Usually the Levelers were hungry and graceful in their own distorted way. Today they were restless. Their gray-white bodies hunched over, shoulders nearly level with his own. Their claws dug into the hard stone ground as their tentacles twitched and curled. The one to his left had two milky-purple eyes; the one on his right had slightly paler eyes, a white that reflected the dull glow of the ostentatious crystal in the rod Marchion carried.

When he walked, they followed him.

There in the east, where the small red sun had risen, the crystal farm took on a dull sheen. Because the entire field had turned to ash.

The blight was familiar to him now, though he had yet to seek it out on any of the worlds with possible sightings of it. Once he'd satisfied his curiosity here and gathered this final piece of information, he would go. Discover if this blight behaved the same way on every world it touched.

His experiments had proved thus far that the blight did not only affect living creatures, and so while it was recognizable as a cousin to the husking effect his Levelers had on Force users, it was not the same. Ro wanted to know if the Levelers recognized it. If they feared it or brought it with them.

From what little data he'd gathered, there seemed to be no immediate pattern. It did not show up only where the Levelers had been or appear only where they had never trodden. It did not move from system to system or sector to sector like a stone skipping across the galaxy. No, the four possible instances he was aware of held to no discernible pattern except: They all were nearer to Wild Space than anything else.

Ro needed to widen his search parameters into Republic space. But for now he had an experiment to run.

The ghost's footsteps were silent on the gravelly rock, though Ro's own boots scraped harshly with every step and the Levelers' claws loudly gouged into the strata. Ro kept his eyes on the graying horizon, though he couldn't help but listen to whatever prattle his ancestor would spout. Sometimes what she said reminded him of useful things.

With a quick glance over, he saw the ghost petting the long tendril-like whiskers that grew from the skull of the Leveler on his right. She twined her delicate-looking gray fingers into the whiskers, and for a moment it seemed like the Leveler leaned into her touch.

Impossible.

Marchion Ro focused. He sped up, dragging the Levelers to his same pace with the rod. They followed like desperate lackgoats.

"Oh," the ghost whispered. She was in her white jumpsuit, the cowl pulled up over black braids. A few flowers held in her fist. "I see."

Ro thought bitterly to himself that he didn't *see*. But he pushed it aside and beckoned a Leveler to him.

They stood several paces from the edge of the blight.

The change in the crystal farm was somehow more obvious and disconcerting—more real—from ground level than it was from the air.

Marchion Ro let himself vividly recall the elaborate, drawn-out death of Grand Master Veter all those months ago. On the anniversary of his first unleashing of these Levelers against the Jedi Order. When he'd used them to scare and confuse, ultimately leading to the fall of Starlight Beacon.

Ro smiled.

Beside him the Levelers backed away.

Interesting.

"Interesting," the ghost echoed, head tilted thoughtfully.

Ro gripped the rod tighter. Its pink glow lit the knuckles of his hand like eerie blood. "Remain with me," he commanded the Levelers. It was unclear even to him exactly how this rod controlled the creatures, but it did. It worked and always had.

The Levelers groaned. One turned its face to the darkening sky, peering up as if to seek salvation there. The other dug its claws into the dirt and shuddered. Its skin seemed to retract, its bones thrusting out in starved prominence. It bared its teeth and shook its head.

"Go," Ro said softly, walking forward with them.

They approached the blight together. Ro relaxed, eager, the Levelers dragging themselves at his heels.

Ro blinked and the ghost was ahead of them, kneeling at the exact line of raw gray blight. She brought her hands together with flowers clutched between her fingers and closed her eyes. She smiled and bowed, then tossed the flowers into the blight.

It was an illusion, but Ro found himself captivated. The flowers began to shiver with gray blight before they even touched the surface of the planet. They cracked and crumbled.

The ghost bent over, tears tracking down her gray cheeks.

Ro smiled. He held out the glowing rod. "Go," he said, willing the Levelers to approach the blight. "Now. Closer."

The Levelers obeyed as they must, but it was slow. Excruciating.

One Leveler's whole body shuddered again, and it seemed to resist the command of the rod. The other threw itself forward with gusto but skidded to a halt. It spun and fled.

Ro yelled, "Stop!" And it did. But it trembled.

The Great Levelers were afraid.

Ro stepped up to the edge of the blight. He stared down, watching it slowly creep toward the toe of his boot.

He felt . . . new. Excited.

It had been a long time since Marchion Ro had felt anything like this keen anticipation.

This was not only a mystery. It was a threat. A thread of history and legacy, dropping its mark everywhere he passed.

If Marchion Ro was good at anything, it was turning an opportunity into a weapon.

The Levelers continued to pull away, stretching the space between this blight and themselves as far as he allowed.

And the blight itself shifted its borders. Not only did it spread faster, but it reached for the Levelers, the edges of its consummation bending like hands to reach, reach, *reach* for them. It wanted them. It needed them.

Oh, this was a revelation, and Ro would find a way to harness it and use it. Everything could be a weapon with the right understanding.

Chapter Twenty-Three

REPUBLIC SPACE,
BORDER OF THE OCCLUSION ZONE

The stars surrounding the small shuttle *Clear Spring* stared coldly back at Elzar Mann.

He breathed carefully as he studied the view beyond the cockpit, leaned up against the round door, and did not give in to fear. Though he had much to be afraid of.

The last time Elzar had faced this swath of space—the invisible, mighty Stormwall—he had sent ships and their crews into death. He'd been so sure it was their chance, their best bet, he'd been desperate for the Force to be on his side and the side of light. It had to be.

And the Force had been with them, of course, but nothing else was.

These stars did not shimmer or twinkle; they were only points of distant light. Star systems in Nihil space, filled with people suffering under the oppression of Marchion Ro.

This time the mission would succeed.

This time Elzar would not watch helplessly as his comrades disappeared and died.

This time Elzar was going through first himself.

He'd gone to the Jedi Council to tell them—not ask them—that he was co-leading this mission. He'd been prepared with a handful of arguments, ranging from his duty to the Force to insisting that if they trusted him enough to invite him onto the Council, they should trust him enough to know where he was needed from mission to mission. Elzar had been ready to fight for it.

But waiting for him outside the Council Chamber had been Grand Master Ry Ki-Sakka. Elzar had stopped short, quickly tucking away his surprise. "Grand Master."

"Elzar." Ki-Sakka had smiled at him.

Elzar had scratched his beard, amused at himself. "You know why I'm here."

"You're going with Master Kriss to attempt an assault upon the power source of the Stormwall."

"I . . . am. Would like to," Elzar added sheepishly. The grand master preempting him like this deflated his ego fast.

Ki-Sakka laughed. "Which is it?"

Elzar had lowered his eyes and listened to the soft thump of his heartbeat—the tide of the Force inside him, Avar had named it. It wasn't ego. It was necessary confidence. Trust in the Force. "Am. It's where I need to be."

"Very well."

"Thank you." Elzar felt an urge to add more, but anything more would be too final. He bowed, turning away.

"And Elzar," the grand master said.

Elzar paused.

"This doesn't have to be your answer."

Relief buoyed him, and Elzar felt his shoulders relax. He hadn't realized how much of him needed to be free to choose that position or not, on his own time, without external issues necessitating a closed door. He glanced back at Ki-Sakka. "Thank you again. And . . . I will have an answer. Soon."

"We know."

This was just something Elzar had to do first.

It was three days past the meeting with the chancellor and Avon Sunvale's breakthrough, thanks to the information provided by Graf. They were finally here at the edge of Republic space ready to punch through the Stormwall. Once the home key proved successful, the Republic would send through dual strike forces: one to jump into Nihil space after the Lightning Crash itself, one to storm Naboo and free it of General Viess's occupation. Elzar would be fighting with the former and Avar with the latter.

"Nearly there?" Avar appeared at his side at the cockpit entrance. She skimmed her fingers against Elzar's, though her question was directed at the two humans currently bickering about the hyperdrive interface.

Xylan Graf, sitting at the hyperdrive and punching in data, flicked an annoyed glance at the Jedi. "Sooner if we're left in peace."

"You work better with an audience, Xylan," shot back young Avon Sunvale, from where she'd half dove under a floor panel, slicing into the comm unit to add some data that would allow it to project her home key to the Stormwall as they attempted to cross. Elzar's understanding was that Mari San Tekka's home Path had allowed Avon to unravel the rest of the Path codes and create a sort of reverse key code to essentially use every Path at once to cheat the entire Stormwall setup. If it worked, any ship with the reverse key code and Avon's comm slice could cross.

The *Clear Spring* would be attempting the test run as soon as they were ready.

Avar squeezed his hand, and they synchronized their breathing. As she'd suggested in the meditation garden, Elzar did his best to think of the rhythm of it as both an ocean tide and a song. Their two parts of the Force sinking into one.

But the snappy arguing of Xylan Graf and Avon Sunvale was a distracting discord. They hadn't stopped needling each other since they'd all left Coruscant, though to Elzar's ears it sounded more like sibling affection than real antagonism.

They'd made Xylan come as part of his deal: He needed to be on the first test ship in order to prove the legitimacy of his information. A show of faith that he wasn't setting them up for an explosive death trap. Graf had pretended to be wildly offended, of course, but ultimately agreed. Either he believed in his data or he had an extremely good bluff. Elzar suspected Graf continued to have a hidden purpose for wanting to return with them, but Avon seemed oddly comforted to have him along, almost as if his presence reminded her they were doing this for the right reasons.

When Elzar had said as much to Avar, she'd offered him her softest smile and said, "You're very good with people, El. Reading and understanding them."

Only when he wasn't straying too close to the dark side, he'd thought, but he shrugged a little and made himself take the compliment. He *liked* people. Most Jedi found it simple to like people as part of the Force and Life and Light, but Elzar had grown up thinking people of all species were weird and delightful, and it was their strangeness that made them special. Worthy of his efforts. It had been years of enemies and politics that made him forget he used to go out of his way to talk to new people every day. To learn things, to figure out how others ticked. To push buttons and boundaries. That had helped him understand himself and his connection to the Force better.

It wasn't that he'd forgotten. He'd only let himself get bogged down by the bad stuff.

"I might understand people, but they listen to you," he'd said to Avar.

"I just have that kind of face," she'd joked. It was so nice to see her humor return in fits and starts. When they'd been young, Avar Kriss had been the funniest person he knew, somehow both good-natured and scathing. They'd sent each other into giggle fits as younglings. But just as Elzar had stopped seeking out interesting people, the weight of duty had sanded down Avar's jocular edges, and war doused them completely—as it had done to everyone Elzar knew.

"This is finished," Avon said as she dragged herself out from inside the cockpit floor. Elzar bent to help her refit the panel in place. Avon climbed into the copilot's seat. "Xylan?"

The Graf's fingers slowed as he completed his input. He took a deep breath and let it out in a whining sigh. "I suppose there's nothing else I can do to delay the inevitable."

"Fainting spell?" Avon suggested sweetly.

"That wouldn't get him back to the *Third Horizon,*" added the RDC pilot who'd be flying the mission for them. His flight partner leaned near the comm station, attention on Xylan, her ostensible prisoner.

Avar stepped up behind Xylan. "We'll be fine," she said as she patted his shoulder.

Elzar opened the ship's comm. "This is Elzar Mann to Captain Tearlin. We're a go over on the *Clear Spring.* Ready to jump."

"Tearlin here," his gravelly voice answered. "Widening your comm to all ships. Countdown when ready, Master Jedi, and we'll see you in twenty-one minutes. May the Force be with you."

"Very well," Elzar said. "And thank you."

"Patching ship comm in," Avon said.

"Starting countdown," added a very reluctant-sounding Xylan Graf. Elzar and Avar took the rear seats and strapped in.

"Ten," Xylan marked.

"Home key active," Avon said. "Coupled successfully with hyperdrive and comm."

"Engines ready," said the RDC pilot as his partner strapped into one of the jump seats in the rear of the bridge.

Anxiety chewed at Elzar's guts, and he glanced at Avar. Wished she'd stayed behind. They needed one Jedi on this mission in case they were expelled into hostile territory. Neither Avon nor Xylan was equipped for battle. But there'd been no point in both himself and Avar risking it all like this. He'd argued hard for her to wait with the fleet. Let him do this. "I have to, the risk has to be mine," he'd said.

Avar had replied, "Not yours alone."

"I'll be worried about you."

"We'll be stronger together."

"It isn't about strength. All that has to happen is pushing some buttons," Elzar insisted. "They barely even need me."

"That's not the kind of strength I'm talking about. I wanted you back out here, away from your Senate building, and I didn't mean for you to be out here alone. So I'm not leaving you. If you go, I go. So that's it."

"Avar—"

"Would you let me go alone?"

"That's not the point—"

"Elzar Mann exceptionalism, then? I see." Avar's expression had closed off.

"I'm sorry."

"For what?"

"Being patronizing."

"Stellan was better at it," she said, with a little smile to show she was teasing.

The whole conversation flashed through Elzar's mind as Xylan said, "Five," and Elzar reached for Avar again. She met his hand with hers, his gaze with hers. Tiny wrinkles around her eyes seemed tighter than usual.

"Three," Xylan said.

"I'm glad you're here," Elzar said. "With me for this."

Avar's surprise was obvious, but just as she smiled and opened her mouth, the pilot called out, "Jumping!"

Their fingers squeezed and the ship lurched. Elzar ignored everything except for Avar's gaze. If those dark, fathomless eyes had to be the last thing he ever saw alive, he was all right with that.

Bluish light shifted through the cockpit.

Avar's face snapped toward the viewport. Elzar followed.

Avon Sunvale let out a triumphant cry.

They were in hyperspace. The blue streaking tunnel of stars stretched ahead of them into infinity.

"Six minutes to the jump point inside Nihil space," the pilot said tightly. His left hand danced along the controls. "Everything seems fine. Hyperdrive processing . . . normal."

"It worked," Avon said. "It isn't going to spit us out in the middle of nowhere. We did it."

Avar dropped Elzar's hand and unbuckled. She stood up and stared out the viewport. Now that the ship had jumped, everything felt smooth and still. No hint of momentum or friction. Just the quiet caress of hyperspace.

Elzar watched Avar tilt her head slightly, a tell that she was listening to the song of the Force.

"Don't bother adding my name to the historical archives," Xylan said, poking Avon in the arm. "I don't want the glory."

"Just the residuals in cold hard ingots," Avon said, batting his hand away.

"Get your tracker ready," Elzar suggested to Xylan, though he couldn't help enjoying their banter. It was relaxing amid the tension.

Xylan swiveled his chair to the comm unit, and Avon bounced in place, fitting for a fifteen-year-old kid genius who'd just cracked a barrier that had stymied everyone for more than a year.

Elzar opened his feelings to the Force. It rushed around him, an insistent, constant pressure he could sink into, grab onto, flex and drag. His body lit up with it, roaring with potential. Elzar sat in it, experiencing the trembling sensation. He closed his eyes, felt Avar beside him, brilliant spiking Force, and Avon and Xylan nearby, both knots of expectation and anxiety, the two RDC personnel focused and on edge. Elzar was not particularly sensitive to emotional energy, but even he could sense the worry and excitement everyone exuded.

The *Clear Spring* dove through hyperspace, following the string of math to slice across the Stormwall. Elzar could almost imagine he felt the wall itself, a pulsing, deadly barrier. It had its own Force resonance, its own tide.

Elzar took another breath and reached for Avar. Her song reached back, and they connected. *Elzar.* He felt his name in her voice and replied, *Avar.* Hearts together through the Force.

"Coming out of hyperspace," the pilot said.

Deep in his Force awareness, the shift from lightspeed to realspace felt like slow motion, a step and another, climbing up slippery sand from the reef to the shore, from deep water into air. Then the ship pinged several alerts, and Elzar opened his eyes.

Stars.

Unlatching his safety harness, Elzar stood. There was nothing but stars before them. He moved to activate the ship's shields and check on the sensors for any other ships near or far.

"We made it," Avon said.

"Activating tracking beacon," Xylan lazily replied.

"No other ships in the vicinity," the RDC pilot reported.

"Nothing on the comm," Avar said, a smile in her voice. "Avon, recheck your slice, get us ready to jump back to the fleet the moment Xylan grabs the location of the Lightning Crash."

Elzar leaned toward Xylan. This was the other reason they'd brought him. The Lightning Crash was his proprietary Graf design, built to his specifications even though it had been reskinned by the Nihil. He'd claimed to have engineered a homing beacon directly into the foundation. But his beacon couldn't penetrate the Stormwall any more than regular comms now that his personal Nihil codes had been scuttled. Here on the Nihil side, though, Xylan should be able to track it. "Is the beacon responding?"

"Naturally," the Graf scion said. "These are my personal codes, built into the undercarriage of the sublight sequencer. And I put another one in my silknest pillows. It's a state-of-the-art beacon, tracking and learning the movements of the Lightning Crash, and can even hypothesize where it will go next. But the station rarely moves."

"I'm sure they moved it when they lost you," Avon said.

"You're underestimating their arrogance and reliance on the Storm-wall," Xylan argued. "Even losing me, they won't expect an ambush this soon. It's the perfect time to attack."

Elzar only half listened as he monitored the ship's long-range sensors, breathing in time with Avar even though she stood on the opposite side of the cockpit.

Xylan slapped a hand on the console. "Lightning Crash location locked! We can extrapolate a hyperspace route from this, and it will be there waiting."

"Good," Elzar said. That was his mission: leading half the fleet to destroy the Stormwall's power source. "Did they move it?"

"Yes, I've got a lock on it."

"Let's get back then," Avar said.

Avon brought the *Clear Spring* around, and Graf put the return coordinates into the hyperdrive. Getting back out of Nihil space should be as easy as jumping in had been.

They'd done it.

Chapter Twenty-Four

Avar said goodbye to Elzar in the landing bay of the *Harmonic*. She was ready to load up into her Vector and zip over to the *Axiom*, from which she'd lead the assault on Naboo. Several other Jedi had joined up with them and been divided into her and Elzar's teams. The Council had promised full investment in the mission, alongside the regular firepower of the Republic Defense Coalition. The objectives were clear: take out the Lightning Crash, damaging the power of the Stormwall, and remove General Viess from Naboo permanently, preferably with her capture. Either would be a blow to the Nihil, a reminder that the Republic wasn't sitting back and letting them wreak their devastation on the galaxy.

Though freeing Naboo had been one of Xylan's so-called requirements for helping them, his opinion was hardly why the Republic had agreed. It was due to General Viess's new base there, making the planet a politically and militarily expedient target. And a decisive victory would give the chancellor a position from which to drive hard negotiations. Because Naboo had only been recently invaded with the expansion of the Stormwall, it suggested a possible narrative for the chancellor to use: As easily as you take away, now we can reclaim.

Avar didn't love that this two-pronged mission was just as much a political statement as the work of the light, but she'd do it. Anything they could do against the Nihil was good.

"The Force is with you," Avar said to Elzar as they took their leave of each other.

"It is," he answered. "And you are."

"That's right. Always. No matter what happens."

Elzar nudged the arrowtip of her diadem where it pressed softly to her forehead. Uncertainty flickered across his expression. Avar wished she could wipe it away, but she felt the stretch of uncertainty, too. They were at war with the Nihil. It was natural to be worried.

His finger slid down her nose, then he gently touched her jaw. She smiled and leaned in for a hug. Their cheeks pressed together. "I'll see you for a victory drink," she murmured.

"Grab some of that fancy Naboo wine the San Tekkas offered us back then," he said into her hair.

"Deal."

They squeezed each other, and then Avar pulled away. She jogged off immediately and climbed into her Vector for the quick flight to the *Axiom*.

An hour later, Avar stood in the crew lounge of the star cruiser as it flew through hyperspace. Several tables had been turned out so they all faced her. Avar stood near the front of the lounge where a meal counter was filled with auto-stocked drinks and packaged food, while a galley droid silently prepped a large tray of some kind of grain protein cake.

A dozen Jedi and Padawans watched Avar as she pulled up the battle schematics on the holoscreen in the small podium before her. Naboo turned, and dark blots of blue marked where they believed the general's ship was likely to be based on intel from the San Tekkas. "We are going in mostly blind," she started. "But we know General Viess of the Nihil has made Naboo into one of her military bases, given its location near the edge of Nihil space and its position as a well-known Republic ally."

Avar pointed to the marks where the *Axiom* and two sister cruisers in their wing would jump in. If the intelligence was wrong and the general had more than twice the expected firepower, they'd jump right back out. But the San Tekkas didn't believe Viess would have reason to bring more. That said, she had an occupying force on the ground, already dug into the capital city of Theed.

"We're timing our jump to coincide with the arrival of Kronara's team at the Lightning Crash," Avar said. "We'll jump directly into orbit. Though we're hoping to be a surprise, it's possible they'll be expecting us, if they've realized we've amassed near the system on the Republic side of the wall. That's why our initial strike team is so small. We'll be ready to leave immediately if necessary, or send for backup. As we can't be sure what we'll face when we reach the planet, the plan is loose, but the star cruisers *Harmonic* and *Tractate* will immediately locate the general's ship, which usually orbits Naboo when she is in residence. They will attack as quickly as possible. A few Jedi Vectors will launch from the *Axiom* immediately upon entry and join them."

Nods from the assembled Jedi, but no questions yet. Avar continued, "The *Axiom* itself will drop into the atmosphere over the capital, Theed, and the rest of us will launch our Vectors alongside RDC fighters to destroy the Nihil bases and infrastructure—"

"Nice of them to make their garbage so distinct for us," Jedi Knight Far Linghe, a well-liked Cathar, said from near the back.

Avar allowed herself a tight-lipped smile of agreement as a handful of Jedi chuckled. "If we're lucky, the RDC cruisers in orbit will destroy the general's ship immediately so that she can't escape, and we will capture her while she is planetside. If she is aboard, the aim will be to cripple her ship instead of destroying it, if possible. On the ground we need to focus on chasing out the Nihil, getting them to retreat or surrender so that we can reestablish the planetary defenses as well as comms. We believe the queen and most of her government are intact but deep in hiding, and we're unsure what their reaction will be, just as we don't know if we'll be remaining in the system or if we'll need to clear out quickly, depending on the situation with the Stormwall."

The Jedi's job was primarily on the ground. "Those of us who stay with the *Axiom* will split into two initial teams: One will head for the royal palace where, according to our sources, the Nihil have already begun redecorating it as their home base, while the other focuses on greater Theed itself, rooting out Nihil, protecting civilians, keeping a lookout for unexpected threats. Our sources insist there have not been Nameless on Naboo, but we must plan for their presence regardless. We will have support from non-Jedi and security droids for that. But I'd like to deal assignments on a volunteer basis."

Plenty of the Jedi grimaced or shared nervous looks. One or two seemed overly confident, and Avar marked their names in her memory to make sure they didn't join the ground team. She didn't want her fellows to be afraid or to give in to that fear—but to ignore it was arrogance, and that was one of the fastest roads to the dark side and defeat.

"Come see me to volunteer, then get some rest," Avar said.

She stepped back and focused for a moment on shutting down the holo to allow the Jedi to get themselves together and make their decisions. She expected Vernestra to volunteer for the ground force, and Mirro Lox and his Padawan Amadeo Azzazzo. Avar disagreed with putting any Padawans in sight of the Nameless, but it wasn't her decision. When she'd been one, she'd have been offended if the Jedi Masters had tried to keep Master Cherff out of a fight just because of her.

In the end, Avar was unsurprised and pleasantly proud that every Jedi in the room volunteered. She told them she'd make up a roster and post it shortly before they left hyperspace.

Before she could tell them to take a break, a mug of steaming dark tea was pushed into her face by a Wookiee. Avar blinked up at him. "Burryaga!" She smiled.

The Wookiee Jedi Knight spoke in a low trill. She thought he said yes and asked a question, but her Shyriiwook wasn't very good. Fishing around her belt for her translator with one hand, Avar accepted the tea with the other.

"He says he made you tea, and can we talk to you for a minute?"

Avar glanced at Bell Zettifar, Loden's former Padawan. He looked nearly the same, except for strain around his dark eyes and a new set to his mouth. Every time she saw these two, they seemed older. *Don't we all,* she thought sadly. But it was good to see them: Zettifar and Burryaga had been the ones to catch her when Avar had come charging out of Nihil space in the stolen, dying *Cacophony.*

"Of course," she said, gesturing with her head for them to take a seat at the nearest table. Burryaga perched on a chair that barely fit his height, and Bell had to dance around the presence of the waist-high charhound dogging at his heels. Once they were all seated, the charhound put its long jaw against Bell's thigh, and he scratched at its ear. Avar couldn't remember the charhound's name. She reached out and the beast sniffed at her.

Smiling a little at the hot breath on her fingertips, Avar said, "What can I do for you? Have you been on Naboo before? Is there something you wanted to add to the plan?"

"No," Bell said. "It's not about that."

Avar kept her eyes on the charhound as it reacquainted itself with her. Then Avar was allowed to stroke the beast's long nose.

The two Jedi Knights were silent long enough that Avar glanced up. Bell's worried frown gave her pause. Burryaga's shoulders were slightly drooped. They looked like they needed a vacation that none of them were going to get anytime soon. Avar reached for them through the Force, allowing them to feel her gentle hello. Sometimes a connection like this could help. She said, "You've been on the border with the RDC still, right?"

"Yes." Bell smiled. "Do you keep track of everybody's assignments?"

"When I can, and only loosely," Avar said. "It's an old habit, but I like to know where Jedi are, where we're stretched thin or congregated."

"So you know who you can pull on when you need us? Like at Hetzal?"

Avar nodded. That was most of it. But she liked knowing what sort of blanket the Jedi spread across the galaxy. It comforted her when she knew names and pieces of history for the people the Order sent out. And once she'd met someone, it eased something naturally tight in her heart to keep track of their movements and works. Especially if, like Burryaga, their song had ever melded with hers. Hetzal was where she'd first worked with the Wookiee.

Burryaga spoke in soft Shyriiwook, and Bell took up the answer, putting his elbows on the table. "We've been helping with the evacuations—getting people out of the way of the possibly expanding Stormwall."

The Wookiee added something, and Bell snorted. "Yeah. Burry says it hasn't been going especially well."

"Local resistance?" Avar asked.

Bell shrugged. "A lot of things, but that's not what we wanted to ask you about."

"All right." Avar realized she was bracing herself internally. She made herself relax, letting the steam of her tea tingle over her lips.

"It's the Drengir," Bell said.

"Drengir!" Avar nearly slammed her mug down in surprise. "But . . . oh, no."

Even though she'd been trapped behind enemy lines all of last year, it was the Drengir that represented the worst time of Avar's life. They'd been a relentless enemy, their whereabouts unpredictable, and Avar had lost too many people to them. Their ability to latch onto even Jedi minds with their dark side influence had dragged trusted Jedi into awful places. They'd been in her head, too, and the memory of it caused a revulsion so visceral that Avar struggled not to shudder physically before the two younger Jedi. The choices she had made when she'd let herself become so focused on them had kept her from being able to help on Valo during the massacre at the Republic Fair and led her to her fixation on Lourna Dee, which had nearly ended with Avar making irreparable mistakes. Avar had never come so close to falling as when she nearly murdered Lourna. She'd had no time to process or come to terms with that darkness in herself before Starlight Beacon had crashed and she'd fled into Nihil space.

For Avar, it had all truly begun with the Drengir. She couldn't deal with them right now. She . . . would, though. She had to.

"Tell me," Avar said, feeling the weight of her professional mask settling over her expression. Leadership, authority, concern. Things she knew how to project, that sometimes helped her settle herself.

"We've encountered two incidents recently—well." Bell grimaced. "One really, the second was more like the remnants."

"Remnants of Drengir should be nothing but a massacre," Avar said grimly.

Burryaga spoke and Bell haltingly translated. "The first was on Felne Six. We answered a distress call from a small science outpost. A single Drengir was there, but . . . it was dying." The Wookiee fell silent and Bell continued alone, "We couldn't see any reason. It felt strange, like it was still part of the Force—the dark side—but there was no sign of disease or massive injury. It just . . . was dying. Burry says it felt alone."

"If it was alone," Avar said, "it should have still been connected to their telepathic root network."

"Right. We read about that in the reports. But Burry insists it was solo. Alone," Bell said. "And the second incident was on Ronaphaven, and there obviously had been Drengir on that world very recently, but they were gone."

Avar's breath drained out of her. "Gone?"

"The signs of them having been there were obvious. Blights and diseased crops, sinkholes, dead people and animals . . . but there were no Drengir. Not even their bodies, from what we could tell."

Avar bit back a soft curse.

Burryaga spoke up again asking a question. Bell said, "Can they leave a place when they've rooted there?"

Slowly shaking her head, Avar said, "If they use their telepathy to overtake a person's mind, yes. Sure."

"That must be what happened. We should double-check, when we have a chance, if any ships were missing from their port." Bell glanced at Burryaga when he said it, and the Wookiee growled agreement.

"Was there any . . . sign of something that they might have been running from?" Avar asked, but she knew the answer would be no. Something that *scared the Drengir* had to be awful, had to leave a huge impression or evidence. They'd have noticed. Probably started with it. Except . . . "What about the Nameless? As much as we hate to admit it, Drengir are Force users, too."

"Nothing," Bell said. "We were planning to ask you, and then maybe put together some kind of mission to look into it more, but this mission . . ."

"Yes. I'm glad you're here," Avar said, confirming their instincts. "And no, I'm aware of nothing that scares them enough to make them leave a place plentiful with food."

Bell slumped a little, and the charhound nudged at his arm until he patted its sinuous neck.

Avar took a deep breath. "You've written up a full report?"

"Yes, we just transmitted it to the Temple before we rendezvoused with the *Axiom*."

"Once we liberate Naboo, I'll read it. We'll scour the galaxy for any similar reports, get some researchers on it. And . . ." Avar stopped talking as her blood went cold.

"Master Kriss?" Bell said.

She struggled to contain the spike of dread she was sure she'd just stabbed through the Force. She said, flattening her hands on the cold surface of the table, "The Great Progenitor was captured and held in stasis—that's how we stopped them. But . . ." Avar closed her eyes. "She was supposed to be transported to a secure facility, and until then she was being held on Starlight Beacon."

"There's no addendum about her in the file we read," Bell said, and Burryaga's large hands curled into fists against the table.

Avar had forgotten. She'd lost track of the Great Progenitor and assumed Maru had overseen the Drengir's official transfer. Maru always did his job. But Avar had never checked, and there were always delays, especially with the emergencies that caused them to move Starlight itself several times in its last weeks. "She's dead at the bottom of the Eiram ocean."

Burryaga said something in a choking, almost angry tone.

Avar raised her eyebrows at Bell. The younger Jedi looked haunted but with a grim expression said, "Burry says that not everything trapped under the Eiram ocean stays dead."

Chapter Twenty-Five

INSIDE THE OCCLUSION ZONE

The *Third Horizon* battle cruiser flashed out of hyperspace, instantly activating shields and weapons and launching a squadron of Skywings.

Elzar Mann gave the order for the Jedi Vectors to launch directly on their tail.

He moved his senses in line with the vessel. Elzar always felt lighter, sharper, more dangerous in a Vector. He didn't have the opportunity to fly one very often—not these days on Coruscant. And never before for the purpose of a direct assault. Every slice of power and stamina the Vector was capable of would come into play today.

As he launched from the Vector bay, he nudged the controls to urge the Vector faster, shooting forward. He flicked the comm from task-unit-wide to Vector-only and said, "This is Vector One, are you with me?"

The seven Jedi in six Vectors behind him sounded off, and with each voice Elzar pushed his awareness farther until the Force linked them all. It was a gentle connection born of Elzar's affinity for mind-touch, not the strong alignment required for a true Drift—but if they needed that, they'd be ready.

The Vectors spread in a tightly aligned formation, darting in sync toward their goal.

The Lightning Crash gleamed against the backdrop of stars, white towers reaching up from the crystalline bowl of its meteor base like an ancient city—one the Nihil had marred with their violent-blue scrawls and jagged cannons. One of the towers had been sheared off, leaving its edges torn and ragged but sharp. It was a small fortress kneeling over the nest of crystal arrays it existed to protect.

The lower levels with the array were Elzar's target. The *Third Horizon* would be aiming to knock out as many of the station's defenses as possible as swiftly as possible, while the pacifier cruiser *Crescent Blaze* engaged with any Nihil ships in the vicinity and the RDC fighters swept the field of any Nihil fighters to clear the way for the Vectors—with their greater firepower—to blast the bowl of crystals to nothing.

Xylan Graf had provided them with accurate schematics, as best he could recall, of the weapons capabilities of the station and the types of Nihil ships usually in residence. And he'd suggested they plan for worse, given his recent decampment. But the Nihil wouldn't expect the RDC to be able to bring a battle cruiser through the Stormwall—not so soon at least. Admiral Kronara of the *Third Horizon* had agreed, any eagerness he'd felt for striking back at the Nihil hidden behind the crags on the battle-hardened old human's face. Kronara and Graf had made their plans for taking out the Lightning Crash's weapons arrays—Elzar and his Jedi only had to focus on destroying the crystal base.

"Seven Nihil ships detected," came the voice of the *Third Horizon*'s comm officer through the task-unit-wide comm.

"*Crescent Blaze* engaging," the star cruiser acknowledged.

"Blue Squadron engaging," the leader of the RDC Skywings said. "Clearing a path."

"Vectors en route," Elzar replied on the all-ships channel. Toggling to the Vector-only channel, he added, "Ready weapons."

Elzar put his lightsaber on the panel and flicked the field button, locking the blade into the controls. The full strength of the Vector weapons was the only thing that could penetrate the Lightning Crash's shields and the hard meteor rock of the undercarriage.

The Lightning Crash swiveled cannons and began to fire on the two cruisers as the Nihil ships broke off and some went directly for the starfighters. One Nihil ship hurriedly uncoupled from the station's bay.

Elzar let his awareness focus on the space station and his goal, and the noise of the battle, alerts and quick conversation and reports, faded slightly.

The Jedi didn't fire on the Nihil ships, letting the RDC fighters do their work. Elzar led the Vectors in swooping maneuvers behind and under the RDC. Flashes of energy and fire drew his attention to the *Third Horizon,* to the cannons on the Lightning Crash.

The station leveled blue-laser rail cannons against the RDC battle cruiser, which fired back with the front cannons, keeping its nose aimed for the station. The *Crescent Blaze* turned, fighting off three Nihil ships at once. None of them were as large as the cruiser, and its cannons and maneuverability outmatched them. But the Nihil were reckless and furious. They tore through the *Blaze*'s fighters while the fighters dipped and spun.

There were no Nihil Strikeships, not even scrambling from the Lightning Crash.

Elzar thrust his Vector forward, coming up along the curve of the station's bowl-like bottom. He leaned into the motion of the vessel, spinning to fly his belly along the curve. Large smoky-pink crystals jutted out of the metal and rock infrastructure, crackling with energy. Elzar opened fire, his Vector's weapons at full strength.

The cannons tore along the energy shield, and alongside him the other Vectors did the same.

"Incoming, Vector One!" called one of the starfighter pilots, and Elzar let the Force guide him in a sharp spiral down and away, avoiding a stream of laserfire.

"Follow," he called to the Jedi.

They turned as one, then instantly scattered in evasive maneuvers like a handful of shattered glass. They came around from every angle, darting between starfighters as two Nihil ships came around, blasting at them.

The Lightning Crash's shields flickered—the *Third Horizon* had taken out one of the towers and continued fire as it cut across the top of the station, coming around with cannons alight.

Elzar and the Vectors spun, slipping under the station again, firing again and again against the flickering shields. Elzar felt every shift and dip in his body. He was the Vector; it was exhilarating.

"Contact!" Ai-Dan Yelooc in Vector Three cried. "We're through."

At that, Elzar dropped his Vector hard and spun, hovering in space and letting totally loose with his weapons.

Three other Vectors pulled the same trick, holding in place and firing over and over again at the crystals.

"Watch it!" someone warned, and the Vectors fell away as one just in time for one of the Nihil ships to blast through their formation, three starfighters chasing it.

The Jedi swooped farther out, giving the fighters room to clear the way again. Elzar looked up through the transparisteel cockpit and checked the RDC ships: The *Third Horizon* blew up a Nihil ship right before his eyes, the percussion knocking back another one, and the *Crescent Blaze* was turning through a similar scatter of Nihil scrap.

Starfighters darted around the remaining Nihil ships. There weren't many: only three left. No new ships. It hadn't been long, but Nihil support should be incoming.

"Let's make another sweep," Elzar said to the Jedi just as Admiral Kronara's voice called out through the comm, "Nihil station, stand down now and we will accept your surrender. Now is your opportunity."

Elzar didn't hear any response as he and the Vectors came up onto the bowl of the Lightning Crash again and fired.

Their blasts hit and hit again, a striation of pulsing red laser and fire.

An impact Elzar felt like a huge crack flared from one crystal to the next, and he heard whooping from the other Vectors. Elzar spun with his Vector, and they made another pass, blasting the base of the Lightning Crash with everything they had.

Danger fell away, enemies fell away, it was only the flight, the aim, the fire, the community of their individual Vectors spinning in tandem, turning, passing between and over one another in spirals of firepower.

Chunks of the station cracked as the entire bowl began to fall apart.

Pink-white energy from the crystal array cut in jagged streaks, leaving broken pieces behind.

"Pull back," Elzar said, diving away with the other Vectors like slick silver leaves behind him. "*Third Horizon,* this is Vector One, the array is breaking apart."

"Shields on Lightning Crash are down, *Crescent Blaze* removing final remaining Nihil."

"Capture them if you can," Elzar said.

"Lightning Crash standing down," another voice said. "This is Blue Leader, all cannons remaining on the station powered down."

"Two Nihil ships jumped to hyperspace," the comm officer from the *Blaze* said.

"Cowards," Admiral Kronara said.

Elzar agreed but remained silent.

This was too easy.

Elzar reached out with the Force and found the swirl of battle chaos, a quicker rhythm than usual, a churning sea.

"Any communications from the Nihil on the station?" Elzar and his Vector unit hovered in space. They stared at the bowl of the Lightning Crash as huge pink and smoky crystals fell away, drifting off. The Vectors moved easily to avoid the detritus.

"Negative," Kronara said.

"This was too easy," Captain Tearlin said, echoing Elzar's thinking.

"Why would they let us have it?" Elzar said. "They must have assumed Graf escaped in our direction. They had to expect this." He strained to listen for any hint through the Force, any incoming threat, something he'd missed.

Nothing. Either nothing was coming or Elzar couldn't find it.

Xylan Graf's voice broke through the comm, thick with satisfaction. "Don't worry about it. What matters is that my readings show the power relays on the station are fully disrupted, not transmitting to individual stormseeds."

Elzar said, "Does that mean . . ."

"You can send for whatever backup you need, Jedi. The Stormwall is down. Heaven and seven hells of Ryloth. It's down."

Chapter Twenty-Six

NABOO, INSIDE THE OCCLUSION ZONE

Cair San Tekka was in pain. Not only from his aching body, but the kind of gut-wrenching spiritual pain that came from being made to sit across a small table from one's enemy and eat.

Sure, Cair could pass on the perfectly grilled coral bass and beds of callus egg rice, the candied seaweed chips, and the finest petaldown salad the San Tekka kitchens could produce. But if he didn't eat, he'd die. He was only human.

The food wasn't the problem. It was everything else.

He sat carefully on the low, soft chair in Marlowe San Tekka's private dining room. The table was low, too, set over an inset marble well that was self-regulating for either heat or chill depending on the meal and season. The curved wall was striped with thin windows that let in colors of the sky beyond, but no sound or light—that was provided by the three small chandeliers hovering intimately around the diners' heads. They were made from the dried eyes of sand sharks from the southern seas of Naboo, which could be hollowed out and set with energy. The membranes shone with natural iridescence that only appeared once the creature was dead and its parts harvested.

Cair hadn't known any of these gruesome details about his uncles' decorations until General Viess calmly described them to him as she fed herself morsels of raw urchin with a long shell pick.

He did his best to ignore her and eat what he could reach with his only remaining hand. Viess had none too gently removed his prosthetic, claiming it was a deadly weapon.

She was right, but Cair wished she hadn't relished it so much.

His bones hurt. His skull throbbed with the edges of the serum she'd administered to him to compel him to give up his secrets. He had, of course. The ones he knew. It was the price of being caught and burned, and why he'd risked so much to get the word to Belin. The Ugnaught had the right relays and codes to make sure everyone in immediate danger knew to go to ground. He hoped.

Cair had held out through the pain, the anxiety trip, the sleeplessness, as long as he could. But a few hours ago, he'd given in. His network was dust. He couldn't do any more.

The only thing he didn't understand was why he remained alive.

Viess sipped the flute of wine made from the hardened tulip of a sanna tree, and Cair thought about diving across the table for her shell pick and stabbing it into her throat. Maybe the Mirialan arterial vessel was just as vulnerable as the human one.

But he didn't. Even though she deserved it, he wouldn't act again unless he had to. Unless he knew he could win. She'd been killing people more skilled than Cair for five times longer than he'd been alive.

Viess pushed a plate of redglass noodles toward him. "These are spectacular," she said.

Cair ignored the noodles. "Why are you feeding me?"

"It's civilized."

"Compared to torture?"

Viess snorted. "If you'd prefer, I can keep you chained up and hanging from the ceiling somewhere. Starving, filthy."

"Why keep me at all?" The food in Cair's stomach soured.

The general stared at him. She didn't blink even as she took another bite. Cair could think only of Xylan describing this woman as blundering and wicked, easy to bribe, and ultimately vicious. To Cair, she seemed only the latter. Maybe because she'd never pretended to need him like she'd pretended to need Xylan. By the Force, Cair was the one who needed Xylan. To live, to tease him, to kiss him, or even to divorce him. Anything, as long as he was alive to do it.

Viess didn't answer, but the longer her silence reigned, the more amused she seemed. Something about her expression made him feel like a child.

Cair suddenly realized. "You're using me."

Viess's lips curled into a smile.

It made Cair laugh. Hard enough he pushed back from the table. He said, "Xylan won't come for me. You can't trap him through me!" He felt better enough that he reached for a drink.

She had not killed his husband. Xylan had gotten away from Viess. Now all Cair needed was confirmation that Rismo, Belin, and Rhil had gotten away, too.

"The Jedi will come," Viess said almost delicately. Testing him.

"I don't work with Jedi."

Now it was Viess's turn to laugh. "You projected Avar Kriss's face to countless citizens across Nihil space. Don't tell me you don't work with Jedi."

"We have similar goals: namely, getting rid of you." Cair grinned. He pulled the redglass noodles closer to himself and lifted a forkful directly from the platter.

Viess watched him. "I think I must know the Jedi better than you."

"That's easy because I don't know them at all," he snapped, sticking to his story. Besides, Xylan wouldn't come for him, and the Jedi had no reason to. His story was true. Her trap wouldn't work.

"They will come—Avar Kriss and her good ally Porter Engle, with whom I have some unfinished business." Viess smiled.

Cair nearly startled at the mention of Porter Engle, but before he could answer, Viess's comlink beeped and she casually thumbed it.

"Report." She smiled at Cair as if she already knew what was to come.

"General, the Lightning Crash is under attack. Permission to assist."

Viess paused. She stared at Cair, then shrugged one shoulder. "Do whatever you like."

"But Gen—"

She cut off the protest by thumbing off her comlink.

Cair did his best not to gape. "Don't you want to protect the Stormwall?"

"Why?"

Honestly, every answer Cair could think of was pure scum villain reasoning.

"If it . . . goes down, the Republic will evict you from Naboo, for sure."

"I don't care about Naboo, child. It's just another rich world from which I can take what I wish and go." Viess sipped her drink. "The Lightning Crash merely powers the Stormwall. It doesn't control the technology. Even if something happens to the power relays temporarily, Ro will have his Stormwall back up."

"Without power?"

Viess shrugged elegantly. "Don't assume this attack on the Lightning Crash will be successful until it is. The Jedi rats that have been slinking back and forth to help you have hardly been able to establish any foothold in the Occlusion Zone, and they definitely cannot have created any kind of alliance of oppressed worlds," she said with scorn. "I run a tight slice of galaxy, and what leaks there are I am currently in the process of plugging up." Viess smiled at him.

Cair wasn't shocked at her arrogance. It was the lack of respect for her enemy that surprised him. If spying on the Grafs for years had taught him anything, it was to always assume they'd find a way to get something done if they were desperate or being paid enough. Even if Viess didn't expect the Jedi and Republic to be desperate enough to move stars, surely she should have backup plans in place if they did.

Cair would have made all his warlord plans based on the assumption that the RDC would figure out how to penetrate the Stormwall immediately.

They sat again in silence, but for the clink of Viess's crystal pick against porcelain. Each gentle tone made Cair feel sicker and sicker. Like waiting for the pick to scratch out his eyes, one slow scrape at a time. He'd bet Viess had scratched out eyes before, and maybe even eaten them. Cair pushed away the thought, focusing instead on the rhythm, wishing he could strum at his dulcimer. Or any dulcimer.

By the Force, he hoped Xylan was safe. And his allies. He wondered where the uncles were, and that spitfire Jordanna Sparkburn, the San Tekka cousin he'd worked with last year. He stared at the cuff bound tightly around his wrist stump, remembering the sickening moments before she had sliced off his hand to save his life.

Anything to focus on other than the moment.

"General Viess." Her comlink blared without warning. "A Republic fleet has appeared in the atmosphere!"

The Mirialan slammed her glass down hard enough that the stem shattered. She touched the comlink. "Say again, Krivlid? The Storm-wall remains functioning?"

"Yes, General, the Stormwall beacons are fully functional."

"Then where did these ships come from?"

"We don't know!"

Viess narrowed her eyes at Cair. "Send the beacon. How many ships are—"

Before an answer got through, the heavy real-wood doors of the room suddenly blasted open.

The smell of scorched wood filled Cair's nose as he struggled to stand and turn, given the state of his bruised and battered body.

Viess was already on her feet, unsheathing her sword with a fast *shick* of metal. Her teeth were bared as she looked at their intruder. "I told you, child, they'd come for you," she said, voice dripping with derision.

A Jedi filled out the doorway: broad shoulders and a large belly, dressed in dark robes and leather, his white skin drawn around his mouth in determination. Skull bulges, one eye covered by a worn patch, lightsaber. Ikkrukkian.

"I haven't come for him, Viess. I've come for you," Porter Engle said in a rumbling, soft voice.

"Engle," the general hissed.

Cair didn't even think. He leapt over the table and grabbed the general's shell pick. He dashed for her, flicking the sharp end out. She frowned as she turned to him in surprise, and the blade nicked her neck under her ear. Blood blossomed, but the general punched his gut with her sword hand, the pommel lending strength to the hit.

Cair fell back, landing hard on his knee and hip. Bile choked him and he spit it out, his gut heaving. He still had the pick in hand and pressed himself to his knees.

Porter Engle stood calmly with his lightsaber aglow, casting a blue glare over his hardened features.

Viess spun around behind Cair and wrapped her arm around his neck. "I'll kill him gladly. Back off."

"I thought you wanted to face me," the Jedi said.

"I could snap his neck and still do so," she said.

Cair went limp, all his weight dropping instantly. Viess stumbled, and he twisted his torso, elbowing her in the ribs.

Viess cursed and shoved him away—just as the hum of a lightsaber sounded near his head.

Cair rolled away in time for Engle's lightsaber and Viess's blade to clash. They threw each other back.

General Viess laughed as she rushed for Engle again.

Cair rubbed his aching neck and looked at the battered door. There were definitely better places he could be if this was a liberation. Or even if it was a trap.

Chapter Twenty-Seven

CORUSCANT

Chancellor Lina Soh waited alone but for the twin targons seated one to each side of her desk. Waiting alone was not the most politic option. There were senators, aides, friends, both with her and against her, for whom the outcome of this distant battle mattered just as greatly. Perhaps there was no one in the entire Senate building who was not fully invested in the moment.

But Lina had lost some polish in the past two years, especially when it came to controlling her facial expressions. As she waited, listening to the mission chatter transmitted directly to the personal comm unit in her office, she could let her brow furrow, her lips pinch. She could delicately hold her fingers steepled against her temples. She could reach for the thick ruff of Matari's mane and stare fixedly at the rigid way Voru held herself. The two massive cats were as tense as Lina herself, thanks to their bond. She didn't need to do more than release a soft hiss of unease at the calls of pilots between Skywing and Vector, at Kronara's gruff commands, and her targons leaned closer to support her.

It was all right, because she was alone, for Lina Soh to flinch when she heard the staticky voice of Jedi Master Elzar Mann, thin and distant. It was fine for him to be out with the fleet, taking this shot after his last failed attempts to end the Stormwall. He was a Jedi. He belonged with the fight. Lina hadn't said anything to Elzar when he left, but she suspected that if this attack had not succeeded, if the fleet had slammed into impenetrable gravitational distortions again, crashed against the rocks of Marchion Ro's arrogance *again,* Elzar Mann wouldn't allow himself to return to this office, whether he died in the fight or not.

For a moment, the sounds of battle blipped out, and Chancellor Soh closed her eyes. It didn't mean anything bad. Communications relays struggled through the Stormwall despite the so-called home key working to create paths for information to travel as well as ships. That the small fleet had pierced the Occlusion Zone at all, that this battle chatter could make it to her office was thanks to weeks of tireless work by so many people, but most recently that little miracle worker Avon Starros.

A ferocious warmth burned in Lina's chest when she let herself think about Avon. Fifteen, clever, determined, and angry. When the girl had first returned to Coruscant along with multiple Jedi and reams of information about the Stormwall, Lina had interviewed her privately. Avon hadn't flinched, not in the grand audience chamber, not under Lina's scrutiny. Instead, the girl had asked if she could pet the targons.

Allowing it, Lina had asked why Avon had left her mother.

"I suppose you don't want to hear about how awful the Nihil are and that I'd rather work for people doing the right things," Avon practically sneered, her shoulders hunched as she scratched Voru.

"If it's true, I don't mind hearing it," Lina answered lightly.

Avon snorted but paused before she added anything. "I don't want my mother to find me."

The words struck directly through Lina's heart. She'd give almost anything to find her own missing son. "We certainly won't hand you over or use your relationship against each other," she said slowly. "But,

Avon, if you work here, with us, even given an assumed identity and all the technology and power I have, you may be—will be—recognized. If your priority is safety or escape, you shouldn't help us."

"Why would you say that?" Avon crossed her arms over her chest.

"Because it's true."

"Well, I do mind hearing it," Avon said.

Lina had laughed. Quietly but honestly.

The mission chatter flooded back with a pop, and Lina sat up.

"Shields on Lightning Crash are down, *Crescent Blaze* removing final remaining Nihil."

"Capture them if—" Elzar Mann's voice cut in and out again.

Lina held her breath. She forced her hands flat against Matari so she didn't pull on the targon's fur. She could hear the burst of sudden cheers outside her office.

Then—

"—down. Heaven and seven hells of Ryloth. It's down."

Lina was on her feet, lightheaded with the surge of triumph.

A pounding on her office door saw both targons raise their hackles, but they only stood, tails snapping. "It's fine," she soothed, then called more loudly, "Come."

Her door swept open, and Vice Chancellor Larep Reza strode in with a grin. He said, "It worked."

Lina swept her hand across her comm panel, shutting down the relay. She'd wait for Admiral Kronara's official call, knowing he had plenty of immediate after-action items to attend to, including giving the secondary strike fleet waiting just outside the Chommell sector the go-ahead to jump to Naboo. "I was listening," Lina said, letting herself smile back at Reza. His finlike antennae flickered back and forth in his excitement.

Behind him several senators clapped one another on the back as aides rushed about. Lina said, "I want to hear the chatter from Naboo."

"The fleet under Captain Ba'luun reported engagement several minutes ago. We'll get the channel."

"Good. Is the *Pearl of Faretta* still in orbit?"

"It is, Chancellor," Reza said, almost viciously. Ghirra Starros had been waiting for permission to dock on Coruscant for hours.

"Good. Keep the comms interdiction around her ship. When this is over, I'd like to speak directly with Minister Starros."

Chapter Twenty-Eight

The *Harmonic* and the *Axiom* slipped out of hyperspace moments before they were followed by the *Tractate*.

Drop ships filled with RDC members, Vectors, and teams of Skywings from each cruiser flooded the atmosphere of Naboo as soon as their mother ships settled. The pale RDC cruisers turned to face the general's new flagship, *Precipitate Fire,* and open their full range of cannons and railguns against it.

Avar's stomach dropped out of her body as her Vector fell through the layers of Naboo's atmosphere. She held her position at the nose of one of the drop ships, ready to fend off any cannon fire once they broke through the clouds above Theed.

As the Vector Drift darted over the city, Avar listened with one ear to the Skywing chatter, angling the Vectors east as instructed. She flew them around a spire of glinting marble, and the drop ships landed on a stretch of open courtyard.

"Incoming!" Vernestra called through the open comm channel. "Nihil from point-nine-four."

"And point-six-two," Jedi Knight Far Linghe added as they pulled alongside Avar. She knew them by reputation only, but that reputation was centered on strong piloting and dedication, so they'd ended up on Avar's ground team.

"Let's get to work," Avar said, briefly letting her thoughts land on Elzar and his team, doing their own work. She closed her eyes and hoped he was fully open to the Force. Then Avar refocused and let her connection to the living Force expand, reaching each of the Jedi in their individual Vectors. She felt readiness, anticipation, sharpened nerves, hope as she lashed them all together. The Jedi flew in perfect sync, diving around to face the scrambling Nihil ships.

They split apart like a widening jaw around the Nihil—two Strike-ships and three larger Cloudships, cannons blazing.

"Knock them out if you can," Avar said. "Let's chase them off Naboo for good."

A Naboo starfighter burst violently into Avar's path, shooting at her.

Avar rolled to dodge, reaching with the Force: It was a Nihil pilot-ing it. "They've commandeered Naboo planetary defenses," she con-firmed fast. They'd expected it. "But don't attack anyone you aren't sure is Nihil until they shoot first."

"Copy," came multiple replies.

Avar listened hard to the Force, following the song as it pulled her in different directions. She lost herself in the focus, in the stretch to keep the Jedi with her connected: fire, dodge, pull-pull-pull her wings along with her. The comms from the RDC cruisers blared constantly in her small cockpit as she hunted.

Nihil drove hard at them, and as one dove under Avar's belly, she could feel the ragged bass scream of its music.

The Vectors shifted and swooped, returning fire. From outside it would look like chaos, but Avar felt the tightness of it.

To her left a dome exploded: Marble shrapnel and plumes of flame flared at them, and Avar shielded her eyes. She set her Vector into a spin straight through the smoke. Reaching with the Force, she felt obstructions and danced around them, tucked and spun to shoot at the Nihil suddenly behind her.

High above, the *Axiom* and its Skywings successfully destroyed a bank of laser cannons on the general's *Precipitate Fire.* Cheering echoed in Avar's ears.

"Has anyone located the general?" Avar demanded. "Is she on her ship?"

"Negative, Master Kriss, *Axiom* has no confirmation of Viess's location."

"She won't hide," came Bell's voice, and Burry's agreeing cry.

Avar pulled them around for another sweep.

Cannons from the roof of a long crenellated building shot at them. Avar gritted her teeth as she turned her Vector around tighter than her body should have handled, but handle it she did. The Nihil gunners saw her bearing down on them and fled in every direction. She blasted the cannon itself, let the Nihil flee. There was nowhere for them to go.

Smoke billowed from the streets and towers of Theed.

She watched as a Nihil ship turned fire not to the Vectors or Skywings, but back onto the city itself. The Nihil fighter blasted at a row of what looked like housing, and there Avar spied another Nihil fighter with its tail exploded twist its lurching descent to purposefully land in a garden.

"They've started wide destruction," she told everyone. "We need to get them away from civilians if we can."

Just then Captain Ba'luun's voice came over the comm. "Nihil chatter indicates the general is onworld. We're engaging the *Precipitate Fire.*"

Other calls came from Vector to Vector:

"—hearing the general isn't in the city—"

"—let's get to—"

Avar breathed and focused. The details were extraneous. She wasn't commanding from the bridge of one of the cruisers. This time she was a tool—a weapon. Find the general, take her down, and stop the Nihil from hurting people.

She sliced through a spray of Nihil blasts, and her Vector took a hit, the whole ship trembling. Avar felt it in her bones. A cry echoed in her mind, and she heard Jedi Knight Aviay yell, "Ejecting!"

"Tracking you," Far Linghe said from the next Vector, Aviay's partner since the Guardian Protocols went into effect.

The Drift burst in coordinated motion to break out, spin, and reform around the missing Vector. Avar didn't let go of Aviay's connection, even as she drove the Drift around toward the Nihil ship that shot him down. When she felt the relief as Aviay touched safely to the street, she passed it to the rest.

Avar reached out, seeking a new target.

"There," she said, tugging on the Jedi's awareness toward a midsized Nihil ship letting loose on gorgeously carved statues holding up a bridge. "Split out," she said as she and Bell and Burry peeled off from Linghe and Vernestra, shooting fast toward the Nihil vessel.

Avar didn't hesitate to fire, and Bell and Burry followed suit. They strafed the Nihil vessel, and it shot up and around the bridge support, using the massive statues as a shield. Avar gritted her teeth and wordlessly let the other two know her plan.

They moved in tandem: Avar heading into the Nihil's path of fire, focus narrowed to the tiny motions that let her dodge individual blasts, so fast to the naked eyes of the Nihil it must look like she was being caressed by their weaponry. They fired faster, leaning their vessel toward her, its nose dipping. Everything else fell away from Avar but the Nihil and streaks of destructive energy coming at her again and again and again.

She didn't fire, just let her Vector list suddenly, as if disabled. The Nihil continued to shoot, and she dodged, nosing back up to come at them. The Nihil ship emerged just enough from behind the bridge's supports in order to destroy Avar's Vector—

Immediately Bell and Burry swooped from behind with their cannons hot, catching the Nihil ship as they screamed past. The Nihil ship's engine burst into sparks, and the ship dove hard toward the water.

Avar spun around behind them. "Good job," she said, watching the Nihil ship careen into the water. Two little figures leapt away, falling into the water, too.

"Let's get back to—"

Avar was interrupted by a blare from the open comm: "Master Kriss!"

She blinked, slammed the comm, and aimed her Vector up and up. "What?"

"This is Blue Six, from the Skywings! We've encountered local resistance who report General Viess ignored the royal palace base and has her people across the big lake on an island compound. My squad is heading out."

"Go," Avar said. "We'll follow. Burry, Bell, Vernestra, with me! Linghe, stick with Aviay."

She felt them acknowledge through the Force, even as their voices came through the comms.

The blue sky glared ahead, and behind her Avar felt the battle—felt the glee and fear and pain mingling in the city, relief and overwhelming excitement. It boiled in her blood, and Avar had to tamp it all down to hold focus.

Bell Zettifar's and Burryaga's Vectors appeared on each side, flanking Avar. Vernestra pulled up behind. The four charged away from Theed, letting the chatter from the fight fade behind them.

The ground sped beneath Avar, streaks too fast to identify as trees or roads or towns. Her Vector shot out over cliffs striped with waterfalls, and over the broad expanse of a massive lake. There ahead, her Vector chirped at her, was the San Tekka compound, domes stacked upon cliffs, layers of vivid flowering gardens, a great elegant comm array at the crown, and all of it decorated with General Viess's insignia flapping on emerald-green flags.

And a huge blue eye of the Nihil had been scrawled over the main dome.

"Vectors, Blue Squadron, I'll cover the outside," Avar said. "The rest of you get inside and see if you can find General Viess. And remember, she'll probably have the Nameless with her."

"This is Blue Six acknowledging, Jedi. All four of us Skywings should be clear of the Nameless effect."

"Good," Avar said. "And—"

"Master Kriss!" Captain Ba'luun's voice thundered over the comm. "The Stormwall is down! We're detecting low-level electromagnetic charges from areas known to have stormseeds, and—"

Ba'luun's voice cut off in a shriek of static, and Avar stopped breathing. She opened her mouth to call, but the captain's voice burst back midcurse.

"Can't do that! The *Precipitate Fire* is defending itself while maintaining close orbit. Seems to confirm they're waiting for something—likely for the general herself to get out. Keep a lookout for escaping ships."

"Acknowledged, Ba'luun," Avar said. "We'll keep cleaning up down here."

"Belay that," said the rough voice of Captain Mitker of the *Harmonic*. "Three large Nihil Stormships jumped into the system, weapons hot."

Alarm washed through Avar, but she turned her attention to the Jedi at her flanks. "Bell, Burry, Vernestra, can you handle things down here? I'll take the other Vectors up to the battle."

"We've got it, Master Kriss," Bell said.

"May the Force be with you," Avar said and pushed out a note of confidence through their connection. The three other Vectors dropped low while Avar pushed hers in a wide upward trajectory to cover them as she shot for the stars.

Chapter Twenty-Nine

NABOO, INSIDE THE OCCLUSION ZONE

Cair San Tekka dashed directly for the great library five floors down from the private dining room. He stumbled more than he ran, given the bruises up and down his body, his lightheadedness, and some leftover disorientation.

The hallways were wide and not very full. He could hear Nihil yelling, and maybe—maybe—that roll of thunder was the start of a battle far across the great lake at Theed. He paused, but heard nothing else except for his pulse and harsh breathing. His ribs ached. He pressed against them and kept going.

A San Tekka attendant saw Cair and widened his eyes.

"What are you doing here?" Cair demanded. "I told you all to go!"

"We didn't listen, sir, some of us, at least." The man lifted his whole posture with dignity. "This is our home."

Cair gaped but didn't have time to do anything but react. "Does that mean Ino'olo is in the compound still?"

"I believe so, but I don't know where."

"All right." Cair nudged the man on. "Tell anybody you see to stay out of the Nihil's way. The Republic is here. Now isn't the time to get hurt with heroics."

"Yes, sir, but, sir . . ." The slightly older man frowned. "Aren't you . . . where are you going?"

"Heroics," Cair said with a hysterical laugh as he took off again.

The sound of blasterfire startled him, but it was clearly coming from a different level of the compound. He burst into the library, shoving the door open with his shoulder, to find it trashed. Books and treasures collected over generations thrown around, shelves pushed over, and somebody had apparently set fire to one of the reading sofas several days ago. The blackened furniture stank but didn't smolder anymore, thanks to the puddles under the little carved feet.

Cair pushed through the waste, hoping it could all be salvaged, and reached the old-style hearth. He slammed his fist on the marble pine seed carved into the glittering granite, and the carving shifted. For a moment nothing happened. Cair heard the telltale whine of fighters screaming past outside.

The hearth shuddered then, and a panel next to it opened up in the wooden wall. Cair dove through. He hit his sore wrist stump against the lighting panel, and the tunnel flickered to blue-white life.

Cair took the narrow stairs as fast as he could, spiraling down and down. When he reached the landing, it opened up into a relatively small, hidden storage room.

But Cair grinned in satisfaction. This part of the library collection was dedicated to one thing: weapons.

In the open atrium of the main San Tekka tower, Porter Engle seethed through his teeth as he shifted his weight to catch Viess's *beskar* sword against his lightsaber again.

The blade crackled. Viess laughed, her face screwed up in glee.

She pressed in, and Porter flung himself around with a Force-supported spin. He was behind her so fast nobody should've been able to keep up, but Viess and Porter had been fighting this duel for so many decades. She knew his style.

When Viess blocked him again, Porter leaned away, striking out with his leg. Viess dodged again but had to scramble back.

Turning, Viess leapt onto the wide marble rail of the atrium's balcony. Porter jumped after her, and she attacked. He danced back, meeting her strike for strike. His blood pumped hot in his old veins. The Force was a blade to Porter Engle, and in his hands it was always sharp. He didn't laugh back at Viess—he wouldn't give her anything anymore. It was time for this to end between them.

At the same time Porter pressed his attack, he brought the Force itself to bear, and with a wide cutting gesture from his free hand, he sent it flying at his old enemy.

Viess stumbled, caught herself in a twirl, and flipped off the balcony.

She fell, landing hard, but on her feet. She glared up at him, wiping blood from her mouth.

Porter jumped down. He didn't need to flip or do anything fancy, just let the Force guide him. He landed strong on both feet, lightsaber held in one hand, the other making a fist.

"Ah, Engle, it's so good to do this again." Viess grinned, blood smearing her teeth.

He didn't answer with anything but his attack.

"I stayed here waiting for you, let my people know I'd enjoy the rich trappings of Naboo for a little while," she continued, rushing to meet him. "This manor with its fancy rooms and slippery spies has been a good place to bait my trap."

"You didn't need bait, Viess. I'd come for you if you were the last being in the system." He said it calmly, stating a fact.

Viess barked a laugh. "I know you better than that. Bait makes you eager, makes you jump in when I want you to, not when it's best for whatever plan you might make."

Porter shrugged and shoved the Force at her. She braced, leaning into his power with her sword blade angled at him as if it could cut the strength of the Force like water. Porter stepped closer. Then again. He pressed inexorably toward her.

"You've been hunting me, too," Viess said, "leaving little marks of yourself in places I've been or might return to. A fast-moving Jedi ghost, Porter. I like it."

Porter grunted, turning into a strike she barely dodged, skidding back across the marble gallery.

Then she ducked and twisted her blade, light flashing along it, directly at his eyes. Porter flinched away but his power remained steady. He kept moving toward her. Eventually she'd have to let him through, back off, or pull another trick. He reached for the Force again, eager to slam her into that wall just behind her.

But the Force didn't answer his summons.

Instead, a wave of something prickled down Porter's spine. Cold, sticky.

He swallowed a surge of hot bile.

Fear.

He hadn't . . . Porter clenched down on his control. His hand on his lightsaber hilt trembled once.

The light did not waver.

The Force, though, the Force was *gone.*

He knew what this was.

All the hair on his body seemed to rise.

Porter let go, stopped grasping, and sidled left, away from the— nothing.

General Viess's bright-green eyes widened. "No!" she yelled.

Every fiber of the Ikkrukkian's being told him to turn around, to look, to see it, that if he looked, it would be there. But a tiny part of him hissed and whispered no: *No, no, no, nonononono! If you don't look, it might not be there, you'll be fine.*

The tiny child left in his mind after so many years of life was terrified.

Porter drew a deep breath, pretending he drew on the Force, too. He held his gaze on Viess: He knew her. Knew what she was. She couldn't scare him.

Except white shadows tickled around her, her hair turned white, her eyes sank in—no, not her eyes, Porter saw a different face holding a sword against him. His—

No.

"Get those things out of here," she shrieked, a death's-head of rotting skin, hair falling out in chunks, lips torn and dripping slow ichor. "He's mine and I don't need them—get out!"

Porter lowered a shaking hand.

Barash, no—

"Fight, old man!" she screamed.

Her sword jabbed into the meat of his shoulder, pain clarifying his attention. Porter gasped.

"If you don't fight, I'll gut you here and now, and we'll both be disappointed," Viess said, snarling.

Then, as suddenly as it appeared, it was gone.

The fear—gone. The trickling cold on his skin—gone.

The Force screamed back to him like a punch to the sternum, and Porter choked in a huge breath.

Laughing, General Viess flung herself at him, and Porter turned, lightsaber up. Only instinct saved him.

As he blocked her, Nihil yelled from beyond the evergreen trees potted along the atrium colonnade.

"Republic soldiers!" one called.

Another said, "Jedi!"

Porter ignored it. He let himself grin at Viess. She could have had him if she'd let those creatures distract him. Better for her if she had. Now he could fight at full strength. And now he knew something else about General Viess: She was too proud for her own good.

With a roar he flung himself back into the fight.

Burryaga pushed out of his Vector and hit the ground with a crunch. They'd landed just outside a hangar bay, and the ground was littered with glass and dirt and shrapnel from exploding windows and a Nihil fighter the RDC Skywings had brought down to clear the path for the Vectors.

He strode toward the garage-level entrance to the San Tekka compound, knowing that if he ran, neither Bell nor Vernestra could keep up.

Two people burst out, and Burry had his hand on his lightsaber, but they flung their hands up in panic.

Burry yelled at them to leave, hoping the meaning came across alongside his urgency.

The humans skittered back, clearly still afraid. Burry lifted his lightsaber, pausing so they didn't think he was attacking.

"Jedi!" one of them said, and grabbed her companion in obvious relief.

Burry nodded and gestured for them to keep going.

"There are maybe twenty Nihil with the general," the woman hurried to tell him. "And they have two of those monsters! The Jedi eaters!"

"The general is inside?" Bell said, coming up beside Burry. He unsheathed his lightsaber, too.

With him was Vernestra Rwoh, her shoulders heaving with breath and her lightsaber already burning violet.

"Yes!" the other human said. "She was up in the main family tower!"

Vernestra nodded quickly. "Get to safety," she said to the humans. "With anyone else you come across."

"Let's go," Bell said, taking over the lead.

Burry followed at his heels. They had to dodge a few more people running out as they climbed up into the main compound.

"If you get too close," Vernestra said, "it's debilitating. Have either of you felt the Nameless before?"

Burry shook his head but then nodded.

Bell said, "I have. I . . ." He shook his head. "Let's go."

"We need to keep the RDC with us," Vernestra said as she glanced back. "Here they come, from Blue Squadron."

The pilots caught up, blasters at the ready. "I'm Tenedra," said a Tholothian woman with her head-tendrils tucked under a uniform cap. "We've got you covered."

Burry pushed at Bell.

"Yeah, let's go," Bell said.

They charged in.

Burry ignited his lightsaber at the first sign of Nihil, moving steadily toward them. He moved his blade almost lazily to catch their haphazard blasterfire. They were anxious, he could feel it. Anxious and aggressive.

"Here," Bell said, pushing at the Nihil with the Force. It sent one slamming into a wall, and Burry punched another in the head. They needed to keep moving, avoid the Nameless, push past the random Nihil to find the general if they could. Capture her. That was the mission here. Vernestra darted ahead of them, turning down a broad corridor flooded with sunlight. It opened into a courtyard filled with hanging plants with vivid-pink blossoms and heady perfume.

But Burry stopped.

The courtyard was too dark.

It was cold.

He couldn't breathe.

He heard his name distantly.

Someone was calling for him.

From so far away they'd never find him in time. Waves crashed all around him, and screaming filled his ears.

He was the one sinking, far away.

Burryaga couldn't breathe. He was going to die down here, in this little dark cave, under the Eiram ocean. His chest hurt, his hands were numb with cold.

"Burryaga!"

They're coming to take you away.

He gulped a breath.

The Nameless.

They'd run directly into them.

Chapter Thirty

Cair was tired, and it was awkward carrying the load of weaponry and power cells he'd managed to secure. As he'd headed back to the main part of the compound to help, he'd shot two Nihil and given blasters and one long knife to a handful of San Tekka staff. Then they'd heard sounds of battle, blasters and screaming, and he'd raced into the fray.

Nihil and Republic fought in the center of the compound—he could see flashes of blasterfire glinting off the polished marble walls. Cair pushed himself harder and heard a worse sound: the mangled cry of one of those Nameless monsters.

Dashing across a wide landing, Cair heard General Viess's laugh and glanced down. She swung her sword at Porter Engle, who caught it. With a sweeping gesture, he shoved Viess away with the Force. She tumbled down half a flight of shallow stairs.

The blasterfire ahead drew Cair. Engle could handle Viess, but none of the Jedi could deal with the Nameless. Cair, though, could deal with Nameless and Nihil blasters one-handed. And a good thing, too. He pressed his lacking forearm to his stomach.

From behind him, more blasters fired. He dove forward and rolled, landing awkwardly thanks to the layers of weapons and equipment he'd strapped to his body and stuck in every possible pocket. With a grunt he scrambled up and raced ahead toward the strange roars of the Nameless.

Cair skidded into the atrium on a spin, shooting at the Nihil behind him with one of the blaster rifles strapped to his chest. He caught himself painfully on the marble wall with the stump of his hand, dodging fire that cracked the wall just over his head. Dropping to his knees, he shot the Nihil in the chest.

Behind him, screaming got his attention fast. He turned just in time to see a handful of Jedi and Republic pilots facing off against a few Nihil and two of those monsters.

The Nihil's backs were to him as they crouched behind an overturned side table for shelter.

Cair braced himself and shot one in the back.

The Nihil pitched forward, and his companion gaped back at Cair, raising a blaster but not fast enough. Cair shot that one right in the ugly mask.

A purple whip of light arced up, bright and crackling, and Cair raised his arm to block it. A Mirialan Jedi was lashing out with a long, flexible lightsaber, her mouth open in a silent cry. Cair *knew her.* Vernestra Rwoh!

Beside her, two other Jedi—a human and a Wookiee—struggled to face a second Nameless.

As the Nihil Cair shot fell, the RDC pilots who had huddled for cover behind a pillar dashed across the atrium and slammed into the side table previously occupied by the two now-dead Nihil. The RDC pilots turned to Cair as more Nihil ran up behind him. Cair dropped to the side for the pilots to shoot freely, calling, "Keep the Nihil pinned down!"

"The Jedi can't keep this up," came a desperate answer.

There was nothing for it: Cair holstered his blaster, then leapt forward and dove under Vernestra's purple Force whip. He aimed his shoulder for the Jedi's legs, knocking them out from under her.

She hit the floor hard, the whip flying from her hand. "Vernestra," he commanded, hoping it would bring her back to herself. He hadn't met her, but he knew her through his cousin Jordanna Sparkburn, and Xylan, too. "Come on, Vernestra," he repeated as she blinked up at him. Her eyes were dazed, but she focused.

Cair grabbed her around the waist and dragged her away. Away from the Nameless. He didn't know how far their power worked, where she needed to be so it wouldn't be so debilitating.

"Let me—" she gasped, pushing at him. Cair released her.

They dragged each other up, and Vernestra grabbed Cair's blaster from the holster and pointed it in the direction of the Nameless. Her arm was shaking too badly to aim.

"Here," Cair said. He used his elbow to prop her forearm, giving it a rest, a balance. And he lifted another blaster off his belt with his hand. "Together."

Burry knew he was on the surface of Naboo, on dry land, but his whole body shook with the need for air—just air! He had to breathe! He couldn't fight them if he couldn't breathe!

A purple whip spat across his vision. Vernestra.

He felt it then, their terror, too—Bell's and Vernestra's. He had to do something. Protect them, stop this—

Pain burned along his shoulder. He spun around, flinging out with a fist. He didn't hit anything. Bell, where was Bell—he wasn't next to Burry any longer. Burry couldn't feel either of them, he was alone. Alone again. Burry ignited his lightsaber and held it before him in both hands.

Bell cried out, and Burry *felt* his friend's pain.

Focused on the blue light, Burry looked for Bell, pulled on the Force—it was barely there, a trickle, a delicate thread ready to snap.

"No—stop!" Bell pled in a desperate tone that Burry had never heard.

There. Bell's hands were out defensively before him as he backed away from nothing Burry could see. The tips of the fingers on Bell's left hand were ashy, graying. The Nameless had him. The ash scoured up his wrists, cracking and crumbling—

No. Burry's real, sudden, desperate fear for Bell's life cut through the wave of the Nameless effect. He felt the fear everywhere, but he knew it was coming from . . .

right . . .

there.

Everything about the Nameless made it seem like a Jedi should leave, should run, get out of the way, but instead of doing any of that, Burry reached toward it.

He reached with that tiny thread of Force, and it vanished fast— swallowed into a screaming void, into a hunger so pure it became a single bright spot.

Burry stepped closer. His eyes burned, his throat was hot, and his heart beat so fast it hurt. His blood raced and his hair stood on end. But he felt it—the starvation and the need—and past the fear it was so, *so* hungry. Burry needed to help. He had what the being needed. He should give it: Giving was what Burry did, what he wanted, who he was. He should surrender because he was here and he could—the Force was with him. He could offer it . . . there . . . *there.*

Burry threw his lightsaber at it, thrusting the large blade away from him so it spun toward the pure, bright hunger.

The void of nothingness screamed around him—no Force, no oxygen—and Burry's knees wavered. He had to hold on. The Force— it couldn't be gone, it was just, it was only . . . Burry barely remembered the edges of himself.

His friend cried out hoarsely, but it was his—it was Bell, there—his friend. *Bell.* The edges of Bell were there, and then suddenly here, suddenly with Burry—flashes of terror and monsters—and it was so freezing. The fear raised his hackles. Burry pulled on it, the fear, because it was real—a feeling, a piece of being alive. He felt it drag toward him through the void, and not only Bell's fear but Vernestra's, too, a chasm of loss, both funneling into him. He didn't know what else was going on, he knew only this taking, this feeding.

Something hit him.

Blasterfire shot across his vision like a meteor storm as arms grabbed around Burry's waist, pulling him away. Burry felt a known presence, a person, his friend, he held on to Bell, and fear spasmed between them, vibrating so hot and high it burned. Burry's legs crumpled, they both fell. Burry smelled blood and then—

A shriek, a wet gurgle.

Burry shook his head, tried to lock down his emotions. Everything roiled around him—so many feelings—but he held on to Bell.

Friend, he tried to say around a thick tongue. Burry grasped at Bell's hand, at the hand he'd seen turning to ash.

Warm, brown knuckles and paler nail beds—unblemished and whole. Burry almost choked on his relief, a gasping, childlike, lost noise. It was all right.

Bell was panting beside him.

"I think—I think it's gone," Bell whispered. Burry felt a tremble through his friend's whole body. "It's not like—like—I saw Master—"

As the fog of Nameless terror finally dissipated, it was replaced by a different anxiety. Burry pushed to his feet. Bell came with him, sweaty and cold.

"Look," Vernestra said.

Burry looked at Vernestra and a human he'd never seen before standing behind her. Both of them were carefully retreating from a hunk of white bones, claws, tendrils, and huge milky-violet eyes. The dying—dead?—Nameless. The long hilt and wide crosspiece of Burry's lightsaber tilted against its remains, near singed skin and a cauterized wound.

Another Nameless sprawled nearby with raw blaster burns smoking from its barrel chest. Burry could see them.

They were dead.

Chapter Thirty-One

INSIDE THE OCCLUSION ZONE

Elzar swung his Vector around behind the careening escape pod and caught it in his ship's tractor beam as easily as hooking a snail fish in a tide pool. He'd been surprised to learn the Vectors on the *Third Horizon* had been retrofitted with tractor beams as possible deterrents against scav droids, but not as surprised as he was that the Lightning Crash even had escape pods. It wasn't exactly Nihil style. But then this station had been originally designed for Grafs. And escaping certainly did seem to be *their* style.

Only about six of the pods had launched from the station after the crystalline base had been destroyed, knocking out the power relays for the Stormwall. The Jedi hadn't had any trouble snagging them all.

Elzar could hardly believe how easy it had been. There had to be something else coming. Reinforcements, backup, some trap the Nihil had left behind. The RDC were being as cautious as possible while still moving fast, and Elzar instructed his Jedi to make sure to stay alert.

But still, the unusual feeling of success stuck in his throat as he led the handful of Jedi Vectors towing prisoners back to the bay of the *Third Horizon*. The rest patrolled the circumference of the Lightning

Crash, while Jedi Knights Pal Erlang and Striland Gryl flew through a hole blown into the hull in order to join the RDC teams sweeping the intact levels of the station to round up any surviving Nihil and take stock of casualties and salvageable data and tech.

Elzar commed to the launch bay of the *Third Horizon* and handed off the escape pod to the star cruiser's tractor beam. Then he maneuvered with a light touch through the narrow Vector corridor. Inside the *Third Horizon,* the corridor opened into a broader landing bay. He flew to the far berth, making room for the Vectors returning with him. After powering down and setting the fighter for the hangar crew to refuel it, Elzar grabbed his lightsaber and hopped out.

It didn't take long to jog up several levels to the bridge. Technicians hurried about making a few necessary repairs. Every station was full, though the crew who had gathered against the doors before were gone. Over on the Lightning Crash, presumably.

Elzar took a beat to feel the flow of the Force. It was good. Balanced if a bit harried in here. He strode into the thick of it, glad to see Keven Tarr huddled around the hyperdrive control station with an RDC researcher, pointing eagerly at various areas on a projected map of the Occlusion Zone. Or what used to be the Occlusion Zone, Elzar realized with a grin. Even when the Stormwall went back up under a new power source, as Graf had promised it would, they still had the home key and could get in anytime, anywhere. This changed the game. The wall would be more like a border, and even with the Nihil defending it as viciously as ever with their killzones and scav droids and the *Gaze Electric* itself, nobody could be trapped like Avar had been.

And now that the Lightning Crash was down, Elzar was eager to get to Naboo and join in that fight.

Admiral Kronara stood facing the wide viewport, looking out at the remains of the Lightning Crash. Beside him, Xylan Graf argued hard for something. Towing the space station wreckage, it sounded like.

"We will blow it to pieces once it's clear of sentients," the admiral said gruffly.

Xylan grimaced. "But what a waste of raw material, if nothing else."

Kronara shot Xylan a disbelieving look.

"Xylan," Elzar said as he reached them, "I'm surprised you didn't head over yourself to oversee the reclaiming of your proprietary tech."

"I'm smart enough to know the Republic will never hand any tiny bit of that station back into Graf possession." Xylan smiled. "Besides, I don't have many good memories from living in that place the past year and a half."

Kronara said, "It's not worth the risk of Ro taking this back from us and getting it up and running again. I prefer the simplicity of setting charges."

Before the obviously aggravated Graf could keep arguing, Elzar asked, "When do you think the Stormwall will go back up?"

"I'm surprised it's not back up already," Xylan said.

"What?" Kronara scowled. "That fast?"

Xylan waved a hand dismissively at the remains of the Lightning Crash. "Oh, it won't be the same. The power relay is shot, obviously. But the Stormwall originally ran power through the *Gaze Electric* itself. Once they get a new crop of those crystals set up somewhere else for a new array, they'll have it back at full power."

"Then—"

"But!" Xylan smiled with oozing charm. "Until then Ro shouldn't be able to maintain it at its former level or to the former extent. We should expect power fluctuations along the border, dispersed randomly among the stormseeds, and the like."

"Let's send some people to destroy as many buoys as possible," Elzar said grimly.

"Yes, absolutely," Xylan continued, but he wiped the smile off his face. "Look. We have weakened the Stormwall irreparably today."

"Because of the home key," Kronara said. "As long as we have it, we can get through no matter where the Stormwall goes up again."

"And we can share it with civilians," Elzar said.

"Admiral!" called one of the techs at the communications array.

"The *Harmonic* is reporting that three new Nihil Stormships jumped to Naboo!"

Elzar couldn't help glancing out at the stars in the direction he believed Naboo to be. *Avar.*

"You know," Xylan Graf said, a little too casually, "we don't have to be keeping an eye out for Ro or the *Gaze Electric* from here. Those incoming cruisers can babysit the ruins of the Lightning Crash and coordinate demolition efforts. Isn't this the flagship? It proves a whole slew of other interesting points if the *Third Horizon* is seen at Naboo."

Elzar wasn't the only person on the bridge to look at Xylan in confusion or suspicion. But just because it sounded uncharacteristically altruistic of him didn't mean he was wrong.

"Why not face off against Viess?" Xylan asked, saying the general's name with a gentle sneer. But Elzar could sense an urgency underneath the man's affected calm.

"The Nihil sent reinforcements," Elzar added, unable to pretend he wasn't eager to be back at Avar's side. Whatever Graf's motives were, Elzar had his own as well.

"Fine," Kronara said. "Ready a route to Naboo. As soon as the *Radical Sar* arrives here, they can pick up the rest of our stragglers and prisoners. Now leave me to my job, Graf."

Xylan bowed a little and turned away, but Elzar kept pace with him.

"Why are you so eager to go to Naboo?" Elzar asked as Xylan led him off the bridge.

Xylan eyed Elzar for a long moment. Judging him, it seemed. Elzar didn't mind. This wasn't a man whom Elzar needed to impress.

Xylan finally said, "My dog is there."

Elzar, listening with the Force, shook his head. "Maybe, but that's not the only reason."

"Does it matter? Do you think this is an elaborate trap?" The pitch of Xylan's voice was losing the edge of control.

"No." Elzar didn't think Xylan was setting them up. Not now, not anymore.

Xylan scoffed.

"It's not a weakness," Elzar said softly, catching Xylan's elbow so they both paused in the busy corridor. "Caring is what makes us different from the Nihil."

Suddenly, it hit Elzar hard that he was right. Care, love, compassion, hope—those were what separated the Nihil from the Republic. The Nihil from the Jedi. That part was so obvious everybody knew it. What hadn't been obvious to Elzar was the way he'd been resisting his own *good* emotions because caring so deeply had driven him to desperation and had made him so upset and furious that he let it consume him for the moment it took to murder Chancey Yarrow.

But it had also been caring that pulled him back. Caring, his connection to the light and goodness, made him know—not just believe but *know*—what was right. And that he'd been wrong. It was impossible to accept the strengths of love and hope without the weaknesses, too. But that was the delicate balance of the light.

He wanted to tell Avar. To ask her how she balanced it. He wanted to listen to her answer and accept her words. To hold her hand. To . . . hold her. All of her.

To Xylan Graf's scowling face, Elzar said, "There's someone on Naboo I care about, too."

Xylan slid him a disbelieving look. "You're a Jedi."

Elzar grinned and clapped him on the back. "Let's go get our people."

Chapter Thirty-Two

NABOO, INSIDE THE OCCLUSION ZONE

Avar angled her Vector as she pushed it into a steep climb up through Naboo's atmosphere. She focused hard as her Vector shot through thinning air, light pulling away to be replaced by the starfield. The scanners of Avar's Vector alerted her to the nearest Nihil cruiser. As she emerged fully from Naboo's atmosphere, she opened fire immediately.

She strafed the prow of a Nihil cruiser, dodging return fire in a darting, random pattern like a hopping cricket as she peeled around the long wing of the ship. She cut tight to its hull, continuing to fire.

Avar blasted away, gaining quick distance after distracting the cruiser to get into position. Currently only two RDC ships faced the *Precipitate Fire,* with the *Axiom* low over Theed, and three other Nihil cruisers that had jumped in.

Avar toggled to the RDC channel. "This is Jedi Master Avar Kriss, ready to assist."

"Hit the *Precipitate Fire* with all you've got," Captain Mitker of the *Harmonic* said. "Its fighters are ragged but have strong firepower. If you can take them out, we'd appreciate it. We've got reinforcements incoming, we just need to buy some time."

"Copy."

Avar opened her connection to the other Jedi in the Vectors that had remained up with the RDC ships—Ceryl and Dotdat San. "With me?" she asked them.

"On your mark, Master Kriss," Dotdat said.

"Here," Ceryl answered. Their songs reached back for her.

Avar gave herself to the Drift, uniting the three of them deeply enough that she could see flashes of their selves and memories: a new lightsaber, a kiss on the forehead, a glinting pink pond. Avar let them see her, too. Her confidence. "Let's get those fighters."

The three Vectors spun together, angling hard toward the *Precipitate Fire*. "There," Avar said, almost to herself, as she marked the enemy fighters and quickly engaged her Vector's targeting system. It was mostly just a visual aid to help her aim with the Force, and she appreciated it when everything was dark shapes against the starry infinite. "Disable the fighters when possible, but don't hold back against the cruiser," she said, opening fire.

They spread out, splitting around a midsized fighter as if it scared them off. Its fire bounced off the Vectors' shields, and all three suddenly snapped around, flying backward as they fired on the fighter. Ceryl's and Dotdat's Vectors aimed for engines, which flickered and exploded. Avar hit their forward cannon.

"Incoming," Dotdat said, and Avar let the Force guide her to what Dotdat saw. They arced in formation and charged.

For a while, Avar lost herself in the pull and give of the Force, the immediacy of battle: listen, reach, let the Force show the way, fire and re-form, scatter, push back, *be* the Drift, one with her tiny, sharp Vector.

They fought, diving, and veered too close to the *Precipitate Fire*—the cruiser moved, turning itself to fire on the *Tractate*. As it moved, it an-

gled its fire in a wide defensive swath. Avar called out just in time for
Ceryl to dodge, but the cruiser tapped her Vector's wing. Ceryl gasped
through the comm as her ship was knocked out of formation, spinning
and careening out of control.

"Avar," Dotdat said breathlessly.

"Go," Avar said.

The second Vector peeled off to follow Ceryl.

Avar broke the deep connection—they could manage themselves.
She shot over the bow of the *Precipitate Fire* and reached out. Just then
a ship exploded, the backlash in the Force hotter than any light or fire
Avar observed with her physical senses. Nihil. It had been Nihil. She
didn't have time to be relieved. The battle raged.

"Alert to all Republic ships," Captain Ba'luun said through the
comm. "Readings indicate the Stormwall is active. Repeat: The Stormwall is back."

Acknowledgments shot back—some frustrated, others distracted.

For a moment Avar hung in space, listening to the comm and the
Force. She felt—yes. Avar spun her Vector toward the *Tractate,* which
had suffered heavy damage. Several decks were visibly mangled, with
chunks of shrapnel torn off and flickering lights indicating power
losses. That was the ship the *Precipitate Fire* had turned toward. The
Nihil vessel opened fire again.

Two more Republic ships were engaged with the three Nihil ships.
Nobody could help the *Tractate* except Avar.

One Vector against a cruiser—even a damaged one—made for bad
odds.

But if she could just distract the Nihil ship, it would be enough.
And they only needed to survive long enough for the reinforcements.

Avar pulled back. She could do this. She'd spearheaded a Jedi team
to shift entire chunks of a broken ship out of danger, and together
they'd saved a container of people with nothing but determination and
the Force. She could do it. She could stop an entire Nihil battle cruiser
with only a single fully functioning Vector.

Because Avar had a wild idea.

And it was definitely the kind of thing Elzar Mann would do.

Burry gripped Bell's wrist as they stared at the dead Nameless.

One had been killed by Burry's incredible throw, the other shot with a blaster wielded by Vernestra and the human with messy hair. Though his entire being felt raw, Burry opened up to the Force, but with the death of those creatures, it flared all around him—life and growth, a forest of creeping vines and blossoming ground overtaking the cold marble atrium. He focused on Bell, who was clammy with sweat but still focused and aware.

Even though they'd defeated these two Nameless, their awful, twisted bodies felt out of place. Not quite wrong, but as though they didn't fit with the rest of the Force. Off center, out of alignment. Burry wasn't sure. And maybe he was just exhausted. The fear was so draining, so overwhelming. For Bell, it must remind him of Master Greatstorm. Burry couldn't help thinking of his own Master Nib's husked, ruined body. Of the images of Grand Master Veter's death. The things these creatures could do to the Force were so incomprehensibly wrong. Yet Burry felt a twinge of sympathy. It made his insides twist. He didn't want the feeling. He didn't want to care about these monsters. But dead like this, empty sacks of bones and ragged fur . . . he couldn't help it. They looked used. Abandoned.

Burry swallowed a choked groan. The urge to set them on fire or bury them or anything to give them a real memorial reared in his mind. He shook his head violently. What was wrong with him? They seemed so pathetic now. Yet the power they wielded . . .

"We still need to find Viess," Vernestra said wearily, startling Burry. He agreed vocally. That was their objective. Capture General Viess.

"Oh, I saw her fighting with Porter Engle," the human said. He was in black, covered in ammunition belts and several blasters. One hand was missing. His hair fell all over his face, even though it was obviously supposed to be in a topknot.

Bell blinked. "Porter Engle? Jedi Master Porter Engle?"

The human shrugged. "Yes?"

Bell pulled away from Burry but swayed in place. Burry grabbed him to hold him back.

Bell scowled. He shook Burry off.

"Are there more Nameless in the building?" Vernestra asked the human.

He shook his head. "Not that I know of."

The tight fist of anxiety squeezing Burry's chest relaxed slightly.

"Come on, you two," Vernestra said. "Cair San Tekka, lead the way."

The human—Cair—darted off. Vernestra said to the RDC pilots, "Secure this room, if you can. Anyone to spare, follow us."

The Tholothian pilot Tenedra nodded.

Burry glanced at Bell, whose breath was still coming too fast. He grabbed Bell's shoulder and told him to stay to secure the Nameless bodies and help the RDC. Then Burry followed Vernestra.

It didn't take long for them to dash through a wide corridor onto a landing between long curling flights of stairs. Below them, Burry heard the distinctive sound of a lightsaber whirring through the air. He leaned over the rail: There was a stout Mirialan in gleaming armor fighting Porter Engle, who was in plain gray robes, sweaty, and grimacing stubbornly.

A blaster shot out from their level, its energy bolt zipping across the air. It nearly hit the general in the head, but she dodged, spinning so her leg connected with Porter's. Porter jerked and dove in again with a thrust of his lightsaber.

"Kriff," Cair said, lowering his blaster. "Porter's in the way."

"It looks like they're well matched," Vernestra said. "Impressive considering Porter Engle's reputation. Let's go." She dashed down the stairs.

Burry drew the Force to him and hopped over the rail. His leap carried him down two flights, and he landed in a crouch, igniting his lightsaber. It flared to life, and he held it ready in both hands. Burry roared.

Vernestra's whip crackled to life, snapping in the air.

Porter kicked out, and Viess spun, punching him in the shoulder. Porter fell back several stairs but twisted in a quick motion to pin her against the rail, lightsaber caught against her sword. Burry realized the blade had to be made of *beskar* to withstand that. Viess smiled. Blood smeared against her white teeth. She glanced beyond her opponent to Burry and Vernestra, then her free hand twitched, fingers flicking. Something landed against Porter's stomach.

It exploded. A stun grenade of some kind, knocking Porter back. Burry caught him in one long arm, lifting his massive lightsaber out of the way.

Another explosion rocked them, and Burry heard a huge stone crack.

Vernestra cried, "Look out!"

A statue fell from an alcove high up the wall. Burry and the others dove away just as the statue hit the marble floor and shattered into sharp chunks. More rumbling followed.

"Viess is gone! She collapsed the hallway behind her," Cair said.

Burry looked—it was true. Dust and rubble fell out of the corridor where Viess had fled.

"She ran, that coward," Porter said, then spat dust and blood onto the floor. "I won't let her get away."

"There's still a chance we can cut her off. Follow me," Cair said, then dashed through another doorway.

Chapter Thirty-Three

NABOO, INSIDE THE OCCLUSION ZONE

Cair ran as hard as he could, shedding a few layers of power cells in his wake. His comlink was shot or lost—who knew?—so he couldn't call Ino'olo or anybody to try to cut the general off. The direction she'd taken led toward several destinations, but he was betting all his chips on the main port. If the Nihil hadn't abandoned all their ships, she could find a ride off the island or the planet itself.

Pressing his arm to his aching ribs, Cair pushed himself faster. Behind him, he heard the others running. The Wookiee caught up as Cair grabbed a doorjamb to help careen himself around a corner.

"I think she'll go for the ships!" he yelled, and the Wookiee yelled back. Cair had no idea what the response was, other than some kind of agreement, because the Wookiee kept on going.

"This way." Cair grabbed at the flapping robe as the Wookiee Jedi moved too far ahead.

Tugging, Cair led the Wookiee into a side door and down a tiny staircase more like a ladder than any of the grand marble they'd seen before. It opened two flights below into a corridor used by service personnel and droids. It was wide and plain, built for loads of goods being moved into the manor.

They ran, but the Wookiee said something that was clearly angry when he saw they were aiming for a solid steel wall ahead.

"It's a lift up to the dock," Cair panted.

Just before reaching the turbolift, Cair glanced back. Sure enough, Porter and Vernestra were keeping up, too, as were a few RDC pilots with their blasters out. The Wookiee slammed his hand on the lift panel a little too hard, but the doors parted, and the whole party piled inside. Cair punched in the command with his wrapped wrist. The lift hummed, the ceiling parted, and the floor lifted quickly into the daylight.

The Wookiee Jedi and Porter Engle didn't hesitate. They both grunted with the effort but leapt high with the Force, and their lightsabers ignited before anybody's heads had cleared the ground level. Cair for his part crouched, and the RDC pilots did, too, in a defensive formation.

Above, the vivid hiss of lightsabers rang out, and Cair saw blasterfire—but not much.

Vernestra said to him, "You can stay back."

Cair shook his head.

They cleared the floor, and Vernestra sprang forward, her lightsaber flashing.

Two destroyed Nihil ships smoked on the ground. Some San Tekka skimmers awaited repairs just to the side. Cair dove for them, and a few RDC pilots followed.

"She's in that yacht!" Porter Engle yelled.

Cair looked from the cover of a skimmer's tail. Viess was in Cair's fancy Averis Starburst model. The wings shifted with takeoff prep, and the engine flared bright white.

The Wookiee Jedi roared, shutting off his lightsaber. He ran for one of the skimmers—a two-person pleasure vessel good on land or low over the lake.

"That can't keep up with my ship," Cair said. He pointed back at the yacht and got to a knee to begin firing.

"Surely she can't get far in that," Vernestra said. "Does it even have a hyperdrive? We'll comm up and they'll be waiting for her."

Cair grimaced and shot her an apologetic look. "Shoot out the tail—that's where the hyperdrive is!"

Vernestra and Porter ran for the yacht.

But the Wookiee called out, and Porter stopped, whirled around, and dashed back with an incredulous but eager look.

The two Jedi reached toward the second skimmer, and instead of getting in it, they lifted it into the air. Vernestra caught on and flung out her hands, helping them. The Starburst yacht lifted off with a low whine, immediately turning.

Together the Jedi *threw* the skimmer at Cair's yacht.

Cair held his breath.

The skimmer crashed into the yacht's belly, tearing off its landing gear even as it withdrew. A shriek of metal and sparks rained down, but the yacht kept rising. The skimmer hit the dock and snapped violently in half. Sparks flared and drops of some fluids rained down.

"Again!" Porter yelled.

Cair winced, eyes on the yacht. It was built for pleasure, not battle, thank the Force, or the general might've turned cannons onto them. He stood, watching it rise.

The Wookiee groaned with effort as the Jedi tried once more, with half the skimmer. It moved fast as they flung it, but Cair could see the tremble in their control. The aim was off.

The bright-blue Naboo sky glared back as half of the skimmer arced away and hit the first roof of the storage bay, crunching panels.

The yacht angled away, hot and wobbling, then quickly darted into the atmosphere.

The Wookiee sank exhaustedly to his knees, but Vernestra dug out her comlink and yelled into it, "Master Kriss! The general took off in a personal yacht! She's headed up! Master Kriss, do you read?"

Standing beside Cair, the Tholothian pilot urgently relayed the same message to the Republic fleet at large. Cair didn't hold out much hope. It was a fast ship, and if the general didn't care where she fled to, the navicomputer could calculate a jump in seconds.

He should have listened to Xylan and—

Cair let out a whoop of realization. "There's a tracker!" he cried, laughing. "There's a tracking beacon on that yacht!"

"—headed up!" Vernestra's voice filled Avar's Vector. "Master Kriss, do you read?"

Avar breathed deeply, pulling all the strength from the Force that she could. Her hands held like cups over her lap. She didn't have a moment to respond. The *Tractate* didn't have a moment, and Avar couldn't let the *Precipitate Fire* go, especially not if Viess could escape on it.

Avar listened to the great, ringing song of the Force. She sang with it, softly at first, coaxing, and then let her connection to it, to the whole cosmos, grow and reverberate.

Inside her Vector, Avar's awareness spread, binding her connection to the fighter. She gave herself to it, making the sharp little ship into part of her. Its conduits blood vessels, its power breath, its connection to the Force her own.

Avar felt her hair lifting against her neck. With a nudge of the Force, she unbuckled herself, moving the slight controls with her mind to maneuver the fighter where she needed it.

Her body rose until she hung in perfectly balanced alignment inside the pointed bubble of the Force she'd made, expanding beyond the walls of the Vector. She toggled the controls, shifting all the shields to the nose of the Vector. All her strength to the fore.

Avar breathed slowly, carefully, aware of only her lungs, the Force, and her plan.

Ahead, the *Precipitate Fire* strafed the *Tractate,* and distantly Avar heard yelling through the comm.

She pushed, opening fire with everything the Vector had.

The Vector shot forward with all its own speed and all the strength of Avar's song.

The nose aimed for the neck of the Nihil battle cruiser, its narrowest section.

Avar closed her eyes and held on.

The Vector screamed. Avar held on. She clung to the steel and plastic, the energy and bones and blood. She clung to the Force and let it guide her through space and defensive fire, gritting her teeth as the Vector shot through the neck of the *Precipitate Fire.*

Everything shook. Avar's gloved fingers bruised her own palms, she fisted them so tightly.

The Vector's body kept shaking, bits stripping away.

The Force surrounded her like a fireball, a pure raging cry that was less than a song but more than enough.

Avar held on.

The Vector blasted out into space again, a tail fin torn away. It spun, out of control.

Avar held her grip. She tasted blood.

The fighter was so hot, *too* hot—a poor breaking thing.

It couldn't fall apart yet.

Avar held on.

Through the scream of the Force, she heard voices, felt the shock wave of an explosion, debris, distress signals, and cheering.

Her bones rattled along with the hull of her Vector.

Avar couldn't let go or it would all break apart.

"—that you?"

"Avar?"

She held on. She kept her Vector's cockpit intact with only will and desperation and the Force.

"Avar!"

Elzar.

She reached out a trembling hand but missed the comm switch. She tried again. "Elzar?" she croaked.

Other voices broke in, but she focused on only one:

"I'm here, Avar."

and

"I've got you."

and

"Hold on."

Chapter Thirty-Four

CORUSCANT

When word came from Admiral Kronara that they'd chased the Nihil off Naboo, Lina Soh allowed herself to close her eyes for a moment. "And Viess?"

"Unfortunately, she slipped away after a battle with several Jedi on the ground. We're tracking her, and she's vulnerable with her flagship destroyed, so hope remains."

Lina managed to withhold her sigh of frustration and said, "Get me the full report as soon as possible. With the Stormwall back up, we want everything as secure as we can make it and you back home. This isn't an occupation."

"Yes, Chancellor," the admiral said, his gruff voice sounding tired. "I'm sending the *Axiom* back in a few hours with the worst injuries. The *Tractate* needs more assistance and time to get up to lightspeed. Once everything is as settled as we can make it for a Naboo that remains in occupied territory, the *Third Horizon* will be back in Republic space before the Nihil can mount a counter."

"Good. And good work. I know it isn't the kind of win you want."

"Still a win."

"True. By the time you return, we should have a full report ready on the current situation with the Stormwall and whether Ro moves it or rearranges anything, as Xylan Graf insisted was a possibility."

From his chair by the door, Senator Toon snorted.

Kronara said, "Ro won't give us anything useful, Chancellor. Kronara out."

Lina shared a grim smile with Reza and waved at the door. "All right. Time to talk to Ghirra Starros." She leaned her hip against her desk, though the angle strained her prosthetic where it attached to her leg. This would be worth appearing dominant, at ease. Ghirra Starros's ship had arrived mere hours ago from Hosnian Prime. Lina had denied the ship clearance to land and ordered a comm interdiction. A typical, even petty political move. Exactly what Ghirra Starros deserved.

Lina's third aide Elisa, a world-weary Alderaanian woman whose family had been senators and aides for generations, walked swiftly to the desk and inputted the call. She hit the holopad and bowed out of Lina's space.

Almost instantly—too quickly for Ghirra to hide her impatience at having been stalled—the call was answered and a miniature Ghirra Starros flickered to life. The former senator wore her lavish robes and the large eyesore pendant of the Nihil. It even seemed to gleam heavily through the holo. "This is Ghirra Starros on the *Pearl*."

"Ghirra," Lina said, letting satisfaction curl around the name. "Thank you for waiting."

"Of course, Chancellor Soh," Ghirra said, lips pulled back in almost a snarl. Rather reminiscent of her daughter. Thank the Force Avon had been convinced to remain in Republic space after proving her home key worked, instead of insisting on joining either strike team. Avon was stubborn and smart enough to have talked her way into battle. But it wouldn't be long before Avon was safely back on Coruscant—or as safe as she could be in the same sector as her mother.

The thought bolstered Lina even further. "Allow me to officially inform you: A team of Republic Defense Coalition ships has successfully destroyed your Lightning Crash."

A beat of silence spread, and Lina didn't look away from her former colleague. Beyond the shimmering hologram, Reza smiled. Senators Toon, Noor, and Ilpatr'ii listened, too, and more crowded in the door. Their attention helped Lina control herself. This was a win, yes, but not a moment to gloat. That wasn't what she did. That wasn't what the Republic stood for. Too many lives had been lost, and there were more to come.

"I see," Ghirra said. Then nothing more.

"Shall we have a summit to discuss the border?" Lina spread her hands almost innocently. "How honestly have you approached us, Minister Starros?"

Lina wanted to say, *Look at your precious wall now. It's weakened, and we are coming, whether you like it or not. Meet us halfway, and maybe we can resolve all this the way I know you want to, former senator Starros.*

"I'm already here," Ghirra said. "Perhaps we can commence immediately instead in the shining heart of the Republic?"

Lina pretended to consider it. "Or you could invite us to you? Somewhere near the border, such as Naboo perhaps?"

Even through the holo, Lina could see Ghirra react. She knew Lina had named Naboo for a reason, and she'd find out what had happened at her first chance. When Lina gave it to her.

All right, Lina was definitely being a little bit petty. She'd earned it.

Ghirra said, "Naboo is under Nihil authority, and I didn't expect you would want to leave your stronghold, Chancellor."

As best she could through the holo, Lina held Ghirra's gaze. "I'm lifting the comm interdiction, and you might consider checking in on your so-called strongholds, Minister," she said as coldly as she was able.

"You do realize destroying the Lightning Crash is not enough to destroy the Stormwall itself," Ghirra said with dripping condescension.

"Slipping in and out makes you look like insurgents and spies, not a formidable, or friendly, neighbor."

"Aren't you the one who wants to be neighbors, Ghirra?" Lina asked casually.

Ghirra stared at her, and Lina stared back.

After a long enough beat of silence, Lina said, "Here should do nicely for our discussions. I do have to wonder if your Eye would prefer more neutral ground?"

"The Eye doesn't concern himself with such matters."

Lina let her smile grow. *That* was the point.

"You're only buying time," Ghirra said.

"That's not what we earned today," Lina said in her most pitying tone. The Nihil—and Ghirra Starros among them—could never understand. They'd built themselves to be opposed to the gentle drip of hope wearing down a mountain. The Republic could lose and lose, but they would be relentless in the pursuit of safety and freedom for everyone. For hope.

Lina Soh made herself smile at Ghirra Starros. "I'll give you a few days to settle in, then make arrangements for a more informal meeting."

Lina gestured to her aide, and the call cut off.

Immediately, Senator Toon said, "When we think we've won is when Marchion Ro is most likely to throw down a new card."

Lina nodded wearily. Oh, did she know that. "This time, Senator, we know we haven't won. Maybe it will surprise him."

Chapter Thirty-Five

This once had been a thriving rain forest. Now it was a monument to blighted mystery.

Marchion Ro walked steadily along the edge of calcified trees, each footstep deliberate to avoid the tangle of roots and falling pink seeds. He followed the dried-out bed of a thin river, which distinguished the area of the rain forest turned to ash and stone from the part that clung to life. The water had obviously only recently fled, stopped farther upriver by who knew what: a sinkhole, a fallen boulder, or perhaps this strange galactic disease ate away at water, too? Turned it into flakes of gray . . . something.

At Ro's heels, one of the Levelers kept a reluctant pace.

As he walked, he tapped the rod against his thigh and studied the details.

Here was the carcass of a giant insect—a flying one, with a long thorax and several legs with clawed grippers, antennae that branched like antlers, and nine faceted eyes perfectly preserved when the blight consumed it. One wing remained only as an imprint of dust against its body; another had shattered off and left a film of itself on the meadow. From there, the blight spread onto this side of the creek bed.

The insect must have been infected but still able to fly across. Where it crashed, the meadow died.

Ro made a wide circle around it, pulling at the Leveler, who edged farther and farther away.

So the blight could be sped up and moved, as the infected bug had done.

Fascinating. It crept not only along the ground but inside living things as well, taking each slowly without killing it until finally—it did so.

Ro's comlink beeped, but the crackle of words did not clear up. This moon was in Republic space, inhabited by a colony of Republic scientists who were already beginning their evacuation to escape the blight. Ro had intercepted their calls for resources and made haste. He'd put the *Gaze Electric* into orbit around a nearby world in the same system, synchronized to remain in the shadow of the gaseous rings to obscure its presence. He did not want any interruptions to his study of this blighted world.

Interference from the rings also made his comlink go down occasionally.

Whatever Thaya wanted must be urgent, though, as she continued to try.

Ro hissed in displeasure. He'd get to a better location soon enough.

Just as he considered returning to his shuttle, or insisting the Leveler at his side walk into the blight, he came upon a grassy meadow half-consumed. Large, twisting trees with hanging black berry clusters surrounded it, and the grass was scraggly, bent in strange ways. At the edge, where the creek had once flowed, were the charred remains of a single Drengir.

Exactly what he'd been looking for.

Though the body had been burned, its tendrils and leaves curled by the heat of fire, the shape of its trunk system was recognizable, as were the remains of its wicked beak and handfuls of teeth.

Except it had been turned into gray stone, just like everything else in this forest.

Marchion Ro wondered if the blight or the fire had found it first.

"—ormwall, my lord," his comlink blared. Thaya's voice.

Ro touched his comm, said, "Thaya, try that again."

Had she said something about the Stormwall?

The crackling repeated, but he couldn't make it out.

With an irritated sigh, Ro turned and headed back for his shuttle where he could patch in to hear this report.

Of the three worlds beyond the crystal farm that Ro had visited, thanks to Thaya's reports and gossip regarding the presence of this blight, two of them had been places his Nihil had seeded the Drengir more than a year ago. This world was not included in such a list, yet here was a dead Drengir. Other than the presence of life itself, those beasts were the only potential link he could find among the infected worlds.

Interesting. And how thrilling to hunt something difficult again. A prey that defied all usual methods of escape. If he could not track it, neither could the Jedi.

"What a sight," the ghost of his great-great-grandmother said. "What is so insidious that it infects anything it touches?"

The Jedi. False ideals. Hope, he thought, but did not say.

Ro climbed over a tangle of roots, glaring at the Leveler, which moved fast now that they were headed away from the blight.

Once he reached the shuttle, Marchion climbed aboard and activated his security channel. "What is it?" he barked.

The comm crackled again, and Thaya's voice said, "My lord, we have received word that the Lightning Crash was attacked. The Stormwall fell, but the backup systems in place on the *Gaze* have restored it. We'll need a few more hours before we can jump anywhere while the power fluctuations resettle."

The news did not distress him. He was cold and hollow. This meant only that one of his subordinates had failed. "Where is Viess?"

Thaya hesitated. Anger flashed through Ro then. Before he could growl at her, she said, "The *Precipitate Fire* lost Naboo to a second Republic attack. The general has yet to reach out, but her second insists that Viess escaped."

Ro dug his claws into his own palm, and blood welled through his fingers. None of the people he had admitted into his rule proved worthy. Viess lost as often as she won, despite her despicable tactics. Boolan was secretive and ought to be put out of his misery, or else try to do something more useful with those Children of the Storm he led. And Ghirra—ah, Ghirra was in this for her own good, not Ro's. She would love this turn of circumstances, for it would give her a chance to play politician again.

Good thing he was prepared. "Keep the *Gaze*'s power focus on the Stormwall. Upon my return, I want specifics about the progress of the crystal array on Hetzal."

"My lord, it will take a few weeks more before it's fully operational."

"The *Gaze* can take it, Thaya. Did they manage to remove any of the stormseeds?"

"No, my lord."

"Then what are you worried about?"

"The security of the wall is compromised."

"Hardly. They've been slicing holes for weeks now." Ro snorted. Viess and Ghirra had been concerned, but it was all so boring. The Jedi hadn't even used their little holes to come after *him*. So focused on the Stormwall, on rescuing people, on spreading their hope and light in the wake of his devastations. They were shortsighted. With hardly any effort, he could reset everything they'd seemingly accomplished today. Instead of destroying a space station or liberating a world, they should have come after him. "Toss some scav droids into Republic space and give the Tempests their leash. Tell them their Eye would appreciate them leaving nothing but destruction and pain at their discretion."

"Immediately. And the Republic ships? Several remain in the Chommell sector, and there are two near Wild Space with the remains of the Lightning Crash."

"For now, let the Republic and the *Jedi* enjoy what they think they've won. It will make their disappointment more poignant in the morning."

"In the morning, my lord?"

"Metaphorically speaking, Thaya. And when General Viess reappears, invite her to do her job more successfully or bring her excuses to me personally."

"And, my lord . . ."

"What?" Ro nearly snarled.

"Ghirra Starros has sent constant inquiries after your whereabouts."

"Continue ignoring her."

Thaya hesitated again, and Ro narrowed his eyes. Thaya did not usually have opinions. "Speak up or get to work."

"Perhaps alerting the Minister of Information to your location will calm her down."

"She's best riled up," he said. "But tell her what you want, so long as it is not the truth."

"Yes, my lord."

Ro shut down the comm and fired up the shuttle. He wanted to stay here on this moon to set up more experiments. To throw the Leveler at the blight and discover if it functioned differently on different worlds. Did it move quicker when there were more living things to consume than on the crystal farm of Norisyn? Or did the blight prefer pristine crystalline forms for its meals?

This blight, more than any fleet or storm, more than any great *ministry* or senate, had the potential to offer Ro exactly what he'd always wanted.

He was the only danger, the center of the storm. The danger—and the relief. Everything. The Jedi distracted themselves, the Republic pretended at galactic diplomacy.

But this, *this* would prove otherwise.

It did not come from Republic losses, or from private technology like the Stormwall. It was not something developed by people who would be able to develop or discover parallel flaws.

This blight was raw. Wild. Nothing escaped it.

This thing made even the Drengir fall. The Levelers were afraid.

It was a world killer. A system destroyer. It left no life in its wake.

And Marchion Ro would be its master.

Chapter Thirty-Six

NABOO, INSIDE THE OCCLUSION ZONE

Stars glittered in the clear sky, and two of Naboo's moons reflected against the rippling lake. Avar Kriss stood at the marble rail of an open-sided veranda jutting out from under one of the great domes of the San Tekka manor, appreciating the beauty. The scent of smoke and energy discharge tinged the wind, but for now the battle was over, the fires extinguished or smoldering, and the enemy fled or imprisoned. For all of it, Naboo remained beautiful. And the San Tekka private island remained luxurious.

Avar leaned against a pillar, gazing out at the water, at the distant shadows where horizon and sky blurred with dawn. Everyone had stood down a few hours ago, and Elzar would be here soon.

She was tired. But at the same time, life buzzed inside her. She didn't like to think too closely about what she'd done—or what Burryaga had done. Everyone took risks. Putting oneself on the line for others was part of the Jedi way. In the end, what she'd done hadn't been too special except that it had worked. Burry on the other hand . . . his success would have ramifications.

Tomorrow.

It had been hours since she'd heard Elzar's voice, cutting through her incredible effort. Bolstering her to hold on. Everything she'd needed.

Of course, it had been the *Tractate* that swallowed her up through its landing bay before an emergency landing on Naboo. She'd heard Elzar but hadn't seen him yet. She hadn't touched him. She'd only sent a message that she lived, that she was waiting.

"Fine atmosphere for longing gazes," Porter Engle said, coming up beside her. "But you should eat some of this soup."

Warmth spread in her chest as Avar smiled at the old Jedi. He'd found an apron somewhere and taken over one of the big kitchens in this wing to stir up some kind of egg-and-vegetable soup. By the time the Jedi on Naboo had gathered, had their wounds treated—the physical ones anyway—and settled down, Porter had carried in a huge steaming cauldron, apologizing wryly for the limited and varied ingredients he'd been able to procure on short notice.

Three San Tekka retainers had scurried after him with bowls and utensils and some day-old sourbread, and the feast had been laid out on the low table and even a few chairs used as smaller tables. Avar had watched, gladdened and tired, as Burryaga made bowls for Bell—who was slumped in the corner, exhausted—as well as Vernestra. Dotdat was on her second helping, and Far Linghe was drinking the broth straight from the bowl. Jedi Knight Isrie Fallau was helping a wounded RDC pilot enjoy the food. After some prodding from Porter Engle, the San Tekka retainers finally sat with their own portions, and Cair asked someone named Ino'olo to find wine to go with the ground tea.

Cair San Tekka had then plopped on the floor next to the massive white snow dog wearing a thickly padded medicinal collar and fed her pieces of egg while fending off Bell's charhound. The charhound was immensely interested in the snow dog, but after a dribble of soup had to be poured on Plinka's rump to put out a small fire, Burry had summoned the charhound to his side and made her sit with him.

Now Bell slept with his head on Burry's shoulder, while the Wookiee

and Vernestra spoke softly. Everyone on the veranda chatted about nothing much. It was as if they collectively chose to pretend it was over for a
few hours. There was no worrying about the Stormwall being back up,
or what new monstrosities Marchion Ro might have up his sleeve. And
no talk of the two dead Nameless. Once any of the creatures died, their
bodies slowly turned to stone and dust, exactly like their victims. These
two had already begun to husk before they could be transported to the
Axiom for their jump back to Coruscant a little while ago.

"Go on," Porter said. "Eat."

Avar accepted the warm bowl. "It's so good to see you," she said for
the second time.

Porter snorted. "I liked your broadcast, by the way."

"Thanks," she said with a little grimace. She declined the spoon
Porter offered, lifting the bowl to her lips instead to sip at the broth.
Despite Porter's claim of limited resources, it was delicious. Herbal and
rich. When she finished, she should find a place to lie down. Even
though she'd told Elzar to come, if he was busy or if there were duties
for him to attend to, that's what he should do. Not prioritize her. There
was no need for her to wait.

After she slept, she'd be on to her next mission, facing whatever the
morning might bring.

Porter watched her as she fished out a small soup egg and popped it
in her mouth.

"When the skies are a bit clearer, I'm taking off," he said.

Avar frowned. "We could use you . . . frankly, in a lot of places."

"I'm going after her again."

"Porter . . ." Avar studied the old Jedi. His dark gaze continued to
dart toward the sky, but otherwise he seemed calm. As if he'd grounded
himself in the care he'd shown with his cooking, by staying here this
long. Avar tilted her head and listened to the Force: Porter Engle was
steady. A low string that vibrated on the level of old, wise elephoths.

No, not steady. Relentless. The constant piercing light of a billion-
year-old sun.

There was no need to lecture him on seeking revenge. And she had no stones to throw at chasing unfinished business. Avar reached out and touched his jaw. "Come back."

"Enjoy the soup," he said with a grin.

She held the bowl in both hands and after a moment saluted him with it. Porter wandered toward Bell, Burry, and Vernestra and said something quiet. Maybe congratulating that miracle trio again for defeating the Nameless.

The details of that would need to be dug into and investigated. Avar both did and did not want to know more. But she'd have to. Tomorrow.

Avar glanced around the room again. Everyone was exhausted. Drained. But a vibrancy thrummed in the spaces among them—not urgency at the moment, but a sweet note of success, of hope. Even though the Stormwall was back and they hadn't gotten anybody out of the Occlusion Zone or captured Viess, they had the home key, and it felt like something in the galaxy had shifted fundamentally. The melody was the same, but the song had changed key.

She felt the urge to walk through the small crowd of Jedi and RDC soldiers and touch them all. A brush of fingers here, a tug on a braid there. A physical connection to mirror the song she heard and to anchor them through the Force. Maybe it was a sign she was getting older: She wanted to reassure them and let them know she trusted them to take care of themselves. Whatever came with dawn, they'd keep fighting.

As if he'd heard her thoughts, Cair San Tekka said a little loudly, "How would everybody feel about a little lullaby? Ino will bring my dulcimer, and there are a few soothing tunes I can play one-handed." His smile was tired but his eyes bright.

Before Avar could concur, her gaze swung to the door. *Elzar.*

She felt him suddenly. Nearby. Headed her way.

A lightness filled her up like carbonation, expanding in her heart. The doors to the covered patio were flung open, the real wood thumping hard against the marble wall.

But Xylan Graf filled the doorway, hands gripping the carved frame, electric-blue eyes darting around the room at every relaxed figure until they landed on one human.

"Cair San Tekka," Xylan said. "I absolutely forbid you to keep giving me these kinds of shocks or—"

He was interrupted by a high-pitched canine whine as the mass of the snow dog Plinka heaved herself up, trying to canter nearer. Xylan's face went big in shock.

"What have you done to my sweet baby?" he gasped as he ran for Plinka, hands out to catch her stumble. Xylan grunted as he helped Plinka lower back down, murmuring at her and stroking around her bandage.

Just as surprised, Cair's eyes widened. "You're here."

Xylan ignored him, tugging his dog's fluffy ear.

"She—she'll be fine," Cair said, using a cane to drag himself to his feet. His missing prosthetic had yet to be found, but he'd clearly made time to bathe so that it was only the hints of bruises and cuts that marred his features, no remaining blood spatter. "She's resilient, and besides, I took care of her."

With his hands dug into Plinka's fur, Xylan stood, too. He glared at his husband. "Cair."

"*Xylan.*"

Avar would have looked away, except the next instant, Cair flung himself at Xylan, and the Graf caught him with a soft *oof.*

They were sweet, filling her with gladness, relief, and yearning— until she realized her feelings weren't coming from only her own heart. The pull was clear. She glanced toward the door again.

There was Elzar Mann, looking right back at her.

Avar let her own relief and yearning guide her steps as she moved with purpose to Elzar. He started to say something, but Avar reached up, took his face, and kissed him.

Just a light, quick kiss, and she lowered off her toes to smile at him.

Elzar was gobsmacked. His jaw dropped and his eyes widened into saucers.

Avar laughed. She wrapped her arms around his waist and leaned in, pressing her cheek to his while he collected himself.

A moment was all it took for Elzar to hug her back, tucking his head against hers. "Avar," he said. Avar opened up completely to the Force and thought, *Elzar.*

The crash of his song rattled through her pleasantly, and she heard—felt—her name again and again, in the throb of his heartbeat and the rhythm of his tide.

For a long moment they breathed together, the Force flowing through them as if sewing them together. Avar leaned back, finding his hands. "Have you eaten?"

"Yes."

"Then come with me." Avar kept one of his hands and pulled him with her out the door into the corridor. She didn't really know where she was taking him, but she listened to the Force and dragged him along until she found a room that seemed to be an office. Intact shelves with old-style scrolls and books—actually bound—as well as a huge desk fit with several holo stations and a soft-looking chair. The office had a balcony, as befitting Naboo architecture and aesthetics. Avar shoved open the translucent door and brought Elzar with her to the rail. Wind dragged her hair from her loose braids and snapped the edges of Elzar's mission robes.

They stood for a moment in the darkness, in the reflected glow of stars and external security lights. Elzar leaned against her and said, "We did it."

"We did."

"And . . . I think I . . . I wanted to tell you, I realize it's messy. I'm working for balance, but it's messy." Elzar shook his head. "I push, sometimes in dangerous directions, but it's all I know how to do. It's what I'm good at. It's taken me to dark places, Avar, you know that. I . . . think I'm getting closer to understanding why. That dark comes with the light. What keeps me driving toward the light keeps the shadows right there, too."

"You sound like you've already broken into the wine." Avar squeezed his hand.

Elzar laughed a little. "I need my feelings. Hope. Compassion. Even if they keep me on the edge—the edge is where I do my best work."

"Yes," Avar agreed. "It is. Knowing that about you inspires me, El. Makes me better. You thrive when you can push and drag us with you to new places. You find the light in those edges. Your problem has been pushing without the right anchor, without something that keeps you focused on the light so that when you fall over an edge, it's to the light that you leap first. And when you asked me to be your anchor, I wasn't ready."

Elzar hummed thoughtfully. "Do you think Stellan was ready?"

"He was born ready," Avar said, because they both knew it was a joke. Ah, she missed him. It ached, and Avar looked out into the sky, craning her neck, and let go of the ache. Every time it hurt, she had to let it go. Not ignore it or pretend it didn't hurt—only let it pass through her.

Just like love. Accept it, embrace it, let it pass through and be part of her. *Oh.* Avar realized Elzar was asking her to do the pushing now, into something he was almost ready for. She had to answer. It was bursting out of her.

"What's your problem been, Avar?" he asked.

"Any guesses?"

"You bring people together, through the Force, through your charm and power . . . and then you forget yourself. It's the opposite of me, maybe," Elzar added with a light frown.

"That makes us a good balance for each other," Avar said, and she wrapped her hands around the back of his neck to tug him closer. Then Avar kissed him again.

This time it wasn't sweet and gentle; it was filled with intent.

Avar pushed her mouth against Elzar's, gripping his head. She tilted and did her best. It had been a long time. But Avar wanted to taste him again, to give him this piece of her that nobody but Elzar had ever come so close to. Even if it was awkward, or messy as he said. She wanted to push and take. There wasn't anyone else alive she trusted with this.

Once, she'd refused him. More than once. Elzar had always been the one asking. Avar thought it wasn't their duty, it wasn't who they'd chosen to be, so she *had* to refuse.

But if she'd learned anything about the Force in the past years, living and cosmic, it was that the Force reached. The Force connected. This kiss, this need in her—in them—was a way of sharing that connection.

Avar had all the arguments right there at the ready, sparking in her mind as she kissed Elzar.

He drew back, gasping a little. "Avar," he whispered.

"Elzar."

Their names could be enough in these shadowy close quarters. The frayed ends of their friendship eager to be knotted back together, a braid of Avar, Elzar, their pasts, Stellan, the song and tide of the Force. Waiting for Elzar to welcome it back.

Avar felt incredible.

"I don't know how to do this," Elzar said, pushing away.

Avar blinked.

He was shaking his head. "I'll be consumed. I won't survive it, Avar." His voice was so sad, so lost.

"Tell me," she said, holding his face.

Elzar took a deep breath. He didn't try to move away. "I already struggle so much with attachment. With fighting back the grim desperation of the dark side. I struggle with selfishness, with impulses. I want this. I want you. I always have. I don't think I've known you without wanting you, Avar."

Avar couldn't help the little smile that flickered over her mouth at the sheer romance of his words. "But," she prompted gently.

"I'm trying to be better. To let the Force beat a rhythm in me, like you said. Flow through me. I'm trying to lean toward the light by accepting that I have this pull to the dark. That it's part of me. And I think I'm doing it. Coming to terms with the presence of darkness. The understanding is making me stronger. A better Jedi. I'm worried that giving in to this desire will make it harder again. What if something happens to you? I'd already be lost as it is, but if I take more, if we become . . . more . . ." Elzar's eyes drifted shut. He took a shuddering breath. "I'm afraid of what I might do. This is why we—the Jedi— avoid attachments. I'm a case study for it." Elzar laughed a little.

"All right, Elzar," Avar murmured, stroking his cheeks. "I'm here for you, however you need me—or don't. As long as you're saying my name, that's all *I* need. But it's time for me to tell you something else. Something I just know, fundamentally. May I?"

He stared at her for a moment, almost wary. But Elzar Mann was nothing if not brave. He nodded. "Yes. Tell me anything."

There were so many things she could say, that she wanted to explain. Her whirling thoughts, where they should go next, what the Jedi should do with this strange win, her feelings of rest, the key change in the song of the Force. She could use the moment, the battles they'd just fought. They'd changed Naboo, changed lives, injured and killed, lived and survived, the Lightning Crash was gone but the Stormwall remained. The hope here was surrounded by darkness; the change was no more than a kiss, both insignificant and intrinsic.

But there was only one thing Avar needed to tell him that he also needed to hear.

"I love you," she said, breaking into a smile.

Elzar exhaled hard and fast.

Avar slid her hands back and gripped his hair. "I've struggled with it, too. Thought it was dangerous, selfish, something to be carved out. That's a common interpretation of what we're taught. But that's also too easy of an answer. That love is attachment, that it's selfish, possessive. It isn't. I was wrong. Those things are real, and dangerous to Jedi, to anyone, but they aren't love. In my worst moments, I've loved you. In my greatest grief and failure, I still loved you, and it didn't turn me down the wrong path—it's what got me back onto my feet. I stood back up and reached back. Loved back—people, the Force, watched hope spread and beings all over the galaxy keep fighting, keep trying. That's love. That's the purest form of light. How can a sliver of it here between us be wrong?"

A tremor of something shook Elzar. He didn't look away.

She got even closer, so all she could see were the galaxies in his eyes. "I love you, so much, and it's not a hindrance. Attachment, possessiveness—those are hindrances because they limit a Jedi's potential. They make the galaxy smaller. But love is *limitless,* Elzar. Just like the Force itself is limitless. There's no end to it!" Avar laughed a little. "If there was an end to the Force, to love, to hope, don't you think we'd have found it in the last few years? But we're black holes for love. Unending notes and bottomless seas. We make the galaxy bigger with love, with the Force bursting inside us."

Avar kissed him again. His beard tickled her lips, and she brushed them along his jaw.

Then she dropped her hands and stepped back. "I love you," she said a third time. "It's part of me forever. The way the Force and light are part of me forever. Nothing—not distance or grief or death—could end it." With a helpless, smiling shrug, Avar added, "That's all I needed to say."

"All," Elzar said hoarsely.

Avar nodded. She reset her expression into something more neutral, simpler. But she was certain her feelings shone in her eyes.

Elzar stepped forward into the space between them that she had created. He grabbed her and kissed her, crushing them together. Avar held on to his wrists and opened up to him.

The kiss lasted only an electric moment before Elzar stumbled away. "I . . ." He put his hand to his mouth, "I have to go."

Before Avar could reply, he fled. She was alone on the balcony, but it was all right. She felt Elzar solidly even as he ran away from her. He had to leave her, too, so that he could come back.

Avar leaned onto the rail with her eyes closed, listening to the Force, to the song of light filling her—and the whole galaxy—up.

Chapter Thirty-Seven

THE *GAZE ELECTRIC,*
INSIDE THE OCCLUSION ZONE

It was morning somewhere. A sun—or two—were rising, burning off fog from a lake. Birds flocked to tall grass, while rodents shuffled in the detritus. Predators were quiet, waiting—patient, ready for blood.

There wouldn't be blood on the *Gaze Electric* today, but Marchion Ro remembered the smell of it permeating the walls.

He glanced at the chrono to confirm that yes, it was finally morning somewhere in particular. Theed. The capital city of Naboo.

Standing before his throne in the vast dark hall of the *Gaze,* Ro stripped off his cape and draped it over the jagged back. His helmet propped near the foot, he dropped his jacket and then his shirt over it. He reclined, naked to the waist, and activated the control panel in the thick left arm of the throne. Rather lazily, he tapped in his oldest security code, then brought up the Stormwall controls. The holomap shivered to life all around him, a necklace of tiny stormseeds, the slice of his galaxy right in his lap.

With a satisfied but tiny smile, he commanded the ship to give him access to the tangle of Paths. This slippery tech looked like nothing but a wild batch of numbers, a cluster of chaos—all of it the deeply layered result of Mari San Tekka's strange, brilliant mind.

Ro's code turned one string of numbers into a bloody line. Mari's home key. The Path that tied the rest together.

Well, one of them.

Deactivating the Stormwall holo, Marchion opened the compartment in the right arm of his throne. One of several, this one always housed a blaster, sometimes a lightsaber or two, and a small platinum mirror.

He took the mirror and held it out, catching the dull bluish light from the arcing ceiling, pulling it to him, though he hardly needed it to see clearly with his Evereni eyes.

The *Gaze* shuddered around him.

Exiting hyperspace didn't usually cause so much internal distortion, but with most of the ship's capacity aimed at powering the Stormwall, such things were bound to be bumpy. Fortunately, Ro didn't mind getting a little rough.

His orders were to orbit Hetzal and get up-to-date information on the edges of his territory as well as drag the Nihil in charge of the new crystal array up here to answer his questions in person. Then his Tempests were to ready themselves for new Stormwall codes and stand down until they received them. But that would take a few minutes. Time enough for his little surprise.

Ro angled the mirror toward his torso.

Silvery lines decorated his gray skin, stretching in lines like webs, arcing constellations. Star charts carved into his flesh.

He remembered the day when he was held down, his jaw clenched so hard he thought his teeth might crack. He'd refused to scream even as the pain built and grew, the sensational burning never quite going numb, never quite flipping over into adrenaline or euphoria. Lines were etched and numbers needled in, an array of the galaxy with a few very important codes. The sinews of his own body built into the foundation.

His father had watched. Mari San Tekka had been propped up against Asgar's side, her hand gripping his shoulder until her already pale fingers whitened. Asgar's hand was inexplicably tender under Mari's elbow, holding her. Marchion hated Asgar even harder for it. But Mari's eyes had been all on him, on Marchion, so focused that she saw nothing but math and possibilities in him—on him. "There," she whispered. "This." She murmured words from languages Ro never knew—or couldn't quite grasp through the searing pain.

Back then, the design had blurred under the smear of his dark blood—the most he had ever shed. The lines had been raw. Angry.

In the mirror now, the result was beautiful.

Sometimes Marchion Ro wished that instead of his father or grandmother or great-great-grandmother, he would be visited by Mari.

He found the lines he needed, the numbers cut into his skin, just for him: a pretty bouquet of a star chart, of coordinates, a Path. The oldest Path.

Marchion Ro had the *Gaze* bring back the holo of the Stormwall Paths, and stared at the thin bloody line of Mari's home key.

He used a claw to erase it, and then carefully, one little number at a time, inputted the new one from his body. When it was finished, Ro touched the command restart. With not even a momentary blip, the Stormwall seamlessly rearranged its Path codes around the new key— the original Path—and in the next moment, the central relay sent out its fractal impulses.

The Jedi had found Mari's secret somehow—treachery, hope, luck—but this new one could be discovered only on his dead body.

Chapter Thirty-Eight

NABOO, INSIDE THE OCCLUSION ZONE

Cair woke up the way he'd woken up for the past two years, give or take a week: alone. At first it didn't strike him as out of the ordinary. He was used to it. Then a rustling from the other side of the room and a familiar quiet scoff reminded him that yesterday his husband had shown up with a fleet of Republic ships and Jedi in order to *rescue him*.

Propping himself up on his elbows, he glanced over at Xylan, fully dressed and coiffed, going through Cair's wardrobe. It was the one he'd gathered in the past couple of months while playing the lazy San Tekka scion, so most of it was brightly colored silkensteen or the sort of fancy fellwool that glimmered—not the clothes he kept tucked away here and there for his real work. "Xylan? What are you doing?"

Xylan tossed a scarlet tunic at him. "Get dressed, and put this on under one of those coats folded over the chair."

"What?" Cair sort of caught the tunic. It was so soft it slid through his hands as he sat up. "Why? It's so nice."

"That embroidery at the collar is pearlseed thread. We can pick the stitches and use it to buy a whole high level in a Coruscant tower, or a state-of-the-art new hand."

"But why?"

The look his husband sent him would curl the hair on a bantha. "Get. Dressed."

Cair stood, stretched. He wandered into the opulent bathroom and turned on the shower.

Xylan appeared in the arched doorway. "There's no time for that."

Cold anxiety slid down Cair's back. "What happened?"

"Nothing. We're going to be on the next ship out of here, which happens to be the *Third Horizon*. It's leaving soon." Xylan's clipped tone made Cair frown again. But Xylan kept going, his boots clicking on the tiles. "Wash your face, clean your teeth, that's it. Everything else you can do in hyperspace."

"Xylan—"

Xylan turned Cair by the shoulders to face the marble sink and pushed. "Get going. I already uploaded all the data from your consoles, under your name and mine, and used all the Plinka codes, then I burned the datapaths, so your information should be safe with us. When we get back to Coruscant, we'll go over it, all right?"

Shock froze Cair in place. "What is going on? I can't leave. The—"

Xylan's vivid-cerulean eyes caught Cair's and glared. His expression was tight, tense. "Cair, you will be on that ship with me when it leaves the sector if I have to drug you and sit Plinka on your body to hold you down the whole trip."

For a second Cair only stared back. He hadn't spent a lot of his time—not nearly enough—face-to-face with his husband during their marriage, but he'd thought he knew him. Thought he understood Xylan's flippancy and cunning, but this was something else. It was fear. "What happened?"

"Nothing yet," Xylan said. "Just get ready. I let you sleep until dawn. That was all I could give. Now it's time to go."

"But—"

"Cair San Tekka," Xylan snapped. "Do you trust me?"

Cair opened his mouth but nothing came out. He . . . didn't know what to say.

Xylan's expression closed off. "Fine. But you have to—I am taking you with me whether you like it or not." He smiled bitterly. "Though I suppose that doesn't add anything to the trust side of the scale. Just do it."

"I will. I do. Fine." Cair said it all fast. He turned back to wash, and Xylan caught his gaze in the mirror this time.

Xylan flicked his glance to Cair's missing prosthetic. "Do you need any help?" His voice was tentative, as if he wasn't sure he should ask.

"No," Cair said softly. "I won't be long. Is Plinka ready?"

"Yes," Xylan said, and he spun out of the room.

Fifteen minutes later, Cair was half jogging to keep up with Xylan as Plinka whined behind him. She was just as confused by Xylan's attitude as Cair. Her neck was doing better. They hurried through the wide hallway of the San Tekka manor toward the launch pads. It was a long trek from Cair's rooms, and in the few moments, while they moved from the family tower to the broader central dome, the number of people hurrying around tripled. The urgency in the air went from nothing to battle ready.

Xylan had known something was wrong.

Cair grabbed his arm. "Xylan, what happened?" he asked, instead of *What did you do?* He couldn't say that. Xylan was here. He'd come back into the Occlusion Zone after escaping to total freedom. He wouldn't do that only to put Cair and Plinka in danger again.

"The Stormwall," Xylan muttered, tearing free and continuing on. "The shuttle up to the cruiser won't wait for us if we're too late."

Cair knew the Stormwall was supposed to go back up. They—the RDC, the Jedi—expected it. There had to be more to what was upsetting the entire manor.

When they burst out of a lift and into the wider landing bay, it was filled with people. Pilots, San Tekka aides, soldiers, half the crew of the cruiser *Tractate,* and the Jedi. Several of the transports and fighters docked were fully powered up or being refueled.

Cair sped up to get around Xylan and run for Jedi Master Avar Kriss. She looked the least harried of everyone, even as she listened to a tech in RDC uniform try to explain something on the datapad he was holding.

"What's going on?" Cair asked.

"Sometime in the last hour our comms with the Republic stopped working," the Jedi said.

"You mean across the Stormwall."

Kriss nodded.

"Is the *Third Horizon* still jumping through?" Xylan asked, joining Cair. "We want to be on it. Everyone should be on it."

The Jedi frowned. "We're concerned that the comms are down because our home key codes will no longer work to penetrate the wall. It's one thing to be cut off from communicating, and a far different issue to send a ship through when it will be destroyed if the Stormwall is not penetrable by the home key anymore."

"You have bags," Vernestra Rwoh said to Cair, nodding with her chin at the bag over his shoulder.

Even as her eyes slid past him to Xylan, Cair nodded. "Xylan wanted to get back to Coruscant before . . . anything happened."

Vernestra stepped right into Xylan's space and narrowed her eyes. She was only slightly shorter than him, yet her body language was so aggressive that Cair felt an urge to get between them.

But Avar Kriss put a hand on Vernestra's shoulder and looked at Xylan.

Xylan lifted one shoulder and said, "Let me look at the new readouts from the Stormwall. I'll be able to tell if the impulses are still based on the Paths in the same sequential patterns as before, which they should be—that's how it was designed. In which case, even if the home key isn't working for whatever reason, the Sunvale device should still work. Even if something has changed in the fundamental code, the principles of the fractal impulses and the indecently complicated network of Paths will function the same way."

Cair leaned away from his husband. Xylan flicked a glance at him with a little frown.

They'd drawn a crowd now of not only the Jedi but also RDC personnel, as well as several of Cair's known associates here in the manor.

"It's just a bigger ship you have to use," Xylan said, exasperated. "And both of you," he added to Kriss and Vernestra, "have made the jump a dozen times."

Cair bit his lip. It wasn't the worst thing that could have happened. If the comms were down across the Stormwall because the home key didn't work anymore, that meant the RDC couldn't send ships in and out with the ease they'd used for this liberation. It put them back where they'd been at the start, only without the Lightning Crash, and there were several RDC ships trapped on this side of the Occlusion Zone.

Vernestra said with very controlled calm, "The Sunvale device is on the *Axiom,* which left last night."

Master Kriss looked at Vernestra. "It was the only one we had over here. There aren't enough of the devices to spread them to ships that weren't running missions with us."

Xylan cursed. The Wookiee said something in a rumble, and the human Jedi at his side shook his head. Cair immediately started thinking about plans for spreading out all the people trapped on this side. They couldn't remain such a clustered target. But most of Cair's avenues were burned. They'd have to head out by other means, maybe Belin and Rhil—the journalist definitely had contacts beyond Cair's team. And all of it had to happen before the Nihil showed back up. Maybe at least that old Ikkrukkian Porter Engle who'd vanished again last night would distract the general a little bit longer, buying them time.

But Xylan bared his teeth in a wide smile and said sweetly, "Isn't it a good thing then that Avar Kriss and Vernestra Rwoh are the two Jedi in the galaxy able to jump the Stormwall without one?"

All eyes turned to the Jedi in question, but Cair frowned at Xylan. Master Kriss finally said, "It's too dangerous."

"Come on," Xylan said. He drew himself up imperiously. "It's worth the risk. I want off this planet, out of Nihil space, before the *Gaze Electric* itself shows up, and I know most of you do, too."

"I don't," Cair said, pinching the red silk collar of his tunic, brushing his thumb over the oh-so-fancy and expensive pearlseed thread.

Xylan turned to him with a slight moue of frustration. But Cair asked, with growing horror, "Did you know this would happen? Did you know the Nihil could change their home key, this thing for which you bargained your life and—and my life, and all these people? That they could just swap it out?"

"How could you *not* know?" Xylan snapped. He swept his anger over everyone. "It wasn't the Nihil that did this, it was Marchion Ro! You've been fighting him for months, no, years! How could you not expect this? Of course he could swap out the home key when he felt like it! Of course! Marchion Ro sleeps on a bed made of backup plans! He's got so many schemes running at any given time it almost doesn't matter which one works, because one of them will. Then he wins again—or he tears apart the closest person in the room so he might as well have won! The smartest people I've known have only served his machinations! Seven hells! His blood is probably made of fresh-squeezed strategy!"

In the wake of Xylan's outburst, everyone stared at him.

Cair didn't know whether to feel angry or sick. "Not all of us are so well versed in thinking like monsters, Xylan."

"Cair—"

"Stop upsetting everyone," Avar Kriss said, cutting in, and Cair was relieved he didn't have to listen to whatever Xylan was going to say. "Is there a comm room nearby?" she asked Cair, the pinch in her brow under the tip of her diadem the only sign of stress.

Cair pointed toward the launch tower with its wide viewport. "Up there."

"All right. I'm going to reach out to Admiral Kronara and discuss things. Most people will fit on the *Third Horizon,* and it needs to get back if at all possible. If we attempt this, the rest of you can make your own choices about whether you want to be on the ship or here on Naboo."

"Trapped again," Xylan added.

"We didn't know it would be a one-way trip," one of the RDC crew said.

"Would that have mattered?" Avar Kriss asked.

The crew member backed down and looked away.

The Jedi Master nodded and said to the crowd, "At least half of you will have your orders. The rest of you, consider quickly. Graf, come with me, let's see if you can confirm the Path network. You too, Vernestra." With that, the Jedi left, and everyone else broke up into clusters or dashed off.

Xylan hesitated.

Cair turned to Plinka, who sat shuddering hard enough that her fluffy white fur had puffed up. She looked back and forth between Cair and Xylan. The snow dog had to go with Xylan. To safety, to the Republic.

"Cair," Xylan said. Then he stopped.

The morning light caught the reddish highlights in Xylan's dark hair. He needed the undercut trimmed back. Cair wondered if that was his real reason for being so eager to get back to Coruscant. Then immediately felt bad for thinking it.

"There's so much to do here," Cair said.

"There's just as much to do on the Republic side."

"Not what I'm good at."

"You're good at a lot of things," Xylan scoffed, almost reaching his usual level of insouciance.

"Xylan Graf!" Master Kriss called from across the bay.

Xylan waved his hand at her. Then he let his hand fall, slapping it hard against his thigh. "I can't stay in the Occlusion Zone."

"I'm not . . . asking you to," Cair said softly.

For a long moment, Xylan stared at him, something in his posture tensing angrier and angrier. Plinka barked a little just as Xylan burst out, "Why the hell not?!"

Then he spun away and strode after the Jedi.

Chapter Thirty-Nine

THE *THIRD HORIZON*,
INSIDE THE OCCLUSION ZONE

Jedi Knight Vernestra Rwoh was unused to being in meetings like this.

They'd ended up on the *Third Horizon* less than an hour after the impromptu gathering in the San Tekka manor's docking bay. Vernestra's head ached gently with leftover stress from the battle the day before, even though she'd slept for several hours. She'd spent the quick shuttle flight up meditating to clear her body of hunger and adrenaline, then followed Master Kriss directly into Admiral Kronara's war room.

With them were Jedi Master Mirro Lox, Captain Amaryl Pel of the *Tractate* along with her second in command, Captain Mitker as a shimmering blue holo from the *Harmonic*, Xylan Graf, and of course Kronara and his aide Ensign Casset. Vernestra couldn't help feeling unnecessary—except that if they were really going to try to break through the Stormwall the same way she had several months before Avon developed her device, then it made sense for Vernestra to be here.

Xylan, somehow dressed in an even more eye-piercing jacket than the last time she'd seen him, was hunched over a trio of datapads on the central table. He flicked through the information on one while Master Kriss introduced Vernestra and Master Lox to the RDC members who didn't know them. Vernestra bowed shallowly, her attention on Xylan. Her history with the Graf was fraught, to say the least, but if she believed anything about him, it was his investment in his own survival. He wouldn't screw anything up on purpose as long as he was standing in the same target zone as the Jedi.

"You think you can repeat your previous success?" Kronara was asking Master Kriss. "My understanding was that it was near to impossible without this Sunvale device."

"It is," Master Kriss said, as all seven of them joined Graf at the table. Its surface gleamed black, reflecting the long lines of lights above, waiting to be activated. "And no, not *my* previous success." Master Kriss looked to Vernestra. "Jedi Knight Rwoh, can you explain to everyone what you did to get through?"

Vernestra nodded once, sharply. She put her hands on her belt to keep them from fidgeting. "We had a Nihil ship, but the Path engine was scuttled when we first tried to make the jump because our pilot's code was wrong. Luckily it shunted us into one of their killzones instead of worse." Vernestra did her best to quickly relate the information without dredging up corresponding emotion. It hadn't been her best day. She'd been working a little outside the rules of the Order, and when she found Imri, her Padawan—former Padawan, he'd earned his Jedi Knighthood in the Occlusion Zone—instead of returning with her, he'd chosen to stay behind. After she'd defied so much to find him again. She was proud of how strong and wise Imri had grown, but Vernestra could recognize how upset she'd been at the time. "Avon Sunvale was with us, and she had a bundle of Path codes that Xylan gave her. But the Nihil changed their exit code for passage through the Stormwall after Deva—well, after the mess we'd all made on Seswenna. We had no way of knowing which of the Paths in Avon's bundles was the new exit code. So my understanding is that with the bundles—using *all* the Paths—she figured out how to confuse our hyperdrive so that it could in turn confuse the Stormwall's directives. But that used up all the power and space in the computer, so one of us had to input the actual route coordinates manually. It all had to happen perfectly and fast."

The table display lit up suddenly, holomaps flickering to life before fading into the regular glow of a powered and waiting display. Ensign Casset looked at Xylan, who appeared to be busy at the console before him. Transferring data from one of the 'pads in his hand.

Master Kriss cleared her throat to draw attention back to her. The blue glow gentled her expression but put a ghostly spark in her dark eyes. She said, "That's essentially how we still did it, before we had the home key. The Sunvale device was developed to integrate the entire network of Path codes into random bursts to essentially crack little holes in the Stormwall that we could push through—but it still requires the time-phased inputting of the route coordinates, perfectly, while the hyperdrive is engaged with the device. Which is why Jedi have been the only ones leading the missions until now."

"And not all of us can do it," Master Lox said.

Captain Pel of the *Tractate* frowned. "You want to try the hard way again, because the theory is that the home key we all used to cross over this time has been changed. And we can't decipher the new one or change it back. And we don't know which Path the Nihil are currently using as their exit code."

"For all we know, the whole wall is in lockdown," Xylan murmured. "So there might not even be an exit code for the Nihil themselves right now."

"That's what I would do," Admiral Kronara said. Suddenly the display table's rim flared vivid white-blue and an alarm pierced the room.

Vernestra had her lightsaber in hand, unactivated, as did Master Lox. Master Kriss held herself tense but waited as Ensign Casset glared at Xylan Graf. "What are you doing?" she demanded.

"Sorry," Graf muttered without looking up. "I needed to slice into the table. Just shallowly," he added immediately at the outraged noise from the aide.

"Graf," said Admiral Kronara. "Ask before you break my ship. I'll have you in the brig otherwise."

"There's barely time," Xylan said. "More Nihil could show up at any moment, and we have no comms to the Republic. We're sitting ducks."

It was unfortunately true. Vernestra waited to see what Master Kriss or Kronara would say. Everyone in the room knew they were on borrowed time.

"What are you doing, Xylan?" Master Kriss demanded.

Xylan didn't look up again. "Confirming as fast as I can that the Stormwall is using the same damn technology it always was, the same damn Paths. As long as it's only the home key that's changed, the Sunvale device theory should still work, even if we have to imitate the device the way Vernestra and Avon did originally."

Master Kriss glanced to Vernestra. "Do you know more about how it works?"

Vernestra shook her head.

Master Kriss nodded grimly and said, "Elzar was working on the machinery side; he'd know more."

Captain Pel said, "Too bad we can't comm across the Stormwall to ask. We did confirm as best we're able that the *Axiom* should have made it through to the other side over an hour before anyone here noticed the comms were down."

"Good," Master Kriss said.

"Do your comm codes still work, Xylan?" Vernestra asked.

"Not across the wall," he said with disgust. "Not since I defected."

"All right." Admiral Kronara held up a hand. "My priority is getting the *Third Horizon* back to Republic space if you can all figure this out. We need to make some decisions about personnel and the risks of remaining versus making the jump attempt. I'm implementing an executive threat level for all RDC ships in the O.Z. I've already retasked the ships engaged in recovery to patrol, and I'd love some Jedi help with that."

Master Kriss nodded. "Jedi Knights Dotdat and Ceryl are already in the air, I believe. Jedi should all be returning to Republic space," she said to Vernestra and Master Lox. "I left several on the ground on Naboo to continue coordinating whatever evacuation we're going to manage, but I'll summon them up when we have a plan."

Xylan took his cue. "I'm only a theoretician by training, but as far as I can tell, the Stormwall system is the same. It's just echoes I can detect and grab from this station—from this ship, really. If I had some of my proprietary hardware from the Lightning Crash, perhaps I could be more specific, but it's been blown to smithereens."

The admiral ignored him.

Vernestra leaned in to ask, "Are the bundled codes you gave us before still viable? For this?"

"They should be. The codes are simply the Paths Mari San Tekka created, and the Stormwall is designed to use them alone. I've got them here." Xylan tapped the datapad. "Can you remember everything Avon said at the time, how she pressed them directly into the hyperdrive computer? Or"—he looked at the admiral—"if you have an especially skilled slicer or information officer, they might be useful here."

"It was fast," Vernestra said. "Avon didn't have time after the Path engine died, because we were under attack from scav droids. So she was shoving them in tangles."

Xylan's lips curled in distaste. "Yes, it's good the Force was with . . ."

He trailed off, and everyone was staring again.

"What?" barked Captain Pel.

Xylan's electric-blue eyes pinned Vernestra. "She did that only *after* the Path engine died?"

Vernestra started to nod, but then her mouth fell open. *The Path engines.* Before the Sunvale device existed, all they'd needed to cross was the right code and a Path engine. The Nihil had changed the code just before they took off, in an attempt to stop their escape. Avon had thought she could use Xylan's Path sequences to trick the Path engine and the Stormwall into letting them through without the code. They didn't have a Sunvale device, but they were in Nihil space. They'd just fought a Nihil squad that had to have Path engines among them.

"By the Force," Master Lox said, understanding. "We were trying to capture Path engines intact for months before that young woman invented her device."

"Can we use a Path engine in the same way as the Sunvale device?" Master Kriss asked, disbelief and astonishment in her voice. "Get through without the right Path code?"

Vernestra felt pops of excitement in her chest. "Avon said that's all she was doing in the first place. Faking a Path engine."

"A fake of a fake," Xylan drawled. "How apropos."

Ensign Casset began furiously working the console before them, bringing up a quick summary of the system and after-action reports, based on what Vernestra could see. "There are two Path engine signatures based on these readings, one from a partially destroyed long-range shuttle and one from the *Precipitate Fire,* sir."

"Get someone over there immediately," the admiral said.

"Sir, it appears to be damaged. The power signature is missing, it very likely won't work, given the Nihil habit of engine self-destruction when the ship is lost."

Vernestra watched Master Kriss's grimace and couldn't help saying, "Isn't this the second of General Viess's flagships you've personally wrecked?"

The grimace turned into a reluctantly amused smile as Master Kriss nodded. The Jedi Master held Vernestra's eye for a moment, and Vernestra could feel the gratitude through the Force. Vernestra shrugged a little. She had her own reputation for breaking ships. Besides, it was what Master Stellan would have done.

Captain Mitker's hologram spoke: "Do you need the whole thing if you're imitating it?"

Xylan sniffed. "I suppose not. Just the data core, or whatever similar part functions to translate the Path bundles. My husband has worked with Path engines and will know what it looks like."

"Let's get him up here," Kronara said.

"Tell him to bring me my dog," Xylan said.

Vernestra hated to be glad Xylan was here, but she was beginning to think they might make it home again. She said, "I'll stay with Xylan while we work out how to fake a fake."

Master Kriss agreed. "Good. Master Lox, will you remain here, co-ordinate the Jedi on patrol, and retrieve any additional intact Path engines with Admiral Kronara? I'll return to Naboo and organize from there. As soon as you have a workable exit, let everyone know. There are two of us who can do it, if there are two engines. And I believe out of the other Jedi present, another willing to make the attempt can be found."

"No," Captain Pel said. Her voice was soft but firm, cutting in. "The *Tractate* and crew are staying on this side."

Vernestra studied the captain, whose visage exuded resolution. Vernestra understood. It wasn't quite the look she'd seen on Imri's face when he told her he was staying in the Occlusion Zone. But the sense behind it felt the same. This wasn't a sudden choice or a whim. Pel knew what she was doing and trusted her crew to agree.

The admiral said, "Captain—"

"My ship needs hours more at least for repairs before it could even possibly undertake something so dangerous as this free jump through the Stormwall. And we're needed here."

"You can't stay on Naboo," Xylan Graf insisted. "They'll be back. The Nihil will be back, and they'll burn it all to the ground. They'll annihilate it. Because they can."

"If we're here, maybe they can't."

"One ship!"

Admiral Kronara snapped, "Graf, this has nothing to do with you. Do your work."

Xylan's teeth clicked as he shut his mouth.

"Pel," Kronara said.

"The *Harmonic* will remain to assist," Captain Mitker said.

Captain Pel glanced over to nod at the holo of Mitker, then faced the admiral at attention. "It's the right move, sir. We'll be able to dig in and prepare. If the Nihil come in force, we can remain nearby, or call in the *Radical Sar* from its position near the Lightning Crash and the three of us create a blockade. It's only a matter of time before there's a larger-scale Republic mission on this side again. When it happens, the *Tractate* and its crew will be prepared. Here. In place."

Even as Master Kriss's brow furrowed, even as Master Lox strode out of the war room and the admiral made plans with Captain Pel, Vernestra smiled. Not from happiness or foreboding. But because it felt right with the Force. She felt right, and Captain Pel's words "here, in place" resonated with her. Vernestra clung to that resonance. For a long time, she'd been stuck out of place or had been moving, moving, moving as if that were the only way to exist in the flow of the Force. But this was the right call, even if it was aggressive. She was where she needed to be, too. Whether she survived it or not. The Force was everywhere.

Xylan stepped next to her. "Come on, Vernestra, let's 'do our work.' "

Even though he was mocking, Vernestra felt that little spark of rightness, of light, that was so difficult to reach these days. She frequently felt out of place, unsure of her role in the hierarchy of the Order, even when she trusted in the Force and her fellow Jedi, even when she knew deeply that what they were doing was necessary *and* good.

These little sparks were rare, but Vernestra had learned to listen.

Chapter Forty

INSIDE THE OCCLUSION ZONE

Though Cair San Tekka was absolutely positive his husband could have described exactly what the data core for the Path engine looked like, or even pulled up a schematic to display if he wanted to, Xylan insisted on Cair doing the work.

So Cair had loaded Plinka onto one of the evacuation shuttles up to the RDC flagship and silently traded her to Xylan for a vac suit before heading over to the *Precipitate Fire* with Ensign Casset and an RDC security team. The Stormship was surprisingly intact, given the gaping tear in its neck, but the Path engine was nonfunctional, barely flickering bluish-green. While the ensign guarded his back, Cair hurried to cut it out. Xylan's voice rather sneered in his mind, *Why the hell not?!*

They touched down on the deck of the *Third Horizon*'s launch bay fifteen minutes later. Cair had used the time to strip off the vac suit and let the RDC medic with them give him a dose of painkillers for his still-aching ribs. When they had the all clear, Cair saluted the crew and let Ensign Casset lead him down the ramp. They jogged across the gleaming bay floor for one of the six exits deeper into the ship.

"Straight to the hyperdrive chamber, right?" Casset asked.

"That's right," Cair said, cradling the data core to his chest. The ship's chrono told him he had only about twenty minutes to get back to the shuttle if he wanted to return to Naboo before the *Third Horizon* made its jump attempt. Which he did.

They took a lift down several levels and hurried along a busy corridor filled with techs and soldiers and droids zipping about. They entered a huge engineering complex through round black doors that hissed open, and Casset directed him left.

Cair heard Xylan before he saw him.

"—told you I'm a theoretical physicist, not an engineer!"

The Jedi Vernestra Rwoh caught his eye as Cair entered. She looked stressed but slightly amused. Xylan was crouched near an open floor panel, talking down to two RDC techs standing inside the panel.

"Xylan, here," Cair said sharply.

His husband turned fast and reached out an imperious hand for the data core. Cair dropped it down without meeting his gaze.

Xylan offered it to one of the techs. "Just get it hooked up. All the codes are in this datapad." He set the 'pad on the floor. "Connecting the core to your ship is your problem. When I'm back, making it talk to the hyperdrive is mine."

With that, Xylan stood. Vernestra said, "Will you want me inputting the route from here or the bridge?"

"Wherever." Xylan strode past her, grabbed Cair's right forearm, and started dragging him along. "Come with me."

"Xylan, I have to get to the shuttle."

"Just listen for a moment, all right?" Xylan's jaw was clenched, and he walked hard and fast without looking at Cair.

It was strange, but then again Cair was angry, too. And he couldn't give Xylan what he wanted: either to go with him to Republic space or to ask Xylan to stay. Xylan was no good as a spy and would hate being on the run or undercover or assisting a rebellion on the dirty ground. Which were all the things Cair expected to do in the next few weeks, assuming he survived.

So for a few minutes, he let Xylan drag him up several levels and into crew quarters. "Here," Xylan said, stopping them at one narrow door. He keyed in a code, and the door slid open, revealing a small guest bunk mostly filled with the fluffy white fur of a Theljian snow dog.

"Plinka," Cair said, glad she was settling in. "I'll see you again, girl."

"That's right," Xylan said, nudging Cair fully into the room.

Cair rubbed behind Plinka's ear with the secured cuff protecting his right wrist. The snow dog nuzzled at him, sniffing the dark-red flight suit he wore. "Xylan, tell me what you want to say, then I have to go."

Xylan hadn't stepped into the room. He was staring at Cair with something distant in his perfectly bright-blue eyes. Alarm zipped down Cair's spine just as Xylan hit the outer panel and the door slid shut between them.

"Xylan!" Cair yelled, throwing himself at the closed door. "What the—" He slapped his hand against the cold metal. "Xylan!"

The comm speaker crackled, and Xylan's voice came through. "I'm not sorry, darling."

Cair hit the comm controls. "Let me out!"

"I have control of the room's comm and lock. It was the first thing I did when they assigned it to me en route to the Lightning Crash, oh, it feels like years ago. When I leave, you won't be able to use the comm or pry open the door. It's a military ship, after all." Xylan's tone was light.

"Kriff!" Cair yelled back at him, kicking the door. Pain radiated from his toes even though his boots were solid. Behind him, Plinka whined. His pulse raced. He wanted to tear open the door and shove Xylan as hard as he could. But Plinka had been through enough. So Cair took a deep breath. Then another. "I won't forgive you for this," he said almost quietly into the comm.

"Pshaw. I told you how it would be. Should I have gone through with drugging you?"

"Xylan—"

"I know you can spy your way out eventually, but by the time you do, we'll be in hyperspace, in Republic space, or, well, dead, I suppose. That's romantic, too, my love."

Cair leaned his forehead against the cool door and closed his eyes. It was too much to imagine Xylan doing the same on the other side. The reality of the situation drained through him like cold rain. He'd been right: Xylan could have given anyone the schematics for the Path data core, but he'd wanted Cair to deliver it here.

"You knew who you married, Cair San Tekka," Xylan said, sounding like a goodbye. The comm beeped and went dead.

With a frustrated snarl, Cair pressed the ball of his left hand and wrist stump of his right into his eyes and turned. He sank down to the floor, knees drawn up. Plinka padded over—only two steps for her in this small room—and touched her cold nose to his face. Cair sighed and buried his face in her ruff.

Chapter Forty-One

It was time to go, and they were leaving everyone else behind.

Avar stared out the viewport from the bridge of the *Third Horizon* as Admiral Kronara recalled all external fighters and gave orders for everyone to take their positions for a bumpy ride.

Beyond the debris field and the remains of the *Precipitate Fire* was the gorgeous green-blue Naboo, filled with life and at least a hundred RDC crew members and civilians who'd chosen to remain back with the *Harmonic* and the *Tractate*. Jedi Knights Far Linghe and Aviay had stayed, suggesting Naboo could use a few Jedi still and saying there was plenty for them to do in the Occlusion Zone. Avar couldn't even disagree with their choice. She was just glad the rest of the Jedi were on the *Third Horizon* now. Dotdat, Ceryl, Master Mirro and his Padawan, and Burry with Bell in a medical bay.

Less than an hour ago, Avar's copilot for all these weeks, Friielan, had contacted her from the surface of Naboo.

"I want to stay here, Avar," Friielan said, adding, "They'll need pilots." Friielan was a good one. They could fight here, and technically they'd already been released from the *Axiom* when it jumped back to

Republic space with the injured yesterday. They'd been attached temporarily to the *Harmonic*. It fit. "It's the will of the Force," they added, as if Avar had been arguing.

Avar had wanted to. She didn't want anyone to stay. But she understood. Naboo couldn't be evacuated and needed a shield.

Instead, she'd squeezed her hand into a fist and imagined squeezing Friielan's hand. "Be careful" was all she'd said, tucking away the thread of concern. She looked out now at everyone in the system, letting only light and pride and hope shine through her.

"May the Force be with you all," she said to the stars.

She touched her comlink. "Vernestra?" she said softly.

The young Mirialan answered, "We're almost ready."

"Do you want me to do it?"

"*No*," Vernestra said. "I've got this. But . . ."

There was just enough of something Avar couldn't quite name in Vernestra's voice that the Jedi Master turned on her heel and ran for the door.

Vernestra sat with her legs crossed on the floor in the engine room, her back against the hyperdrive relay console. She breathed carefully, blocking out everything that wasn't the Force, that wasn't the codes for the route to Takodana. It was the one she'd used the first time, the only time she'd done this without the Sunvale device. The only difference between then and now was the first three jump coordinates. She could do it. She had to. A few hundred lives depended on her focus.

Through the Force she felt Avar Kriss approaching fast, like a beam of light, and Vernestra felt Avar reaching. Vernestra reached out, too, and felt the beings in the room with her, anxious, determined, afraid, brave. She felt Burryaga nearby in the medbay, sitting with his large hand on Bell's shoulder. Bell, who was still half-unconscious with relaxants after his brush with the Nameless. Master Mirro Lox and his puppylike Padawan Amadeo working together in the adjoining room, helping disconnect and reconnect relays so the star cruiser's power was

diverted between rear defensive shields and hyperdrive reactor shields
to contain any excess energy from the unconventional Path data it was
being fed.

When they were ready, they'd tell her.

Vernestra skimmed her fingertips along the keypad. At the go, she'd
begin to input the coordinates one at a time, perfectly, smoothly. She'd
done it before. She could do it this time.

She was one with the Force. No matter what happened. They all
were.

Light-years away, Elzar Mann meditated in one of the small chambers
on the *Axiom* as it rushed through hyperspace back to Coruscant with
its injured and information. He thought of the heartbeat of the ocean
and the last things Avar had told him before he left her in the Occlusion Zone. He didn't worry at her words like gristle in his teeth but
only held them, listened again and again, and let the Force flow in and
out with his breath.

In his devious husband's guest bunk on the *Third Horizon,* Cair petted
Plinka and told her they were going to be fine.

Avar burst into the engine room and slid to her knees next to Vernestra. She reached out with the Force, pushing gently, and Vernestra
opened her eyes, met Avar's. Avar pressed her lips into a determined
shape and flicked her eyes to the cluster of techs and Xylan Graf hurriedly attaching cables and fussing at an astromech droid whose various knobs and arms were connected to the ship. Vernestra nodded and
her eyes drifted shut again. Her hands hovered over the keypad. Avar
set her fingers lightly on Vernestra's knees and let the Force flow
through her—through them both.

Burry heard Master Kriss's song and squeezed Bell's shoulder. They
opened up to the Force together, the forest of it unfurling in Burry's

mind, roots and branches reaching and growing. This wasn't like helping Master Kriss at Hetzal, full of straining and effort; now Burry only
needed to let the Force flow through him toward Master Kriss and
Vernestra. Master Lox's strength joined them, and the wavering voice
of his Padawan Amadeo blossomed in Burry's awareness of the Force
like a sturdy little flower.

Master Kriss wove them together.

"It's as ready as it will ever be," Xylan said to the RDC tech, glancing at
Avar Kriss. The Jedi Master held on to Vernestra, her eyes closed, and
said, "So are we."

"Let the bridge know," the tech said.

"Admiral, we're ready. Now or never," said another soldier.

Kronara's voice came over the comm. "On your mark, Lieutenant."

"May the Force be with you, Jedi," the lieutenant said.

Avar gently squeezed Vernestra's knees. She said, "Go."

The *Third Horizon* jumped.

Chapter Forty-Two

INSIDE THE OCCLUSION ZONE

The tiny planet in an unnamed sector where Porter tracked the beacon in Cair San Tekka's stolen star yacht was even more backwater than most in this part of the Outer Rim. But Porter Engle had seen worse.

It revolved around a tiny sun, almost too far out to be caught in the sun's gravity, so its path was ragged enough the atmosphere couldn't settle and the oceans raged. Yet life had found a foothold as it did in so many places: The whole world was covered in varieties of moss and lichen and tiny little insects that feasted on them.

Porter approached the planet cautiously, though the general was already gone. The shuttle he'd borrowed from Naboo was for research and collection, so it had decent long-range scanners and almost no weaponry—but it was fast. Porter should have been only a few hours behind her.

He landed several kilometers out and jogged over the soggy red wetlands. The sky was steely gray, striated with thick clouds and low planetary rings. A terrible place, but simple and straightforward.

Though according to the shuttle's sensors, Viess had already departed, Porter expected she'd left something. She wanted this final confrontation as much as he did.

That didn't mean he wouldn't go in assuming the worst.

The yacht was wedged against the lee of a cliff. Long strands of moss were scorched in a halo around it, though the ship didn't look damaged. Light flickered in a perimeter around it. Porter expanded his awareness of the Force as far as it would go, listening for any sign of danger. He slowed, picking his way carefully over the slippery landscape. He held his lightsaber in hand, waiting.

The light was from pale-pink flames dancing atop stakes wrapped in charring moss.

Viess must have been here recently if the torches still burned.

Porter ground his teeth. This was an invitation.

He knew better than to trust it, moving even more carefully. She hadn't played games like this before. Something had changed.

Porter hoped she was afraid.

The yacht's rear cargo doors hung open like a gaping mouth. Igniting his lightsaber, Porter held it out and let go. It floated near him, ready for the split-second thought that would send it flashing at an enemy. Though it took concentration through the Force, this was second nature to Porter by now, and worth the effort for the time saved if he didn't have to tell his hand to let go first.

Porter stepped up the shallow ramp, unsurprised to find the small cargo hold lit up as if the yacht were welcoming him home. He flicked his gaze around, noting pressure plates and trip wires so thin as to be nearly invisible. Porter stopped at the edge of the cargo bay floor. Listening, looking, reaching out with the Force.

But what she'd left was impossible to miss. The message was scrawled across several seamless access panels in what looked like blood: *Old man, I'll be waiting for you here . . .*

An arrow pointed beneath the message, to tiny, blurrier words. He couldn't read them without moving closer. Or doing what he was best at.

Letting his smile get just a bit smug, he sent his lightsaber shooting across the cargo bay in a pretty spiral. The tip sank into the yacht's panels with a hiss. Metal melted and Porter reached out, guiding the weapon in a swift circle. It sliced the section of metal with the words away, and—

A series of beeps warned him he'd triggered something. He hadn't moved, so a temperature sensor maybe.

The beeps got faster and faster, and Porter recalled his lightsaber. It slapped into his palm, and he used the Force to jerk the metal section free. The metal disk flew toward him and Porter ran.

He barely got a few meters before the beeps were a single long note. Porter grabbed the hot edge of metal and ducked into a ball. He pulled the Force around him, then pushed out in every direction just as the yacht erupted.

Heat and noise slammed into him—into the Force he wielded. It knocked him down flat, but the Force muffled its power.

His ears rang, and his skull thrummed as he rolled over. Everywhere but in the oblong circle around him the moss and lichens had burned to nothing but ash that hung in the air, shifting in fast little spirals and tornadoes as the atmosphere settled.

Porter crossed his legs, balancing himself with the Force, breathing carefully until he was sure he could stand again. He wasn't hurt.

The metal disk cooled down in his lap, and he finally looked at it. For a moment the writing didn't make sense. But there was nothing wrong with his vision: The writing was in an old style Porter hadn't seen in 150 years.

He couldn't read it, but he recognized it from pennants and long tapestries adorning the walls of the palace of the royal family of Firevale on Gansevor, the planet where he'd met General Viess. The last place he'd seen Barash.

Chapter Forty-Three

THE *THIRD HORIZON*, REPUBLIC SPACE

Burry did his best to let the Force flow through him and, by example, help Bell do the same. The other Jedi sat beside Burry on the cushioned bench, and Burry's big hand rested solidly on Bell's back.

Vernestra Rwoh was with them, meditating on Bell's other side, her legs crossed up on the bench, boots discarded on the floor.

They'd barely made it back to Republic space before being summoned to the lobby outside the Jedi comm office aboard the *Third Horizon*. Inside the office, Master Avar Kriss was speaking with several of the Council. Soon it would be Burry's turn.

The Council had already received his initial report on the fight with the Nameless, but he expected to have to explain himself again. If he could. Burry wasn't even certain himself what he'd done.

His instinct was to downplay it, though given how devastating the Nameless had been to the Jedi, he wouldn't be allowed. To his knowledge, no other Jedi had done what he'd managed, so it was his duty to pass it on if he could. But it made him deeply uncomfortable. He didn't know if he could replicate it, anyway.

And when Burry closed his eyes, it wasn't the Nameless haunting him: All he could see was that strange disease destroying the forest on Ronaphaven, which looked so much like the Nameless effect but felt so different.

"Burryaga," Vernestra said softly. She reached across Bell and nudged the Wookiee. "I can feel your anxiety."

He trilled a soft apology.

She shook her head with a tired smile. "You don't have to apologize. I only . . . thought I could help you steady."

Burry held her gaze and let himself open a little more to the Force between them. Vernestra felt only sincere and calm. He wrapped himself up in it until he was nothing but calm, too.

Except for those tense hours between the Stormwall's home key changing and their jump through it, Vernestra had remained with him and Bell with this same quiet, determined presence. Together the three of them had fallen back on the oldest Jedi lessons about being one. With one another and with the Force. They'd meditated and focused on Bell, who was doing better. The Nameless effect had left echoes in his mind, triggering harsher memories of his master, and Bell had needed the help regulating himself. Right now he breathed peacefully beside them, a little spark of amusement in his glance.

Beneath the bench, Ember snorfled, letting out a little smoke.

"What's bothering you, Burry?" Bell asked.

Vernestra tilted her head to listen to the answer casually, slowly stretching her neck and shoulders. She'd been injured during the fight, but they had smoothed already into dull aches and bruising.

Burry hedged his answer.

Bell frowned slightly. "You don't know how to explain what you did to the Council?"

Vernestra shrugged. "Just tell them that. That you don't know how to describe it."

Burry huffed.

"Listen." Vernestra's bearing grew serious. She was young for a Wookiee or a Mirialan—even for a human like Bell—but suddenly she seemed older than all of them. "The Council doesn't know what they're doing, either."

Burry couldn't help dropping his mouth open in surprise. Bell's eyes widened. "Vernestra, it's the *Council*," Bell said, hushed as if they'd be overheard.

It was Vernestra's turn to shrug. "And they're only people, too. I respect them and trust them, because I respect and trust the Force—something all of them have been doing for ages. But nothing like this has ever happened before. Not with the Nameless or the Nihil. They're doing their best. That's all anyone can do. They can't *know*, none of us can."

"This is some pep talk," Bell said with a little laugh.

She smiled again, this time with a lot more humor. "Just be honest, Burry, and trust the Force. I guarantee you that's what the Council wants."

Though his thoughts remained unsettled, Burry nodded.

Just in time, the office door swooped open, and Master Kriss poked her head out. She didn't have a mark from battle on her, and she wore pristine gold-and-white robes. "Burryaga, Vernestra, your turn."

Bell squeezed Burry's forearm. Burry followed Vernestra into the chamber with its ring of holoprojectors. Other than ten shimmering blue Council members, only Master Kriss was with them, and a shiny protocol droid waiting stiffly.

Grand Master Lahru greeted them. "Burryaga, Vernestra, it is good to see you well."

They made their bows while Vernestra murmured, "Masters."

"Killed one of the Nameless, you both have," Master Yoda said in his creaky old voice.

"I had the help of a man named Cair San Tekka, who was unaffected by the creatures," Vernestra said. "I was barely functional, but he pulled me far enough away that the effect was mitigated. We shot one together. I could not have done it on my own."

Master Kriss gestured for Burry.

Burry didn't want to remember. But he began to speak all the same.

Beside him, the protocol droid made a slightly awkward sound like clearing its throat, then translated Burry's words in a dull tone. "I was afraid."

For a moment Burry couldn't say more, pushing the memory far enough away to engage with it without being overwhelmed. The Council waited. Vernestra and Master Kriss watched him patiently. Finally, Burry heaved a deep breath. He explained that his worst memories and fears had been intense around him. He was in them. But he knew why. It had felt like a waking dream. He'd read about the effect and knew the terror was because of the Nameless.

"Recognizing what was happening gave you some clarity?" Master Soleil asked gently.

Burry shook his head with a little whine. He spoke, aware as he often was of the soft drone of the translator droid repeating his words in Basic. He explained that it hadn't been clarity. He'd heard the screaming of his friend, who was nearer to the Nameless, which caused Burry to panic. He used the panic.

For the next part, Burry couldn't help closing his eyes, feeling an echo of it again as he reminded them that he knows emotions well, and he used it. The fear—his own, Bell's, everyone's—gave him direction, and he guessed where the creature was by the strength of the fear. Then he threw his lightsaber.

Master Kriss blew through her lips, and Burry looked to see her nodding. She said, more for the Council than to Burry, "It was you at Hetzal who felt the people on that ship first and warned us. You're strong with empathy."

Burry nodded.

"Do you think that's what it takes?" Vernestra asked. "Empathy?"

"Not too much, I hope," Master Ki-Sakka said wryly.

"Testing this possibility is not an option," Master Yoda said.

Master Kriss said, "Disseminating the information is. The mere possibility needs to be shared, even if it is not enough for most or the circumstances were unique."

"We will discuss it," promised Master Yarael.

"Is there any other detail you can describe about your encounter, Burryaga?" Master Rosason asked.

Burry stared at the central console of the meeting table around which the holos hovered. He thought of what Vernestra had said just outside and nodded.

"Yes?" one of the Council members said, though Burry didn't know which by voice alone.

He lifted his gaze and looked at each Council member, then at Master Kriss. He told them this wasn't about the Nameless, but something awful and strange he and Bell came across that reminded him of the Nameless, of the husking effect the Nameless had on Force users.

"A blight that spreads over everything it touches?"

Burry's gaze shot to Master Ki-Sakka, who looked especially grim. Burry said yes.

"Heard similar reports, we have," Yoda said. "Not many, but all concerning."

Burry asked if he could look into it.

"We have investigations ongoing," said Lahru. "You and Bell Zettifar requested to continue seeking evidence of the reappeared Drengir."

Burry nodded, slightly relieved—though the Drengir were hardly less dangerous.

"That reminds me," Master Kriss said, coming to stand next to Burryaga. She gently nudged him so that she would be in the holocapture for the Council. "After you received their initial report, was someone dispatched to look for the Great Progenitor in the Eiram ocean?"

"The RDC is coordinating it, but Jedi will be going to investigate," said Ki-Sakka. "We will keep you informed, Burryaga, as it pertains to your mission, and after we discuss your revelations regarding the Nameless, we may follow up with you."

Burry bowed, knowing a dismissal when he heard one.

Master Kriss said, "I'll come find you when I'm finished. You, too, Vernestra." Turning back to the Council, she said, "Masters, I have a few further items regarding the situation along the Stormwall, and I'd like to discuss making the search for Marchion Ro himself our priority."

"Elzar just arrived back on Coruscant," Master Ki-Sakka said as Burry and Vernestra left. "He and I will be discussing the situation with the chancellor and her cabinet so that we can create priority assignments and allocate resources between the Order and the RDC—"

Burry was glad when the office door whooshed shut behind him. He shared a glance with Vernestra, who snorted gently. She said, "I'd rather be out here getting back to work than in there politicking, too."

Sighing a wordless agreement, Burry turned to share the news of their assignment with Bell.

Chapter Forty-Four

CORUSCANT

Elzar tugged at the high collar of his formal temple robes, even though it was not too tight. It simply gave him something to do instead of obsessing over what Avar had said to him on Naboo. She was due back on Coruscant in the morning, and he was going to have to give her an answer. Even though it hadn't been a question—he knew that. She'd simply held out a hand to him, and they both knew he'd take it. He just . . . had to decide exactly how.

He waited with Chancellor Soh amid verdant greenery in a garden pavilion on the rooftop of a tower so tall none of the cityscape was visible, only the sky smeared with vivid-orange clouds thanks to the setting sun. It was a rare sight on Coruscant, to be without the constant motion of traffic and glint of light on windows. Elzar was having difficulty enjoying it, though not because of the company—not yet anyway.

Lina Soh tilted her head, and the cascade of simple gems woven into her elaborate headdress tingled. One of her hands lifted toward her hidden ear, and she smiled. "They're coming up," she told Elzar.

Elzar grimaced for her, and the chancellor smiled wryly. Together they walked across the soft lawn to position themselves before a table set with crystal dinnerware for three. The targons Matari and Voru got to their feet and arched their long furred backs in perfect sync before padding along after Soh. As Soh and Elzar stopped, the giant cats did as well, but they did not lie back down. They remained standing and, to Elzar's surprise, incorporated him into their bookending of the chancellor.

"I didn't get a chance to thank you for including me," Elzar said lightly. "I'm incredibly excited for this dinner. It's going to be fun and carefree, and nothing dreadful could possibly come of it."

Laughing, Soh patted Elzar on the shoulder. "It relaxes me just enough to have someone along who hates this even more than I do."

"No wonder you didn't want Master Yoda here—he doesn't hate anything."

The truth was, when the chancellor had invited Elzar, as the representative of the Jedi Council, he'd sent word to the Council itself offering to step aside for one of them to take his place. Master Ki-Sakka had replied that they more than trusted Elzar for the job, not-so-subtly reminding him there was an open seat awaiting his rump if he'd only accept it. And soon.

Soh gave a little smile, then let it drop off her mouth. With quiet gravity, she said, "After the way I provoked her in the immediacy of the battles for the Lightning Crash and Naboo, I expect Ghirra to make this evening difficult, to say the least."

At the far edge of the garden pavilion, the indicator lights on the elevator arch flashed, and the two Senate Guards standing to either side shifted their attention to the newcomers.

Silently, the platform rose, revealing an intricate lacework enclosure and behind it three figures.

"Here we go," Elzar murmured.

The enclosure slid gracefully open to reveal Ghirra Starros and two more Senate Guards.

The former senator was alone otherwise, but from her bearing she might as well have an army behind her. Elzar's stomach soured.

Ghirra glided forward in a voluminous gown of Nihil blue with a tiny silver pauldron on each shoulder, attached across her collar by a chain that clasped with a wrought gold-and-copper sigil of the Nihil's eye. The human's long braids were wound into a crown and fell loose in the back, glinting with matching copper beads.

It made Elzar glad to be in his own formal uniform and appreciate Chancellor Soh's understated black-and-silver finery.

The former senator paused several paces from them, and for a moment, all three were silent. Elzar knew better than to speak, though he generally preferred breaking this kind of tension with a quip or aggression.

Chancellor Soh waited serenely, and one of the targons sighed, its ruff twitching with either boredom or irritation.

The light shifted quickly as the sun set, and Ghirra Starros smiled. "Chancellor Soh. I'm relieved and delighted you've agreed to meet with me as a representative of a neighboring state, given the recent Republic-driven attempts to disrupt our border."

"A neighboring state, is it, Ghirra? You remember Jedi Master Elzar Mann, of course."

Ghirra blinked as slow as one of the targons. It wasn't quite as effective with only two eyes. "Minister will do, Chancellor. And of course."

"Minister," Soh murmured. She stepped back a pace and gestured at the table. "Shall we?"

"We shall."

The trio took their seats, and the targons padded over to sit at Lina Soh's shoulders.

At an unseen command, service droids appeared from entrances obscured by graceful pinkseed and evergreen topiary or archaic water features. They brought out wine and tea and chilled infused sparkling water, along with slender trays of delicate hors d'oeuvres meant to be eaten with equally delicate chopsticks. Elzar experienced a vivid memory of a young Stellan showing him how to tell what food required what type of utensil at a fine dinner like this, based on placement and orientation to the plate. It really should be Stellan here.

But Elzar could manage. Stellan had made sure of it.

As the droids set the service, Elzar said, "Minister . . . does this mean the Nihil are seeking recognition as a political entity, a nation, instead of remaining mere marauders and warlords?"

Her calm expression didn't alter in the slightest as Ghirra said, "We have ruled ourselves as such for months now. I'm glad the Republic is catching up."

"We've been busy protecting our people from a rather malicious and relentless enemy," the chancellor said, nodding thanks to a glinting black droid as she lifted her cup of wine. "I do hope this conversation settles a few things and sets the agenda for a commitment to peace."

Ghirra took up her own cup and held it toward Chancellor Soh. "To commitments."

Elzar joined their toast, uncomfortable at the various connotations of the minister's words.

They drank, and Chancellor Soh said, "Well, Minister Starros. What do you have for us?"

"I don't see what perceived shift in power is making you arrogant, Chancellor," Ghirra said, reaching with her chopsticks for the many-layered leafy urchin appetizer. "You attacked us, destroyed part of our border defense, invaded a world under our claim. We did not even re-taliate, but merely reestablished a border."

The words were more direct than Elzar had anticipated for opening gambits at a dinner like this. It was difficult not to immediately argue with her.

But Chancellor Soh ate her food and said nothing. Elzar struggled in the drawn-out silence, unable to do the same and eat. He was here to support the chancellor but also as a representative of the Jedi Order, and he wanted to tell Ghirra Starros to take her fancy dress and Nihil jewelry and run. That it didn't matter if the Nihil pretended to act like a nation. Starlight Beacon was remembered. Valo was remembered.

The *Legacy Run* was remembered. Even putting all that aside, as a Jedi, Elzar was determined not to stop until they'd made sure that the Nameless could never harm another Force user. That there could be no negotiation or compromise as long as the Nihil remained a threat to all beings in the galaxy.

He held his tongue though. Threats weren't the point of this, and they'd slide off Ghirra anyway, coming from him and being so direct. Still, the tension between the two politicians was enough to make Elzar feel out of his depth once again. As if his concerns about justice and the Force and freedom and hope were small compared with complex galactic politics. He had to remind himself he was here for a reason. That the Jedi had worked hand in hand with the Republic for centuries because their priorities aligned more often than not. And recently, they aligned consistently. Chancellor Lina Soh, with her "We are all the Republic" motto and Great Works outreach, with the vision of Starlight Beacon and the Republic Fair driving her . . . no matter how those things had turned out, been twisted by the Nihil, what mattered in this case was Soh's faith and determination that mirrored the hope of the Jedi.

Elzar put his utensils down and stopped pretending he was going to take a bite. "Minister, if the Nihil are becoming a nation, can you tell us what you represent? We know where we stand as the Galactic Republic and the Jedi. Do you?"

Ghirra Starros pursed her lips. "Naturally I can answer such a question," she said slowly, and Elzar felt a zing of triumph when he realized she was stalling to give herself time.

"Oh?" the chancellor said.

"Hmm, yes." Ghirra sipped from her cup. "We are . . ." Here her smile turned sharp. "Balance. Options. Choice. The Republic may be great, and its morals and mottos are reflective of not only high standards but also unimpeachable ideals . . . yet there will always remain people who do not fit. There will always be cartels and organizations that chafe at the ways of the Republic and of the Jedi. People whose wants and needs cannot be met by the Republic. The Nihil provide an opportunity for such individuals, for such different and marginalized ideals to come together. To make their own path. Their own nation. Is it not better for a receptacle to exist to catch such dissenters? An alternative with which the Republic can coexist?"

Elzar felt his stomach turn over again at the impressive politicking that turned the oppression and viciousness of the Nihil into such a benevolent entity. It was a lie. It was a trap. But it still sounded like an argument some people would believe—even some senators.

"I see," Chancellor Soh said thoughtfully. "What remains to be seen is whether the Nihil are not only willing but also *able* to coexist with us."

"And what must I say or promise to convince you we can?"

Lina Soh leaned forward. The only hint of the shift in her composure was that one of her targons' hackles rose, and both their tufted tails whipped with anxiety.

"To begin, you can return my son to me immediately, unharmed."

"Oh, my," Ghirra said, sitting back. "I didn't realize your son was missing."

"Since the Stormwall activated well over a year ago," the chancellor said tightly.

Ghirra, instead of faking any sympathetic moue or pretending shock, said, "I believe, Chancellor, that you are aware of my own daughter's whereabouts."

Elzar did his best not to wince. He also knew exactly where Avon Starros was, and it was not too far from here. Soh could use her. Could easily relent and give up Avon's special status to turn her over to her mother for some leverage.

The chancellor said, "I am, Minister. But because of the great service your daughter has provided and because I respect her autonomy, I will not betray her to you."

Not even for my son, rang the underlying declaration. Elzar watched Chancellor Soh. He had long admired her passion and integrity, but this was a whole new level. Everything he knew about her crystallized, and he realized her decision was born from a place of great altruism, the kind Jedi had tried to teach and to reach themselves, for years and years.

Lina Soh loved her son so much that it made her a better person.

Clarity reverberated through Elzar, echoing what Avar had said to him. That love was limitless, that it expanded the galaxy. It was how this chancellor led. Toward Light and Life, always. Even when she'd been taught repeatedly that it didn't always mean she'd be successful. That she was *likely* to lose. She kept trying.

Elzar smiled. He felt as though a little bit of the chancellor's light brightened in him.

No matter what happened for the rest of this negotiation, he believed eventually Lina Soh would win.

Ghirra must have felt it as well because she inclined her head. "I will look into the whereabouts of your son. I do not know where he is, if he is in Nihil custody or simply lost as so many have been, but I promise I will do my best to find him."

"Thank you," Soh said.

"I hope," Ghirra continued, "that these assurances are enough to press forward and discuss what we need to discuss in order to set an agenda for negotiations."

"I believe so. Let us have the next course."

This time Chancellor Soh made her gesture to the service droids more pronounced, and they came with bowls of milky soup dotted with glistening pearls of some sweet violet salt bubbles.

Soh sipped from the soup and then said, "The first thing we must consider is that if the Nihil are to be recognized as a sovereign nation, the border must be clear and stationary."

Ghirra laughed. "We aren't the ones treating our border as permeable."

"It should be permeable, especially to the so-called citizens of Nihil space," Elzar said. "People have been trapped against their will in the Occlusion Zone, and their freedom has to be taken into consideration."

"The Nihil are hardly the first to establish themselves through violence," Ghirra chided. "Yes, there are people who did not enthusiastically consent to our governance, but can you even pretend to say that the Jedi—much less the Republic itself—have never pressed their rule onto anyone?"

Chancellor Soh said coldly, "You're asking the Republic to forgive not the violence of a government legitimately establishing itself, but absolute atrocities. Atrocities targeting us and our ideals, and specifically meant to instill fear and chaos and death. Marchion Ro gruesomely and despicably executed one of our great leaders in a live broadcast, Ghirra Starros." Soh set down her utensil and stared coldly at the former senator. "To even consider treating your proposals or sovereignty in good faith, I *will have* assurances that the Nihil intend to act like a neighbor, not a malicious enemy. If you cannot even convince me there will be a sustained and recognized border, one that will *not* expand into unwilling systems, I won't ever bother to open the subject of anything like trade tariffs or prisoner exchanges with the Senate."

"Be glad we aren't demanding the total destruction of the Stormwall," Elzar said.

Ghirra smiled tightly. "Even you must know there are things the Eye of the Nihil will not give up."

Like his Nameless creatures, Elzar assumed, pressing back a shudder at the thought.

"Why have we not heard from Ro?" Elzar asked. Grand Master Ki-Sakka had told Elzar that Council members were turning their attention more and more toward Ro himself in the wake of the recent battles. They'd had the Stormwall defeated until Marchion Ro changed the game on them again.

The chancellor added, "Yes, Minister. Your 'Eye' certainly likes to send us devastating messages. Where is his personal message of friendship? If he is so willing to allow these negotiations."

"I am the message of friendship," Ghirra said smoothly. "I have come through official channels as his Minister of Information. There is no one more highly ranked among the Nihil than myself."

It wasn't anything a person should brag about. Elzar didn't bother to hide the disgusted curl of his lips.

The chancellor answered more smoothly. "You understand politics, Minister. You must understand how symbolic a message from the mouth of Marchion Ro himself would be. With his penchant for dramatic galaxy-wide declarations, I know he does."

"You hardly expect to do direct business with the regasa of the Togruta," Ghirra snorted.

"And yet sometimes that queen visits us in friendship," Soh said, a fire in her dark gaze—it had been a mistake to remind her of the Togruta queen, who had been at the Republic Fair so brutalized by the Nihil, where Lina Soh had lost part of her leg and where Stellan had become the face of the Jedi.

Elzar opened his feelings to the Force, aware of the delicate nature of this moment. Chancellor Soh projected fierce determination, and Ghirra Starros controlled her emotions tightly.

Soh added almost casually, "A word from Ro himself would go a long way toward convincing us of his offer of friendship. As long as he hides, he behaves like an enemy."

"He is hardly hiding," Ghirra scoffed.

"Then where is he? We've heard nothing from him after our defeat of his Stormwall and his general. His past suggests retaliation, not reaching out via a peaceful representative."

"Marchion Ro is at his stronghold on Hetzal, naturally."

Ghirra said it easily, but Elzar could feel she was lying. Neither Soh nor himself could admit aloud that not having proof of Ro's location, or some word from him directly, only added to the lingering fear of his next action throughout the galaxy. For all his presence promised violence, not knowing where he was let all their imaginations run wild. The longer he hid himself, the worse his reappearance would be.

"For now," Ghirra said, "you'll have to rely on me. We can surely discuss some other things, in addition to your demand regarding our border. Reparations, perhaps, to certain worlds and people," the minister offered so silkily.

"Oh, certainly, Ghirra." Chancellor Soh smiled, and Elzar almost imagined sharp teeth behind her lips. "I'm so glad to know we can rely on you."

Chapter Forty-Five

NEAR WILD SPACE

The badlands spread before Marchion Ro. Orange and red striated rock pillars thrust up here and there beside blue-green cacti sprouting neon-orange flowers and spindly bushes with long tentacle-like arms that reminded him of the cephalosaurs he'd hunted on Regnio III in his youth. If he'd come to this unnamed world to hunt, he'd be focused on the fat-bottomed succulents for water and possibly for edible fibers, or the shimmer in the distance that suggested humidity on the horizon. Prey would congregate at any watering holes, no matter the planet or moon. Especially a world with an atmosphere Ro could breathe.

This was not that kind of hunt.

He'd come here on a hunch after abandoning the chaos on Hetzal, where his entire so-called government was arguing among themselves while two of his ministers ruled from a distance. A very great distance, he thought wryly. What the third minister, Boolan, did could rarely be called anything close to governing anyway. But Ro had one of the new creatures Boolan had engineered with him.

The Nameless monstrosity groaned quietly but constantly beside him as Ro walked. Its pace was off balance thanks to extra claws grafted to its forelegs and cybernetic additions down its spine. Making it a more efficient killing machine. Ro didn't really need it more efficient. He enjoyed the slow death of his enemies. But these Nameless of Boolan's who survived their treatments could at least be said to be more resilient and, to beings less dangerous than Ro, more frightening.

Ro had brought it with him to test its conditioning to his control. The experiments were no good to him if Boolan's work eradicated their reliance on the rod.

And so it moved strangely at his side, though its presence wasn't needed for this particular mission.

Ro was on this desert planet because it was one of the worlds where he had tucked seeds of the Drengir all those months ago. Just to see. To discover if they would grow in a place with little traditional vegetation. There was water here, and there were cacti and glorious blooming flowers . . . but not forest, not the lushness where Drengir thrived.

It had been an experiment, and so was this.

What mattered was that Marchion Ro had been right.

There had been Drengir here, and now, for some reason, they were gone.

In their stead: this blight.

"This is a beautiful world."

Ro ignored her voice, the tender wonder there. Neither of those feelings were useful to him.

Cold wind tore at his hair and the fur of his heavy cloak.

Ro tugged the Rod of Power out from his belt and held it calmly before him. He needed nothing for this but himself, his ambitions, and this ancient artifact passed down from his ancestors.

It was strange inasmuch as on a desert like this, the blight was only a gray-white version of the same rough sand and climbing pillars. Unlike the crystal fields, where the change was obvious and disconcerting, here it might have been one desert mineral replaced with another.

Ro walked toward the blight. He held the rod, commanding it as he commanded the Levelers. He reached the edge of desert, the start of the blight.

Calmly, he stepped across it.

"Oh," the ghost breathed. His boots crunched softly against the blighted desert rock. A few chunks crumbled under him, but he kept his balance.

The rod tingled against his palm. He waited for a moment but felt nothing attack him. Nothing slinked deadly fingers into his skin and bones.

Marchion Ro smiled to himself and walked farther into the blighted landscape.

Chapter Forty-Six

Burryaga felt a dull sense of heaviness as the two-person Vector settled onto the landing pad just outside the Elia-An colony. As the lateral wingtips folded in and the engine hum quieted, Burry let himself focus on the feeling and the Force until it sharpened into dread.

He took a breath big enough he had to let it out in a long sigh. Ember growled a little, rubbing her head on his thigh. Burry patted her and pushed her gently away.

Bell said, "You have to stay in here again, Ember. We're back on a forest world."

The glow of her fire veins dimmed, but she sat. Bell scratched behind her ears. "Ready?" he asked, staring hard at Burry.

For a moment, Burry just stared back, settling himself as best he could. He rumbled agreement.

But Bell didn't move. The human Jedi patted Burry's shoulder, reaching high. He didn't say anything right away, but Burry knew Bell was thinking about their encounter with the Nameless on Naboo, and the aftermath for both of them. Though Bell had initially been affected more extremely, it was Burry who couldn't shake off the last of it, even days later. Burry had admitted he'd been dreaming of tearing out his own fur, and not in order to make talismans like the ones that had saved him on Eiram, leading Bell to him. In the dreams, Burry did it for no reason other than how it felt. Bell was worried about Burry and wanted to request a leave, just a short one, to try to speed-recover from what the Nameless had revealed about both of their emotional states ever since Starlight Beacon fell. Burry hadn't ever wanted Bell to know so explicitly about the terror and loneliness he'd felt trapped under the Eiram ocean, alone in that cave, running out of air, desperate to believe somebody was looking for him. Resigned that it didn't matter. Dying alone.

Bell had suggested Burry take him to Kashyyyk and introduce him to the huge old trees there. He'd suggested it would help him think of the Force the way Burry did: like a massive old forest. And he wanted to know his friend better. Even if Burry hadn't lived on the Wookiee homeworld since he was five years old, it had been his first home.

The temptation to retreat to those peaceful dark forests had been difficult to resist. But Burry had to keep moving, keep fighting. They couldn't afford to lower their guard. The Force needed them out here, ready for what was already coming. It was more than the Nihil, more than the Drengir. Burry felt it.

Burry suspected Bell felt similarly, because it hadn't been hard to convince him they should keep hunting Drengir, to investigate if the Nihil were behind their reappearance.

They weren't here on Oanne for Drengir, though. Two days ago a message had reached Burry from the medicine artist Arryssslesh, begging him to return.

Following the destruction of the Lightning Crash, the Jedi Council was hopeful the Stormwall couldn't expand again very easily or casually, since the power source was gone. Hopefully there would be days of warning if it moved toward Oanne again. But Burry knew Arryssslesh would only ask them to come if it was important. And if it had been Drengir, she'd have said outright.

"Let's find out what they need," Bell said, his hand falling off Burry's shoulder.

Together they exited the Vector.

The humid air smelled fecund and sweet, and the breeze ruffled the blue-green canopy of the nativity tree forest. Waiting for them was the medicine artist herself. Her bristles flickered bluish in a pattern Burry couldn't read, but it felt anxious to him.

He barked a greeting in Shyriiwook, then added one in An-An.

Arryssslesh bustled nearer and spread her seven-fingered hands in welcome. Something . . . brittle drifted off her through the Force, and this time Burry had no desire to pet her.

"What can we do for you?" Bell asked. The RDC evacuation team had mostly departed, taking their droids with them, and so Bell had a boxy translator device clipped to his shoulder, set low to broadcast what Arryssslesh said quietly in his ear.

"Something is devastating our nativity forest in the east," the Elia-An leader said. The pattern of light on her bristles spiked and popped to Burry, and he felt her fear wafting strongly enough that Bell could likely sense it, too.

Burry asked her to lead the way.

Bell caught his gaze and Burry shook his head. He didn't *know* what to expect. But he was extremely worried that he could guess.

The medicine artist brought them to the edge of the landing pad, where three other Elia-An people waited. Two of them wore pale sashes that seemed to be some type of rank indicator, and the third had paler bristles than the rest, which Burry understood to mean they were from a different clan from the neighboring continent. "These are leaders from two different communities," Arryssslesh said. "I invited them, too, in order to see. Rysslusykyn artists, these are the Jedi I described."

Burry didn't know the title she used, and Bell's translator unit didn't either. Once introductions were complete, Arryssslesh ushered them all onto a sharp-nosed air carrier with an open viewing stern. She explained that they would fly to the location of devastation before making any further decisions.

The trip took only a few minutes at high speed. Both Bell and Burry stood at the rail where wind buffeted them, peering forward as if they'd be able to spot the problem early.

They could.

Burry's hands tightened on the cold rail of the carrier, and he whined softly. Bell murmured a quiet curse. It was just like on Felne 6.

From the horizon reaching toward them, the forest had become gray. It was pale dust and desiccation. Husked. As far as they could see.

Burry carefully modulated his breathing. He felt Bell's shock and dismay. The knots of fear, disgust, uncertainty, grief coming from the four Elia-An with them. And . . . Burry reached out.

The nativity forest thrummed with uncertainty. Below them, elegant nativity trees reached up with their white flute branches and blue filaments of leaves and vines. They were unmoving, of course, except where a duller breeze tickled their filaments, but to Burry it felt as if they pulled away, leaned far from the blight. The nativity trees sensed the danger and yearned to escape it.

His heart felt tight. He'd known this would be it. Ever since he'd first encountered it, Burry hadn't been able to get this blight out of his thoughts.

The carrier hummed to a gentle halt near the edge of the gray blight. The trees already diseased—dead? sucked dry of life?—retained their shapes, as if they'd become a forest made of rough pumice. The very edge of the blight was different, though: Some trees were fully consumed but for a few snaking vines clinging to blue-green life; others had branches ruined, yet their trunks remained vivid green-black and healthy. The blight appeared in small blotches along the boundary, but not too far, only as far as a seed might float or a root creep under the rest, emerging to embed the disease in a nativity tree several paces from the rest.

It was like a living disease, reaching for its next meal at a relatively steady pace. Just like on Ronaphaven, where the Drengir had been and left. He asked Arryssslesh if they'd had Drengir on Oanne. They had, but more than a year ago.

Burry reached with his senses for the feelings clamoring at him. The blight felt strange and . . . sad.

"Do you know what it is?" Bell asked.

Arryssslesh said, "We do not."

Before he second-guessed himself, Burry gripped the rail and vaulted over it.

"Burry!" cried Bell. But Burry reached with the Force and found it plentiful here. He used it to slow his leap, descending to the forest floor smoothly. He landed in the leaf litter and steadied himself against a twisted old tree without the distinctive furrow of the nativity trees. Vaguely aware of Bell and the others in the carrier overhead, Burry walked carefully in the direction of the blight.

Something about the smell of this part of the forest added to Burry's wariness. It wasn't a rock smell, or a death smell the likes of which he was familiar with. No, it was . . . arid, like a desert, not like the teeming forest it should be. Arid and . . . old. But this blight wasn't old. It had been only a few short weeks since he and Bell were here before, and if this had already begun at that time, it hadn't been affecting enough to be noticed or concerned about.

Burry kept going, eyes wide and open to the Force, hunting for the first sign he'd reached the border.

It came in the form of pale light and then a stillness.

He moved cautiously toward the nearest blighted tree. It was frozen in stone, more a rough sculpture than a living plant transformed this way. The Wookiee closed his eyes and held out a hand to feel it without touching. Empathy was how he'd stopped the Nameless. Maybe it would serve him here, too.

Except it felt like nothing. It was empty. Raw.

And beyond—no, part of—that was a chasm of something . . . he couldn't quite name the feeling yet.

Vaguely aware of Bell's approach along his path, Burry lowered himself to sit on the forest floor. He crossed his long legs and adjusted the fall of his robe. He placed the hilt of his lightsaber across his knees and closed his eyes. When he sensed Bell near enough, he told his friend to send word to the Jedi.

Then, reaching into himself, he found his internal forest, the Force growing through his guts and bones, and filtered out beyond his body to the ground, the roots and mycelium and insects and worms . . . he reached, and when he found it, the boundary, it pulled at him. No, at the Force in him.

Burry breathed deeply and strengthened his emotional resolve. He readied himself, and then, using the Force, he pushed back at the blight.

Chapter Forty-Seven

CORUSCANT

Elzar nearly escaped the Jedi Council Chamber without issue, stepping into the turbolift only to hear his name called. He paused, turning. "Master Yoda," he said, bowing slightly.

"Walk with me, hmm?" the Jedi Grand Master said, marching slowly to join Elzar in the lift. Elzar smiled as he waited, then let the door whoosh closed behind Yoda.

As the thrum of power indicated the lift was in motion, Elzar leaned his shoulder against the gilded wall. "Are you going to make another pitch for me to join the Council?"

Yoda snorted and tapped the end of his cane on Elzar's boot. "Know a decision when it's been made, I do."

All the pent-up fight drained out of Elzar at the admission, because he knew his answer, too. He was glad he didn't have to deny the Council again. "I'm honored by the offer," he said quietly.

The turbolift opened. Yoda led Elzar out into one of the antechambers midway down the spire, toward a balcony. It opened up into the early morning of Coruscant, kept quiet by energy shields surrounding the Temple. But the city was alive with the movement of traffic and slowly shifting clouds. Thermal vultures spun in circles higher even than the Jedi Temple. Elzar crouched down to stretch the small of his back and be nearer eye level with the old Jedi Master.

"The reasoning behind your choice, I would like to hear," Yoda said, his big green eyes holding on to Elzar.

Elzar nodded. He had so many reasons, some that he'd already given and some that now seemed irrelevant, such as never having taken on a Padawan. And some that he'd only just understood himself. "Being in between suits me," he said without thinking too hard about it. "Representing the Jedi to the chancellor and vice versa is a good space for me to occupy. It lets me be flexible, move between bodies of government and justice . . . lets me move at all."

"Think the councilors are stuck in our seats, do you?" Yoda teased.

Elzar laughed. "I know better. But the symbolism of it . . . the stability . . . the honor of it even, to be honest. Those things don't suit me."

"Hmm, I see."

"I'm working on leadership," Elzar admitted. "But I'm still not there. I feel . . . that there is a place for me, where I'm meant to be for the rest of my time with the living Force."

"And the Jedi Council, it is not."

"That's right," Elzar admitted with a little chagrin. Thinking, *Avar. It's with Avar.*

Yoda tapped his cane on Elzar's boot again. "Satisfied with your answer, the Council will be."

Elzar let out a big puff of breath. "I have a question for you, too, Master Yoda."

"Listening, I am."

Closing his eyes, Elzar centered himself and made sure his feelings and words were in close alignment. "Avar said something to me that I have been contemplating. Or really, agonizing over." He let himself smile at Yoda.

It was the grand master's turn to laugh. Then he gestured with his walking stick for Elzar to continue.

"She said she loved me, and that it was through the Force that she felt it. Not attachment, not anything selfish or that would prioritize her feelings for me, for us, over other lives or the rest of the song she hears in the Force. But a love that . . . is the Force. Expansive. It makes the galaxy better to love. And . . ." Elzar looked at the polished stone floor. "Since she said it, I've been feeling it, witnessing it in others all around me."

The old Jedi Master hummed thoughtfully.

"Master Yoda, do you think it's possible to be free of attachment, to be pure in the Force, but also to love an individual? Or a place or . . . the whole Republic, I suppose."

"Depends on what is meant by love, I believe," Yoda answered readily. "Some beings think love is connection. Love is recognizing you, in me. In the whole galaxy. To name a thing is to love it, some teachings say; others that love is vulnerability or a natural, bodily need." Yoda shook his head. "What the real answer is, I do not know. But if you find the answer for yourself, and it opens the Force to you more widely, brings you closer to the light, then wrong you cannot be."

"Is it really that simple?"

"Feels simple to you, it does?"

Elzar laughed again. He had been the one to say he was agonizing over this question. "Master Yoda, have you found the answer for yourself? Do you love?"

"Always," Yoda said.

"How?"

"Hmm. For you, a question I have in return. Do you think your parents loved you less because they sent you to the Jedi Temple?"

"No," Elzar said immediately.

"Why?"

"Because it was my destiny. I was born with Force potential, and they wanted what was best for me."

"Even without you in their lives, and knowing you would grow without holding on to their names?"

Elzar took a deep breath. "They let me go. They loved me and let me pass through their lives, through their love. They didn't hold on to me even if they ached to. Or not." He shrugged a little. It reminded him of Chancellor Soh desperate for her son to be safely returned to her, but not willing to compromise her principles, the safety of billions of lives, to demand it. He had thought last night that her love made her better.

He wondered if love had any chance of making Ghirra Starros better, too.

"The Force passes through us, as do all feelings and thoughts. Such things are fleeting with the living Force. And when they pass through us, through everything, to the cosmic Force do they return."

"I worry that if I give in to love, I will allow it to overwhelm me. That I'll want it to."

"Choose you must, how to let the Force flow through you, be a part of you, yes? This you already do, and strive for every day."

"So that's why it's hard," Elzar murmured.

"Hmm, yes, hard to choose. Hard to live." Yoda shrugged. "Choosing and living are the same, perhaps?"

"To live is to choose," Elzar said, "every day. What to say, who to say it to, what to eat, when to sleep, how to listen, who to be." Elzar looked at Yoda. "How to love and serve the Force."

"And if you choose in a moment a way that overwhelms you, then the next moment, the next day, hmm?"

"You choose again." *Like getting knocked down by the sea when meditating in a handstand,* Elzar thought. Orla had been telling him this same thing. Get back up. Try again. He said, "No matter how many times I fall, I can get back up. Must get back up."

"Much to contemplate," Yoda said with characteristic slowness. "And work to do."

With a slight grimace at that reminder, Elzar stood back up. "Right as always, Grand Master. Thank you for the counsel."

As Elzar made his way across the open gallery on the ground level of the Temple, deep in thought considering how to make his approach to Avon Sunvale, someone else called his name.

This time, Elzar looked up with an automatic grin. It was Avar, coming in through the massive front doors, midmorning glowing behind her.

Jedi moved around them, some glancing their way, others focused on their own tasks or disregarding the two as they grasped hands.

Avar looked tired but good. The rose-gold diadem he'd given her gleamed in a graceful arc against her forehead, and her hair was pulled back in a tail. She was in her formal robes, maybe on her way to make a report herself. Her hand was cool in his, and Elzar thought of how she'd kissed him in a room full of people on Naboo.

He swallowed.

"Good morning," Avar said.

"I've been up for hours," he teased. Then he squeezed her fingers. "I just told Master Yoda I won't take the seat."

"Are you all right?" She caught his gaze, concern obvious in her expression.

But Elzar said yes easily. "It was the right decision. I . . . I'm good at what I'm doing, even when it includes sit-down dinners with Ghirra Starros."

Avar wrinkled her nose dramatically. Elzar wanted to touch his nose to hers, as silly as it sounded.

Their fingers were still entwined. Elzar felt almost giddy about it suddenly, like when they were kids. That thought led immediately to memories of the two of them giggling with Stellan, flirting with each other, and at him, his ears pink when he wouldn't flirt back.

The memories, just flashes and little fond nicknames echoing in his mind, faded as he pushed them away, watching Avar as her face went through a similar journey. She was thinking the exact same things. Her lips parted in a soft sigh that was almost, almost Stellan's name.

Loving Stellan had certainly never done anything but make the two of them better.

The weight of who they were now settled around Elzar and Avar in the heart of the Jedi Temple. It was good. Solid. Woven with both giddiness and grief.

He squeezed her fingers again, then let them go. "Are you heading to your quarters?"

"Yes. I need to finish my write-up on proposals to track down Ro himself, if it's even possible from this side of the Stormwall. But we have to. We pushed the Nihil back. We cracked the home key. If not for Ro, we'd still have the Stormwall open. We'd have a better chance of defending Naboo, and . . ." She shook her head in frustration.

"I'm actually on my way to track down something that might help with that."

Avar lifted her eyebrows.

Elzar only said, "I'll let you know if it pans out."

She accepted it. "I heard from Bell Zettifar right before disembarking that he and Burryaga found more of that blight on a planet on the border, and some evidence it might be linked to places the Drengir are—or have been. There hasn't been any movement on the investigations into what it is, has there?"

Elzar stepped nearer, out of habit lowering his voice. "No, not really. But the reports initially all came from the Occlusion Zone, where we have little room to investigate—or even ways to get that kind of specific information."

As Avar nodded through a thoughtful frown, Elzar touched her hand again, realizing something. "You should ask that Cair San Tekka you brought from Naboo with you. He was the one with the information network, right?" When she nodded, Elzar added, "He might know more about the blight or rumors of its presence in the O.Z., since if anybody was going to pay attention to things like that, it would be him."

Avar opened her mouth to reply, then stopped. Her look turned more than curious: suspicious. "Why?"

"Because . . ." Elzar paused in surprise. "Because the first sample of the blight we ever got was his hand."

In their whole lives, Elzar wasn't sure he'd ever seen Avar so stunned. "This whole time," she murmured incredulously.

"I assumed you knew."

Avar blew air out through her lips. "It wasn't—his name wasn't in the report I read. Skimmed, really. I wasn't part of the teams working on it or focused in that direction."

Elzar nodded. It made sense. There was a lot going on in the galaxy, and Jedi were spread thin. In his role as the Jedi representative to the Chancellor's Office, he read everything these days.

"Well, kriff," Avar muttered. Then she took a deep breath. "I'll ask him."

"Good. I have to go. I'll . . . dinner?"

"Yes."

A mere hour later, Elzar found himself in some tucked-away guest lab in an RDC research compound a short flight from the Senate building. He'd needed JJ-5145 to help him find the facilities Avon Sunvale had taken over, as well as permissions obtained by one of his contacts in the senatorial committee for RDC actions. But he was here, touching the panel outside to indicate a visitor had arrived.

He heard a muffled bang inside and raised his eyebrows even though nobody else was around to see it. A voice echoed, and the door slid open to reveal a workshop not unlike Elzar's personal rooms at their worst, with the single exception that Avon Sunvale worked with crystals and the detritus of her experiments were shards of quartz glinting everywhere, the spears of smoky crystal propped against every wall and available surface.

"Master Elzar," Avon Sunvale said in surprise as she pushed focus goggles up her forehead to snarl in her puffy curls. "What do you want?"

Elzar didn't take offense at her tone—it was more neutral than irritated anyway. "I have a request for you."

"I'm really busy, trying to reclaim this array data so I can jump my place at the university—I should be teaching this section, not made to sit through the lecture, you know?—but I assume you're here about the survival of the galaxy or something like that?" The young woman pressed her mouth into a line and ushered him in. She picked up a few discarded boxes and a chunk of pink stone in order to make room on a plain chair against the wall. "I don't have anything to offer you except some blue milk, sorry."

"I'm not thirsty. But are you feeding yourself?" Elzar frowned.

The scowl Avon shot him reminded him intensely of Ghirra.

"What's that?" he asked, pointing at a half-unspooled cord of what was maybe synthetic crystalline filament. Elzar asked partly because he was very curious, and partly to win back a few points with Avon for caring. This urge to invent was something they had in common, after all, but Avon didn't know that, despite Elzar's early experiments with flexible alloys to make the device more adaptable to differently config-ured ships.

Avon lit up. She started talking about subspace frequencies and power arrays that could somehow harness natural resonance of the vacuum of space, or something like that—it was clearly theoretical, and Elzar was intrigued despite only understanding about a third of what she was saying.

Suddenly Avon stopped. She narrowed her eyes. "This isn't why you're here."

"I need your help," he admitted.

"Oh, no." Avon spread her hands flat in denial and backed away, nearly tripping on some machinery. "When Jedi ask me for help, ev-erything goes to hell."

"It can be annoying to do the right thing," Elzar said. He felt a little bad bringing this to her, but he'd seen Ghirra's face when she'd asked after Avon, and he'd thought of it again during his conversation with Master Yoda. Ghirra Starros loved her daughter—and maybe Avon could help convince Ghirra to let that love make her a better person, too.

"So annoying," Avon agreed as she plunked herself down. "What is it?"

"You won't be surprised. It's about your mother."

The humor vanished from Avon's aura. Serious stillness quieted the room. "I don't associate with her anymore."

"She's looking for you. She might know exactly where you are."

"If she did, there would be kidnappers barging in constantly."

"Or she respects your autonomy and is waiting for you."

Avon snorted so hard her curls trembled.

Elzar smiled grimly. "Be that as it may, we—the Jedi and the Republic—do respect your autonomy. I'd like you to hear me out, but whatever you choose to do, your status as a Republic citizen and your work to help us defeat the Nihil and the Stormwall will remain. You don't have to help me to maintain your protection."

"All right . . ." Avon narrowed suspicious eyes. "I'm listening."

Chapter Forty-Eight

CORUSCANT

It felt good to stand before a window overlooking the sprawling city of Coruscant. Ghirra Starros had spent a good chunk of her life working on this planet, manipulating, arguing, dissembling, and succeeding.

Just because this office wasn't the same as her old one in the Senate building, and just because she was no longer a senator, didn't mean it wasn't satisfying to be here. To have made it back here despite everyone's doubts, despite what she'd sacrificed. It was worth it.

Before leaving her dinner with the chancellor and that Jedi, she'd negotiated for this space—rather like an embassy instead of guest quarters. This way it could be run as Nihil territory, with her guards, her security measures, her people. Within reason, of course. No Nihil music—truly a relief to agree to—and no defacing the façade of the building. Ghirra had used her own money to acquire the top ten floors of this cloudscraper, and it included a personal shuttle landing pad and private comm antennas. If this worked out in the long run, Ghirra already had a list of improvements to make, and she supposed she'd eventually send for Nan as promised.

Ghirra was in the middle of mentally composing her holorecording to send back to Hetzal for Marchion—assuming he was interested in receiving it. After dropping in to change the entire basis of the Storm-wall, as if it had been his intention the whole time, the man had absented himself immediately again. Ghirra had managed to speak with Thaya Ferr briefly, though to little effect. If Marchion Ro wanted to leave his ministers in charge while he galivanted about causing trouble, reappearing only for abrupt and dramatic action, so be it. More frustratingly, Nan's reports from the *Gaze* on Marchion's recent travel made no sense. If he had a purpose for his galaxy-hopping, he wasn't sharing it with Nan, and thus far the little spy hadn't discovered it. Ghirra told Nan to get into Thaya Ferr's notes. If she came up with answers, Ghirra would let her come to Hosnian Prime.

In the meantime, Marchion refused to answer her comms.

The most annoying part of Ro's absence was Ghirra being made to deal directly with General Viess. At least Viess's needs were basic and understandable, though she'd recently put Ghirra off by claiming she was tending to Ministry of Protection business and Ghirra ought to mind her own. Fine. Ghirra wondered how long Ro would need to be absent from the "government" before she could subtly suggest to Viess that they assassinate Boolan. It was bad enough trying to work with a fanatic like Ro, whose monstrous faith was in himself—Boolan was a much less predictable type of extremist.

Ghirra shuddered and got back to the section of her report about the weaknesses in the Republic's initial offer. This negotiation was part of her ultimate goal, to intertwine Republic and Nihil politics deeply enough that both sides needed Ghirra's expertise. Being indispensable made one hard to reject. Or murder.

The door to her suite pinged, and a moment later one of the Nihil security guards she'd chosen to accompany her showed up to fill the doorway with his broad shoulders. All the Nihil whom Ghirra had brought were members of races lacking in overtly aggressive physical characteristics such as disarticulating fanged jaws or poisonous skull spines. Having a bodyguard with a reputation for literally eating her enemies had served a purpose for Ghirra's daughter, but as a minister visiting Coruscant for politics, Ghirra preferred to rely on sharp words and jeweled embellishments—trappings of success and wealth. No need to constantly remind the senators she came into contact with that the Nihil were bred on violence and fear.

Shon Felspix, a human Nihil with cords of scarification running in rivulets along his scalp and blue paint scrawled across his mouth like he'd taken a messy bite of some blue-blooded creature, grunted his greeting at her. "Minister," he said in a voice like a rockslide, "there's a kid to see you. Claims she belongs to you."

Ghirra's entire body went cold. Endeavoring to hide her shock and rising hope, she smiled gently. "And what is this child's name?"

"Avon?"

"Are you asking me?" Ghirra snapped.

The bodyguard cringed.

Ghirra tilted her chin up. "Show her into my sitting room, and have Jayd thaw some of the lompop flower jelly we brought. My *daughter* always liked it."

The Nihil grunted again and left. The tabard he wore to serve as a uniform for Ghirra's people here was emblazoned with the bright, swirling eye so that when he departed, it stared out from his back.

Ghirra took a moment to compose herself. This couldn't be a goodwill gift from the chancellor or the Jedi. But on the other hand, why else would Avon be here now? So soon after Ghirra's arrival? Avon was smart—smarter than her mother, Ghirra was unafraid to admit—but no spy. She preferred to keep her mind in books and research experiments. Someone had told her Ghirra was here, and wanted to see her.

Maybe Avon wanted to see *Ghirra*.

No, it was too much to hope.

Ghirra grabbed the beaten-metal hair clasp from where she'd set it when she let down her braids and pulled half of them into a high bun, securing it quickly. The rest of her formal gown was as pristine as when she'd put it on this morning.

The minister swept out of her office and entered the sitting room.

Her daughter stood stiffly before the window. It had been months since Ghirra'd seen the child—and Avon had grown. Just fifteen now, she was taller and gangly. Her hair was short and curled, barely restrained by a headband. She wore plain work clothes made of hardy material in dour colors. Clothing that could be dirtied or replaced without much cost. It was not what Ghirra wanted to see, but then again at least she was laying eyes on her daughter at all.

It took a considerable amount of willpower for Ghirra not to immediately grab Avon and lock her in the bedroom, or at least hug her for the next hour. But the former would drive Avon to run again, and the latter was simply not supported by their current relationship.

"Mom," Avon said with a faint tremor in her otherwise hard voice.

"Avon," Ghirra answered gladly, letting a genuine smile spread like dawn. "You're well," she said firmly. "And taller."

Avon jerked one shoulder in a shrug. "You're older."

"I suppose so." Ghirra walked toward Avon, and the girl let her. Cautiously, Ghirra placed a hand on her daughter's shoulder. She let her hand trail down Avon's arm, squeezing gently. "I have lompop jelly. Would you like some?"

"Sure," Avon said, bright gaze flicking around the small sitting room. There was nothing personal here yet, as Ghirra had only moved in today. The shelves and sofas matched in texture and gentle mint-green curves. Some sprays of flowers emerged from tiny pots hung on the walls. There was a long, angled window showing a view of the nighttime cityscape that gave off a quiet glow under a swath of royal-violet sky.

Just then Jayd entered with a box of the jellies. She was a Kexing Nihil with gray skin and delicate-looking vestigial teeth cutting out from her jawbone. Jayd had streaked her hair with Nihil blue and wore an armored chest piece with the eye sigil.

"Set them on the table," Ghirra said. "Help yourself to one if you'd like."

Jayd did so, plucking a jelly with vivid-orange glaze. She ate it and bowed.

"I see you're pretending the Nihil can be polite," Avon said, grabbing a jelly of her own and plopping the whole thing into her mouth. She continued to talk while she chewed. "It's pointless, Mom. Everybody knows it."

"I disagree," Ghirra said lightly. She poured them both a thin glass of culia-flavored water from a carafe and sat near her daughter on a separate little sofa. "You aren't registered at the university you told me accepted you."

"Not under your name," Avon said with a little smirk.

Ghirra smirked back. But her amusement faded. "Tell me what you've been doing. How you've been."

"Busy helping the Republic unravel the Stormwall," Avon said, eating another jelly.

"As expected," Ghirra said, shoving down every emotional response. "I hope Xylan was able to give you some aid."

"I guess so." Avon rolled her eyes.

Ghirra sighed softly. She wanted to tell Avon to regulate her emotional responses better, so she didn't make her secrets or thoughts visible. But to do so would only push Avon in the opposite direction. She was uninterested in listening to her mother anymore.

"Mom, I appreciate the candy, but I'm not here to reminisce."

"Oh?" Ghirra leaned back into the firm sofa. "What are you here for?"

"I came to ask you to do the right thing for once."

Ghirra lifted her eyebrows. "The right thing? The right thing for whom?"

"For the galaxy! For me."

"Hmm." Ghirra eyed her daughter, letting it be cold. "I am doing the right thing. I have been for my whole life."

"The Nihil—"

"The *right thing*," Ghirra interrupted, "is to keep my family safe. To keep my people, the entire Hosnian system, safe. I will accumulate enough power so that no one can take it away, so that I can protect what is mine. You, Hosnian."

Avon pressed a fist to one knee. "I don't need your protection, Mom, not like this. Was raising me last year in Nihil territory protecting me? Surrounded by psychopaths and murderers? They were always trying to kill me."

"People have been trying to kill you from the moment you were born, little one. You just didn't notice until it was the Nihil being so overt about it."

Avon sucked in a breath. "That's not good!"

"I have given you every immediate protection. You are alive. You are well. What I am doing is a longer-reaching game, Avon. To keep you safe forever, to keep us in a position to retain power. Even when I am gone, I will make sure you are safe. This is the way I can best achieve that."

"The Nihil don't make anybody safe."

Ghirra shook her head. "You don't understand politics."

"I don't want to, if this is what it tells you the right thing to do is!"

"Avon." Ghirra gazed at her daughter. "I love you. I admire your intelligence and determination. But one thing you have not learned is how to build a legacy. A legacy of power and safety."

"I want to be remembered for science, Mom, if anything. Or because—because I did the right thing."

"The right thing again!" Ghirra scoffed. "You have truly spent too much time with Jedi. Next you'll say, *For Light and Life!* As if that isn't only a smokescreen Lina Soh uses to make her own power plays and manipulations more palatable."

"It's better than the Nihil smokescreen of literal poison! The Nihil can't help with a—a legacy! They don't build anything."

"They do under my leadership. We do. We will."

Avon thrust to her feet. "I knew this was a waste of time. I told him, but Elzar said I should try—or maybe I'd regret it someday. Prove to myself that you might actually care about me or anyone!"

Ghirra swallowed back a sarcastic comment about Jedi priorities. She'd been swallowing her opinions on them for decades. "I care about you. You'll understand someday, when I'm finished and you have everything you need."

Avon crossed her arms. "When will you be finished? When you've turned yourself into one of them? I guess you've always been a liar and manipulator, that's politics, right? But doing it on behalf of the Nihil! On behalf of Marchion Ro, that mad dictator! How can you not see that it's better to win with the Republic than with the Nihil?"

"How can you not see that the Republic doesn't *win* anything? Not against Ro."

"We—we have. Some things. The Lightning Crash is ruined."

Ghirra sighed again. She had to hold on to the belief that Avon would understand one day. Would strip herself down to the core Starros in her. Ghirra only hoped it didn't hurt her daughter too badly. "I will come out of this on top, Avon. You'll see."

"Some ways aren't worth it, Mom."

"That is something people who can't succeed tell themselves. My goal is worth what I've had to do."

"You want me to win, even if I hate myself for how I do it?" Avon's eyes were so narrow, so pleading.

This was the first time, Ghirra realized, she'd spoken to her daughter as if Avon were an adult. She drew a slow breath. Avon was grown up, at just fifteen. After everything she'd seen and learned and experienced. Ghirra needed to proceed with care. She said gently, "It is better to be alive and safe and hating yourself than proud of your choices, but dead."

Avon gasped. She stalked away, heading for the door. Then she stopped and said quietly, "Mom, the Jedi want to know where Ro is. I want you to tell them. Help them. Doesn't that matter to you, what I want? What I'm asking you to do?"

Ghirra held her silence. It did matter, of course it did.

But Avon didn't wait. She nodded once and said, "I'd rather be proud of you, Mom."

After delivering that mortal blow, Avon left.

Once the sun had fully set over Coruscant, leaving the world shrouded in blackness and the glitter of a billion stars, Ghirra walked on weary feet, as if through thick solar syrup, and at her new office's personal comm unit sent a message to her spy on the *Gaze Electric*.

Throughout their brief conversation, all she could hear was the unspoken part of her daughter's final words: *I'd rather be proud of you, Mom, even if you're dead.*

Chapter Forty-Nine

CORUSCANT

Avar easily tracked down Cair San Tekka—he was staying in the San Tekka manor right in Republic City. Their manor was more like several bouquets of apartments built in elegant stacks and domes across three platforms atop the roofs of several cloudscrapers just far enough from Monument Plaza that air traffic was slightly less restricted. Arcing bridges connected the platforms, gleaming under the hazy sun. It wasn't the rosy opulence of their compound on Naboo, but its more efficient and elegant richness suited Coruscant instead.

Though she'd sent word ahead that she was coming, Avar waited awhile in their courtyard for a guide. She settled herself into a shallow meditation, aligning herself through the shifting Force. It was always different on Coruscant, where so many beings lived and interacted, where the planet itself wore the metal of civilization like armor.

Porter hadn't checked in, though Avar knew he couldn't. A flutter of concern for him seemed constant in her mind since he'd vanished off Naboo in the wake of the battle, determined to go after General Viess on his own. Avar couldn't blame him, and on a certain level she felt he was right to do so. A single Jedi hunting a single enemy, tied together in the Force. There could be a balance to it if Porter clung to the light.

It would be easier for him if he had a partner or a team, though. Jedi at his back. That was the point of the Guardian Protocols, if you asked some Jedi. Nobody should be alone.

That was what Avar was doing back on Coruscant. She needed the Order at her back to go after Ro. She needed a team.

"Master Kriss?"

She blinked out of her meditation and smiled slightly at the attendant wearing a San Tekka shoulder badge. They led her to the secondary platform, waxing on about the family. There were thirty-seven San Tekkas currently in residence, her guide told her proudly. Avar smiled and nodded, unsure what she was actually agreeing with—that it was impressive to have such a large, successful family?

Cair San Tekka was in the violet library, she was told, and when the grand double doors swished open, she saw why it had been named so: The double-decker room shone with chrome and display screens, along with shelves of glowing holobooks along the second story. But every meter of space unoccupied by consoles or stacks of reading material was covered in plants blooming some shade of purple. There were spike-tongued succulents whose thick leaves themselves were vivid royal purple, and a sweep of sweetpond clematis fell between two curved ladders. Beyond that, Avar couldn't name any of the species, though she knew they came from all sorts of different biomes and shouldn't easily live in the same environment. There were even a few potted trees here and there, tucked next to alcoves with busts and long-limbed statues.

The room bustled with several people, some of whom Avar noticed only through the Force, tucked among the shelving, minding their work. In the center of the library, directly under an arced skylight letting in sun and the flash of the occasional ship darting past, Cair San Tekka leaned against the giant Theljian snow dog Plinka as he studied a three-layered holomap of part of the galaxy. It seemed to be running a simulation, with certain stars blinking white instead of the standard blue and several interpretations of a flight path appearing and disappearing. Standing next to Cair with a datapad in hand was a woman Avar remembered seeing in the aftermath of the battle to free the island. She looked sleepy, despite the harried glances she kept sending Cair, and her hair was in one of the gravity-defying updos Avar had seen the senator from Naboo himself wear. Ino'olo, that was her name, Avar recalled. She'd helped organize the transport of those still needing medical attention up to the *Third Horizon* before the jump.

Cair poked at the map with a simple prosthetic with only two curving hooks. His other hand dug into Plinka's fur as he frowned.

"Sir," Avar's guide said, and when Cair looked up, there was an almost frantic gleam in his eyes. Two pink spots flushed on his tan cheeks.

"Master Kriss!" he said excitedly. "I've been poring over my data—there's a lot of it, we tracked the Nihil deployment patterns as best we could and have a lot of scav swarms mapped out, Viess's bases, and rumors of Jedi sightings and the Nameless. Also lists of places that haven't rolled over for the Nihil as publicly as others, where there might be more rebels to ally with. Most of it is the sort of information we've been smuggling to you for weeks, though. I assume you're looking for Ro?"

The gleam in his eye sharpened.

"Cair," Avar said, stopping directly across the circular table from him. In her message, she'd only said she wanted to discuss information he'd gathered from the Occlusion Zone. Cair had come to this further conclusion himself. Though it wasn't what she needed from him, Cair's assumption that the next logical course of action was finding Ro himself, taking their fight to the Eye, reinforced for Avar that it was the right idea. The will of the Force.

She asked, "Is this the Occlusion Zone?"

The holoprojector flickered, painting eerie blue waves over Cair's face. "Yes, including places our sources say the *Gaze Electric* or Marchion Ro himself has been supposedly spotted recently. I've been working right now to winnow out incidents where only Levelers have been spotted, or other Nihil cruisers. People are afraid of him, so when they see anything that might be him, they assume it is."

"A good way to survive," Avar said.

"Can I help you to some tea?" Ino'olo asked, projecting an aura of "please, say yes" at Avar.

"Thank you, yes," Avar easily agreed. She moved to sit on the stool beside Cair that Ino'olo indicated.

"She'll make me take my medicine alongside your tea," Cair explained with a fond grimace.

"You're healing well?"

"Everything is perfectly fine except for the last of my ribs," he said. "But we've got everything we need here, and Plinka is nearly as good a nurse as Ino."

The Naboo woman snorted softly as she brought back a tray with two different little steaming pots and poured for them.

Avar listened to the Force as she studied Cair. She'd heard he hadn't wanted to come back, but his husband hadn't given him a choice. Despite Cair's eager, easygoing demeanor, she sensed a lot of raw edges. "Are you sure you have what you need?" she asked gently.

Cair switched to scratching Plinka with the hook prosthetic, and knocked back his medicine quickly. His mouth twisted into what could be only charitably called a smile. "What I *need* is to do this work, to keep at it as best I can from here until I can get back to where I should be."

"If you can help me, maybe you're already there."

He lowered his gaze, and Avar felt a swell of guilt before he smiled at her again, this time softer and more true. He said, "Is there something specific you think I can help you with now?"

Avar held his gaze. "Actually, I wanted to ask you if you had gathered any information on other incidences of the wasting blight that corrupted the moon where you lost your hand."

The tea tray in Ino'olo's hand rattled in surprise, and Cair's mouth dropped open, but he quickly recovered himself. "Ah," he said, expression transforming into self-deprecation, "you have it here? On Coruscant? My hand, I mean. I guessed that's where it would end up, but I didn't get a chance to ask Vernestra, and I keep thinking about how weird it is to be back in the same place. I don't exactly want it back, but it's also . . ." He laughed a little. "Weird."

Avar touched his forearm.

His lashes fluttered as he looked down again, then back up at the holomap. He tapped a key on the console so that the map swung around about thirty degrees, then pointed with his prosthetic. "That one," Cair said quietly. "It's a small system, the inhabited moon was orbiting a red ocean planet with this moss that . . ."

As he trailed off, Avar stood to lean in. "Have you heard of it elsewhere?"

"Yes, but even more distant, convoluted, thirdhand rumors than Ro's location."

"It's appeared on this side of the Occlusion Zone."

He sucked air through his teeth. "Inhabited worlds?"

"Just one as of now, that we know of."

Cair cursed quietly. He turned around and petted Plinka aggressively. The snow dog whined and tilted her long head to give him access under one of her big ears. She seemed to like the hooked prosthetic. After a moment, Cair sank to his haunches against the dog and looked up at Ino'olo. "It's fine, Ino," he said. "You don't have to be angry at the Jedi for asking."

Ino'olo shrugged a little.

Cair continued, glancing at Avar. "I was there with a cousin of mine, Jordanna Sparkburn. We flew my *Brightbird* out there looking for her older brother Harth. When we got there, the Nihil had an interdiction on it—they didn't seem to know much about the blight, as you call it. But they knew it was bad and killing people. We wondered if they'd done something to the moon, you know?"

"Do you think they had?" Avar crouched beside him.

"Hard to say. If they did, it was experimental, and they didn't have control over it." Cair grimaced. "Though they don't mind unleashing things they can't control."

Ino'olo huffed angrily.

Cair smiled wearily at her, then dragged his eyes back to Avar. "Well, we were trying to convince Jordanna's family and the remaining miners to leave with us. The Nihil were there, the mines had to be abandoned, and that blight was getting closer to town. Jordanna and her brother and I went to get a better look, and we guessed later it had gone underground, into these waterways and caverns beneath the valley, and while we were there, the ground collapsed. We managed to get away, but . . . I must have touched it. Didn't notice until we had everybody on the *Brightbird* on our way back to Seswenna. I . . ." Cair sighed. "There's not much else to tell. It didn't hurt as much as I expected, and it was fast. We didn't get anything else infected."

Avar reached out again and gripped his forearm. "You transported your infected hand safely in a containment field."

"We did. As far as I know, it worked permanently. I mean, they took it to Coruscant, so you'd probably know by now if the sickness hadn't been contained . . ."

"Thank you. Anything else you can think of?"

"It was slow. It didn't hurt. I mean, the blight itself. It didn't even itch." He laughed a little. His remaining hand flexed. "I know it looked like what the Nameless do. But it didn't make me out of my head or afraid or anything. I'm not attuned to the Force, so . . ." He shrugged. "I don't think it's the same thing. I don't see how it could be."

"We don't understand what the Nameless are or why they feed on the Force as they do." Avar squeezed his arm again. "The Force is with you, Cair."

"Big time," he agreed.

Plinka barked happily at a commotion at the library entrance. Avar turned just in time to see Xylan Graf firmly pushing a San Tekka aide—the one who'd brought Avar here—back from the marble door-frame. He posed for a moment, the salmon-orange jacket tailored tight to his shoulders and waist drawing all the light in the room. When he saw Cair, he strode toward them, floor-length jacket tails fluttering behind him, scalloped and ruffled enough for a dozen sunrise peacock fans. Even Avar, who did not particularly care about sartorial anything, was impressed.

"Cair," Xylan said imperiously, sweeping around. He spared a slight look at Avar. "Master Kriss, don't mind the interruption."

"I mind it," Cair said before Avar had a chance to reply. She felt frissons through the Force between the men. Anger, heartbreak, and a mess of less identifiable emotions.

Displacing Ino'olo as if she weren't there, Xylan patted the snow dog, who nuzzled at his jacket tails. "I've brought the specialist with me," Xylan said, and there in his wake Avar finally noticed an unassuming woman in a sharp gray suit holding a large case. At her cue she set it on the library table, disrupting a slice of the holomap, and flicked it open. Inside were several models of prosthetic hands. They ranged from sleek black metal to polished rainchrome rendered with a skin covering a few shades darker than Cair himself.

"I told you I don't want your help with this." Cair held up his hook. "I'm managing just fine."

"You can't play your dulcimer with that," Xylan scoffed.

"He said no, Graf," Ino'olo said.

Avar stood up. Everyone stopped and looked at her. Avar calmly said, "Can this wait a little while longer?"

"Yes." Cair pushed at Xylan's stomach with the curved side of the hook. "Go away."

Xylan glanced at the specialist with a nod, and she just as efficiently packed up her display and headed for the door. Then Xylan smiled briefly at Avar. "My apologies for the interruption. Do continue."

With a flourish he tossed back the wild orange tails of his jacket and sat on an elegant wingback chair a bit off to the side of the table. He made it look like a pretty throne. Then he stared at Cair and said very seriously, "If you truly want me to leave, I will, but I'm taking my dog."

Plinka heaved herself up and padded over, settling again so that her forepaws nudged Xylan's polished boot and her fluffy white tail flapped gently against Cair's.

Ino'olo crossed her arms over her chest and sat down, too, where she had a perfect view of Xylan to glare coldly at.

Avar was glad she didn't have to stay here for very long herself. As someone who'd spent her fair share of time yearning, Avar hoped the two men could work this out, but it really wasn't her business. She cleared her throat. "All right. Cair, if you can gather the information you do have about possible locations of the blight in the O.Z., I'd appreciate it. We don't know anything about it, why it's appearing, if there's a pattern to it. We can't find the correct pattern until we have all the data."

"Sure." He leaned in and started tapping. "We could try one of the algorithms we used to use to plot new hyperspace routes. It suggests potential terminus points with a set of data as if the data were a route. If we have enough about the blight, then maybe it can be reversed so there's an origin point instead of terminus."

Cair quickly outlined his information, including commentary such as who had provided it and how many degrees of separation he was from the source, and together they decided how viable the data was. Ino'olo had a lot of input, clearly having spent time previously scouring immense amounts of data to find reliable and useful information. Once or twice Xylan threw in a comment, earning sharp looks from both Cair and Ino'olo, but he was making decent suggestions based on what he knew personally of how the Nihil did and did not work. Avar hoped Xylan was scheduled for a very long conversation with several Jedi to analyze everything he knew.

And Avar listened, open to the Force, to the intricate play of melodies in this room. Ino'olo's underlying earnest desire to help and soft loyalty was a running, thrumming bass, Cair's passion was like scales dancing up and down a harp, and Xylan's skittering flute kept high and apart from the company but tied in rhythm and theme to his husband. Even Plinka had a Force song, and it was a pinging happy harmony. Avar listened and wove it together with her breath.

And she let the Force narrow her focus on two of the planets from their "viable" category. She studied them and realized the connection.

"There were Drengir here," she said suddenly.

The song around her sharpened.

"Drengir," Xylan said with obvious disdain. "I thought you all took care of those monsters."

Avar didn't answer directly but said, "Here and here," pointing to the map. "I personally engaged with them on Selvernis. Before the Stormwall. There wasn't blight there then, at least not noticeably."

Cair frowned as he flicked through information on the smaller display screen before him.

"We should find out if any of these other worlds have had such Drengir sightings," Avar said.

"Why?" Ino'olo asked.

"We are sure the Nihil were responsible for propagating the Drengir problem as widely as it was. They dropped Drengir offspring and seeds across the galaxy to distract us. Why not use the same tactic again? If they are behind the blight, the Drengir connection might help us find a pattern, or determine if it's truly scattershot."

Cair said, "When you get somebody back through the Stormwall, we should ask Belin and Rhil for the most up-to-date information. Or . . . you should go yourself."

"Yes," Avar said. "I'll see to it. Get me what you want me to say or send."

"I want to go with you," Cair said, standing.

Xylan immediately huffed in outrage.

"No," Avar said. "Thank you. But no. You need to keep healing, and this is Jedi business now. We can handle it. We will."

Cair stepped toward her. "Let me help, if you think of anything I can do."

"I will." She held out a hand, and he took it.

"May the Force be with you," Cair said quietly. The yearning in him was sweet, rippling through the Force.

Avar smiled. "Let the people who love you take care of you for a little while."

Then she nodded to Ino'olo and Xylan, the latter of whom exuded a much more frustrated kind of yearning. When Avar left, she was already mentally composing the message she would record for Elzar, explaining they'd have to miss out on sharing dinner yet again.

Chapter Fifty

Burry gasped with his renewed effort, pushing back against the blight. His hands trembled, held out before him in the air as they directed the Force—shoving, reaching, yearning.

He trembled. His lungs ached as if he hadn't been breathing.

His shoulder was hot, but he shrugged it away, focused. He felt it: longing, ache, a . . . loneliness, and the deepest silence he'd ever imagined. A silence so vast it might swallow an entire planet.

Burry pushed back.

He breathed, though it hurt. He pushed back again. He would not be silent—could not. Life was loud.

Something suddenly rang in his skull, and he cried out, snapping awake.

"Burry!" came a voice he knew. It had been yelling his name for a long time.

Burry blinked, rubbed his eyes. He felt awash in . . . in . . . he wasn't sure. He was dizzy, though.

Taking a few breaths to center himself, Burry blinked his eyes open again. It was Bell. Bell. Zettifar. He knew Bell. Bell was his partner.

Ember whined beside them.

He groaned an apology in Shyriiwook.

"It's all right, Burry," Bell said. "Are you okay?"

Burry nodded automatically but then sighed harshly and actually performed a quick self-scan. Other than the echo of pain in his head, he was stiff and hot, and he ached with exhaustion. His stomach rolled over in a twisted combination of hunger and nausea. He told Bell he needed to eat.

Bell smiled, despite the tightness around the human's dark mouth and eyes. "You were deep in that meditation."

Slowly, Burry became aware of the drifting pinkseeds and the forest around them.

Oanne, the Elia-An colony. Arrysslesh, the medicine artist who'd sent for help because their nativity forest was being . . .

Burry cried out softly, turning to glance at the blight.

The sight that greeted him was horrifying and shocking. The forest, turned to gray, retained the shape of trees—trunks, branches, even individual leaves, though many had scattered to particles of sand or ash. All that remained. He could see the outline of what had been animals, too: rodents and birds, dropped where Burry and Bell were, trying to escape. Worse: The line of ash, of devastation, had grown nearer to where they were, had crept beyond the trees he remembered from when he sat down to work. But it was uneven.

A small semicircle seemed cut out of the blight line, right before where Burry himself sat.

It had worked.

Burry had held the blight off with the Force. But only the slightest bit.

He swayed, lightheaded.

"Careful, Burry. You were in that trance for about five hours," Bell answered. The human crouched next to where Burry sat with his legs folded under him on the soft grasses.

Burry's heart fell. He'd depleted himself in so little time and barely kept the blight away.

Tiny leaves on the trees curled before his eyes, turning gray ever so slowly, and the wind scattered the tips of the nativity trees into ash.

He could keep trying. But it would only stave off the inevitable.

Maybe that was worth it.

The charhound Ember's fur flashed to life in little lines of fire as if she was agitated. Burry looked around, anxious, but Bell only patted the hound's head and tugged one ear. "She's worried about you, Burry. So am I. You were . . . shaking."

It had been difficult, and Burry tried to explain.

"I see." Bell pointed at the arc of forest Burry had seemingly protected.

Burry needed to rest, get his bearings, and then push again. He asked if Bell thought the two of them could push together, forge a connection and double the strength of their push.

Bell shook his head. "We have to go. We need to report this and keep looking for Drengir."

Burry surged to his feet and shook his head emphatically. He swayed again and Bell jumped up to catch his elbow. Burry shook him off. He insisted they needed to help the Elia-An.

"Help them what, Burry? You were killing yourself."

Burry shook his head, roaring softly in frustration. How could Bell not get it? The Elia-An wouldn't leave. They couldn't. They would die if they left, but if this blight destroyed their nativity trees, they'd die anyway. This planet was too much like Burry's homeworld. He understood what was at stake here. He had to stop it. He *had* to. He couldn't watch this world die.

"Burry, what you're doing isn't enough."

Burry reared back, shocked.

Bell held out his hands. "I watched what you were doing. It was working, but only right here, and with all your effort. Whatever this is, we need to know more, and we need more Jedi, more people who can do what you're doing. Otherwise what will you do but make a tiny island of safety, and for how long? It won't be enough to save them."

Burry stared at Bell. His friend's words pounded at him. "Won't be enough" was not something Burry wanted to face again. Not ever. Not after Starlight, not after the cave in the Eiram ocean where he'd spent weeks starving and desperate, completely alone. Where he'd pulled out his own hair, throwing tiny hopeless pleas into the roiling sea. Where he'd wondered if there was any point in trying to feed himself anymore or if he should just let the Force keep him forever. He'd stopped talking to himself just to hear something other than the roar of the vortex, stopped picturing rescue, stopped hoping. Because nothing he'd done then had been enough.

Burry had thought, so quietly, tucked away in the darkest part of his mind, *Even the Force isn't enough sometimes.*

But then he'd lived, and he'd promised himself he'd never give up again.

He couldn't give up on this. If it didn't matter to push at this now, how could anything ever matter?

"Burry, you're panting. I think you're hyperventilating." Bell grabbed Burry's shoulders and used all his strength to shake him once. "Breathe, Burryaga. Breathe."

Burry tried. His chest heaved, stuttered. He closed his eyes.

Bell smacked a hand on his chest, shoving aside his tabard and the strap of his lightsaber holster. He thumped his palm to Burry's chest again and again. "Breathe. Breathe."

It took a long moment, but Burry focused on the hits, on Bell's voice. On the shriek of insects in the living part of the forest—the part still alive! Those insects, they didn't know. They didn't know what was coming for them. He felt the wind in his long hair, ruffling his braids so a few of the tiny beads clacked together. He heard Ember's sparking cough.

"I'm here," Bell said.

The ache of the blight burned at the edges of Burry's senses. It nibbled painful, yearning bites against his emotions, the living Force inside him. Burry pushed at it more gently this time. Not to fight it but to free himself of it.

He breathed, he leaned down until his forehead touched Bell's. They made an arch, and Ember's tail whapped against Burry's thigh.

"I am here," Burry said.

"I'm glad, my friend," Bell answered. "I know it's hard. I want to help them, too. We need to know the best way to do it, though."

Burry straightened up, glancing at the line of awful gray death. He could see the shell of a nativity tree crumbling.

He looked the other way, and there were more of the trees, lighting up along their heartlines with that bluish phosphorescence.

And there was Arryssslesh, her spines lighting in the same patterns. The connection between the Elia-An and their nativity trees.

In the closest he could come to Arryssslesh's language, he told them he had to go, but that he wouldn't abandon them.

"We understand," the medicine artist said.

"The Jedi want to help," Bell added, triggering his translation device again. "I promise, if we can stop it, when we know how, we'll be here."

"We will be here, too," Arryssslesh said. "We have nowhere else to go."

Burry didn't know what to say. There was nothing. If this were Kashyyyk, he did not know if he would be able to make his feet move.

But then again, Bell would be there to help him.

Burry walked to the medicine artist and bent to his knees again, lowered his head to her.

She put one long-fingered hand on his cheek. Patted him lovingly.

As they hurried back to their Vector, Burry couldn't help glancing over his shoulder to watch the blight.

They would need help. So much help. People to measure the speed of the blight's spread. Scientists to experiment and try to understand. And Jedi who could be spared to keep pushing at it to protect the living Force of this world before it was all drained away.

Chapter Fifty-One

ISOLT, INSIDE THE OCCLUSION ZONE

Once, Isolt had been a pastoral world of lively green, but over a year ago, the Nihil had bombed it repeatedly, aiming for the caldera in the north. Some enterprising Nihil wanted to know if they could trigger a super eruption as had occurred on Dalna. The bombing had destroyed nearly all life there. And they had managed to cause at least one major volcanic eruption.

Now Isolt was quiet. The comm buoys had been diverted long ago, and interstellar traffic avoided the area even more than most places in the Occlusion Zone. It was a prime location for a secret enemy base, if Porter was honest. And he liked to be honest, especially with himself.

He set his shuttle down a three-day hike from the exact location specified by Viess in her invitation. There, at the edges of the volcanic activity, life had already begun creeping back. Vivid-green grass sprouted everywhere, and the charred trees were surrounded by seedlings. Porter even picked his way around a small meadow of tiny orangish flowers whose faces followed the dark sun.

On the third day, after suffering through stinky sulfur pockets and gaseous springs, passing ruins of settlements and sometimes skeletal remains, Porter reached the outskirts of the small base Viess had created on a low platform over the bed of an extinct river long since turned to steam.

Sweating, Porter found high ground and settled down to observe. He had thermal blankets, dried rations, a dull all-weather cloak that blended with the landscape, macrobinocs, and his lightsaber. What more did he need for this hunt?

For two more days he watched.

The base consisted of two buildings, one that he guessed was an operations center, the other a barracks and garage for various speeders and short-range ships. Two Strikeships were docked at the edges of the low platform. Porter estimated there were only about thirty Nihil here, and half of those were affiliated mechanics and cooks and service personnel.

In the dead of night, he slipped down the rough slope, closer and closer, waiting for the sudden onset of fear.

Porter walked the long perimeter of the platform, moving nearer every few meters to test for the presence of the Nameless. He had to be extremely gentle, knowing that if he was near enough to sense them, they could likely feel his strength in the Force, too. He didn't want to alert the creatures, and therefore the Nihil, that he was here and biding his time.

During the day he returned to his dugout, chewed on a few rations, and meditated. He didn't let his thoughts turn toward the past, toward his sister.

It had been so long.

The same number of days that he'd known Viess, he'd missed Barash.

Porter did not think of it, and instead let the Force flow through him. He was not alone.

A second night he returned, testing the edges of Viess's defenses again. Listening, he reached out with the Force.

The fear never came. She didn't have Nameless here.

Another clear invitation.

Porter was almost amused at the transparency.

He didn't let himself wonder what Barash would do.

As quickly as he could under stealth conditions, Porter returned to his shuttle and gathered what he needed to make a few delicate little explosives.

In the early morning, before sunrise, Porter slipped to the southern rim of the base platform, hunkering down as near as he could get. He kept his mind blank as he put his rebreather on, ready for fire and smoke—and the gas so favored by the Nihil. Using the Force to carefully compress the trigger mechanisms, Porter sent the explosives in high arcs up and up, until they hovered over the center of the compound. He released his grip, and they fell hard as the triggers popped. Just as alarms screamed to life, explosions ripped across the southern wall.

Porter braced for the wave of percussion and the swiftly following smoke. He closed his eyes and reached out with the Force, leaping up to the top of the wall. Smoke billowed around him. He heard yelling and the hiss of fire suppressants. Then a barrage of furious, cranky music the Nihil included in their alarm system burst in his ears.

Porter leapt down into the chaos, moving faster than most sentients could see. He somersaulted over wreckage and flames, landed hard, rolled, and when he came to his feet, he kept running for the middle of the base.

With his rebreather he couldn't call for Viess's attention, but he figured his explosives were announcement enough.

Nihil ran at him, blasters firing. Porter squinted through the smoke, flicking his lightsaber to bright life. It made the smoke glow and turned him into a target.

Nihil kept firing as he blocked their blaster bolts with ease.

He tucked and spun on the ball of his foot, kneecapping a Nihil and spinning to skewer another. With the Force he lifted one, flailing and flinging blood, and threw it into another. The Force turned with him, a whirlwind of strength. Porter slid between two Nihil, lightsaber cutting through them, and flung himself backward into a high arc, the glowing blue of his blade blurring with speed. He kicked a Nihil in the helmet, spun again, and sliced through another.

This time when he landed, Porter took a breath. Nihil backed away from him, away from the circle of wounded and dead. Morning breeze caused the smoke to drift away, and Porter removed the rebreather. The Nihil stared at him, their sickly blue eyes scrawled on their helmets and chests and their tattered armor and spiking shields splattered with blue paint.

"I'm not here for you," he told them, releasing his lightsaber, using the Force to lift it until it floated over his shoulder, brighter than the rising sun. Porter held out his hands, palms up, and when he shifted them like the bowls of a scale, his lightsaber shifted, too.

Two Nihil dropped their blasters and fled.

The rest held their ground.

"Leave him to me."

The general's command rippled through the black stone courtyard. Nihil jerked in surprise. But they all stepped back.

Porter turned to face Viess.

Chapter Fifty-Two

CORUSCANT

Avon Sunvale was waiting for Elzar in front of the Jedi Temple with a scowl and a datastick. "Here," she said, holding the stick out for Elzar.

He took it, his eyebrows raised.

"It's from my mother. I didn't look, and I don't want to know."

Elzar tamped down on the thrill of hope and nodded solemnly. "Thank you."

"It might be worthless."

"I doubt it." Elzar waited for her to finish rolling her eyes and look back at him. "*Thank you,*" he said again.

"Sure," Avon said quietly. She glanced behind him at where the Jedi statuary stood before the Temple. Her chin lifted and her gaze with it, as if taking it all in. Something in her glance, in the pinch at the corner of her mouth, at the sense of her swirling in the Force, told Elzar she was saying goodbye.

"You don't have to go," he said, following his gut.

Surprise flicked across her expression. Then she put her scowl back in place. "Uh-huh. Anyway, good luck."

With that, Avon walked quickly away, even picking up her pace to jog a few meters across the long marble yard toward someone waiting for her in a cloak with the cowl drawn up.

Elzar watched until Avon was in the custody of her tall mystery friend and murmured, "May the Force be with you, Avon Starros."

He dashed back the way he'd come, forgetting the list of meetings and tasks JJ-5145 had sent him at dawn. He hurried to his quarters and threw himself behind the console, inserting the datastick so he could read through it as soon as possible.

When he finished, Elzar felt pinned down by the weight of what Avon had delivered.

He hit the comm and ordered up a priority channel for Avar Kriss on the *Elder Lily*, where she was heading for the Stormwall border to rendezvous with Vernestra Rwoh and prepare to head back into the Occlusion Zone.

"Avar, wait for me. I know how we can find Marchion Ro."

Elzar spent the jump through hyperspace meditating.

It was easy.

He wasn't drowning. His tumultuous feelings and thoughts pressed into him, a crushing weight, but he allowed it. He simply breathed through it.

Like doing handstands in the surf as waves crashed into him again and again, Orla laughing from the shore.

Elzar shifted himself in the small quarters on the star cruiser, using his own body and the Force to slide up into a handstand. The ship was stable, with only a constant even thrum of engines as it sailed through hyperspace. That hum, too, flowed through Elzar from his palms up his arms and into his shoulders and chest.

He summoned the ocean of the Force as he held himself up. It roared in his ears, and he heard Avar say, *An ocean has a tide. A rhythm. A heartbeat.*

A rhythm—a tide—is part of a song.

Elzar heard it, deep in his ears, in the tiny bones vibrating with the Force, with the hum of hyperspace and power of the engines, with the lives and light of every being on the *Axiom.*

It was so big, so loud, it could crush him. He could drown.

But he didn't. He always assumed he was vulnerable to drowning, because once he let the dark side overwhelm him. But that didn't mean he always would.

His heartbeat was the same as the tide of the Force, a rhythm, part of a song. And not just any song: Avar's.

She was at the other end, a pulse that connected them. And she was here, too, because the Force was everywhere. She surrounded him, and Elzar knew his heart beat with her, too.

Elzar Mann pushed the boundaries of what even he had always known. The Force was an ocean, but it was a song, too. And a galaxy of stars, bright streaks of color, a forest, a million candle flames, and a conflagration of life. It was darkness, as well, but the darkness of an oceanic abyss, still full of life and water, and the darkness of the deepest roots under the trees, the smoke and the ashes. Every color at once. The galactic darkness that made those stars shine most brightly.

And it was him, alone in a tiny room, hands on thin carpet, feet in the air, breathing. Every part of him, every worst instinct and best intention. All of Elzar Mann turned to the light.

Avar could feel Elzar drawing closer.

It was as though a string had been pulled taut and a note slid sharper in pitch until it hit just right to vibrate her bones.

Before heading for the command center, she slipped the diadem over her forehead and tied her hair back around it into a soft bun. The cool kiss of the metal on her skin felt good. Right.

Vernestra had arrived hours ago, and Avar had surprised the younger Jedi with the news that they were pausing before their mission into the Occlusion Zone to wait for intel from Elzar, and that Avar had sent for other Jedi who remained nearby: Master Mirro Lox and his

Padawan Amadeo Azzazzo; Bell Zettifar and Burryaga. The latter of whom requested all the information they had about the blight immediately. It wasn't much.

Elzar hadn't wanted to share his information on comm. The cryptic reasoning had made Avar want to tease him for trying to be a spymaster, but the stakes were too high. He'd bring the data to her, and they'd use it in the field. "This isn't a moment for me to hold back," he had said. "Maybe that time in my life is over."

His ship was due any moment to rendezvous with the Longbeam *Elder Lily,* and the Jedi waited in the same command center, one similar to the room on the *Third Horizon* where Avar and Burryaga and Vernestra had made their report to the Council.

Bell stood close to Avar and told the gathered Jedi about what they'd seen on Oanne, and how the blight there seemed to consume and move. He said it responded to pushback through the Force, but barely, and required an immense effort. While Bell spoke, Burry swiped at the information on the datapad in his large hands.

"Burryaga," Avar said gently but firmly.

He looked up at her with round black eyes. He spoke and Bell translated, "No one knows what this is?"

"We don't. We have ideas, as I'm sure you do," Avar said. "What did it feel like when you pushed against it?"

The Wookiee moaned softly in Shyriiwook.

"Not much," Bell said. "He says it's different from what the Nameless do. The Nameless husk is just empty of the Force, but the blight is . . . not empty and not . . . aware? Is that right, Burry?" Bell frowned, and Burry tried again. "But it's reaching. It has an active, maybe living component? But whatever it is, pushing back exhausted Burry fast. With the . . . weight, I guess . . . of this blight's consumption, it's like trying to stop a moon from orbiting its planet. Maybe all of us together could do it, the way Jedi worked together to save Hetzal. But . . ."

"But it's showing up in a lot of places, and our resources are thin," Avar said. She squeezed Burryaga's arm, reaching out with the Force to let her compassion and her concern brush against him with a trill of a few bright notes.

Burry was particularly empathic, and he certainly felt it. He lowered his head, a few braids sliding around his face.

"The first step—the thing we can focus on now—is finding and stopping Marchion Ro," Avar said.

"You think we can?" Amadeo asked.

Vernestra, who sat alone on one of the bunks with a leg drawn up and her arm hooked around the knee, said, "We have to."

It was only the truth.

"The information Elzar Mann is bringing us should make it possible," Avar said.

The young Padawan seemed to gather his courage. He said, "Burryaga, Master Mirro and I went over the description the Council sent out about how you fought the Nameless. Will you . . . can you show me?"

As Burry nodded, giving off a distinct feeling of grim determination, Avar backed away to watch.

By the time the *Axiom* arrived, Avar was overeager to get started. She, Bell, Burry, Vernestra, Mirro, and Amadeo transferred over so that the *Elder Lily* could return to its patrol.

Waiting in the conference room with Elzar were Captain Ba'luun and a handful of high-ranking RDC. Avar nodded at Elzar, who nodded back, and that was all they needed. It didn't simply feel good to be in the same room with him and be so attuned to his presence: It felt *right*.

She thought, *Elzar isn't going to run away from me again.*

Ba'luun tugged at her beard and gestured for her lieutenant to pull up the star map. It blinked to life, vivid green.

Elzar removed a datastick from his belt and inserted it into the console. He touched a few controls, and several worlds lit up white. "I have confirmation that these are the places Marchion Ro has personally been in the past six weeks. He's traveled alone on either the *Gaze*

Electric itself or one of its shuttles. Each time, he was gone for a few hours, and he didn't bring anything back with him as far as my source can identify. Can you put up the various borders of the Stormwall, previous and current?"

Ba'luun's lieutenant did so. The lines appeared in shades of red.

Avar leaned closer along with everyone else. Her gaze flicked from world to world, looking for a pattern—looking for Drengir, if she was honest with herself.

"On every single one of these worlds he's visited in this part"— Elzar gestured at a swath of about a third of the map, including quite a bit of the Occlusion Zone—"there have been reports submitted to the Republic or Council about sightings of this energy blight."

Burry moaned sadly. It was at least seven worlds.

"Does this include the data from Cair San Tekka?" Avar asked.

Elzar nodded.

Good, Avar thought. She was glad Cair had gotten the packet to the Council.

Bell Zettifar said, "I don't recognize most of those worlds. Are they inhabited?"

"Mostly not, thank the Force," Elzar said, then grimaced. "My source confirms that Ro has been looking for it, or tracking it—the blight. What we don't know is why. Or how he's predicting the pattern of its appearance."

Master Mirro asked, "Do you have dates for his visits? To compare with the reports?"

"I do." Elzar keyed in a new command. "But as we don't understand the blight, we can't know when it appeared in these places. It might grow at a stable rate, or it might depend on the world, on the ecosystem, on circumstances we can't even guess."

As he spoke, the worlds Ro had visited began to blink in sequence.

At first, Ro had not been moving in a direction of any kind, and he returned to one of the worlds twice. But the two most recent locations were both in Republic space.

"What made him begin to focus on Republic space like this?" asked Vernestra. "Arrogance?"

Burry pointed at the map and spoke, and Bell translated, "Those two had Drengir on them. We saw the blight on Ronaphaven for the first time."

"The data we received from Cair San Tekka's network indicated a possible link between the blight and the Drengir seeding," Avar added.

Bell said, "If there's blight on Felne Six now, too, then two of the places we've encountered it had evidence that Drengir *had been* there, not that they were active. The one on Felne Six was dying for no reason we could tell, except that it was cut off from the hive mind, we think. And on Ronaphaven there were Drengir burrows but not actual Drengir."

Elzar rubbed his beard. "The teams sent to Eiram to look for the Great Progenitor in the ruins of Starlight are still investigating."

"If the Drengir are moving, she has to be out of stasis," Avar said, trying not to think too closely on the vicious creature. The memories of the voice of the Drengir in her mind darkened Avar's thoughts. Elzar nudged her shoulder.

"Could it be the Nameless instead?" Mirro Lox suggested. "The Drengir are connected to the dark side, but that's still the Force, and as far as we know, the Nameless don't differentiate between light and dark. Perhaps something about the creatures has awoken . . . rogue seeds, free from their Great Progenitor?"

Burryaga spoke up again, sounding frustrated. Bell said, "He thinks it could be something else, too, other than the Great Progenitor . . . if it has to do with the blight. That . . ." Bell frowned in concentration, nodding.

Captain Ba'luun gestured at one of her lieutenants, who set a translator device onto the table with the volume turned high to catch Burry's argument:

". . . feed on the Force, the dark side, too. Maybe the blight itself interferes with the Drengir's normal functionality," the device blared out much too loudly. Burry bared his teeth at it and skewed a look at Bell.

"All right, I'll do better," Bell said with a little laugh.

The lieutenant sheepishly turned off the device.

Avar held up a hand to stop them. "It's possible. You're right, Burryaga, we don't know anything for sure." She shook her head and focused on the map. "Either way, if there were Drengir once in all these places, maybe the blight is something they leave behind?"

"By the Force, I hope not," Mirro Lox said, rubbing his closely shorn hair. "A new version of how they've decimated crops in the past?"

Burry replied immediately, shaking his head, and Bell said, "Burry's right: The blight we encountered doesn't feel like the dark side, and the Drengir do. So if it is something they're responsible for, we don't think it can be the same."

"It could be this blight activates dormant Drengir roots," Avar said. "We aren't sure about all the mechanisms of their sprouting; we only know how they all woke up last time."

"Maybe it isn't something they're doing, but something they're running from?" asked Padawan Amadeo very tentatively.

Avar heard what she could only describe as a shiver in the song of the Force and pressed her lips together. *We should all be running from it,* she thought. She clenched her jaw. It wasn't in her nature to think such things.

Elzar frowned as he made a dozen more worlds on the map light up, this time in blue. "Avar got the data on where we think the blight is in the O.Z., and here are the additional worlds from which we—the Council and chancellor—have had confirmed reports of the blight in Republic space. Including now the world Oanne, thanks to Burryaga and Bell."

"So you think he'll head for one of those?" Master Mirro said slowly. The tension in the room was thick, but Avar could feel all her fellow Jedi making the effort to shake it away. Vernestra had one hand on the hilt of her lightsaber. Captain Ba'luun's tail flicked back and forth rather aggressively.

"I do," Elzar answered. "Unless he has a means of predicting where it will be without rumors and reports, which is possible."

"If he's going places he thinks Drengir should be, but aren't anymore . . ." Avar suggested.

"Assuming we can track him this way, it will be one of those," Captain Ba'luun said, gesturing at several systems. "Which are in the possible trajectory field if you follow the order in which he visited the most recent three."

It gave them two likely possibilities.

Avar stared at them.

A moment of grim silence was broken when Captain Ba'luun asked, "So where are we taking my ship?"

Avar studied the holomap. She let her eyes glaze. She knew this was her decision. "Did either experience Drengir the year before the Stormwall activated? I didn't chase them from either, but I wasn't the only one fighting them."

"Stand by," the RDC lieutenant said, working at the console.

Elzar shifted closer to Avar, and their shoulders brushed together. She closed her eyes and ignored her memories of fighting and despair from that time. The fury. It roiled deep inside her, but Avar breathed it into diffusing—at least the hardest edges of it.

"Vixoseph One," said the lieutenant. "It's barely inhabited since the Drengir scoured the main colony twenty months ago."

"Looks like the blight appeared in a wetland area used to harvest ore," Elzar added, reading off his datapad. "The mining droids lost contact a few weeks ago, and the conglomerate paying for it all reported signs of the blight."

Avar took another deep breath, leveling her emotions and holding her heart open to the Force. Nothing she sensed urged her in a different direction. Avar nodded. "Let's go. Everyone get some rest, but remember, this is reconnaissance at first—we need to be sure we can find him, track him, and then we'll put together a real strike team."

"And may the Force be with us," Master Lox said.

Chapter Fifty-Three

Avar was pulled away with Captain Ba'luun to coordinate the jump to Vixoseph and how they'd deploy fighters and Vectors once they arrived. It was decided they'd emerge from hyperspace as far out from the planet as possible for reconnaissance first. Better not to jump up the nose of the *Gaze Electric* if they could help it. Once they understood the situation, they'd drop Vectors to dive down to the planet itself and search for signs of the blight and Marchion Ro.

When she left the captain's office, Avar was pleased to run directly into JJ-5145. She hadn't realized Stellan's droid had come with Elzar from Coruscant. It rolled back anxiously, then said, "Master Kriss! Master Mann was hoping you wouldn't be long."

"Where is he?"

"In your quarters I'm afraid, Master Kriss."

"That's a good place for him, Forfive," Avar said with a laugh. She hurried past him, hoping she'd look too busy to be stopped in the corridors. She didn't want to wait any longer, though just feeling his presence on the ship this whole time had been so compelling. A relief to part of her that she hadn't realized was reaching out while he was so far. The change since the last time was so strong—whatever had been holding Elzar back had dissipated. He was ready. She hoped.

Avar didn't knock—it was her own quarters after all—but only keyed in her code, and the door slid open.

Elzar sat on the bed, his legs folded and his eyes closed. His robes flared around him on the bed in a gold-and-brown half circle. His mouth was set in a soft, relaxed line, his hands folded neatly together in his lap. His boots were lined up at the head of the bunk.

She swallowed back a joke about how responsible he looked and stepped in. The door swished shut in JJ-5145's metallic face.

Elzar opened his eyes. "Avar."

Avar walked toward him. She stopped. It wasn't a large room, just the bunk and console and a tiny counter for washing up or rehydrating protein packs.

Elzar got to his feet. His bare toes wiggled in the thin carpet. Then Avar saw his lightsaber on the narrow shelf over the bed, and beside it, Stellan's.

His gaze followed hers, and Elzar said, "I've been thinking I should give it to Vernestra."

A soft smile pulled at half her mouth. She met Elzar where he stood, putting her hands on his waist. For a moment neither spoke. They only shared the space, breathing together. The Force hummed between them. Then Avar leaned in and put her forehead against his neck.

"Ghirra Starros," he said, answering her before she could ask.

She blinked in surprise, and Elzar jerked back a little as if her lashes had tickled him. He smiled wryly.

"I was surprised it worked, too," he said.

"What did you have to give her?"

"Nothing, if you can believe it." Elzar tilted his head. "At least not yet. I'm sure she'll come calling."

Drawing back, Avar studied his eyes. "You trust the information, though? The locations about Ro and what he's been looking for?"

Elzar simply nodded. "I do, because of how I got it."

Avar waited, so close she could barely focus on one of his eyes at a time.

"Love," he whispered.

Warmth blossomed across Avar's chest and pooled in the small of her back. She leaned her whole body nearer to him. She brushed her lips to the soft beard along his jaw.

"Avar," he said again, then nothing else.

She should get them some tea or water or food. They should talk strategy. She should tell him what Cair San Tekka had said about the blight.

Instead, they only stood there, pressed lightly together, breathing. It was a gentle meditation. A sway of the tide and a soft lullaby.

Avar slowly slid her hands around him, pressing her palms flat against his back so that she could be fully against him. Her temple touched his cheek. The metal of her new diadem a line of cool relief between them.

Elzar shifted his head and kissed the diadem. He breathed against her skin, his breath sliding down her cheek, her neck. Avar shivered. She smiled.

"It feels right," Elzar murmured. "This. Us."

"I know."

"You balance me, your song does. It can . . . shape my tides, the ocean. Or echo through it. I don't have the exact words, but I *know* it. I *feel* it."

Avar felt so filled with light. The song she heard was tender, inexorable, and so quiet. Quiet like gravity or magnetism. A thing one felt, needed the right tools to understand, but if one listened with the right senses, with the Force, it became the pressure of stars, the pull that made a galaxy spin.

"I keep asking myself, why now?" Elzar kept talking, and Avar kept listening. She didn't have the answers, while at the same time she knew the answer was only: because now is the right time.

"At first I thought, *It's to make up for Stellan being gone,* but that isn't how the Force works. It doesn't replace or exchange. It flows. It fills. So maybe we're needed like this," he said. "Together. The Force needs something from us. Of course it does, but maybe it needs us together for it."

"Maybe," she murmured, drifting closer to him, if that was even possible.

Elzar huffed a laugh. "Whatever it is, I like it. I want to choose it. Let it be, let us just be. No attachments. No expectations. Just whatever we have to do. One with the Force."

"Two with the Force," she teased.

She turned her face and kissed him, deeply and lazily. Elzar's arms tightened around her. He kissed her back, tentatively enough she knew he was still overthinking it. It made her smile into his lips.

"Are you laughing at me?" he murmured.

"A little bit." She bit his jaw and he yelped, laughing, too.

Elzar said, "I like it when you laugh. There hasn't been enough of that the past years."

Avar's thoughts spiraled idly while they kissed, emptying her mind of anxiety and fear, of ambition to win, of even hope and relief, of everything. It was meditative. The song of the Force became the beat of her pulse, building faster, echoing against the boundaries of her mind and heart. It was Elzar, and it was the Force. They held themselves there, in tune, in balance. Give-and-take, harmonizing. They sank to their knees on the floor, never letting go.

Slowly, slowly, the rhythm of their kisses changed. Elzar dug his fingers harder into her ribs, and Avar bit at his mouth. Their breathing heated.

Yes, Avar thought before she fully realized what was happening. Every single part of her knew what she wanted.

"Yes," Elzar said out loud—she thought. Maybe. But he kissed her like he meant it. Avar opened up, kissing back in a fury. She slid her hands up his arms to skim over his beard and dig into his hair. Avar tugged, and for a moment they kissed frantically, as if hard and fast were the only way. It hurt, but Avar felt alive. She pushed at him, and Elzar fell back. He held on to her hips as she straddled his waist. She sensed how hard he was thinking—panicking, really!—too many thoughts and worries, consequences spooling out too much too fast, but under the pressure of so much desire, it felt like a dunk in a crystal-clear hot spring.

Elzar licked his lips, staring up at her wide-eyed. Avar panted as she looked back, settling her hands on his stomach.

Awe, delight, anxiety pulsed between them. Avar took a deep breath, holding his gaze. Elzar breathed with her. In and out. As deeply as her lungs could fill.

They breathed. Together they calmed down enough for Elzar to smile ruefully, tinged with self-deprecation.

"I want this," Avar said. "Do you?"

Elzar's brown eyes wrinkled at the corners with the intensity of his soft smile. "Yes," he said.

Avar leaned over him and cupped his face. He held her hips, hands skimming down her strong thighs.

"Can we?" he asked softly.

Avar waited. She *felt* him readying his words.

"I want to be with you in every possible way, and for it not to ruin me or you, but only make us brighter."

Nodding, Avar slid her hands from his face down his chest. She held herself open, listening to his Force song, the tide of it, pulling her in.

"Can we?" Elzar asked again. "Can we choose this and never let it become selfish or dangerous?"

Avar breathed deeply, and Elzar automatically mirrored her. She pushed aside the folds of his vest, then moved her hands to the first tie of his shirt. She unknotted it and pushed it aside to bare his collarbone and his chest. It didn't feel selfish; it felt buoyant. She put her hand against his warm body, over his heart. A bit breathlessly, she asked, "Do you know what Jedi teach about choosing the light?"

"Remind me," he murmured with a little smile.

A grin spread over her mouth, and Avar leaned in to speak against his lips, "It takes practice."

"Practice," he said, his voice warm with laughter. "I like practice."

This time, when Avar kissed Elzar, she felt only her name in his mind—her name and the song of the Force, and a vast, brilliant ocean.

Chapter Fifty-Four

General Viess held a sword in one hand. It glinted sharply in the flames from Porter's explosion. She wore battle armor over deep-purple skirts.

Porter wished for a moment he was in his Jedi robes. He'd given them up in the Occlusion Zone, but the brown and undyed wool he wore managed to mirror them in a homespun way. The glossy hilt of his lightsaber stood out in his hand, unsuited to the humble costume.

His mind slid to Barash, to what she'd say. Tease him, urge him on with a certainty that had bolstered him every day until suddenly it was gone.

Because of this person before him. Viess's green skin looked healthy, her tattoos rich and bold. Her *beskar*-plated armor more glimmering than ever before, as if recently polished.

Porter didn't need to look good. He *was* good.

"Leave us," Viess said, not to him, but to the remaining Nihil. "Leave us, take everything. This is between him and me."

Porter kept his eyes on her. If the Nihil disobeyed, so be it. If they shot him in the back, so be it. He was here for Viess.

But he was aware of the Nihil scattering.

"Did you really need to blow up half my compound?" Viess asked silkily.

Porter shrugged. He could ask so many things in return. If she really needed to embrace murder and mayhem, if she was fulfilled by mercenary work, if her position as the head of Marchion Ro's Protection Ministry mattered. If she knew what she wanted from the galaxy, what fed her, what could make her free instead of pinning her down in the miasma of violence like a skitterfly in a glass box.

He pushed away his anger.

There was anger, there was rage and guilt and grief and 150 years of loss egging him on. Decades of not knowing, of needing to know, of pretending he could live beyond what had happened back then. The choices he and Barash had made, together and apart.

"I am not alone," he said to Viess and sprang into action.

Viess's confusion parted for an aggressive response. She swung her sword and cleaved the air. But Porter met her head-on with his outstretched left hand. He shoved through the Force, and his palm stopped her blade with a shock wave of power that spread in waves and waves.

Distantly, Porter heard cries of alarm, pounding footsteps, but his eyes were only for Viess.

They shoved apart, and Porter sent his lightsaber flashing her way. It darted at her head in fast, intricate maneuvers, led by Porter's will and sweeping hand. The Force tied him to the lightsaber: It was an extension of him. Nothing more, nothing less.

Viess blocked, bared her teeth, hit back, but could only keep up through concentrated effort.

Then she roared and let the lightsaber cut across her shoulder. It singed her cape, slicing a long chunk of it free. Viess spun, slashed out. She was too near. Porter jumped closer, let her sword slice his side low toward the hilt. If she'd jerked it back, the long blade might have eviscerated him. But Porter punched her in the face.

With a mangled cry, Viess stumbled back. Porter grabbed his lightsaber from the air and swung it.

This was not like their back-and-forth on Naboo. There was nothing to distract them, no Republic soldiers, no fancy balustrades, no blasters. This was no invitation-and-answer, no give-and-take. Porter was here to make sure she died.

Overhead, Nihil Strikeships took off, one after another.

Porter pressed in relentlessly. Viess's expression narrowed and shifted as she aligned herself to his intensity.

The lightsaber and *beskar* blade clashed again and again. Viess snapped her foot out to catch his leg, and Porter spun, lightsaber swirling. He jabbed at her throat with stiff fingers; she bent back, kicking out. Her armor flashed in sunlight as the courtyard was washed in light.

Porter reached out with the Force; he didn't need to see well to know where she was, to sink into the Force and fight. Drive forward, into her.

Viess was panting, and Porter felt sharp weariness in his ribs, in old injuries, but he was not leaving here with both of them alive.

It was time. Whatever else happened, one of them would die today.

Viess moved, throwing him back and rolling. Porter hit the ground and was on his feet, the Force ringing around him. If he had a dozen blades, they'd be answering his call, arrayed around him in a deadly ring.

But he had only his lightsaber. It was enough.

"Porter Engle," the general said.

Porter tasted blood in his own mouth and was unsure when he'd been hit. His left cheek ached. He spat blood onto the ground and did not say her name back to her.

He drew on his awareness of the Force. On her weariness, on her.

Viess, her weight back on her heels, startled. She frowned and began to charge, but the moment she moved, Porter swung out with the Force and knocked her off her feet.

She hit the ground hard, with a clang of *beskar*.

Porter slashed at her with his lightsaber, and she parried from her back, spinning back to her feet. She lashed out, but Porter was ready. He grabbed her wrist and wrenched it around with all his strength and the weight of the Force behind him.

She screamed in pain, dropped her sword. Viess kicked back at him, and Porter had to push her away to avoid the hit. Viess ripped herself free and *ran*.

Porter let out a sound of shock. She'd invited him here, she'd set this up, and she'd sent her underlings away.

She had thought she could beat him. But now she was running.

His surprise gave her a temporary advantage, and Viess darted into the smoke. Porter reached with the Force and felt her, stumbling, urgent, with a definite goal in mind. Porter put his rebreather back on, squared his shoulders, and barely touched the blood seeping through his tunic and jacket just above his left hip. He followed her into the smoke. Inexorable. Relentless.

The squeal of taxed gears drew his attention, and he heard the high hum of a sudden engine.

Porter lengthened his stride, shoving through a half-open door into the base's small hangar. The curved roof gaped wide open, the fleeing Nihil having left it. The bright blue-pink morning sky shone, hardly tinged by smoke here. And—

A fighter, with room for only one pilot, lifted. Its long nose turned, and Porter raised an arm to protect himself from the vivid engine glow.

He threw his lightsaber, aiming with an outstretched hand. The blade sunk into the metal, sparks flying. He shoved with the Force, and the saber dug in, up to the hilt. Porter could tear through this little fighter like it was nothing. The Force was with him. Eager for it.

He could finish her.

Knowing the cost, Porter took a deep breath, ready to give in.

"Stop!" Viess's voice shrieked through the ship's intercom. "Stop!"

Porter sneered, flexed his fingers into a tight fist, and focused on—

"I know where your sister is!"

The lightsaber froze, blade vanishing before Porter even realized he'd extinguished it. He stared up, and the hilt of the saber fell, smacking the ground with a clang.

Viess's fighter wobbled, nosed up, then righted itself and darted off with a blast.

Porter sank to his knees, her words ringing in his skull.

Chapter Fifty-Five

Marchion Ro had been minding his own business for days, to be honest. Ignoring the needs of his ministers and Storms, ignoring the Republic, focused instead on this . . . gift. Before now, everything Marchion had he'd taken, but this had been waiting for him. Scattered across the galaxy, whispering *yes, yes.* What he wanted, the galaxy wanted, too.

The experiments with the blight had gone well. No matter where in the galaxy he came across it or what sort of world it was consuming, the blight was the same. And now Marchion Ro could control it.

To a certain extent. He could walk upon it and touch it without harm to himself, so long as he used the Rod of Power that controlled the Levelers.

He was on Vixoseph I because of the pattern of Drengir fleeing from the blight seemingly before the blight was detectable by most sentient beings. While the blight existed on worlds that had never seen Drengir—such as Norisyn, with his defunct crystal farm—Ro had yet to find a world the Drengir had recently abandoned that did not have seeds of the blight blooming with their deadly ash.

Of all his remaining questions, the one for which he could not yet fathom an answer was how exactly the blight traveled. It seemed to hop randomly from world to world, appearing chaotically as if some ancient god had thrown a handful of blighted seeds across the galaxy eons ago, and only now did they blossom.

Rather like the way Ro had planted the Drengir.

Surely if he could move the Drengir so successfully, he could discover a way to move the blight exactly where he wanted it to be. Shape it. Use it. Weaponize it. Remake the galaxy in his design, again.

Few existential pleasures appealed to Marchion Ro, but he could not deny the appeal of such raw power.

Here on Vixoseph he intended to prove he could do it—replant the blight, and if the Drengir proved amenable, use them to disseminate it more widely.

The *Gaze* had brought him and a gunship here, then jumped away to hide until he wished to be retrieved. They'd scanned for Drengir and found three where expected, some kilometers north of this location where the grasslands turned into low-lying scrub forest. Ro always seeded the Drengir near a food source like the mining colony had been.

While his Nihil subordinates tracked emerging Drengir north of the blighted grasslands, Ro stripped off his cape and tunic and hung them over the branch of a succulent tree. He removed his boots and propped them in the crook of a thick violet stem. Previous experience had taught him that while the rod could entirely protect his body, the clothes he wore were more vulnerable. Two worlds ago the hem of his cape had touched the blight, and only keen observation had allowed him to notice it before he returned to the *Gaze* itself carrying infection across his shoulders. That cape had been lost, and he would not lose another. He didn't even bring his mask off the ship anymore.

Bare but for his trousers and belt from which hung a comlink and a lightsaber, his hair loose in the distant ocean breeze, Marchion Ro took up the rod and walked into the blight.

His feet dug into the ground, and he paused, focused the strength of his will onto the rod, and dragged the two Nameless in with him. One young, gangly, still learning vicious hunger; the other Boolan's monstrosity with the cybernetic spine. They gouged the blighted grass into ashes with their huge claws, whining and roaring, trembling. Their face-tendrils whipped in agitation; they rolled their brilliant-blue eyes.

But they walked at his side.

"It's unkind," the ghost at his side whispered. She was barefoot, too.

After walking carefully for some time, Ro bent and dug his own claws into the ground. He uprooted chunks of ruined grass and their disintegrating roots, along with what remained of the once mineral-rich soil.

Slowly, like a king on his way to a coronation, Ro made his way to the edge of the blight. Here the grasslands broke up into a spread of wildflowers along a tiny creek. Ro walked into the healthy meadow, and the Nameless barreled after him, eager to be away.

Twenty paces outside the blight, Ro planted the blighted grass among the flowers while the ghost of his great-great-grandmother pouted. Ro was not able to resist smirking at her.

They waited. The Nameless leaned into each other, rubbing and whining, unable to move too far from Ro and the rod.

He watched, crouched on his bare feet and one clawed hand, admiring the dark gray of his skin against the tiny pink flowers.

Beside him, his great-great-grandmother knelt. She tilted her head, staring at the flowers.

It began with only a shadow. Under a leaf, at the base of the pale-green stem.

A shadow. As gray as bone, as ash.

Slowly, slowly, it crept higher.

Slowly, the pink flowers turned gray, too. Chalky, blighted gray, as Ro's experiment worked.

He'd done it. Replanted this blight. Picked it up, carried it with him, seeded it. Now he needed to try moving it to a new world. Across light-years. Infect a Drengir and see what happened. Would the Drengir send it along their hive mind? Good thing his Nihil were herding a few of the creatures toward him.

The Evereni ghost touched his cheek, and Ro felt nothing but satisfaction.

They continued to watch.

Within the hour the entire stand of flowers had calcified. Some leaves and petals crumbled; others maintained their pristine shapes, like ghosts of themselves.

If he were the sort to talk to the dead, he'd have pointed out the similarity to her.

Chapter Fifty-Six

HYPERSPACE

When the summons came, the ping of his comlink shook Elzar from his lazy doze. Avar brushed her lips under his jaw, and he squeezed her. As he lay with Avar in the quiet, dim crew quarters, Elzar's feelings were alight with life, and the ocean of the Force was heavy against them, holding them together.

He didn't think the peace and certainty could last, but then again nothing lasted. The nature of the Force was flow, was change. One moment became the next, and nothing remained.

And that was all right.

Together he and Avar sat up, straightened each other out, and left her quarters together without exchanging a word. They didn't need to. There was this thing between them, a bond, wordless and full, something that had been growing for their entire lives. It ebbed and flowed and had nearly been lost once or twice. Elzar had been too confused and desperate, or Avar too focused. They'd thought they needed a fulcrum point between them. It didn't matter. Everything that had come before had led to this, and from this, everything would come. That was what Elzar was supposed to think about it, right?

He glanced at Avar as they hurried along the corridor to the bridge. His pulse raced, and he wanted to grab her, cage her against him, and not let her go into danger. At the same time, he wanted to push her ahead, let go of her as she flew, and witness her glory at her side. Neither impulse was stronger. They balanced.

Vernestra was already on the bridge, and she gave Elzar the same cool look he'd received from her ever since she'd returned to Coruscant after her time in the Occlusion Zone. Today Elzar nodded back easily. She didn't have to like him, that was all right, too. When they survived this, he'd give her Stellan's lightsaber.

Bell and Burry joined them, with Mirro Lox and Amadeo just behind. Everyone was prepared for action, if called for. Mission attire and lightsabers and ready demeanors. Even the young Padawan looked outwardly calm.

The Longbeam dropped out of hyperspace with a soft purr just as they reached the bridge.

"Sensors detecting the presence of—it's the *Gaze Electric*!" a comm officer cried out.

Captain Ba'luun said, "Cannons ready just in case. Lieutenant, bring us around to see the *Gaze* directly ahead, but keep back."

"Sir!" a different officer said, "It—it jumped. It's gone."

Avar strode forward to the comm console as if to see for herself. "Ro ran?"

She sounded as incredulous as Elzar felt at the idea.

"It must have been ready to go," the officer said. "I don't think it had time to notice us, calculate a jump, and go. They must have been in the process already."

"We can't even pursue," Ba'luun said, thunking the end of her tail against the metal floor in frustration.

"At least we have confirmation of his recent location," Master Lox said. "He is following a pattern."

"Anything from the planet?" Elzar asked.

The captain indicated one of the stations next to her command terminal. The RDC officer there slid her hands over the controls. "No distress signals. The comm buoy appears to be functioning . . ."

Avar walked to the tip of the platform overlooking the broad swath of the viewport. Stars glimmered, and just below the nose of the cruiser the planet Vixoseph I glowed with white-pink clouds. Beneath them lay yellow-gold continents striped with veins of dark water. "Can you bring us around to orbit over the droid mining facility?"

Elzar joined her, putting his hand on her back as if he could channel his power into hers.

"Doing so," the pilot answered.

"Do you want to try to pick a new location? Something that can be jumped to quickly from here?" Elzar asked quietly.

"I think we should make sure we were right about the blight and look for Drengir. Confirm our theories in order to keep tracking him, since we know he was just here," Avar answered with her eyes closed. She tilted her head, and something shimmered in Elzar as he seemed to feel Avar reaching past him out into the galaxy.

"I feel it," Avar said. She leaned back into Elzar's hand. "The blight. I feel it, just like Burryaga said. It's not the dark side, but it . . . pulls. It's hungry—or something like hunger. Yearning? I . . ." A shudder racked Avar's body. She looked back at Elzar. "I want to see it myself."

"What about the Drengir?" Captain Ba'luun asked her bridge crew.

One answered, "We aren't picking up anything specific . . . pinging the droid tower at the mining facility."

Elzar rubbed his thumb against Avar and nodded to her. He'd go with her.

The RDC comm officer said, "The droids report that several ships descended from orbit in the past day, and not all of them have left. I've asked them to scan for any sign of Drengir or the Nameless, but they aren't worried, given the nonorganic nature of their process."

"Where are the ships that landed?" Elzar asked.

After a pause, the tech said, "They landed near the old mining colony."

Avar said, "Let's get all the Jedi loaded and head down there."

Five Vectors cut through the thick atmosphere. Elzar flew his Vector at Avar's flank, shifting in tandem with her and the other three starfighters. They managed the sync relatively easily, thanks to Avar probably.

The planet rolled under them as they darted over endless grasslands toward the ocean that created the briny wetlands where the ore could be harvested. An abandoned town from the previous colony perched on an outcrop of old basalt, the pale domes and empty windows ghostly and lost. It was there that the ships—Nihil presumably—had landed. Elzar's Vector wasn't showing anything currently on the landing pads. "We should swing around and land," he said.

Avar's voice came through the comm. "Vernestra, Mirro, you two sweep farther out and look for any signs of Drengir or any Nihil. The rest of us will take a look at the blight and talk to the mining droids. Keep your feelings open, and speak up if you detect anything that could be the Nameless."

Acknowledgments came through from everyone, and Elzar followed Avar's lead as they dropped down to the outskirts of the town. The grassland was flat enough here that they could set down directly on it instead of using the landing pads, which were on the opposite side of town from the blight, facing the sea.

As Elzar popped the transparisteel bubble of his Vector, Vernestra and Mirro buzzed overhead, the soft whine of Vector engines trilling against the ocean wind.

Elzar let himself glance toward that rolling ocean for a moment. It was darker than most oceans, probably thanks to some kind of plankton or something in the atmosphere that scattered light differently.

He joined Avar, lifting his hand to shade his eyes from the dark-orange sun. She touched his elbow briefly and led him to Burryaga and

Bell, waiting with the sparking charhound Ember. Burry already gazed out at the blight itself.

Looking, Elzar was taken immediately aback. Though at first glance it could have been a large swath of gray-white desert, the monochromatic nature of it, and the ... sinking feeling of it made it obvious that this was no natural rock formation, no plight of erosion or ecologically born disease.

It was like a wound in the Force itself.

He started walking forward without realizing he was doing so.

The others came with him.

In the afternoon light, with the distant crashing of the sea, the wind gusted over tall grasses, slapping them against Elzar's boots and knees. The dirt crumbled in dry black-and-gray chunks—healthy and full of minerals that the colony here had harvested with their droids.

And the grass simply ended. It cut off in the uneven line of blight. At its edge, a meadow of pink flowers bloomed, the blossoms shaped like tiny bells hanging off curling stems. Some of them were going gray already, at different rates. Probably a function of their root systems—who knew how the blight traveled underground. Elzar fixated on the flowers for a moment, on the seemingly random way they were consumed.

Burry spoke mournfully, and Bell said, "Yeah. It's like the Force itself is dying here."

A wound. Becoming a scar. Something cancerous, insidiously appearing in a yet-unknown pattern, eating healthy, living worlds whole.

"We tried to fight it on Oanne," Bell said as the four of them and the charhound approached. "Burry meditated and pushed at it as if it were a part of the Force or something tangible he could shield against. It worked, but only slightly. He nearly passed out from the strain."

Burry added that even his entire effort hadn't been enough.

"We can link together," Avar said, "and see if our combined strength matches it more equally."

The Wookiee nodded emphatically.

"Master Kriss," Vernestra said, the Mirialan's voice tinny from Avar's comlink.

"Kriss here," Avar said, holding the link up to her mouth.

"We located the Nihil ship. They're flying in from the north. It's a gunship, and it's firing on something on the ground. We can't see what yet."

"Keep on them. We'll get back to our Vectors and be ready."

As Avar commed up to Captain Ba'luun that they'd found active Nihil, Elzar promised Burry, "When we take care of them, we'll try."

But Burryaga suddenly pointed over the blight and cried out wordlessly.

Bell cursed under his breath.

Elzar peered. "Is that . . . something moving?" he asked.

"Something is alive out there?" Avar said, shocked.

They'd nearly reached the border of the blight, and as they stared, whatever it was drew nearer.

Walking.

Across the blight.

It was huge, a beast of some kind, bent and distorted, ghostly white against the blighted landscape. It was coming toward the edge where the Jedi stood.

Dread hit Elzar fast as he stared at it. He couldn't look away. He knew, even before he felt it.

"Nameless," Bell whispered.

Chapter Fifty-Seven

VIXOSEPH I

Marchion Ro waited at the northern edge of the blighted land for his useless Nihil to drive the Drengir seeded on this planet months and months ago toward him. Using his Levelers to corral the beasts, Ro would infect the Drengir as he'd infected the stand of pink flowers.

Then he would see if the Drengir feared this blight because it was devastating or because it was an even greater danger to their species in particular.

Ro had long been curious about how the Drengir were connected via a mind network maintained by their Great Progenitor and the dark side of the Force. It interested him for the way it gave them such an advantage as predators, and Ro considered himself to be a top-tier predator. It connected them in unique ways, and Ro had come to wonder if the blight could be spread from Drengir to Drengir via that hive mind.

It was certainly one way to hop from world to world without a trace. Through the hive mind of dark side creatures.

If this experiment worked, the blight could spread so much faster than anyone would predict. Ro would enjoy watching the scramble.

Meanwhile, he could pick some up himself with the strength of the Rod of Power, and plant it wherever he wished.

At his sides, the Levelers suddenly twitched more violently than they had been. Their guttural cries made a discomfiting home at the base of Ro's spine. It spurred him to sneer, both glad to be affected and irritated at his body's weakness.

He could purge the weakness, though. It was what his kind did.

With absolutely no other warning, five Jedi Vectors dropped through the sky, appearing below the layer of striping orange clouds.

"Jedi!" the ghost of his ancestor gasped.

Startled, Ro narrowed his eyes and turned to cast a murderous look at her.

She'd disappeared after he moved the blight into the meadow of flowers, but now she stood barefoot next to him, hands clasped together over her heart, black eyes raised to the sky.

Her blue robes snapped in the wind, and waves of blue appeared on her forehead like blood seeping up through her skin.

The old dead Evereni seemed awfully happy to see Jedi.

Ro, on the other hand, snarled. Now was not the time to face them. He was busy. They were interfering and unwelcome.

His claws and teeth itched for Jedi blood.

But no. It was not time.

The ghost skipped over to one of the Levelers and tweaked its whiskers. "Are you hungry, my darling? Here comes a feast." Ro could see the wildness in her gaze, and he could see the fangs in her mouth as she grinned.

The dead woman's attention snapped to him. She stood straight. "What are you waiting for? Let's go get them! This is the legacy of my Levelers!"

Ro stared at her and slowly pulled up his comlink. Activating it, he said, "This is Ro. Pick me up, Thaya."

Dropping the comlink back in his pocket, Ro ignored his ancestor and watched the group of Vectors land in the direction of the mining colony. Attacking them would be an excellent surprise. They wouldn't expect him, unless they had finally decided to come directly at him, finally realized the only way to defeat the Nihil was to destroy him, and him alone.

Ro played with the hilt of the lightsaber at his belt, hungering to face the Jedi and collect more trophies. But no. He had his business here, and he wouldn't be distracted.

"Not today, ancestor," Ro said. But he squeezed the rod and commanded Boolan's Leveler to run south and enjoy itself with a Jedi feast. It took off instantly, its tendrils unfurled, and its mouth dropped open eagerly. The cyborg moved fast, gouging the ashy surface of this blighted field as it suddenly ran, baying and slathering. Perhaps Boolan had the right idea after all.

Ro laughed, and beside him so did the ghost. He'd let the Leveler distract and hopefully eat up all the Jedi, and while he awaited the return of the *Gaze,* this other Leveler would go with him to help with the Drengir. Finish his experiment.

"Watch out for those pretty flowers growing in that cluster, darling!" Ro's ancestor called to the cyborg Leveler, like a strange mother sending her children to school. "You never know what flowers are hiding!"

Of course, the Levelers couldn't hear her. That was only for Ro.

Chapter Fifty-Eight

VIXOSEPH I

Vernestra Rwoh flew her Vector low to the ground, stealthily coming up behind the Nihil gunship by skimming the canopy of the forest. The Force blazed around her, driving her with focused adrenaline. It was the kind of focus Vernestra had more than earned recently, though she wished she could turn it toward peace and defense instead of this constant ready offense the Nihil conflicts required. She shouldn't have to be used to it.

Behind her, Master Mirro Lox and his Padawan Amadeo slid parallel in their Vector. When they reached the Nihil ship, they'd dart apart, Mirro driving high and Vernestra shooting for the underbelly.

The tree line broke, and the Nihil ship became an unobstructed target. Vernestra nosed down while Lox and Amadeo shot up. She tilted her Vector easily and double-checked that her lightsaber was locked in place. Vernestra refocused and fired at the Nihil ship's rear wings. She'd bring them down if she could.

The Nihil avoided the hit with a sudden veer south, and Vernestra's blast scored a burn into the grassland. The Nihil fired, too, at something ahead of them on the ground.

Vernestra glanced down at twisting vines and the gleam of claws, a roiling knotted fury of plant life: a Drengir's mouth opened in a scream!

Vernestra rolled her Vector and shot up, yelling into her comm, "Master Lox, did you see? Drengir!"

"We're engaged with the Nihil gunship," Lox said. "We'll keep the Nihil occupied."

She glanced over to see the Nihil ship cut around and higher suddenly, firing a string of blasts at the other Vector.

"I've got the Drengir," she acknowledged grimly. Vernestra rolled again, angling sharply to come around in front of the Drengir. She fired.

For all its messy, angry bulk, it was fast. The Drengir dodged and tore back toward the forest. Vernestra chased it, coming in low. She swooped close and fired again; this time the blast hit a tangle of tentacles, ripping them away.

Her trajectory took her close to the tree line, and she nosed up, flipping in a tight maneuver to come around and continue firing. Unlike the case of the Nihil, there could be no quarter for Drengir. They didn't stop until they were made to.

The whole Vector jerked, and Vernestra cried out in pain as her restraints cut into her chest. Alerts flared in her mind as she felt the tail fin torn away in a shriek of metal. A Drengir had her, and she grunted with the effort of pushing the Vector up and away.

A second Drengir exploded out of the forest, leaping for her.

Vernestra flipped away again, but her left wing dipped too low, and the first Drengir grasped hold. It whipped the Vector back, its body dragging with her.

Gritting her teeth, Vernestra violently twisted her body and her Vector to tear free. The Drengir didn't release her. She needed to get the guns around, or climb higher out of their range. Anything.

"—coming around!" Master Lox yelled in the comm. "We're on its tail."

Unable to worry about the Nihil, Vernestra blew out a sharp breath and shook her Vector. She made it tremble, vibrate, and screamed along with it.

The Drengir roared, and she ripped free, taking a vine with her. The Vector spun upside down, and Vernestra fired.

The second Drengir whipped around, slapping at her, and Vernestra flew higher. Both Drengir raced away toward the abandoned mining colony. And the blight.

Vernestra caught her breath and looked toward Lox and Azzazzo's Vector, being chased by the Nihil gunship now. It shot heavy cannons at them, but Lox maneuvered in a gut-wrenching twist midflight and strafed vivid-red blasterfire across the Nihil's bow. The gunship veered off, struggling.

"The Drengir are headed for the others," Vernestra commed quickly.

The Padawan's higher voice answered, "I let the RDC know we need reinforcements down here."

"Copy, heading off the Drengir," Vernestra said, bringing her Vector around. "Join me when you can."

Vernestra gripped the flight controls harder and settled back into the Vector's sensory input. There was damage to her tail fin and left wing, but she could hold out a bit longer through the Force.

The Drengir were far ahead now, but Vernestra was going to catch them.

Burryaga fought against the spikes of fear cutting under his fur. Beside him, Master Elzar commed to the *Axiom* for backup against the Nameless. Even Master Elzar's voice broke.

Bell panted harshly. "I can't— Burry, do you see it?" he hissed.

Burry spun and grabbed Bell's shoulder. He growled for Bell to go get a ship—they needed distance to fight the Nameless. Bell could escort the fighters from the *Axiom*. Stay away from the Nameless this time.

"Good idea!" Bell agreed. He sprinted toward the mining colony where they'd left their Vectors. Burry ached to chase after him, to get away from the chilling terror. His ears were filled with the sounds of the roaring Eiram ocean.

"Can we . . ." Avar said, somehow stepping *forward.*

"Avar," Elzar said, grabbing her arm and tugging her back. His face was tight and pale, staring back at the blight. "I can see . . ."

Burry made himself turn, made himself stare: The blight crumbled in a long path, footprints and gouges from invisible claws. Burry's mouth was so dry that he couldn't catch his breath. The roaring that filled his ears was constant and awful. He clutched at his head, knowing it was the Nameless effect, not real, not— He could barely breathe. Fear choked him.

He was better than this. Burry couldn't look away from the evidence of death rushing at them. The ground beneath him seemed to buck, and as he stared, he almost saw it, coming in distorted images, like seeing something through a waterfall.

"Burryaga," Master Kriss snapped. He gasped and fell back, trying to focus. She said, her voice strange, out of tune, "If we link up, maybe . . ."

Fear clawed at him, making his hair rise. He put a hand on his lightsaber hilt. She knew what he'd managed on Naboo when he used his empathy to pinpoint the fear and fight it. He could—he could do it again. Try it again. Take the fear, let it flow through him, consume him. He could make his fear into a fighting chance. But he wanted to run.

"Burryaga," Master Kriss said again.

Before he could give in to the terror, Burry flung his feelings at Avar Kriss.

She caught them. Firmly, like a warm, friendly hand grasping his. For a moment, Burry heard a clarion. He focused on it with the Force, and felt her fear echo back. But it was hot fear, determination. They were both afraid. That was . . . better.

Burry could feel his chest constricting painfully with every struggling breath.

"What's the plan here?" Elzar asked through gritted teeth. "It's nearly here, are there more of them? It feels like so much! Avar—"

With his words, Burry felt the Master Jedi join the connection with Avar: a jolt of power bolstering them.

"Back up," Avar said. "Hold on to me."

The three of them jogged away from the blight. It was easy, so easy, to let the fear spur Burry's legs faster. He nearly stumbled in his effort not to run. The air in his lungs was too thin, too cold. The Nameless were coming. He saw them—too many of them—and the glint of metal. He heard an eerie wail that dropped his knees from under him.

Hands grasped at his elbow. He heard his name spoken. Burry felt Elzar Mann, but his fear was spinning fast, almost out of control.

But Avar was there, Master Avar, and the clarion rang through Burry again, erasing the terrifying wail.

"Focus, we have to do this now," she commanded.

Burry clutched at the waves of cold terror radiating between them.

Something about the brightness of her fear let him focus on passing it along.

"Skywings two minutes out, Jedi," said a voice from his comm.

A distant explosion sounded, and Burry's head jerked up. Far to the north, where the tree line darkened the horizon, a Nihil ship wobbled in the sky with its front half on fire. A tiny Vector darted around it like a little dragonfly.

He couldn't—Burry wasn't breathing right. He slammed his eyes shut as his pulse raced—there wasn't enough oxygen, and the sun was getting darker.

"Burry." The voice saying his name was breathless. It was—Master Kriss.

Burry swallowed and listened for the clarion.

It was there. He could feel it inside him, ringing. He raised his bright lightsaber, swung it in a slow, defensive arc. He could hold the Nameless back. They had to. It was here, close, closer, somewhere—

But then he heard someone laugh.

A low, wicked laugh, and Burry opened his eyes. Directly before him, a cybernetic eye flashed scarlet and tendrils reached for him, a meter long, two meters—impossible, he wasn't seeing the truth. The Force—

There was a sound, too, a vibrating purr of—of hunger, right beside him, and it became the hiss of air spilling away, into vacuum, into a deep-sea cave.

Elzar gripped Avar's hand, aware of her presence beside him and in the Force. And Burry, too, was a maelstrom of panic and determination. He could stay with them. They were real, even when the Nameless were everywhere, disorienting, impossible.

He had to hold on to Avar's song, to keep the rhythm of their breathing back and forth, in and out, anchoring him through the terror, through the messy sky, the blurring of the line between meadow and blight—the Nameless. He could feel it, the pull, the hell of its endless starvation, the despair rolling in his stomach. The Nameless had killed so many, destroyed them, turned Jedi and friends into nothing but chunks of rock and despair. It would destroy Avar, too, right here—suck her dry of all her vitality, the Force, and life, and *love*. At the thought, Elzar felt his terror tip into rage, into hate—it was right there. The power to destroy the Nameless first, if he chose. Lash out with darkness, meet the monsters full-on, destroy them, pour himself into them, an unending channel of the Force, a conflagration to make them feast until he was no more.

It would be worth it, to save Avar and Burry.

Elzar stepped forward toward what he knew to be his own doom. It was fine, though, fine, he'd do it, choose it: lose himself and Avar would be saved. Burryaga and Bell and Vernestra. If Elzar let the fear take him, maybe it would leave them alone. Give them a chance to act.

Avar squeezed his hand, her fingers digging painfully into his. *Elzar.*

He stopped.

Avar. He squeezed back. Push and pull, a desperate tide. Together.

Avar's song pulled on him, and Elzar welcomed it. He ignited his lightsaber.

As Marchion Ro approached the northern tree line, his eyes followed a Jedi Vector driving Drengir toward his position. Excellent, and useful for a Jedi. Too bad he wouldn't have a chance to thank them.

Several Nihil ships dropped out of the sky, and Ro smiled. Thaya was efficient as always.

Too bad they were directly followed by Republic fighters.

He watched a Nihil ship take a hit and spin out of control. Another of the *Gaze*'s Strikeships drove after the Vector heading this way. It fired. The Vector dodged, but one of its wings tore away under the pressure of its maneuver.

The Vector spun out of control. Ro picked up his pace. "Go on," he said to the Leveler, directing it at the Drengir. "Bring me one."

Vernestra cursed as her Vector lost vital function, but she felt where the Drengir were and managed to pull the Force to her and nudge the Vector's crash right at them.

She grabbed her lightsaber and punched the emergency release. The canopy popped free, and wind tore at her.

Leaping out, Vernestra reached with the Force to the ground and air. She pushed back against the ground, slowing her descent.

Her Vector slammed into the grassland at full speed. A shock wave knocked her back, but it flung fire at the nearest Drengir.

Vernestra didn't give it time to recover. She hit the grass running, igniting her lightsaber, and as she leapt toward the Drengir, she twisted the emitter ring to activate the whip function.

Snapping her wrist, the purple whip sliced through the confused Drengir. It spun, flinging tentacle-vines at her, and Vernestra darted to the side. The Drengir roared, and Vernestra dropped to the ground in a roll. She came back up with the whip at the ready. The Force helped her curl it around the Drengir's beak, shearing part of it off.

Pain radiated at her through the Force: dark side rage. Vernestra winced as she fought it away through adrenaline and determination. It couldn't get its hooks in her unless it got its actual hooks in her.

The Drengir ran, but Vernestra didn't chase. She felt Mirro Lox and Amadeo above her just in time to get out of the way as their Vector blew past, shooting the Drengir with everything they had.

It erupted in goo and char, vines and thorns flying. Vernestra used her lightsaber to whip things out of her way, but a stray vine tore across her shoulder. Blood poured down her arm, and Vernestra paused to rip the sleeve away. It was a brutal, jagged cut. Vernestra twisted her light-saber hilt again, returning the whip to a shining purple blade, and carefully brushed her lightsaber to the gouge in her flesh.

Pain burst clear and bright, but Vernestra kept herself still and con-scious with a focus through the Force that she'd only recently learned to achieve. The wound cauterized. She shut off her lightsaber and panted, looking out at what was ahead.

Two more Drengir tumbled and crawled across the grassland—she hadn't even realized there were three. More Nihil ships had arrived, and RDC ships, too, engaged in a desperate fight overhead. Mirro and Amadeo's Vector was turning a large loop in the distance and coming back around toward her and the Drengir as the two monsters fled south, toward the colony.

Hand raised to block the vivid-orange sun, Vernestra could just make out the edge of the blighted land, where the mining colony was and the other Jedi had landed. She heard Master Elzar calling for RDC assistance against Nameless, sounding panicked.

Tears of fury and helplessness sprang to her eyes. She remembered viscerally what they felt like, the Nameless. She didn't want to go. She wanted to stay back, get to a ship, stop the Nameless from far away, before she could feel them.

But that wasn't her job. Her job was to go. To help. Fear like acid clawed at her throat.

Vernestra swallowed it, and ran after the Drengir.

Chapter Fifty-Nine

VIXOSEPH I

Fear washed over Avar and through her. Burryaga called something in Shyriiwook—she heard it vaguely and said Elzar's name.

A flash of blue, the hum of a lightsaber. Elzar's. The glow focused her. It was real. She gathered herself, unclipped her own weapon, and let it flare to life. A roar of wind blasted over them as fighters blew past, the noise of blaster cannons breaking her concentration.

Avar staggered back. She hoped Bell was up there, a safe distance away. But the Nameless was probably too close for the Vector to fire.

A new roar suddenly crashed through the song of the Force, tearing every melody to shreds. Even the shriek of starfighter engines was engulfed by this overwhelming battle cry. She knew that roar. Avar spun in place as an even older fear coiled in her gut.

Drengir, screaming, the drag of their tentacles, the rustle of their leaves, the click of their beaks. *Meat!*

It leapt high and landed in front of Avar, grabbing her before she could move. A tentacle touched her cheek, and Avar jerked away. It whispered darkly through her veins. She had their voices in her mind, their hooked, slimy fingers down her throat, violating every boundary they could. Avar choked on it, her free hand clawing up her neck, her mouth gaping. She had to get it out. Block it from—

"Avar!" Elzar yelled.

Burry cried out, and Avar managed to turn her head in time to see him fling himself back from nothing. His fear drove through Avar, and her knees buckled. Fear, terror—*Nameless*. Not Drengir.

The Drengir tentacles vanished. Their touch and the voice were cut away by Burry's heady fear.

Where was it? Gripping her lightsaber, Avar tried not to panic. She breathed past the nausea and the building dread, the sucking emptiness. She knew what came next. They would suck the life from her insides, devour her Force. Her song would shatter, her bones turn to ash, and beside her Elzar would die, crumbling in her arms.

"Elzar," she said. "Burryaga."

They had to hear her.

"Avar," Elzar gasped—right there. She saw the blue shine of his lightsaber. Her eyes focused again. "Elzar," she said, and she felt him—a wave of fear and camaraderie. They were in it together.

Even if it was dying.

Even if it was losing the Force forever.

Avar's panic choked her. Her breath shuddered painfully as she clung to him—

Burryaga warbled something desperate, and Avar remembered how to fight it.

Use the fear. Together.

Vernestra caught up with the two Drengir when they suddenly jerked to a stop and reared back, their tentacle-vines whipping, and tried to scatter in opposite directions.

Fear hit Vernestra in the stomach, and she stumbled away, too. The clinging dread of Nameless was right here, somewhere—she flailed in a circle, but the effect surrounded her. She saw grassland, the gray blight, the tree line she'd left behind, and the Drengir, both of them whipping tentacles and sharp leaves, churning up the grass as they flailed. Vernestra backed away. If she could get far enough away, she could see it, and maybe her whip was long enough to reach without being overcome.

One of the Drengir screamed so high and loud that Vernestra clapped her hands over her ears, pressing the hilt of her lightsaber too hard against her head.

She thought, *The Drengir are Force users, too.*

She tripped away, pushing grass back, stumbling as the Drengir screamed incomprehensibly, flailing everywhere. She wondered what the Drengir feared, under the spell of the Nameless.

Vernestra swallowed bile. Waves of panic hit her, mingled with dread and fear, and she felt helpless fury, rage—the Drengir's emotions, the cut of the dark side pushing at her.

She needed to kill it and put it out of its misery, let it die.

There was nothing else for her to do.

Vernestra listened to the Force, moving slowly. There it was. The Nameless locked together with the Drengir, both of them roaring. The twisted, blurry white Nameless slashed at the Drengir, as the Drengir whipped around, reaching and flailing with its vines. The Nameless screamed—it sounded like children surrounding Vernestra, begging for help—and the Drengir bent itself back, trying to run. The Nameless leapt at it, grasping a vine in its gaping mouth.

The Drengir whipped around, tearing its vine from the Nameless. Vernestra tried to focus. She could see the teeth of the Nameless suddenly, and then its vivid-white eyes as its attention snapped to her.

But it froze. Vernestra stared as the Drengir twisted a tentacle-vine around the Nameless's neck, even as its huge body shuddered. Vernestra's fear came and went, tightening a grip around her throat and letting her go. The Nameless wasn't focused on her. She activated her lightsaber, twisting the emitter ring, and struck out with the whip. Too far, she couldn't reach. Too close, the fear choked her. Vernestra darted in and out, panting. Sweat broke out across her skin.

Then she realized the fear was fading.

The Drengir wasn't running. Its tentacles pulled around itself, and it wailed. It huddled in, a tangle of vines and leaves and thorns.

It was turning into stone.

She could see the Nameless clearly as the fear faded: Instead of a distorted creature of bones and screaming, it was just a body—ghastly white and emaciated, strangled in the grip of the dying Drengir. Its own work killed it.

Vernestra shook all over, adrenaline and pounding fear making her head ache.

The Drengir's beak clicked once, twice, and a few of the vinelike arms flicked. Vernestra felt pure terror wafting off the poor thing, the awful Drengir whimpering, flailing.

She struck.

A yellow lightsaber stopped Vernestra's whip before it slashed through the Drengir, and shock had her pulling back. Then a foot kicked her hard to the side. Vernestra fell onto her hip, brain jarred in her skull.

"Get out of the way, don't interfere," said a harsh voice.

She'd heard him before, coldly announcing ownership of the galaxy, and she'd watched him execute Grand Master Veter.

Marchion Ro.

He held a lightsaber that cast bright-yellow light on his face and down his tattooed chest. His other hand curled around something small tucked against his palm. A strange rod glowed softly pink-violet at his belt. His black eyes stared at the calcifying Drengir.

Vernestra followed that gaze and felt tears fall down her cheeks. The body of the dead Nameless shivered in the Drengir's grip. The Drengir didn't seem to be turning to stone anymore, but whatever the Nameless had done before it died was enough. Vernestra could feel it. She could feel both deaths clinging to her skin.

She pressed the back of her hand to her mouth. The hiss and spark of smoldering grass caught her attention, and she deactivated her lightsaber.

She couldn't do anything but watch as the Drengir shriveled into itself and gasped a final breath.

Next to her, Marchion Ro stepped forward as he disengaged the lightsaber, shoving it beside the pinkish rod on his belt, and kicked the dying Drengir. It collapsed in on itself, and he hummed thoughtfully.

Vernestra was too numb to do anything but stare for a moment. The sound of rustling leaves drew her attention to the third Drengir. It huddled not too far away, knotted around itself as if afraid, as if in the same pain as its companion. But all of it remained green and alive.

The hive mind. It must make the Nameless effect even worse.

This Drengir had felt everything the dead one felt—the fear, the grief. It didn't deserve such an end, such a shared devastation. Not even a killing monster like the Drengir.

Marchion Ro had done this.

Vernestra got shakily to her feet. She reignited her lightsaber and swung it at him. He dodged smoothly, a blaster appearing in his unoccupied hand from a holster on his thigh. Ro turned and considered her with the expressionless face of a predator.

"Tsk tsk," he said, and shot at her.

Vernestra startled back, her saber barely moving fast enough to counter the bolts.

He kept firing as he moved around the dead Drengir toward the remaining one and its high wailing. Vernestra followed. She focused on each step, on Marchion Ro. She gave herself to the Force, tracking his shots just well enough to block them.

Ro huffed and then said, "If you're so determined to irritate me, little Jedi, I'll bring my Nameless for you when it finishes with your friends."

"Go ahead," Vernestra spat. There was blood in her mouth. Her skull pounded. She couldn't stop him.

Ro lowered his blaster. He stared at her thoughtfully, then toward the blight. The race toward the Drengir had brought Vernestra near enough to see the small figures of Elzar Mann, Avar Kriss, and Burryaga facing off with a Nameless in the distance. There was nothing she could do. She was closer to Ro and the Drengir. If she was going to die here, better to die facing Marchion Ro, keeping him away from the other Jedi. Or to stop the last Drengir. Maybe, maybe Burry could pull off another miracle if she could only keep Ro and the Drengir away and distracted.

The shriek of fighter engines brought her attention and Ro's up to the battle between Republic Skywings and his Nihil. Ro frowned.

There were more RDC ships than Nihil. Good.

But Marchion Ro's frown turned into a smile as he watched the sky, and he glanced at Vernestra. "Here we go."

A shadow passed over the sun, and Vernestra looked up again to see the *Gaze Electric* itself descending, cannon ports open, bays mouthing wide to let go fighters of their own. It was massive and could destroy all of them in a single sweep of its cannons.

The final Drengir suddenly groaned and dragged itself up, recovered enough to move. It went slowly away from the blight toward the relative sanctuary of the forest.

Ro ambled casually toward it while Vernestra tried to understand what was happening.

Blaster reholstered, Ro skimmed his fingers against the glowing rod, then opened his left hand and tossed what he'd been holding at the Drengir.

A pale-gray rock.

Vernestra's eyes widened. If she didn't know better, she'd say it was a chunk of the blight itself. But that was impossible. Nobody could touch it. It ate *everything*.

The rock hit the Drengir and the monster twitched. It spun to face Marchion, but Ro laughed and turned his back to it. He threw Vernestra an obnoxious grin and took off running—directly toward the blight.

Chapter Sixty

VIXOSEPH I

In the orange sky of the setting sun, the *Gaze Electric* loomed, spitting out more fighters to meet the Skywings.

But on the ground, Avar, Elzar, and Burryaga were surrounded by nothing but fear. All they could do was push out with the Force and hold their lightsabers to keep the creature away from them. All the music Avar heard and all the strength of the Force vanished as the Nameless stalked them. It growled and roared, its long, sickly whiskers twisting as it darted nearer, then backed away from the jagged, flailing cut of the lightsabers. Avar trembled, barely holding the hilt. She felt its gaping hunger, its nothingness, so clearly. Beside her, Elzar panted, his shoulder knocking against hers. They were too close. Burryaga completed their triangle, the three of them moving, locked into their fear.

It wasn't working. Focusing on the fear, finding a direction the way Burry had done. Avar had no idea where the creature was, and she couldn't fight it this way. "Can you see it?"

"I see something," Elzar said, his face pallid under his beard. His blade was held out in defense, and Burry's, too. They shifted around

Avar, making a shield as best they could with trembling hands, unable to trust their senses—or even the Force.

Burry called a soft negative, his voice too quiet. Fear radiated off him. They had to get rid of it.

"I have an idea," Avar said, her voice barely a whisper. She holstered her lightsaber and held out her shaking hands. "Burry, do what you did before. Focus on the fear for me."

Burry put his larger hairy hand in hers. The Wookiee was so open, so ready, that he and Avar slammed together into a network of two without Avar having to do much.

Elzar switched his lightsaber to his left hand, and took Avar's. She squeezed too hard. "Elzar, it's you."

"What's me—" he said, but she closed her eyes.

Avar opened her heart.

She opened to the terror and the panic, tears springing to her eyes and her knees buckling. Burryaga and Elzar held her up. Burry understood instantly what she needed, and he let the feelings hit him, whimpering, focused on it. Avar held on to his terrified song as she sank down, and instead of pushing away, instead of directing, she pulled fear into herself through Burryaga, pulling it from the Force, pulling it from the thing that made her so terrified, and pulling it away from Elzar Mann.

"Go," she managed to say.

Suddenly, Elzar could see it clearly. No more distortions, no more panic, no more visions of burning Jedi and crumbling friends.

The Nameless creature, the pale, twisted thing of all their nightmares. He'd seen it on the holoscreen when it stalked Grand Master Veter, sucking him dry of life and Force, of everything. It was before him. Huge and awful, with metal fused to its spine, metal spikes on its whipping tail.

Somehow the fear wasn't quite so debilitating any longer. He felt it, but there was so much more to feel again.

No, he knew how: Avar.

Avar was doing it. And Burryaga.

They channeled his fear away together.

The absence left him room for light.

An empty clarity edged along the gentle pressure of Avar and Burry pulling at him, at his emotions, at the tide of the Force ebbing and flowing deep inside him.

The creature came toward them, and Elzar lifted his lightsaber, filling his presence with the living Force. Avar and Burry glowed with it, the Force a glaring song loud enough that Elzar imagined the whole world here could hear it.

He saw the Nameless turn toward it with all its hunger and pain. Unnaturally fast, its metallic spine elongated, it spun and slashed out with its spiked tail.

Elzar reached for the Force and pushed.

The Nameless slid backward.

Elzar stepped forward again, his lightsaber raised. Avar released his hand, but the connection remained strong. Gloriously strong. He focused on the Force, on gathering the great ocean of it into him and pushing. Shoving. He was the center of the tide; the power was immense, more than him, beyond him, and he dragged it through him, making himself a river to channel all that strength. The ocean of the Force hit the Nameless, and its mouth opened. It gouged at the grassy ground, twisting and upset.

It glowed with the surge of the Force.

It stopped moving nearer, swallowing Elzar's power even as he let it all go. The Force was boundless, unlimited, especially with Avar at his side. Elzar yelled hoarsely with the effort of walking closer. He was almost there. Seconds passed under pounding heartbeats that felt like a hundred years—Elzar didn't know. Time and self were slippery, but the Force was all.

He stood directly in front of the Nameless. One whirling blue eye stared back at him, growing larger and larger, until it fit over all of Elzar's vision. It *screamed.*

Then it surged toward him. Elzar screamed back at it, driving his lightsaber into its flank.

The Nameless knocked him away hard enough that he fell, his breath slammed out of him. He saw the Nameless break through Avar and Burryaga's hands, separating them. Elzar yelled for her as Avar scrambled up and threw herself at the monster.

Chapter Sixty-One

VIXOSEPH I

Ro ran directly into the blight, heedless of its destructive capabilities. Vernestra scrambled up and pulled out her comlink, yelling, "Ro is here, on the ground! At my position to the north—north of the blight. The *Gaze*—"

Ro turned, kicking up ashes from the blighted land. He raised his blaster, and Vernestra stopped so fast she almost tripped. She dropped her comlink and had her lightsaber out and flashing just in time to catch his fire. Vernestra wished she'd taken one of those blasters Cair San Tekka had offered her all those days ago on Naboo so she could shoot back.

Breathing through the smell of her own blood, Vernestra let the Force flow through her, guiding her as she blocked and dodged his shots. Ro seemed almost casual about it, amused, as he backed up slowly. But Vernestra didn't follow him near the blight.

Just then the *Gaze Electric* let loose a huge blast, and a row of Skywings blew up into a fireball. The concussion threw Vernestra back to the ground. Pain shocked up her hip, and she wiped hair and sweat from her face.

The giant ship lowered over Ro, and a ladder dropped from one of its lower hatches. Vernestra lifted her hand to shield against the pressure of the wind as it descended. It was too high for her to leap, even with the Force.

Ro holstered his blaster as the ladder reached him. Vernestra stretched her arm toward him, her hand cupped as if to grip the air, and pushed with the Force. If she could knock him down, back, the blight had to catch hold, or she could drag him to her, anything!

A bolt of energy sliced down at her. Again. Vernestra dropped her hold on the Force and jumped back, her lightsaber raised. Someone was covering Ro from the tiny hatch high above.

Vernestra watched, panting, as Ro took the glowing rod from his belt, then bent over and picked something off the blighted meadow. Vernestra felt her mouth drop open. Ro wound his other arm through the ladder, and turned to smile at her.

"See you soon, little Jedi!" he called brightly, and the *Gaze Electric* lifted, taking Ro with it.

The moment before she touched the Nameless, a sudden slam in the ribs flung her aside, shocking Avar out of her body.

She hit the ground, and pain blossomed everywhere, but she barely felt it: A great ringing filled her.

She was alone. She was everything. She was bones and flesh and stars and song.

There was nothing outside of her, and she was boundless.

Avar understood it would be all right to let go. To become the galaxy. Everyone's destiny was the same.

Then she snapped back into herself.

Cold-hot agony encased her ribs, but Avar Kriss remained a song. A song could not be contained by mundanities like pain—pain had its own resonance, its own tune. The Force was beyond life and death, was of a realm where such concepts were the same experience. She'd experienced them all in a fleeting, gasping moment.

The pain grounded her. A star in her chest. She let the feeling ring out and felt the answer in Burryaga and the lush tendrils of his Force. She felt the planet under her feet, alive and aching, too, dead and breathing, a point of light in the galaxy. The entire galaxy was here with her.

And—

Elzar.

All of them connected to her, and the Force was so strong. The Nameless couldn't devour it fast enough to stop her. Avar pushed up from the ground, through the pain, radiating intention. She pulled on the Force, on every feeling she could reach, supported by Burryaga's endless acceptance. Avar pulled and pulled, willing the galaxy to run through her. It gushed and spilled like an ocean tearing under her skin.

Elzar.

He was there, suddenly. Next to her. Avar blinked. She saw the orange-streaked sky. She felt fire gripping her ribs, digging toward her heart. Saw his back, his brilliant lightsaber. Between her and the Nameless.

She tasted nothing but blood. But Avar could bear it for Elzar to have a chance.

She slammed her hands against his back.

A star exploded in Elzar's chest: Light and Life, so brilliant there was no room for anything else, not even a shadow.

Avar.

The Nameless's body heaved as it breathed through the charred lightsaber wound in its side. It hunched over, staring at them, its tail whipping. Avar's blood smeared on the spikes. Elzar could see it all. He reached out his hand, offering a piece of this Force star: It sucked at his power, swallowing it completely—a bottomless pit. He charged, leaving Avar's hands behind, but she remained with him, their connection inalienable.

The Nameless didn't move, feeding, hungry for every spark of life Elzar could shove at it. Drowning.

He swung his lightsaber, and it cut the Nameless across the throat again and again, until the metal shrieked and its skin singed and its head fell away, completely severed.

Elzar stumbled in the sudden lack of fear, drained and suddenly awash in a painful feedback of energy. Turning, he looked around. Avar leaned into Burryaga's arm. The Wookiee bent protectively over her.

Her eyes were sunken, shut, bruised, and her lips parted as she gasped for air with every inhale. Blood plastered her robes to her side. Her hand pushed against her wound, and Burry covered it with his own.

"Elzar," she murmured.

Burry murmured something—exhaustion. Elzar could feel it through the connection Avar hadn't let go of. He felt it right before Burry wavered and sank to his knees.

Elzar reached them just as Avar fell. He caught her in his arms.

In the sky, the *Gaze* sent a wave of cannon fire at all the remaining fighters, chasing them off as it turned toward the stars, its engines lighting to full power. Distantly, Elzar could hear voices in his comlink, and a Vector buzzed over them, veering down to land close by.

Elzar clung to Avar and vaguely felt Burry's long arms drape around them, too. The three of them slumped together on the grassland.

Chapter Sixty-Two

CORUSCANT

Ghirra Starros sipped a cold cream tea from a crystal glass in one of the busier cafés in the heart of Coruscant. The sun shone on the opalescent courtyard, and floating planters spilled pink wave zinnias and vibrant-orange gladiolix blossoms. The table hovered, too, just in front of her knees where she knelt on a silkensteen pillow, and cold-matrix hearths flickered with pale silver flames to create gentle breezes.

Idyllic, pleasing, and very public.

That was the idea: Be seen. Be overtly Nihil in her representation and not at all worried about sitting here idly, enjoying her drink.

She was alone at the moment, but Jayd, the gray-skinned Kexing with vestigial teeth along her cheekbones, was nearby, as were a complement of other Nihil attendants and bodyguards chosen to blend in just well enough. If anything happened, Ghirra's miniature shock knife and of course the disruptor beacon tucked into her elaborate braids would suit for defense. But Ghirra didn't expect any assassins. That rarely happened in the heart of Coruscant these days.

The sun glinted. Ghirra did her best to think only of her future plans and not her daughter or the Jedi or the presumable rancor pit of messiness Boolan was getting up to. No, Ghirra tried to perform simple enjoyment for those reporters with the holoimagers across the way.

Her comlink pinged.

Barely twitching an eyebrow, Ghirra settled the blue-topaz-encrusted earpiece over her ear and pinched the activator button. "This is Ghirra."

"Priority message for you, Minister, from the *Gaze*," came the answer.

"Very well," Ghirra said, tilting her chin up. She remained calm. "Security lock seven-two-two-illius-cat-verictum-nine."

It was too bad she wasn't somewhere more private. Ghirra shifted in her seat to stand, but barely had time to turn her back to the rest of the café before—

"Ghirra, my Ghirra," Marchion Ro said in her ear, a purr and a command that trailed down her spine to settle prickling in her tailbone. "Are you on Coruscant?"

"I am, my lord," she said, tilting her head as she spoke to deter any lip-readers or recording devices. "I hardly recognize your voice after all this time. One presumes you are well?"

"Well enough."

"In that case, how can I serve you?"

He laughed at her tone. "You said they want to hear from me."

Ghirra braced herself, her entire body going rigid. No missing that, if anyone observed closely. "They do."

"I'll be in the stars above Coruscant by tomorrow."

Ghirra managed not to close her eyes in irritation, but she clenched a fist. How dare he surprise her like this? All to keep her on her toes.

"What sort of message are you bringing, Marchion?" she asked lightly.

"Oh, tell them it's a message even the chancellor herself will approve of."

"Yes, my lord," she said, though obviously she would do no such thing. "Is there anything else I should be aware of?"

"I expect them to welcome me and listen to what I have to say. They won't like it if they refuse. See you soon."

"My lord—" Ghirra began, but the buzz of the comlink cut out.

The dread building in her since the start of the call did not dissipate when she stood up, waving at Jayd to collect her. There were some eleven hours until dawn, and she had too much to do.

Chancellor Lina Soh was tired. She'd been so for ages, years even. But it was worse ever since Valo, when it had become clear the Nihil weren't a onetime threat, a gang of pirates interested only in chaos.

Their Eye was interested in so much more, and he took it.

Lina didn't know what she would do if she'd lost her son.

So many people had lost so much—hells, Lina herself had lost friends and allies, whole systems they only barely managed to seize back.

But her son. He was so good and, honestly, helpless. He needed her. And she wasn't there. Lina Soh put her head in her hands and dug her nails into her forehead. She was so tired.

But there wasn't time to sleep. These reports needed reading before her next meeting, and she worried that if she dozed off she'd miss Elzar's message about whether or not they'd found Ro. Whether or not they'd figured out this . . . blight.

The very thought of it drained her even more.

The Republic had faced such things before and had won. Had survived.

They would again. They had to.

Lina didn't need to be the person who saved them. But somebody had to. She was here, so if she could . . . she would.

She wouldn't worry about her son. Or Admiral Kronara. Or Elzar Mann.

She would worry about what was before her. One step at a time. Even if that step was reports on a system-wide strike in the Ossiathora system that was disrupting the harvest of a grain necessary to—what was it?—distill a particular alcohol for deglazing engines caught in the Pyrlix Miasma in the Tyus sector? That mattered. The ripple effects could reach every edge of the Republic. But it didn't feel as immediate as the Nihil.

Everyone in her territory was her responsibility. *We are all the Republic,* Lina always said, pushed, insisted upon.

She had to act like it.

The report included a bulleted list of potential responses, some easy to dismiss but others would require a nuanced consideration. That was something Lina was good at. Using details to bolster people, to find wide-ranging solutions.

Still, it was almost a relief when her aide Norel Quo tapped against the doorframe and said, "Chancellor, Ghirra Starros is here, insisting on—"

"Let her in," Lina said, standing immediately.

Norel blinked, but then he bowed and hurried out through the greeting room.

Lina went more slowly, tucking hair up into her headdress, smoothing out the wrinkles in her gown. She breathed deeply and made her face blank.

When Ghirra swept in, Lina allowed herself to feel the anger this former senator caused to flare in her.

Ghirra paused in the door. The two women sized each other up. Matari, one of Lina's targons, huffed with something verging on irritation.

But the so-called Nihil representative smiled smoothly. "Chancellor. I've come because you wanted a message from Marchion Ro."

Lina's heart froze. Ro's messages were massacres.

Ghirra continued, "The Eye of the Nihil wants to address you in person. So he is on his way here, to Coruscant."

"I see," Lina Soh managed. She folded her hands behind her back, clenching them together. "He expects to be greeted as anything but a prisoner of war?"

"He expects to be greeted as a king," Ghirra said, with a little curl to her lip.

"We will see about that."

Chapter Sixty-Three

VIXOSEPH I

Burryaga should have been in a medical suite but instead insisted on this vigil. Again.

Bell and Vernestra Rwoh sat with him, each weary, injured, but unable to rest.

Burry did not want to become accustomed to watching the slow creep of this blight or the desiccating corpses of Drengir.

It was nighttime on the Vixoseph grassland, and Burry had yet to sleep. He'd chewed obediently on the ration bread Bell had put into his hand, but like everything else on this planet, it seemed to crumble to ashes in his mouth.

They'd remained behind when Master Mann bundled Master Kriss up into one of the RDC carriers and darted off for medical attention. Burry was glad. They needed each other; he'd felt it. They could heal and chase Marchion Ro all the way back to Wild Space if they wanted. Elzar had commed down to Bell at the last minute before the cruiser jumped away, asking for a detailed report on the Drengir, the blight, and the remaining Nihil. The rest of the Jedi had left with them except for Vernestra, whose Vector was a wreck along the tree line in the north.

She was the one who'd directed Burry to this particular dying Dren-gir and said that Marchion Ro had stopped her from attacking it dur-ing the battle. He'd wanted her out of the way. Then he'd thrown something at it. Something that looked like a chunk of the blight. And now the Drengir's body was being consumed. They were dozens of meters away from the current edge of blighted grassland, but it was here, calcifying as it died. And the blight was starting to spread from the new ground zero of the dead monster.

Bell's emotions were soft with sleepiness right now, but the edges of them felt awful. Burry felt Bell's struggle to put his master's death from his mind. In the face of this blight and their encounter with the Name-less, his friend struggled. Vernestra stared at the dying Drengir with an uneven kind of peace—no, resignation. She'd told them already what she'd seen Ro do.

Burry asked if she truly thought Marchion Ro could control the blight.

Vernestra shook her head, looking haunted. "I hope not. But I watched him walk into it. Maybe he found something that it can't af-fect and put it in the soles of his boots. I'd rather believe that than . . . nothing. And maybe that Drengir got too close to the blight on its own. But maybe . . . Marchion Ro took the blight and planted it into this Drengir. Poisoned it. I don't know how else to interpret what I saw. And we do know he can control the Nameless. And we don't know what the blight is, or what its . . . purpose is. What it wants."

"The Drengir want to eat," Bell said. "They want to survive, like most living things. Surely they aren't part of the blight. It ruins what their food would be. It ruins everything."

"But they might be running away from it," Vernestra said.

"Maybe they can sense it before we can see it," Bell said, sounding unconvinced. "The dark side is still part of the Force."

While they discussed, Burry stepped up to the edge of the calcified grassland and peered into the darkness. This world had two small moons that cast dull orange-white light, and behind Burry the hovering lights pushed his shadow into the blight itself. There were a dozen perfectly preserved little flowers just recently overtaken. And there in the scattered remains of thicker grasses was the calcified body of a rodent with long skin-fans down its back that might've been sun protection or ears when it lived.

Burry crouched, careful not to touch anything. He opened himself up to the Force, aware that his edges felt rawer than usual after the past few weeks. Facing the Nameless twice and both times channeling terror on purpose had taken a toll, physically, mentally, and emotionally. And what Master Kriss had done when they linked had been like a deluge through his system. It had worked, though.

Maybe it could work again. Burry was good with emotions. Maybe he could learn to channel the fear away as Master Kriss had.

He hoped she lived.

He wondered if there was an emotion charged to the blight the way fear radiated off the Nameless through the Force. A key of some kind to challenge it, to push back.

Or even to feed it better, so well that it stopped swallowing entire worlds.

Burry let the Force flow through him, roots and branches and millions of tiny leaves flickering in a galactic wind. It reached through his body and outward again, only to fade drastically against the edge of the blight.

Imagining Light and Life, imagining the warmth of a sun and growing forest, Burry tried to feed the blight.

The power he accumulated drained into it. Readily.

The blight was hungry. Like the Drengir. Like the Nameless.

But the blight was enormous. Maybe a thousand Burrys could feed it well enough to slow it down. Not one. He couldn't do it alone. Bell was right. Burry wasn't enough. The Jedi weren't enough. Oanne was going to die.

An ache built in Burry's chest, spilling out of him, mirrored by the blight.

He could not give in to despair. There would be something. The galaxy didn't die like this. They would find something, eventually. He had to nurture that hope and work toward it.

The best way to do so was to learn.

Burryaga stepped away from the blight, and under the dull moonlight he sank into the deepest meditation he could reach. Could he connect to the blight? Not just push back, not fight it. Welcome it.

Like a friend, like a part of the Force.

The nativity trees on Oanne and the people there were fully integrated, which was why they couldn't leave. The Force—the galaxy—welcomed interconnection. At its heart, that was what the Force was.

There couldn't be anything separate from it. Could there?

Burry didn't want to believe it.

Burry gave to the blight through the Force, open and willing to connect. Slowly, he let his awareness move nearer to the gnawing feeling.

The Force spilled into the blight as if the blight were a cliff, an endless abyss of nothingness, that all the Force could fall into forever.

But—

It wanted something.

Not hunger. Not quite longing. It was more specific than that.

It was—

Burry's eyes snapped open, and he made a strangled cry at the rightness of the feeling. He knew it. He had felt it himself.

Homesick.

Chapter Sixty-Four

Avar drifted.

Surrounded by light, a gentle blanket of a billion stars, she drifted and listened.

It started with a pulse. A quiet echoing rhythm. The first breath before a song, then: a hum.

She remembered her name and the Force, and then the bright tone of her own melody.

Someone was holding her hand.

The cushion beneath her was thin but soft. The reverberation of the room around her told her she was on a ship. Hyperspace.

When Jedi Master Avar Kriss opened her eyes, the first thing she saw was the dull ceiling over her bunk. The second was the face of Elzar Mann.

She flexed her fingers around his, and Elzar smiled as relief flooded over his expression, smoothing it out. Relief flooded into her, too, through him.

Avar swallowed, her tongue tacky. Her chest ached. The entire right side of her body had a dull, medicated pain feeling. She'd tried to feed

herself, her Force, to the Nameless to buy Elzar and Burry time. It had
hit her with something. The metal tail. She probably had broken bones.
Avar took a deep, slightly stuttering breath.

"Thirsty?" Elzar asked.

She nodded and he stood to get her water. Avar sat up, watching
him. She didn't want to take her eyes off him. Returning, Elzar perched
on the edge of the bed and handed her a cup.

As she drank, he studied her. His concern rippled into Avar, and
she listened, feeling the curiosity behind it, and . . . affection.

After draining the cup, Avar looked up and met Elzar's waiting
gaze. He felt it, too. The give-and-take of feelings, the hum of connection. She wondered if she'd done something when she linked with him
and Burryaga to fight the Nameless. If it had connected all of them.

Elzar shook his head and murmured, "It's just us. Not Burryaga."

Avar's breath caught. Elzar had known exactly what she was thinking. Her pulse picked up.

Elzar took the cup to set aside, but kept her hand, rubbing his
thumb against her palm. Avar focused on the soothing sensation, on
the way it tingled up her wrist along the veins there, almost a tickle. A
promise of more to come.

She tugged on his hand, pulling him down, and kissed him. She
pressed up, welcoming the ache in her body, the tingling numbness
spreading from her ribs from some topical medicine, and the taste of
his mouth. Elzar kissed her back but only gently. He leaned away, his
gaze flicking over her face.

All right.

"It worked," she said. "You killed it."

"It did. You cleared away enough of its . . . effect, however you did it.
I could fight it."

Avar closed her eyes. She knew what she'd done, but it had been
extremely unpleasant. It started out well, but she'd only leapt into the
true nature of how to help him when she'd nearly died. She'd thought
she would die—had died for a split second maybe. She'd meditate,

write it all up, discuss it with other Jedi who'd faced the Nameless, who had experienced the edge of death, and present it to the Council. Avar suspected it was not repeatable, or if it was, it was something only she and Burry could do together, or she and Elzar because of their connection. And even then, Avar sensed that if she gave in to that nothingness too often, she wouldn't return from it.

She'd barely returned this time.

"What happened then?" she asked, sitting up and pulling away with a little pat on his shoulder. Avar moved carefully to the sink to wash her face and mouth. It hurt. Her diadem rested with a pile of folded fresh robes on the small table. She wasn't sure she could dress herself. Walking, washing, kissing was one thing. Lifting her arm over her head, bending down to lace a boot . . . maybe not.

While she washed up, Elzar told her what he remembered about killing the Nameless, about Vernestra's encounter with Marchion Ro and his escape—Avar vaguely remembered the *Gaze Electric* in the sky.

"Do we know where to follow him?" She turned, patting her face dry.

"Coruscant," Elzar said darkly. "Chancellor Soh confirmed that Ghirra Starros came to her demanding a meeting between Lina and Ro. Imminently."

Avar stared at him. Elzar felt angry and eager, along with an overlying worry for her that was fading the longer she stood up, stayed awake. His hair tufted out as if he'd been running his hands through it, and he'd stripped down to his trousers and undershirt, loosely tied. She said, "Which he'll get?"

"Yes. It's being arranged."

"When do we arrive?" she asked.

"Three hours. I've sent the messages I could and readied everyone as best I can, since we have no idea what he actually wants. When we come out of hyperspace, we should have a more full report from the Jedi still on Vixoseph One. They're investigating what he left behind and rounding up any Nihil survivors."

They didn't know what Ro intended, that was true. But it had always been awful for the Republic and the Jedi. This was unlikely to be any different. There was only one thing they could do now.

"You should rest." Avar went to him and put a hand on his chest.

The touch strengthened their connection immediately, and Avar felt the heat in his emotions. Intense longing, fear, heartache.

Slowly, as if moving through honey, Elzar cupped Avar's face, his thumbs gentle under her eyes. "I love you, too, Avar."

She nodded, bringing her hands to his wrists. She curled her fingers around them. Avar couldn't tell him she thought maybe she had died—just a little. She felt the wound throbbing, reminding her, in the rhythm of her heart, the push and pull of his tide—their tide. But she was certain he could sense it. He knew.

"Rest with me" was all she said, pulling him with her. She sat on the edge of the bed, and he went with her. She hoped in the future that wherever she went, Elzar would follow.

Chapter Sixty-Five

CORUSCANT

The sun rose in near silence—or as close as one could get to silence on Coruscant. Light crept brighter against the eastern black teeth of the cityscape as those gathered did their best not to pace or twitch with anxiety.

High overhead, too far beyond the atmosphere to be seen as anything but a glinting morning star, the *Gaze Electric* orbited. It had arrived several hours before, and arrangements for this greeting had been hurriedly made between the Nihil as represented by Minister Ghirra Starros and the Office of the Chancellor. Norel Quo had done his best to stall long enough to allow everyone the chancellor wanted at her side to be available.

The greeting party waited in the shadow of the domed Senate building, with the great weight of its support behind them, for Marchion Ro's shuttle to land.

Chancellor Soh stood in her most understated regal attire, backed by the tense targons. Soh would not give the impression she needed gaudy accoutrements or layers of expensive silk to be seen as a leader. No, a simple silver pauldron and a chain of state were her scepter, glimmering Coruscant itself her mantle, and the strength of her allies her crown.

Alongside the chancellor were senior senators from a rainbow of worlds and a handful of fleet leaders, all in crisp uniform. Senatorial guards were arrayed across the platform in their elaborate blue masks, holding spears affixed with both blade and standard.

Three members of the Jedi Council attended, white-and-gold robes pristine: Grand Master Yoda, small but impossible to overlook given the strength of his presence in the Force, and on either side of him were Master Ry Ki-Sakka and Master Soleil Agra. Those three waited the most patiently. Yoda closed his eyes and might've been asleep.

Near them stood Masters Elzar Mann and Avar Kriss, clean and fancy in their temple attire. Every once in a while, their knuckles brushed, and one glanced at the other, and their expressions shifted minutely into a question or grim smile, almost as if they conducted a conversation no one else could hear.

Then there was Ghirra Starros standing apart from the rest, her hands folded together and her face tilted to the sky. Her Nihil-blue chest piece was much too pretty for what it represented. A delicate gas mask hung from her belt, overlaid with a synthetic glass shimmering starry blue. By contrast, the masks of her Nihil bodyguards were spiky and obscene, too ferocious for the moment. It was something the Nihil excelled at: over-the-top statements.

Sunlight touched the curve of the Senate building, here at the center of the vast metropolis. The light glinted along the edge, slinking prettily as it grew.

From directly above, a shuttle descended.

A docking platform had been moved in for the occasion, with a simple hovering staircase that connected the platform to the round dais, where the leaders of the Nihil and Republic would meet.

As the ugly Nihil shuttle landed, its external Path engine crackling obnoxiously, the Jedi in the crowd shifted.

"Nameless," Avar Kriss murmured, and the word passed to the chancellor, who nodded solemnly.

She said to Ghirra Starros, "He will not bring them off that platform, or it will be taken as a sign of intent to harm."

"Of course. So long as you do not show intent to harm, either. As we negotiated."

The shuttle door hissed open, red lights blinking.

From the dim maw, they heard not only a single pair of heavy boots but also the scrape of claws or hooves against the metal grating.

Marchion Ro appeared, flanked by two of the ghostly, monstrous things. Their whiskers shivered and curled, and long jowls hung from sharp mouths. Their awful milky-blue eyes were surrounded by sagging, sick white flesh. They crawled behind their master, stringy muscles pulling and shifting, tails curling and uncurling as they scented the air.

Chancellor Soh's matching targons stood bristling. One growled, the other bared teeth and hissed so challengingly that it caused the hair and fur to stand up on the senators who had such things.

"Keep those things back, Ro," Lina Soh commanded. "They are a weapon, and they are not welcome at this meeting if it is to be peaceful."

"Very well, Chancellor," Marchion said, paternalistic and amused. He turned his head and seemed to say nothing at all, but the two Nameless stepped back, cringing.

Marchion Ro stepped out of the shuttle onto the steps, in a flowing dark cape trimmed in brilliant white fur. His sleek black hair hung loose, and his teeth when he smiled were just as sharp as his black eyes. He wore white and gold in long lines, spiked with Nihil blue and dark metallic clips and chains, but reminiscent of nothing so much as Jedi robes themselves.

Worse, though, was the wide bandolier crossing his chest, lined with five lightsaber hilts.

Some shone with recent polish while others were scarred and dull, and two bore hallmarks of designs that hadn't been used in over a hundred years. One was familiar to every Jedi present and to Lina, for it had belonged to Grand Master Veter.

But even that was not the thing to catch and keep the chancellor's attention. In Marchion Ro's hand was a rod capped with crystal, and in his other a bouquet of tiny white wildflowers. Their petals spread like snow, their stems pale gray and strange. Ro held them gently, like they were a delicate gift.

Lina fought back a shiver of foreboding. Nearby, Elzar started forward, but Avar grabbed his wrist. She started to whisper urgently at him, but before she could so much as say his name, the chancellor spoke.

"Marchion Ro, I will not welcome you to Coruscant, but nevertheless we are willing to hear what you have to say."

Ro smiled. He glanced at Ghirra as if to say, *I told you so,* and Ghirra stepped nearer to him, providing the illusion of a united front. She looked at Elzar, having marked his sudden motion, but probably assumed the messy Jedi Master was upset by the ostentatious display of conquered lightsabers. Ro spoke. "Chancellor, you have your reasons to mistrust my intentions, but I come today because of a greater threat to all of us."

The drama of the statement floored several of the people attending, though Lina Soh only narrowed her eyes. "A threat greater than the Nihil and their unstoppable Eye?" she asked silkily.

"To all of us," he repeated. Ro walked slowly down the hovering steps toward her, and the guards shifted their array. But Ro said, "You know of the blight appearing around the galaxy."

"We do."

"It destroys everything. Consumes everything. I have studied it, and you should believe me when I tell you that no being is safe, neither Republic nor Nihil, not even the Hutts or Takodana mercenaries or Mandalorians—except for me." Ro smiled with all his fangs.

"You know what it is?" The chancellor did not quite scoff. Ro was lying, she was certain of that, but she wasn't sure about exactly what or why. She couldn't risk the galaxy for such a gamble. Not yet. Not when she'd read the reports and heard from Elzar himself of the eerie desolation the blight brought in its wake.

Ro said, "I know how to stop it."

Marchion Ro glanced beyond them at the dome of the Senate building and the dawn sky stretching blue and pink. He spread both arms. In one hand, the rod; in the other, the flowers. "More important, I *will* stop it."

"If?" Elzar Mann demanded, earning several cutting glances for interrupting. Though not from the chancellor herself, who agreed with him.

"No if," Ro said, and there was something so powerful in his countenance suddenly that if Lina didn't know better, she'd think Marchion Ro could use the Force to charge his charisma—to make himself seem like a tyrant and a savior in one breath. "I don't think you understand yet."

The chancellor did not want to play this game, and she refused to ask what it was they did not yet understand.

Ro held her gaze, his smile twisting in amusement. He understood, and simply held out the white flowers. He tipped his hand, and they fell from his palm. He said, "That I am your only hope."

The wildflowers drifted down as light as the petals they were, disintegrating into ashes, lost to the morning breeze.

Acknowledgments

I'm not the only kid to grow up thinking the correct response to "I love you" is "I know." I learned it from my parents, who were best friends as well as partners and huge *Star Wars* fans. When the powers that be told me to make *Temptation of the Force* like *The Empire Strikes Back,* which was Mom and Dad's favorite *Star Wars* movie, it was overwhelming. So I made it about love instead. The different kinds of love in this book—galactic, familial, romantic, star-crossed, gentle, villainous, compassionate, charitable, professional—all of them grew in me because of the foundation my parents gave me. Mom and Dad, *I know* love because of you. Thank you.

Thanks to everyone involved in Project Luminous from the beginning; it's been an honor and a delight. Thanks especially to Jen Heddle, Lindsay Burke, Jennifer Pooley, Emeli Juhlin, Kristin Baver, and everyone else on the teams at Lucasfilm, Disney, and Random House Worlds. Thank you, *thank you* to Mike Siglain for losing sleep to corral and support us.

My fellow authors, thank you for this wild ride, for your creations, for your support, and for all the arguments and moments of epiphany. No thanks for the Stormwall, though (wink!).

Thank you especially to George Mann, who set me up with everything I needed to make both *Quest for Planet X* and *Temptation of the Force* as strong as possible. I'll write a sequel to anything you start! Thanks to Zoraida Córdova for being ready with mutual wide-eyed emojis and screaming, and for always managing to think about this work as a fan, too. And of course, thanks to Justina Ireland, who dragged me into this in the first place, who is a genius, and who didn't realize she wrote Xylan Graf just for me until I gently begged to take him over. I'm sorry about the Stormwall.

And thank you, Tom Hoeler, my editor at Random House Worlds, not only for stellar edits and talking me through things, but for realizing immediately in that first messy draft exactly which scene was the heart of the book—and then making me earn it.

And all my gratitude to my wife, Natalie, who realized I was her soulmate when we were fifteen, on an amazing day that started when she saw I was reading a *Star Wars* novel.

© NATALIE C. PARKER

TESSA GRATTON is the *New York Times* bestselling author of adult and YA SFF novels and short stories that have been translated into twenty-two languages. She has been nominated twice for the Otherwise Award, and several of her novels have been Junior Library Guild selections. Her most recent novels are the dark fairy tales *Strange Grace* and *Moon Dark Smile,* the queer Shakespeare retelling *Lady Hotspur,* and novels in the *Star Wars: The High Republic* series. Though she has lived all over the world, she currently resides at the edge of the Kansas prairie with her wife. Queer, nonbinary, she/he/they.

About the Type

This book was set in Hermann, a typeface created in 2019 by Chilean designers Diego Aravena and Salvador Rodriguez for W Type Foundry. Hermann was developed as a modern tribute to classic novels, taking its name from the author Hermann Hesse. It combines key legibility features from the typefaces Sabon and Garamond with more dynamic and bolder visual components.

A long time ago in a galaxy far, far away. . . .

STAR WARS™

Join up! Subscribe to our newsletter
at ReadStarWars.com or find us on social.

𝕏   @StarWarsByRHW

⃝ @StarWarsByRHW

f   StarWarsByRHW